THE PRINCESS GAME

GLITTER AND GOLD

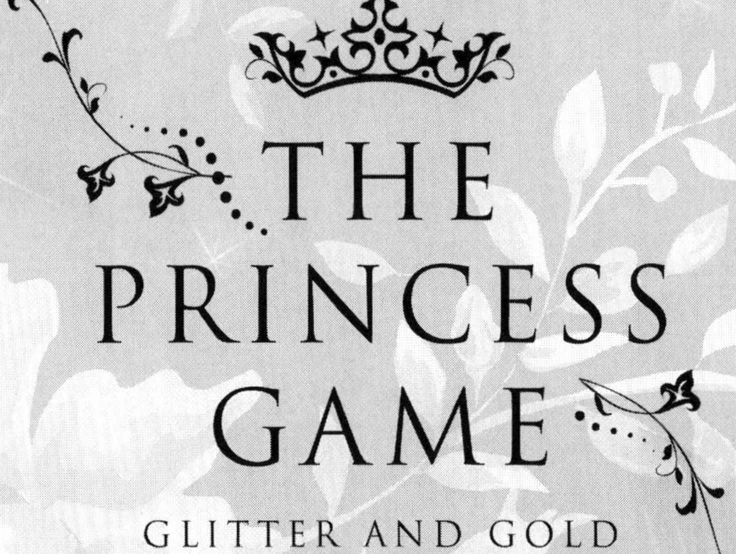

THE PRINCESS GAME

GLITTER AND GOLD

LYRA VINCENT

In a competition where thirty human girls vie to win a fae prince's hand in marriage, the girl who wound up there by accident discovers that neither the glittering faerie world nor the prince she's been taught to hate are what they seem.

ISBN 978-1-998988-10-5 (ebook)
ISBN 978-1-998988-11-2 (paperback)
ISBN 978-1-998988-12-9 (hardback)

Trigger Warning

Recollection of an attempted sexual assault in a character's past.

Chapter One

"Welcome to the Glittering Palace!" On the TV screen in the corner of The Grumpy Bean, a faerie in a burgundy checkered suit spreads his arms wide against the backdrop of a grand, gleaming foyer. "King Eldyn of the Autumn Court invites you to step into a world of dazzling magic, extravagant luxury, and swoon-worthy romance."

"Meet the prince," cries the woman standing beside him, her head piled high with bright pink curls, "experience the lavish life of the fae court, eavesdrop on every magical date, and follow along as the crown prince of Faeworld's Autumn Court finds his true love."

"Welcome, ladies and gentlemen—" the camera refocuses on the first faerie "—tooooo ..." He draws the word out, his voice rising before he punches the air with a bejeweled fist, shooting gold sparkles into the air. "*The Princess Game*! Thirty contestants. One prince. *Who will win the tiara?*"

Beside me, Quinn sticks her finger in her mouth and mimes throwing up. I elbow her in the ribs, trying to suppress a laugh as my gaze darts across The Grumpy Bean to see if any customers have spotted us. But the morning rush is over, and—for now, at least—it's just the two of us.

"I can*not* believe they're making a TV show out of this," Quinn says, tucking her dark hair behind her ears and pushing her glasses up her nose as she continues to glare at the screen. "It's—"

"—a huge farce, completely ridiculous, and a hundred of your brain cells die every time you're forced to watch anything about this crappy reality show. I know." I give her a look. "You've said that about seven thousand times since they announced this thing."

"*Two* hundred brain cells, Avery," she corrects, directing her glare at me. "Every time."

"Good thing you've got plenty to spare, Super Nerd."

She sticks her tongue out at me. I give her my sweetest smile.

"That was the teaser trailer for *The Princess Game*," the news anchor says, drawing our attention back to the screen, "the most highly anticipated reality TV show *ever*. Hosted by two of the most *delightful* fae folk I've had the pleasure of meeting: Carwyn Aster and Evanna Zynn. Next up, an interview with Riya Patel, daughter of British tech tycoon Darsh Patel and the latest contestant announced by the Glittering Palace."

"Daughter of a tech tycoon," I murmur. "I bet they got super excited when they saw her application."

"Yeah, I'm sure that'll come in handy with their world domination plans." Quinn folds her arms over her chest as we both scrutinize the photograph that's just popped up on the screen: a girl with flawless brown skin, glossy black hair, and a beauty queen's smile. "It's all so fake," Quinn grumbles. "Prince Faerie Face isn't actually going to find the love of his life on this stupid show. Everyone knows that. For the fae, it's all about politics and control and getting their conniving little fingers wrapped around our necks, because apparently they haven't done enough of that since they showed up five years ago. And for us, it's all about entertainment and the possibility of getting even a *teeny* bit of their magic, and—"

"And it's about money," I finish with a sigh. "Because that's what makes the world go round." I absently twirl the end of my blond ponytail around my fingers as I think of the less-than-friendly note our landlord shoved under our door last night. Somehow, between Quinn's two jobs and my three, we can still barely afford the rent for the tiny apartment we share.

"It just makes me sick that they're trying to spin it into a fae prince finding true love with a human girl when it's obviously *not* about that," Quinn continues. "The Autumn Court said from the beginning that they would only agree to this insane competition if *they* got to select the contestants from all the applications. That's not how true love works."

"And you know *so* much about true love," I comment, trying not to laugh.

"And why is no one calling them out on their hypocrisy?" she demands, ignoring me. "They spend years looking down their noses at us, and then suddenly one of us is supposed to be good enough for their *prince*? And what about that convenient loophole they suddenly pulled out of their asses about their heirs? No one thinks *that's* weird?"

I lean one hip against the counter and cross my arms. "I've heard a lot of conspiracy theories from you. You're going to have to be more specific."

"You know, the thing about humans and fae not being able to produce kids with magic. They've told us that since the day they arrived, and then one day they introduce *The Princess Game*—"

"They didn't introduce it. Some human did."

"—and we're all like, 'But how will your royal line continue if your prince marries a human and you don't have magical babies,'" Quinn continues without a breath, "and suddenly the story changes. Babies conceived in *their* world will obviously be born with magic, even if one of the parents is human. I mean, that just seems *too* convenient, doesn't it?"

I shrug. "Who cares if it's true or not? If it isn't, they're just shooting themselves in their collective royal feet, producing heirs who don't have magic."

"Yes, but—"

"Quinn." I arch a brow. "Can we go back to the part where you said this whole thing makes you sick? Because you're the one holding the remote, and I notice you haven't bothered switching channels."

"I know." Her shoulders droop. She slides the remote onto the counter. "Tragic, isn't it? It's the biggest load of trash, I *hate* all things fae, and yet I can't tear myself away from this thing."

"Must be magic," I muse, looking at the screen again. "They're casting some spell over us simple-minded humans, forcing us to watch this nonsense while they secretly take over the world."

"Probably. And it's working. I'm losing more brain cells by the minute."

"... and I've *just* received word," the news anchor says, which draws my attention back to the screen, "that another contestant was revealed not half an hour ago! Eighteen-year-old social media influencer Cadence Cruz is the second-to-last contestant confirmed for reality TV show *The Princess Game*. The announcement was broadcast via livestream across multiple social media platforms simultaneously to her eight million plus followers—"

"Eight *million*?" I splutter.

"Wonderful," Quinn grumbles. "So people give her free stuff for a living, and now she's going to get even more free stuff."

"Looks like she does makeup tutorials," I murmur as we watch a screen recording of someone scrolling through the various videos on Cadence Cruz's YouTube channel. "And hauls and room tours and ... did that one say 'My Morning Routine'? Seriously?"

"This is everything that's wrong with the world," Quinn says.

The screen zooms in on Cadence Cruz's latest video, and we get a closeup of a gorgeous girl with delicately bronzed skin, luscious dark locks, and pouty red lips. "OMG, guys," she says, her dazzling hazel eyes immediately drawing me in. "O. M. Freaking. G. I asked you to join me live today because I have some *insane* news to share with you, and I wanted to do it live! I found out a few days ago, and I've *finally* been given the go-ahead to let you all know. So here it is. The Big News. I am going to be one of the contestants participating in—" she pauses, no doubt for dramatic effect, then squeals, "*The Princess Game!*"

"Eighteen," I say. "She must be one of the youngest."

"Yeah, I think the oldest I've heard of is twenty-four."

"I'll be joining twenty-nine other girls in the Glittering Palace," Cadence continues, "as we compete to win Prince Kieren's hand in marriage. Squeeeeeeee!" She bobs up and down, clapping her hands together. "Make sure to follow me, Cadence_Cruz, on all my socials. I'll be giving you the inside scoop on life at the Glittering Palace, as well as daily updates on *everything* going on with *The Princess Game*!"

"Aaaaand there go another ten thousand of my brain cells," Quinn deadpans.

I snort. "At this rate, you won't have any left by the time Prince Faerie Face chooses a wife."

"Excuse me," a deep voice says.

Quinn and I both whip around. Standing on the other side of the counter is a tall man with perfectly angled features, bronze hair, and the kind of caramel brown eyes that look like they should be filled with warmth. His, however, couldn't be colder as he surveys us. He's *way* overdressed in a suit with a bow tie. Or ... wait. Is it a tux? I'm not sophisticated enough to be certain of the difference. Either way, who dresses like that on a regular Tuesday morning?

I grab the TV remote and lower the volume. If we'd done that a little sooner, we wouldn't have missed the sound of the door opening. Before I can apologize or ask the guy what he'd like to order, he says, without a trace of amusement, "You don't approve of *The Princess Game*."

Quinn makes a strangled noise before clamping her mouth shut. She freezes up around hot guys. I laugh as I flash Mr. Bow Tie one of my most customer-friendly smiles. "No, we're not the biggest fans. I mean ... the snooty heir to a faerie throne gets to sit back and watch a bunch of desperate, power-hungry girls repeatedly throwing themselves at him until he's forced to finally pick one of them? I'm sure it'll be entertaining, but probably not the most *intellectually* stimulating." I cock my head to one side. "How about you? What do you think of the whole idea?" He doesn't look like the type who'd cozy up on a couch once a week to watch girls getting makeovers and going on fake dates with a prince, but I could be wrong.

Instead of answering, he stares at me as if I've just spoken a foreign language. As if it's the oddest thing in the world that the girl on the other side of the counter not only has an *opinion*, but has the nerve to ask him about anything other than his order. I guess he hasn't been in here before. I'm known for holding up the queue by chatting too much with customers. "Friendly doesn't mean *that* friendly," our boss told me yet again last week. "The cat lady with the purple hair doesn't want to answer your prying questions about her grandchild."

"She's actually a dog lady, Nigel," I corrected him, "and she has three grandchildren, not one. They're coming to visit her next month. She is *beyond* excited."

At that, Nigel just shook his head and walked back into his office.

"Never mind," I say to Mr. Bow Tie with another laugh, not wanting to make him uncomfortable. Sometimes Nigel's right; not everyone wants to chat. "What can I get you?" I gesture above my head to the menu high up on the wall.

He looks up, then returns his gaze to me. "Whatever is most popular." There's a hint of an accent underlying his words, but it's too subtle for me to tell where he might be from.

"Okay then," I answer, my bright smile still in place. Bit of a strange order, but whatever. I glance at Quinn, but she's already disappeared behind the coffee machine. There's no knowing what kind of coffee Mr. Bow Tie will end up with now. "Would you like to add something to that?" I ask, tilting my head to the side where numerous plates of pastries and baked goods sit beneath glass bell jars on one side of the counter.

"No," he says, expression unchanging. It's as if his face is carved from stone.

"Are you sure?" My smile curves up on one side. "The triple chocolate brownies are to *die* for." I point past the first bell jar to the plate containing a single dark, fudgy-looking square. "You're lucky there's still one left."

His brows lower. "I will not be *dying* for anything in this place."

Wow. Okay. This guy woke up on the wrong side of the bed this morning. "It's an expression," I say in the same slow and patient tone I use for the young kids I give piano lessons to. "It means they're really good?"

He tilts his head a fraction to the side. "Are you *asking* me what it means?"

"I'm *telling* you."

"It did not sound like that."

Wow. Double wow. I would look at Quinn to see if she's hearing this too, but she's probably curled up on the floor with her hands over her head. She deals with confrontation about as well as she deals with hot guys.

I force my smile back onto my lips and make one more attempt at being civil. "Let's rewind. The triple chocolate brownies are *really* good, and you're missing out if you don't try one."

His gaze sweeps the counter before returning to me. "I don't believe there's a single thing I'm missing out on. To be honest, I was hoping there might be. However ..." His eyes travel across the tables and chairs, and the plants and picture frames sitting on floating shelves mounted on the exposed brick walls. "It seems," he murmurs, almost to himself, "there is nothing here but disappointment."

There's suddenly an intense, hot pressure in my chest. A pounding heat in my veins. I lean forward, pressing my palms flat on the counter. "Okay. I don't know if I was supposed to hear that or not, but I did, and it was downright rude. We're doing our best here to provide you with good coffee, delicious treats, and service with a *smile*, and then you come in here with a stick wedged so far up your butt it's a wonder it isn't poking you in the eye. Clearly you have *nothing* nice to say, so perhaps don't say anything at all."

His eyes narrow a fraction. "A stick wedged up my—"

"Also an expression. I'm going to assume you haven't come across that one before either."

"What I haven't come across is the 'good coffee and delicious treats' you seem to think I'll find here. Your opinion of the food and drink in this place is as poor as your opinion of popular television."

"You haven't even tasted the—Wait." I hold up a hand. "The fact that I'm not the biggest *Princess Game* fan means I have a *poor opinion of popular television*? You *like* that trash?"

Another strangled sound from behind the coffee machine reminds me I'm not the only one back here. I assume it was also meant to point out that I'm being as rude as the A-hole standing on the other side of the counter. Right now, I don't care.

But before I can utter another word, Quinn bumps into my side and thrusts the takeaway cup across the counter at Mr. Arrogant Ass. "Here. Your coffee. I, um, hope you enjoy it."

He doesn't move. His eyes don't waver from mine. "That 'trash,' as you put it, will result in the first permanent ties between this world and the fae one. You underestimate its importance."

He's right. The silly show *is* important, and Quinn and I *will* watch it, and as much as we'll complain about it, we'll also become so invested that *nothing* will tear us from the screen every week. I know this from past binge-watching experience. But Mr. Arrogant Ass doesn't need to know any of that.

I take a deep breath and paste my sweet smile back on. "Of course. It is important. But it's as fake as everything else about the fae."

His eyes drop to my chest, then flick back up. *Come on*, is he seriously checking out my—

"Avery," he whispers, my name an icy breath on his lips.

Oh. My name tag. Shiiiiit. He's going to make a complaint about me. He's going to tell Nigel how rude I am. I imagine myself trying to explain this one away. *So, funny story ... Remember when you told me not to be* overly *friendly? I tried, but I may have taken it a little too far. Oops! Let's all laugh about this and not make any rash decisions about firing people!*

But before I can say another word, Mr. Arrogant Ass is suddenly leaning right across the counter. His face is too close to mine, his burning gaze almost enough to sear my skin. I want to take an immediate step backward, but I feel ... frozen, paralyzed, held captive as if by some spell. He leans closer still. Close enough to kiss me. For one insane, dizzying moment, I think he might. Instead, he says, "You should be careful what you say, *Avery*. You never know who might be listening."

Chapter Two

"Holy freaking crap," Quinn gasps the moment the door to The Grumpy Bean swings shut. "What the hell was that, Avery?"

As if waking from a spell, I blink at the empty space where Mr. Arrogant Ass was standing moments ago. Quinn's hand is still extended partway across the counter, gripping the coffee that Mr. Ass clearly had no interest in consuming. In the background, the TV presenter prattles on. "That was Riya Patel, contestant on *The Princess Game*, joining us all the way from London. Thanks again, Riya! So, only *one* more contestant to be revealed—the hosts' choice—and then we'll have our thirty girls!"

I blink again. Then I fumble across the counter for the TV remote and hit the mute button. I don't think I can handle any more chatter about that stupid TV show right now.

"Seriously, Aves," Quinn says, setting the coffee aside. "What *was* that?"

"I ..." My hands rise to press against my warm cheeks. "I have *no* idea. I'm not normally that rude."

"Not normally? You're *never* rude. No matter what kind of jerk is standing on the other side of the counter. You're the epitome of sweet, charming and polite. You're like ... sunshine and rainbows and frolicking puppies. *I'm* the grumpy bean, not you."

I shake my head, hands still pressed to my face. "I don't know. There was just something about him."

"Like the fact that he was probably fae and you were insulting him to his face?"

I lower my hands, a faintly sick feeling coalescing in the pit of my stomach as I stare at the door again. "Shit. Do you think so?"

"Uh, 'You never know who might be listening?'" Quinn repeats his final words with her brows raised almost to her hairline. "Of course I think he was fae! He even had that glow about him."

I give her a look. "You know they don't actually *glow*."

"Aura. Whatever."

"That's nothing more than speculation. They've never confirmed it, and I've never felt anything weird around one of them."

"Well I definitely felt something weird. Something otherworldly."

I arch a brow. "I don't think you felt *anything* except the vibration of the coffee machine."

She glares at me. "Stop trying to change the subject. *You insulted a hot faerie to his face!* What if he curses you or something?"

"Ugh." I squeeze my eyes shut and cover my face with my hands again. Fae curses aren't a thing—that we know of, at least —but there are probably plenty of unpleasant magical things he could do to me or The Grumpy Bean if he *is* fae. I wish there was an easy way of knowing for sure—wings or pointy ears or something—but they look exactly the same as we do. Okay, that's not completely true. They look exactly the same as the *attractive* section of the human population. Or perhaps that's just another one of their illusions.

For the first few months after they revealed their existence to us, I looked more closely at every stranger I passed. What if the man sitting alone at the corner table inside The Grumpy Bean was fae? What about the woman examining cherries in the fresh produce aisle at the store? But I slowly became used to the idea that they were just *there*, like humans, and I would never be able to tell the difference unless one of them chose to use magic in front of me.

"Ugh, Quinn," I mumble between my fingers. "I don't want to end up with a unibrow or seven years of bad luck or a third nipple. I'm perfectly happy with the two I already have."

"Um, A-Avery ..." Quinn clears her throat. I drop my hands to my sides, suddenly—and far too belatedly—aware of the fact that the bell above the front door tinkled a few moments ago. I blink and find two college-aged guys standing in the space Mr. Arrogant Ass occupied a few minutes ago. Ignoring the flush crawling up my neck, I give them a wide grin. "Hi! Welcome! Never mind me and my, uh, weird ramblings. What can I get you?"

Quinn vanishes behind the coffee machine again while I pack a lemon meringue tartlet and a triple chocolate brownie —"Excellent choice," I tell the guy who ordered it—into a bakery box. I consider trying to explain the unibrow-third-nipple comment to them, but decide it's probably a conversation Nigel wouldn't approve of me having with a customer. I give the two guys friendly smiles instead, and the grins they give me in return are ... okay, definitely *too* friendly. Even for me. I'm glad I chose not to mention the word 'nipple' again in their presence. Especially when one of them drops a very generous tip into the tip jar and gives me another once-over—lingering on my chest—as he leaves.

Gross. I won't complain about the tip, though. I pick up the glass jar to get a better idea of the number of coins he dropped inside while Quinn, who clearly doesn't value her brain cells nearly as much as she would have me believe, grabs the TV remote and turns the volume back up.

"We've all seen the human version of this show, of course," the news anchor says to the woman who's now sitting on the studio couch with her, "but throw in a real live prince and *actual magic*, and it's a whole new ball game!"

"Right?" the other woman replies. "Instead of roses, Prince Kieren will be gifting diamond bracelets and pearl necklaces and other enchanted jewels to his favorite contestants every week."

"Are you *kidding* me?" Quinn demands. "No wonder these girls are literally *throwing* themselves at this show. They don't care about marrying a prince; they're there for the enchanted jewelry!"

"I don't know." I frown at the screen, where a grid of smiling headshots shows the twenty-nine contestants revealed so far. "Seems like most of them are disgustingly rich already."

"But *fae* jewelry? That stuff sells for gazillions!"

With a sigh, I take the remote from her. "We need to turn this crap off before you give yourself an ulcer." I hit the power button, then pull my phone out of the back pocket of my jeans. Seconds after I tap the play button on my newest playlist, a quiet piano melody reaches my ears from the speakers installed around the coffee shop.

"Ugh, life isn't faaaiiir," Quinn moans, draping herself dramatically across the counter beside me. "But this is good.

Really good." She points to one of the speakers, and I know she's referring to the music. "It like ... transports me to another world," she murmurs, closing her eyes.

"Thanks," I mumble, my face warming up again. "I just need better equipment and better software and—well, better everything. Access to a live orchestra would be awesome. I can only imagine the thrill of hearing my work brought to life by a concert hall full of *real* instruments."

"It would be incredible," Quinn says on a sigh. Her phone chirps, and she moves around me to grab it from the shelf hidden beneath the cakes and pastries. "Maybe it'll happen one day. Maybe we'll be sitting together in some fancy concert hall and ..." She trails off, her eyes scanning something on her phone as her pale face grows even paler.

"What?" I ask. "What's wrong?"

"It's ... um ..." She clears her throat. "An email from Matt. He says he has to let me go. At the end of next month. They have a surplus of tutors now, and they can't afford—" her voice breaks. She clears it again. "They can't afford to keep us all."

"That's ridiculous!" I exclaim. "You're one of the best. You're definitely better than I am."

"Yeah, well, whether that's true or not," she says in a wobbly high-pitched tone, "it doesn't matter. He's been told they have to get rid of the least qualified tutors, and since I've apparently made *no* effort to further educate myself since graduating high school—as if that's my fault—goodbye Quinn."

Shit. That means—

My own phone buzzes in my hand, and I know what I'm going to see before I even look down. My eyes land on the cracked screen anyway. There's a new email from Matt at Gould Star Tutors. I feel ill as I tap on it with my thumb. "Me too," I whisper, my eyes scanning a similar message. "They're getting rid of me too."

"Shit, Avery. *Shit.* We can't afford rent without this. Where are we going to *live*?"

"It's ... it's okay. We'll figure something out. I'll write more music and—"

"No, seriously!" she interrupts, her face red and tears threatening to spill down her cheeks. "How did life get to be so fucking unfair? Some ivy league girl whose daddy already owns half the tech world is going to spend a few weeks dancing around in pretty dresses and going on dates with a magical prince and then walk away with jewels worth millions, and people like us work our *asses* off and *still* end up with nothing."

I grit my teeth and force myself to put my phone down before I squeeze the life out of the darn thing. If I break this one, there's no way I can afford another. "I know," I say quietly. "It's not fair. Life has never been fair. But we just have to—"

The front door bangs open. I look up, and into The Grumpy Bean rush none other than Carwyn Aster and Evanna Zynn, the two flamboyant faerie hosts of *The Princess Game*.

Chapter Three

My heart almost stutters to a complete halt. I blink. Then blink again. I can't be seeing this correctly. The two hosts of the most famous reality TV show of all time can't possibly be *inside The Grumpy Bean* of all places. Right? I look at Quinn, but her mouth is hanging open as she stares in the direction of the two faeries, so clearly I'm not hallucinating.

"What a *disaster*." Carwyn, in a purple and lime striped suit, drops into a chair at the nearest table, one hand delicately wiping his brow. "I should have known. I should have *known*."

"You should have known that Miss All-American Girl Next Door was about to land herself in the middle of a sex-tape scandal?" Evanna replies. Beside me, Quinn emits another strangled sort of sound.

"How do you even know what it's called?" Carwyn demands.

Evanna dumps a large handbag on the table. "I've been watching reality TV since the day I first stepped into this world." She pats her pink curls, which are arranged in two neat bunches at the nape of her neck. "And I've been here far longer than you." She shrugs. "I'm just more familiar with things."

"Well. I never liked her," Carwyn sniffs, raising a hand to his voluminous pompadour-ish white hair. He smooths a strand back into place along his temple. "I knew there was something off about her. I *knew* it."

"You did not. We both checked her application, and she passed the most important test. Miss Suzanna Sex-Tape Star should have been a strong contender for the tiara."

"Suzanna?" Quinn whispers in horror. "Suzanna Mayberry? Didn't you help her with her application?"

I nod, picturing the afternoon Suzanna from the hair salon down the road sat in a corner booth here while I helped her word her answers in the best possible way. Quinn glared at us the entire time, refusing to take part. I agreed that Suzanna was mad for wanting to have anything to do with the fae, but she begged for help so many times that I felt I couldn't say no. "Um, yeah, a little bit," I whisper back.

"Oh shut up, you basically filled out the entire application for her."

"Shh!" I poke Quinn with my elbow and return my attention to the two faeries.

"... going to get fired over this debacle," Carwyn is saying.

"Yes, that is an unfortunate possibility." Evanna pulls a tablet from her handbag. "The *one* contestant we were allowed to choose, and we screwed it up."

"Unfortunate?" Carwyn repeats. "It would be a *calamity*! I can't get fired!" He gestures impatiently at the tablet. "Hand me that thing."

"I'm in the middle of—"

"The list. I need to see the *list*." He leans forward and grabs the tablet out of her hands. "There must be someone more suitable who—"

"If there *is*, I'm sure I'll be able to find her faster than—"

"I can find it."

"You couldn't find an elephant if it charged right into you."

I bite my lip to hold my laughter in, until Carwyn shouts "Blast it!" so loudly that both Quinn and I literally flinch. Carwyn's screen-tapping becomes more frenzied until he shoves it at Evanna. "Fine. Take it. I can't make these damn things work. Find the letter box."

"That's exactly what I was about to *do*, but I need to check if the location sharing thingy is still on."

I look at Quinn. "Letter box?" I whisper.

"Am I dreaming this craziness?" she whispers back.

"Double blast," Evanna hisses. "I thought I turned it off. Well, it's too late now. That slimy what's-his-name is no doubt leading them all here as we speak. We've probably got ten minutes, if that."

"*You're* the one who made the deal with the slimy what's-his-name."

"And *you're* the one who came up with the live stunt idea," Evanna snaps back.

"I'm sure that's not true."

"So true."

"What a *nightmare*," Carwyn groans. "Now the pop-sees are going to show up with their flashing bulbs and obnoxiously large cameras, and we'll have no one to reveal to them. *So* humiliating."

"Paparazzi," Evanna corrects.

"Yes, that's what I said."

Evanna huffs as she swipes at her screen. Then she pauses.

"Ah. I see the social media girl has announced her participation. Only one contestant left."

"Yes, *our* contestant. Miss Sex-Tape Star. That's going to go down fabulously well with the Glittering Palace. We'll be fired before the day is done."

Evanna looks up, a thoughtful expression on her face. "Perhaps they'll find it—"

"If you say 'amusing,' I will slap you with that thing. Now find me the list. We need to fix this problem."

"I've been looking, but I don't know where the list is! It's not in the letter box—*inbox*—so there must be some, uh ... digital filing cabinet equivalent where documents are stored."

Carwyn shakes his head. "Useless. You told me you were *familiar* with things."

"Just because I've spent multiple years and thousands of hours watching television doesn't mean I know how to use all their technology! Besides, there's no possible way we can fix this in under ten minutes. Even if you manage to find some fresh-faced, clean-cut girl from a wholesome yet influential family who—most importantly—has never stepped a toe out of line, you won't be able to get her here in time for our surprise reveal."

Carwyn slaps both palms down on the table and looks around, as if suddenly becoming aware that there might be other people around. "Ah." His face brightens when he sees us. "You. Coffee girl." He snaps his fingers in our direction. I'm not sure which of us he's calling, but Quinn ducks automatically behind the coffee machine, so I hurry around the counter, attempting to smooth the wrinkles out of my apron as I go.

"Hi! Welcome! What can I do for you?"

"Make this thing work." He grabs the tablet and pushes it at me. "It's dreadfully important. There's a list of names hiding ...

somewhere." He waves vaguely at the tablet. "I need you to find it."

"Sure, absolutely." I turn the tablet the right way up. If I can get a glowing report from the two hosts of *The Princess Game* by being friendly and helpful, that will surely outweigh any negative feedback Mr. Arrogant Ass might possibly send in about me. As luck would have it, the tablet is from the same family of devices as my phone—albeit a far newer member of the family—which means I manage to navigate my way to the 'digital filing cabinet equivalent,' as Evanna called it, fairly quickly.

"It should be somewhere here," I say, making a show of keeping my eyes raised as I hand the tablet back. Wouldn't want them to think I'm snooping through all their private documents.

"Thank you ever so—" Carwyn stops short, frowning. "Wait," he murmurs. "Listen." He cocks his head to the side. "What is that? That music that's playing?"

"Oh, um, just some background music. I can change it if you don't like it. I know it's not the usual—"

"No, no. Do not change it." He stares at nothing, blinking slowly. "It's ... quite lovely."

"It is," Evanna murmurs. "Lovely indeed."

"Oh." My face warms, and I almost thank them. But that would be weird considering they have no idea I'm the one who composed the piece.

"It's one of hers," Quinn says, appearing at my side with two glasses of lemon water. "She wrote it."

"Oh, is that so?" Carwyn looks even more interested now.

"Uh, yes. Just a little hobby of mine," I explain awkwardly. "Um, anyway ... did I help you find the list? Is it in that folder?"

"Forget the list," Carwyn says.

"Forget the list?" I repeat.

"Forget the list," Evanna confirms. She and Carwyn exchange a brief glance weighted with some hidden meaning. They both return their eyes to me.

"Daaarling," Carwyn says slowly and appreciatively, looking at me as if seeing me for the first time. "You seem very nice."

"Um ... thanks?"

"Very girl-next-door," Evanna says.

My gaze bounces between the two of them. "Thanks ... again?"

"Fresh-faced, tanned skin, golden hair. And I love the pony-tail. Very cute." Evanna peers closer, scrutinizing my face. "Blue eyes. Nice touch. Are they real?"

"Uh—"

"Never mind." She waves a hand and laughs. "Doesn't matter, either way. Are you married, divorced, engaged?"

"No—"

"Any skeletons in your closet? Scandals we should know about? A secret sex tape?"

"Absolutely no sex tape," I say firmly, my cheeks heating slightly as I focus on the last question and ignore the first. "Never in a million years."

Carwyn squints at me. "Truth," he declares with a short nod. "That was the truth."

A tiny part of my brain tries to figure out if this is something I've heard of before—can all faeries tell the difference between truth and a lie?—but the rest of my brain scrambles ahead, figuring out exactly where they're heading with this. I need to tell them they've got the wrong—

"Older than eighteen?"

"Yes," I answer automatically. "Nineteen. Almost twenty. But—"

"Perfect. You're our girl. For the show. *The Princess Game*." He laughs loudly. "In case you didn't recognize us."

"I—no. Just wait." I hold both hands up. "I don't want to marry a prince. Especially not a fae prince. No offense," I add hastily. "I just mean that that's not the life I want."

"Oh, darling." Carwyn waves a hand and chuckles as if I've just shared an inside joke. "This is the life *everyone* wants. Do you have any idea how many applications we received?"

"I—"

"Tens of thousands. *Hundreds* of thousands. Girls across the world would *kill* to be standing in your shoes right now."

"Well ... I don't know about that. I haven't exactly had the best life."

"All the more reason to throw your arms around this opportunity and give it a great big kiss!" Carwyn exclaims.

"Look, I'll be honest with you." Evanna stands and moves closer. "You're certainly not our first choice. We know nothing about you other than the fact that you work in a coffee shop and appear to be scandal-free. But we're desperate. We've been dropping hints with the media for weeks that we'll be doing a surprise live reveal of the final contestant. They've been following us around. They've been primed to be ready at any moment, and now they know that today is the day. They know our location. They'll be here in mere minutes. And if we have no one—or worse, if someone discovers the girl we *were* going to reveal until about twenty minutes ago—we will humiliate ourselves and bring the absolute worst kind of publicity to the show."

"Well ... I mean ... there's no such thing as bad publicity?" I suggest weakly, but my mind is beginning to race. I think of my third-hand keyboard and battered old headphones, the countless hours of YouTube tutorials I've watched to teach myself how to play, the pieces of music I've recorded on free apps on my phone. Never mind my dreams of attending a real music school and Quinn's dreams of going to med school, which are probably still out of reach. The mere fact that this could save us from *homelessness* is a major drawcard.

I remember the TV conversation we overhead earlier. *Instead of roses, Prince Kieren will be gifting diamond bracelets and pearl necklaces and other enchanted jewels to his favorite contestants every week.* If I could be one of those favorites for just *one week,* it would change my life. How much could I sell a diamond bracelet for? A *fae* diamond bracelet? And even if I'm sent home with nothing after the first week, this could still be incredible exposure for my music. *Millions* of people might possibly hear snippets of my compositions. Some of them might become genuine fans and stick with me after I've been dismissed from the competition.

Abruptly, as if someone switched a light on, I wonder why on earth I'm saying no to this. I *should* be giving this opportunity a gigantic kiss.

"There is most certainly such a thing as bad publicity," Evanna answers. "And there is also such a thing as being fired. Which I have no interest in."

"If I agree to this," I say hesitantly, "there isn't any real chance that I would be expected to actually *marry* the prince, right? I mean, of course there wouldn't be. I'm nobody."

"Of course, exactly," Carwyn says, standing and moving to Evanna's side, hands up in a reassuring gesture. "You don't have to worry about that. The prince is expected to choose someone with influence and connections. Any contestants who *don't* come with those sorts of attachments are merely there for ..." He waves a hand and looks at Evanna. "What did the producers say?"

"Entertainment?" I suggest. "Drama? The ratings?"

"Yes, yes, the *ratings*. Those were definitely mentioned."

"Which you did *not* hear from us," Evanna hastens to add. "Officially, the prince is out to find his one true love. The Glittering Palace would like everyone to believe that all the girls stand an equal chance of winning his heart."

"Even though we all know that's nonsense?"

"Yes." Her smile is fixed in place, her bright white teeth still visible. "So if you repeat this conversation to anyone, we will firmly deny it. And curse your family for the next seven gener—"

"What Evanna *means* to say," Carwyn interrupts with a loud and very fake laugh, "is that you don't have to worry about him actually choosing you."

"Um ... well ..." I take a deep breath. "Okay then."

"Wonderful!" He clasps his hands together.

Quinn edges closer to me. "Avery, are *serious*? This is—"

"We can go over the paperwork in detail afterwards," Carwyn says, slipping an arm between Quinn and me and pulling me forward. He turns his back to Quinn. "For now, a mirror contract will do." He waves his hand and a small round mirror with a gilt frame takes shape in the air in front of us. "All you need to do is look into the mirror and say 'I accept all terms and conditions of being a contestant in *The Princess Game.*"

Well. *That* doesn't sound like a smart idea. Every other contestant probably had a small army of lawyers comb through their contracts. "Um ... I don't know if—"

"Two million dollars."

I blink at him. "I'm sorry?"

"Agree to fill the role of Girl Next Door and I will pay you two million dollars."

"You ... don't have two million dollars," I say weakly.

"Darling. I'm co-hosting a once-in-a-lifetime reality fairytale event that your entire *world* is salivating to watch. You can't even *imagine* what they're paying me. Agree to be part of the show, make it to the Top 10, and I will pay you two million dollars after you're dismissed."

"But—I—why the Top 10?"

"You are the hosts' choice," Evanna says. "It reflects well on us if you make it past a certain point in the show. There are ..." Her eyes flick up and land on Carwyn's "... certain benefits for us."

An image pops into my head. A small circle of influential fae —members of the royal family, celebrities like Carwyn and Evanna—going through the list of contestants and placing bets on how far each girl will go and who will last the longest. Is that the kind of thing Evanna means? "I can probably survive the first few dismissals, but to outlast twenty other girls? That's a lot."

Carwyn's eyes sweep down and then up again. "Not when you look like that, darling. Your beauty isn't painted on. It's real. That's enough to make you stand out. Enough for Prince Kieren to keep you around a while."

"Even if I have zero connections, zero family, absolutely nothing to offer him?"

He frowns as Evanna bustles away from us toward the door. "Zero family? Everyone has *someone* they're connected to. Don't they?"

"Um, well ... not the girl who was abandoned as a baby and spent her childhood being passed from one foster home to the next. Quinn, my best friend—" I look over my shoulder at her "—is the closest thing I have to family."

"Hmm." Carwyn taps his chin. "I'm going to need a minute

to decide whether it would be advantageous to include that little tidbit in your backstory or not."

"Can you take that minute *afterwards*?" Evanna demands from the doorway. "We're about to be discovered."

"Of course, of course, yes. We'll make this work. We don't exactly have another option right now." He begins to speak even faster, gesticulating wildly with his hands. "We'll make this a rags to riches story. The audience will *love* it. Ooh, the makeover episode in particular. You will *shine* in that one, darling." He brings one hand to his lips and mimics a chef's kiss. "And you're the *Girl Next Door*, so of course you have to be more relatable to the average person than most of the other contestants. Totally ordinary, totally down to earth. The more humble your beginnings, the better. Yes. *Yes.* I love it."

"I haven't signed the contract yet," I remind him.

"Better make it quick, sweetheart," Evanna shouts, shoving away from the door. "I think they just spotted me."

"Fine. Two million, and take care of Quinn," I say hurriedly.

"What?" Quinn asks.

"Take care of her *how*?" Carwyn asks.

"Rent, security—whatever she needs while I'm gone. If I'm not around to help out, she won't be able to afford all our living expenses."

"Fine, yes, of course. We'll make sure she wants for nothing as long as you're still a contestant."

"Then look into the mirror and say that."

Carwyn arches one eyebrow and regards me with something that might possibly be respect. Then he faces the mirror, muttering, "I like you, Girl Next Door." He clears his throat, asks for Quinn's full name, and then makes a statement about providing financially for her as long as I'm still in the game, plus paying me two million dollars if I'm dismissed after making it to the Top 10. He adds a line about doing it in such a way that it will look like a parting gift from the prince so as not to raise suspicion, which hadn't even crossed my mind. I watch in silent wonder as his words shine on the mirror's surface before vanishing, then stumble through my own statement about accepting all terms and conditions.

"Excellent!" Evanna says before my final words have disappeared from the mirror's glossy surface. She waves her hand, the mirror vanishes, and then she's pulling me toward the front door of The Grumpy Bean. "There they are!" And there they are indeed. My heart leaps into my throat when I see the horde of people rushing toward our teeny coffee shop.

"I think we should meet them outside, don't you?" Carwyn says. "Not enough space inside here for all those pop-sees."

"Paparazzi," I mumble faintly.

"Oh, what's your name, darling?" Carwyn leans closer and laughs into my ear. "How embarrassing if I attempted to introduce you, live to millions of people, and I didn't even know your name!"

"Avery," I say, but my voice is a hoarse whisper even I can barely hear. Did he say *millions* of people? I clear my throat. "Avery Evans."

"Lovely. Simply lovely. Now." He tips my chin up and gives me an exaggerated grin. "Remember to *smiiiiiile*. Shoulders back, chin up, *don't* touch that delightful ponytail." He smacks my hand as I reach absently toward the back of my head. Then he walks ahead of me, throws the door open, and steps out with Evanna.

"Oh, you *found* us!" she squeals. "I'm delighted. *Just* delighted. Because we have the most fabulous surprise for you."

Holy heck, this is really happening. I turn to look back at Quinn, but before I can meet her gaze, a strong hand clamps around my wrist. Evanna tugs me outside in front of an ocean of shiny camera lenses. "Please allow us to introduce the final contestant of *The Princess Game* ... Avery Evans!"

Chapter Four

"Holy shopping spree," Quinn whispers as our apartment door clicks shut behind the three Glittering Palace employees. She grips my hand as the two of us stare at the boxes and bags crammed into our tiny living room slash kitchen. "They bought you all this stuff?"

"Quinn, they bought me like *ten times* this stuff!" I whisper-shriek. "This is just a fraction of the clothes she made me choose. So I can 'look respectable—'" I curl my fingers in the air as I quote the woman I've spent the entire day with "—in any photos of me that wind up in the media between now and the start of the competition. The rest was sent straight to the palace."

"This is insane, Avery. Completely bonkers. Who would have thought you'd have your own *personal shopper*?"

"Image consultant," I correct in a pompous tone, before we both double over laughing.

"That sounds ... even more ... absurd," she says between snorts of laughter.

"I know!"

It's been a week and a half since Carwyn and Evanna revealed me as the final contestant and turned my life upside down. My job at The Grumpy Bean came to an immediate end —for my safety, Carwyn said—and a day later, I discovered two bodyguards stationed on the front steps of my building. When the first of the paparazzi showed up twenty minutes later, I understood why.

Then came a blur of days filled with phone calls and contracts and meetings with Mary-Louise, my assigned 'image consultant.' We went through everything from my tagline-length backstory ("Let's go with 'barista by day, budding composer by night,'" she decided) to my social media presence ("Well," she said while examining my barely active social channels, "this is disappointing.") to the contents of my wardrobe (shock seemed to render her speechless at that point).

She picked out a few things I was allowed to wear if I happened to go out in public—"We'll send a car if you need to go anywhere," she added—and then scheduled today's shopping spree. Some of it took place online this morning, while the rest happened in high-end boutiques we drove about two hours to get to. According to Mary-Louise, there was nothing suitable in the town Quinn and I live in.

I did my best to pretend I was interested and excited—and did a stellar job of keeping myself from throwing up every time I looked at a price tag—but I had zero energy left by the time Mary-Louise announced we were done. I flopped into the back of the obnoxiously fancy car and slept all the way home. Part of me wonders now, as I stare at all the boxes and bags with their fancy labels, if I might still be asleep and dreaming.

"And that's not all," I tell Quinn. "Someone's coming by tomorrow to take all my measurements for the dresses."

"The dresses?"

"For ... I don't know. Events? I guess nothing we bought today is fancy enough."

"I suppose you need ballgowns or something."

I find myself laughing again. This is all too crazy. I can't believe I'm going to be living *in the Glittering Palace*. Right next to the main portal between our world and Faeworld. I'm still waiting for someone to show up at our door and tell me it was all a mistake and they've now chosen the *real* final contestant. But until that happens, I'll continue living as if this isn't just a dream. "Want to see everything?" I ask Quinn.

"Of course!"

We clear a space on the couch, then sit down and start unpacking dresses, shoes, skirts, jeans and other accessories. There's nothing too fancy—after all, my image is Girl Next Door—but the fit and quality are far superior to anything I've ever owned before.

Quinn starts laughing again when she opens a box to reveal a lacy white bra and matching panties. "It's hilarious that your image makeover includes new *underwear*. I mean, no one's going to see what's under your clothes."

I sober up quickly as an alarming thought occurs to me. "Oh, shit, I *hope* no one's going to see under my clothes. I hadn't thought of that. You don't think ... I mean, I know it's a reality TV show and there'll be cameras all over the place, but—"

"Relax. The show is totally PG, right? Kids all over the world are going to be watching this thing. And those fae royals are so prim and proper. No one's going to be filming you in your *underwear*."

"Okay, but ... what about off-camera. What if he *expects* ..." I give her a look loaded with meaning.

She wrinkles her nose. "Ew. Gross. As if he isn't entitled enough already."

"Right? And even if I *did* like him, he'll essentially be dating multiple girls at the same time, and doing who knows what with all of them. *So* not my vibe. But I'm worried he might *think* that's my vibe if I'm the kind of girl who wanted to be on this show, and he'll expect certain things from me."

"Well then he'll discover very quickly that you're *not* that kind of girl." Quinn taps me on the head with the cardboard lid and grins. "You might want to keep one of these handy so you can fight him off if he gets too—"

"Oh shut up," I snort, snatching it from her while mentally shoving away the cold clamminess that seeps into my bones at the thought of having to physically fight a man off. I force another laugh. *Be happy, Avery. Be happy.* "I'll never make it to the Top 10 if I take your advice."

"True. Definitely don't take my advice. I haven't had a boyfriend since Lhydan the Liar, and that whole relationship was just a nightmare."

"We're not supposed to mention Lhydan the Liar," I say solemnly, only partly focusing on Quinn. The icy memories that rose abruptly to the surface have begun to recede. My heart rate slows. *I'm fine, I'm fine, I'm fine.*

"Right. Because he was ..." Quinn trails off as a loud, chirpy tone fills the room. "What's that?"

It takes me a moment to place the sound. "Oh, my new phone." I push boxes aside until I find my messenger bag—let's not talk about the look Mary-Louise gave me when I walked out with *that* slung across my body—and dig inside it.

"They got you a new *phone*?"

"Well, Mary-Louise wanted me to post a selfie at one of the boutiques." I dig inside the bag and locate the phone. "She wasn't impressed that I haven't posted a thing since that photo Carwyn made you take of me with him and Evanna. She said I should be updating my followers daily on all my exciting preparations for the show." I flop back against the couch cushions and frown at the phone's screen. The annoying chirpy trill appears to be related to a reminder someone set for me. *Daily post on all social platforms!* I roll my eyes and put the phone screen-down on the couch between us.

"Anyway, my phone kept freezing, and the camera app kept restarting, and then it hit 43% battery and died like it always does. Mary-Louise had a meltdown, called someone, demanded a new phone be bought *immediately*, and when we got into the car again, some guy who looked about twelve asked me to hand over my old phone so he could do ... you know, that thing where all your apps and contacts and data and stuff are copied over. So yeah. New phone." I wave it at Quinn before placing it on the couch again. "Now I'm ready to keep all my followers updated on every intimate detail of my life at the Glittering Palace."

Quinn snorts. "All seven of your followers?"

"Rude!" I exclaim. "I have at least ... I don't know, three hundred."

"Yeah, that's what I mean."

I bump her knee with mine, but she has a point. I tried to use social media to build an audience for my music, but I've always been terrible at that stuff, and it doesn't help that the kind of music I write will never have mass appeal. Add to that the fact that I haven't had *time* to continually post on social media in between my three jobs and writing music, and I was never going to be Little Miss Social Media Personality.

"Okay, so they got you new clothes, new shoes, new underwear, and a new phone," Quinn says, ticking the items off on her fingers. "Anything else?"

"I think that's all of it. Oh, they also gave me the info pack with everything I need to know about the prince and all the other girls."

"Ooh, where's that? I want to take a look."

"So you can lose another two million brain cells?" I ask, one brow raised.

"Shut up. You know I'm hooked on this trash. And now I have a legitimate excuse for it: my bestie is a contestant. So hand over the file." She extends her hand toward me, palm up.

"Fine, fine." I open up my messenger bag and remove the info pack, which is actually a full-color, glossy-paged, hard-bound book with patterns embossed in gold foil on the cover. Because the fae are extra like that.

"Okay," Quinn says, turning to the first page. "Prince Faerie Face. Tall, dark and handsome, twenty-five years old, super uptight, doesn't possess the ability to smile."

I peer over her arm and examine the photo I've already seen splashed across magazine covers and news articles a bazillion times. With his dark hair, chiseled features, and piercing blue-gray eyes that have been described as 'magnetic' countless times, Prince Kieren is the epitome of swoon worthy. "I guess it doesn't hurt that he looks like a model."

"A model who just sucked a lemon, maybe." Quinn wrinkles her nose. "And his looks are probably an illusion that has to be magicked into place every day."

"You know they can't do that," I remind her. "Make themselves look like someone else."

"I don't mean that. I mean he's probably *enhancing* his features with magic."

"Oh, yeah. Probably. I'll let you know if I'm lucky enough to catch a glimpse of his *un-enhanced* face."

"Ooh, send me a photo if you do."

"If it's at all possible—which I doubt—I totally will."

"Why wouldn't it be possible? That fancy new phone of yours probably has some super, *super* zoom. You could get a photo without him even knowing."

"Um, because ..." I've been putting off mentioning this since I read the contract in full and discovered this particular rule. I scratch my cheek and stare determinedly at my lap. "We're only allowed to use our phones during approved times, and I'm guessing there will be people around to kind of ... monitor us during those times. Outside of that, we have to hand our phones over."

"Wait, what?" I sense Quinn looking over at me. "So ... you and I can't chat or text whenever we want?"

I force myself to meet her gaze. "No. Unfortunately not."

"Oh. Wow." She shakes her head, looking a little lost all of a sudden. "I didn't realize ... but I guess that makes sense. They'll obviously have their professional camera crew there, filming all the content for the show, so they wouldn't want you filming a whole bunch of stuff outside of that and broadcasting it on your own social platforms before they get a chance to air it. And I'm sure the fae have things to hide as well. Things they don't want humans photographing or filming. It's just ... weird that I won't be able to talk to you whenever I want. I think we've spoken literally every day since ..."

"Since the day we met," I say quietly. "At Alice's."

She reaches for my hand. "Best and worst thing that ever happened to us."

"Yeah." I squeeze her hand in return.

She drops her head back against the couch and sighs. "Is this all a terrible idea? Drawing attention to yourself like this? To *both* of us?"

"It will be fine," I say firmly. "There's nothing to worry about."

"You sure? You know we don't have a picture-perfect past."

"I know, and that's what I told all these palace people and studio people. I know Carwyn and Evanna didn't fully understand what I meant when I said I haven't had the best life. But Mary-Louise went through everything, and she said that all of it —the foster homes, the whole struggling to rise above my circumstances, my determination to make something of myself, etc., etc.—will all help the audience to warm to me. And the palace people have already done their own digging into my background, and they didn't find anything objectionable. Well, other than my minimal social media presence and my shockingly out-of-style clothes."

Quinn chuckles, but it's half-hearted. "I guess. It's just ... if anyone starts to wonder about Caz—"

"No one's going to wonder about Caz."

"And what about Maddox? He—"

"Maddox never actually knew anything."

"But what if he guessed?"

"Guesses don't count." I loop an arm around her shoulders and force my mind toward sunny thoughts before that sick, clammy feeling can invade my senses again. "This is the break we've been waiting for, okay? It's going to be crazy and fun and a thousand percent worth every painful moment I have to spend in Prince Faerie Face's presence, and one day we're going to look back at that morning in The Grumpy Bean as the moment everything changed for us."

She looks up at me. "I wish I had your glass-half-full mentality."

"My glass is *full* full, remember? Full enough for both of us."

She rolls her eyes at my corniness, the way she always does. "Okay, enough with the emotional stuff." She sits straighter and looks down at the book. "So you have cell phone rules. Whatever. We can deal. It just means you'll have way more to tell me when you *are* allowed to call me."

"Exactly. Now hand that back please." I heft the book off her lap and dump it on my own. "I need to memorize every detail about the prince if I'm going to have any hope of making it to the Top 10."

"Can you do that later? I'm more interested in learning about your competition. So I can make fun of them."

"Fine."

We look through the book, which provides a basic summary of every contestant's background, family, qualifications, achievements, and current work or study situation. It becomes clearer with every perfect, glossy page that I can't compete with any of these girls. The Retail Heiress, the Ivy League Princess, the Politician's Daughter, the Heir to a Whiskey Empire, an *actual* European Princess. How can I possibly compare when my biggest accomplishments in life are a few pieces of music available on streaming services and the ability to produce decent latte art with my eyes shut?

I think of all the footage I've already seen of these girls. Video clips of them having dinner with their perfect families inside their perfect palatial homes, or receiving awards for incredible academic or sporting accomplishments, or helping out at volunteer organizations while somehow managing to keep their hair, makeup and nails perfectly intact.

And what has the media shown of *me*? An embarrassing clip of me grinning like a weirdo while making a coffee at The Grumpy Bean—shot in the early hours of the morning before it opened, because of course I don't actually work there anymore—an admittedly cute video of me giving a ten year old a piano lesson, and then another embarrassing clip of Quinn and me standing outside our crummy, rundown apartment building while I lean over to give her a huge hug and she tries not to pass out from the anxiety of being in front of a camera.

"This does *not* look like the kind of place the Girl Next Door lives," I told the guy who was in charge of the camera crew that followed me around for a day.

"True, but it's all about the rags-to-riches fairytale that is Avery Evans," he told me. "And I've used clever angles and a warm filter. Trust me, it won't look this bad on screen."

He was right. Kind of. But I'm still basically a joke compared to the other twenty-nine contestants.

"I'm so not cut out for this competition," I murmur to Quinn as we turn yet another glossy page. "I mean, what are the chances of me actually making it to the Top 10? I know Carwyn suggested it would be easy, but he was just saying that so I'd agree to be the final contestant and he could save his own ass from embarrassment."

Quinn nods as she scours the current page. "I know. The chance is super slim, considering you're not a real contender for the tiara. It's obvious before the competition even begins that Prince Faerie Face can't choose you, so it would make sense for him to dismiss you early."

"Yeah." I let out a heavy sigh.

"But hey, you can sell all your new clothes and make a fortune that way."

"If only. There's probably some fine print in the contract that says it's all property of the Glittering Palace and I won't get to take any of it with me when I'm dismissed."

"Ugh, yes. Those selfish fae. They'd probably sooner *burn* them than let you—"

My phone starts singing, interrupting Quinn. I turn it over and find the same reminder on the screen: *Daily post on all social platforms!* I swipe it away again, but this time, before I can look up, I notice something else. A colorful notification alerting me to the fact that someone has liked a post. And it's not the only one. I start scrolling through the lock screen, and the notifications go on and on. *Dozens* of them. "Wait, where did these ..."

"What?" Quinn asks as I open the app that suddenly seems to be going crazy with notifications and tap through to my profile page. My eyes land on the number of followers, and I have to blink. Then blink again. My jaw almost unhinges itself from the rest of my skull. "What is it?" Quinn asks.

My face is hot. I can't answer. Mary-Louise's twelve-year-old friend must have logged me into the wrong account. That's the only explanation. Except ... that's my profile photo. The one I haven't bothered to change in about two years. And that's my username. Did Mary-Louise make him *buy* an account that already had followers and then switch the username and photo to mine? And repost all the photos from my old account?

"Holy *shit*!" Quinn gasps, leaning over and staring at the screen. "You have twelve and a half *thousand* followers? Since when?"

"I ... don't know."

She yanks the phone out of my hand and begins scrolling through the notifications. "Since the day you were announced as a contestant. Since the day you posted that picture with the crazy hosts."

"But ... so ... that's definitely my account?"

"Yes, this is your account." She looks at me. "Aves, how did you not know this? Don't you check these things?"

"Well ... there isn't usually much to check. And I've been busy. Things have been a bit crazy ever since the announcement."

"Didn't you have notifications turned on before? On your old phone?"

"I'm pretty sure I did. But it was super glitchy, so ... I don't know. Maybe it just stopped showing notifications at some point and I never noticed?"

She tips her head back and laughs loudly. "How are you *so* bad at social media?"

"I'm not! I just had a crap phone!"

"Oh my gosh, this is so awesome. I mean, it's ridiculous, but it's also awesome. Oh! Have you checked if your number of listens has increased?" She looks up and finds the answer in my eyes before I can squeak out a reply. "Eek, I'm checking now!" She grips my phone tighter and taps the music icon at the bottom of my home screen. "You could be a millionaire already, Aves!"

"I doubt it," I say, but I'm laughing as I lean over her arm and watch her navigate to my profile on the music app, my heart pattering too quickly and a thrill racing through my body. This really is it, I decide before I can see whether the view count of any of my popular songs has increased dramatically. This is the moment our lives change forever.

Chapter Five

The limousine sweeps beneath a flower-laden arch and carries me along an avenue of trees toward the Glittering Palace. If I thought the plane trip and the limo ride were exciting, they're nothing compared to the thrill that races through me as we round a corner and the palace comes into view. Gleaming white in the morning sun, its many windows sparkling like diamonds, it towers above the surrounding landscape. My face is practically glued to the window as my eyes travel the ornate turrets and elegant spires, the intricate marble carvings and delicately curved arches. I've seen it all before online and on TV, of course, but never in my wildest dreams did I think I'd ever come this close to it in real life.

"Are you all right, Miss Avery?" The question comes from the neat, stiff-backed young woman perched on the seat across from me. My aide, Iris. I'd almost forgotten she was here.

"I ... yes," I whisper, still staring wide-eyed out of the window. A distant voice in the back of my mind reminds me how unfortunate it is that this incredible place is filled with *fae*, but I'm sure I can handle that for a short while.

"It's impressive, isn't it?" Iris says. This morning was the first time I met her. She showed up at my teeny apartment looking organized and businesslike with a tablet in her hand and her dark, curly hair pulled into a tight ponytail. She gave me a million and one instructions and then ushered me into the limo. Then she proceeded to read out a list of rules as she tapped neatly on her tablet, hardly looking up once until we reached the airport.

In a faint whisper, I manage to reply, "'Impressive' is an understatement."

"True. Perhaps try to rein in your shock before stepping out of the limo, though," she suggests. "The cameras will be rolling, as you are aware. The contestants' arrivals are being aired live. Looking pleasantly dazzled is fine, but looking completely gobsmacked isn't exactly ... attractive."

I unstick my face from the window and clear my throat. "Right. Yes." And then a second later, when I spot something glistening in the sky on the other side of the palace, I'm pressed up against the limo door again. "Oh wow, is that the Shimmer?"

Without moving to the window to see what I'm talking about, Iris says, "Yes. You did know that the Glittering Palace is built right next to it, didn't you?"

"Yes, I did. It's just ... wow, it's *huge*." My eyes follow the upper edge of the circular shape that ripples with a faintly opalescent sheen. As with the palace, I've seen pictures and videos of the Shimmer too, but the scale is something I couldn't quite comprehend until now. "I mean, they could transport the entire palace through that portal if they wanted to," I add.

I remember the day it first appeared in the air, a hole roughly the size of an entire city block that showed a different world on the other side. No one knew exactly what to think. At first, there were rumors of an elaborate augmented reality stunt of some sort. It couldn't possibly be a *real* portal into another land. But these rumors hadn't even reached the majority of our world before people figured out it was indeed real. Some wailed about aliens and the apocalypse and the end of the world. Others couldn't wait to get to the other side to explore whatever fantastical land lay beyond the shimmering, almost transparent layer.

We were all wrong, of course, and the fae wasted no time stepping into our world and correcting us. They were subjects of the Autumn Court, they were not 'aliens,' and they were not here to end our world. "And sorry, no, you won't be able to explore our land. You'll die if you spend more than about half an hour here. Oh and bonus surprise: we've been walking among you humans for many years. You just didn't know about it."

There was a brief period when we thought they might want to enslave us all and take control of our world with their magic. They clearly thought they were the superior beings, and why else would they suddenly have revealed themselves? But they assured us they didn't want that either, and it soon became apparent that their magic wasn't the powerful force we thought it might be. They could cast all manner of simple spells—force a person to dance a perfect waltz for an hour or instantly change someone's hair color—but nothing they actually *created* was real or long-lasting. Their illusions, whether spectacular or simple, soon withered away to nothing. Still, we knew there was plenty they weren't explaining to us, and many of us spent months living in fear of what might come next.

Governments all over the world had emergency meetings and summits and other official sounding gatherings, and in the end, they decided there wasn't much they could do about the fae. They came and went as they pleased, they had no official identities in our world, and they couldn't spend more than a few weeks in our magic-barren land without needing to return to their own. Policies and laws were put in place to protect us, but that obviously didn't stop any black market trade, and the fae only really answered to their own king or queen, depending on which court they came from.

So life eventually returned to some kind of normal. For many of us, things didn't actually change that much. The fae were simply *there* in the same way actors and singers and sports stars were there: they existed, but the average person wasn't likely to come across them often in real life. At least ... that's what Quinn and I thought until we discovered one day that we were very, very wrong.

I clasp my hands together in my lap and force my mind firmly away from that dark line of thought and back to the details of the palace. The Autumn King gave orders for it to be built as soon as the initial uncertainty over the fae's arrival had settled. With permission from our government, it was constructed on our side of the Shimmer. A 'home away from home' for the royal family and nobles of the Autumn Court. Over the years, presidents, celebrities and other honored guests have been received at the Glittering Palace. Some have even been allowed through the Shimmer into Faeworld, though only for very brief periods due to the toxic effect of all that magic.

The Princess Game marks the first time a group of humans will spend so much time so close to Faeworld. Strict precautions have been put in place to ensure that only food that's safe for human consumption is prepared at the palace for the duration of the competition. In addition, we have to take specially crafted 'vitamins' every day to help our bodies acclimate to being so close to the Shimmer and to Faeworld's magic. Alarm bells went off in my head when a palace official first told me about these so-called vitamins. "Seriously? What dodgy substances are the fae forcing me to ingest?"

But then there was a two-hour documentary special on all of this, with footage of the expansive palace kitchens and interviews with the various chefs who work there and the human medical team and fae herbalists who created the vitamins. Quinn and I were still highly suspicious after we watched it, but by that point I'd been told I would probably die if I didn't take them—and I had been not so politely reminded that I'd apparently agreed to it in my contract.

"Are you ready?" Iris asks as the limo approaches the top of the driveway and the Glittering Palace grows larger and larger, blotting out most of the sky and blocking the Shimmer from view.

"No," I whisper, so quietly she probably didn't hear me. I'll never be ready for something like this. Even after all the etiquette, dance and deportment lessons of the past few weeks, I'm pretty sure everyone's going to realize I don't belong here the moment I step out of this vehicle.

But this is happening. My heart crashes wildly against my ribcage as the limo crawls around the fountain at the top of the driveway and stops beside a plush red carpet that extends all the way up the grand staircase and inside the entrance to the palace. A complex jumble of cameras, cables and lighting is positioned on one side. "Time to go," Iris says as an official looking man in a smart suit steps off the carpet and walks toward my side of the vehicle.

"Shitshitshit," I whisper, my heart climbing into my throat as it tries to escape my body and make a run for it. "I can't do this. I don't belong here. I'm *literally* nobody."

"Hey." Iris reaches across the space between us and places one hand on my knee. For the first time since the moment she appeared at my door, she forgets her tablet and looks at me. *Really* looks at me. Her eyes are beautiful, a bright hazel that's almost startling against her soft brown skin. She gives me a tight-lipped smile, and I suddenly wonder if perhaps I'm not the only one inside this car who's nervous. But her voice is firm when she says, "Of course you can do this. I've walked you through the whole process. Just smile, don't look at the cameras, walk with confidence, and make it inside the palace. By that time, the cameras will be focusing on the next contestant."

"Right. Okay." But I'm so nervous I think I may pass out, and my head is suddenly a tangle of every instruction Mary-Louise has hammered into my brain over the last several weeks and every rule Iris listed since the moment she introduced herself with a prim shake of my hand.

Curtsey in front of the royals.

Don't rise until they tell you to.

That weird knife with the sharp, curved edge is for eating fish.

Do not *enter the North Tower. Ever.*

The palace gardens are out of bounds after sundown.

Don't look at the cameras.

Remember to smile.

Don't forget to take your vitamins every morning.

Smile, smile, smiiiiile!

The door opens. A hand extends toward me. I swallow past the dryness in my throat, take one more steadying breath, and reach for the hand. All sound seems to cease as I emerge from the vehicle and step onto the carpet. I think the man who's guiding me might be saying something, but my brain can't process it. Cotton wool is pressed over my ears, and my eyes are glued to the steps ahead of me. *Don't look at the cameras, just walk straight ahead and up the stairs, and KEEP SMILING!*

The man releases me, and I'm suddenly walking on my own.

I'm walking! Not tripping! My brain takes a moment to appreciate this moment. Me in a floral-print sundress (of appropriate length) and delicate high-heeled shoes with my hair up in the ponytail that is now apparently a key element of my image, walking on a fancy red carpet toward a faerie palace. I think that 'gobsmacked' expression Iris warned me against might possibly be on my face.

I force a more serene smile onto my lips and keep walking. The distance to the steps is short, but it seems to take forever. When I finally reach them, I have to firmly instruct myself not to trip. I manage to make it to the top without incident, where I'm greeted at the gigantic open doorway by a pair of officials.

I made it! I want to scream. *I made it, I made it!* I almost trip over the edge of the carpet in my haste to get inside—and that's when everything becomes even more overwhelming. As if a bubble has just popped, my brain suddenly remembers how to process sound. The enormous foyer is filled with activity. Security guards in palace uniforms, people hurrying around with clipboards, camera gear stacked on top of piles of large black cases, and a line of girls in front of me. We appear to be moving through a security check of some sort. I think I remember Iris mentioning this, but I was so focused on the terrifying act of walking along a red carpet with half the world watching me that I didn't pay much attention to what came after that.

I swallow, take a deep breath, and try to figure out if I recognize the girls in front of me. I studied the info book, of course, but people look different from behind, and there's the fact that my brain is still stuck on the steps outside, screeching, *I'm walking into an actual faerie palace!*

Breathe, Avery, breathe.

"It's happening, people!" the girl in front of me squeals. "This is really it! The Glitter-Freaking Palaaaaace!"

At first I can't figure out if she's talking to someone specific or addressing all of us in general, but then she shifts slightly and I realize she's holding her phone up in front of her in selfie mode. I take a quick step to the side so I'm not in the background, realizing that it's Miss Social Media Personality, Cadence Cruz. I'm struggling to remember the other girls' names, but my brain seems to have decided Cadence is unforgettable. Perhaps it's because of her vibrant personality. Perhaps it's because she announced her participation in *The Princess Game* the same morning Carwyn and Evanna stumbled into The Grumpy Bean and roped me into all of this.

"... what it looks like once you walk inside," she's saying to her phone, tilting it so it can record the ornate details of the domed ceiling. I'm close enough to make out the red button in the corner of the screen that says Live. "How utterly *stunning*?" she says, holding the phone in front of her face again. "I can't wait to show you my—"

"Excuse me." A man in a palace uniform interrupts her, his hand out, palm out. "I'll need to take that. You were supposed to give it to the aide who accompanied you here."

"Oh, I did. This is my spare. She didn't say anything about—"

"Please hand it over."

Cadence's pouty lips pop open. "Ex*cuse* me?"

"Your phone please. Now."

With a few quick taps, she's ended the livestream and locked her phone. She folds her arms over her chest and glares at the man. "You know who I am, right?"

"Yes." His expression remains unchanged. His hand doesn't move.

Cadence's jaw drops a little further as she lets out a strangled scoff. "I have over eight million followers. They want to see and experience everything I'm seeing and experiencing."

"And that's precisely why I'm taking your phone. We don't need eight million humans snooping around the Glittering Palace alongside you."

She sucks in a gasp, pressing one hand to her chest and doing an excellent job of looking wounded. "Snooping? How *dare* you? I'm trying to give the show extra *publicity*. You want people to get an inside look at just how fabulous the lives of the fae truly are, don't you? Otherwise your king would never have agreed to all of this."

"Your phone. Now. You will be allowed access to it during certain supervised times. This was explained in the contract you signed. If you are unable to comply with this rule, I will need to escort you off the property immediately."

"Okay, *that's* not necessary," she grumbles, shoving her phone at the man.

"Your bags will be checked for additional recording equipment and any items of a harmful nature."

"Now I'm really offended. Why on earth would I want to harm any of you *lovely* people?"

I cover my mouth with my hand, trying to smother a snort. They both look in my direction, and I swing around immediately, hoping they didn't catch me eavesdropping. I catch the eye of the redheaded girl behind me, who must have witnessed the whole exchange as well. I expect she might roll her eyes at the whole thing, but she only frowns and looks away.

Sh-something, my brain nudges as I turn slowly back to face the front of the queue. Shona? Shelly? Shay! That's it. Shay O'Connell. Born in Ireland but raised American with her mother and twin sister. Still connected to her father's family in Ireland though, since the info book labeled her Heir to a

Whiskey Empire. Why the fae would be interested in whiskey, I have no idea, but they must have seen some possible benefit if they selected her as a contestant.

Cadence makes it through the security check without anything objectionable being found on her person, and then it's my turn. A woman stands in front of me and another behind me, both twisting their hands in the air near my body while I try not to feel supremely awkward. After several seconds of strange hand movements, a layer of fine gold sparkles settles over me. "Is this safe?" I ask before I can stop myself. It's taking all my self-control not to hastily brush the sparkles away. They're pretty, but I don't want them *on* me.

"Of course, Miss Avery," one of them answers, and a moment later, the sparkles vanish. "That way please," she adds, pointing toward an open door on the right-hand side of the foyer.

"Oh, okay. Thanks. Thank you." The doorway leads to a bright, airy lounge that instantly feels more civilized than the chaos of the foyer. Girls are perched on couches with delicate porcelain tea cups in their hands while serene music overlays the quiet conversation and polite laughter. A long table on one side of the room is laden with an assortment on pastries, sandwiches and other tiny, tasty-looking treats—though there don't seem to be many people actually eating them. Most importantly? There are no cameras in here. At least, not yet.

I head toward the drinks end of the table, deciding I should probably find something to hold in my hand instead of standing here looking awkward. I'm so busy trying to figure out what type of pink fruit is floating in the crystal water jug that I don't see the girl who's stepped into my path until I almost smack right into her. "Oh, sorry!" I stop abruptly and take a step backward.

"No, no, I'm sorry. Hi!" She smiles at me and sticks her hand out.

My mind goes blank for a second. I'm definitely not supposed to shake hands with the fae royals, but what about the other contestants? Did Mary-Louise ever mention that? I don't think so. Before the moment can become too awkward, I grasp the girl's hand. "Hi." I mentally flip through the info book in the hopes of finding her name, but so far I'm having no success. I recognize her glowing skin and rich chocolate hair, but for some reason the only thing my brain can come up with is 'Spanish actress,' which I know isn't true. Clad in a figure-hugging red dress and with a gold clip scooping her hair back on one side, she looks far more glamorous than I do.

"I'm Avery," I say, deciding to lead with my own name since I can't remember hers.

"I know. I'm Lina."

"Lina, yes." I nod as if I know her too.

"Lina Bezzler?" she prompts, because apparently it's totally obvious that I can't place her.

I blink again, and the memory finally clicks into place. "Right, yes. The Retail Heiress."

She rolls her eyes. "Yeah, *awful* title. Thanks, Dad, for owning an online retail giant." She lets out a dramatic sigh. "I'm hoping the media will come up with a more sophisticated label for me at some point down the line."

"Like ... 'Her Royal Highness,' perhaps?"

"Oh, hell no." Then she freezes, eyes going wide. "I-I mean ... I ... of course. Yes. That's why I'm here. That's why we're all here. Right?"

I raise an eyebrow at her stilted words and deer-in-headlights expression. "Why don't I believe you?"

She covers her face with her hands and groans. "Oh man,

I'm *so* bad at this. I cannot act to save my life. We're all supposed to be endlessly grateful for being chosen to be part of this thing, and it *is* such an honor, but honestly?" She leans closer and whispers, "I only entered on a dare."

"Really?" I force myself to keep smiling, but inside I'm wondering why this girl is being so open. I'm certainly not about to explain to anyone how *I* ended up on the show. Is this a part of her strategy, being approachable and non-threatening? That's precisely what Quinn and I would be saying if we were sitting on a couch together watching this conversation.

"Yes," she answers. "I was shocked when I got the call about the in-person interview, and then even more shocked when they told me I made it through. I almost said no, but then ..." She shrugs. "I figured why not. When else in my life will I get an experience like this? May as well see how far I can go. But there are millions of girls who *didn't* make it onto the show who would want to murder me if they knew I wasn't a thousand percent invested in being here."

I hesitate and then decide that since I'm not a thousand percent invested in being here either, there's no harm in taking her at her word. And everyone already knows there's zero chance of me winning this competition. "I kind of have the same attitude about the whole thing," I tell her. "You know, just seeing how far I can make it. I mean, I'm under no illusion that he'll actually pick *me*. The girl with no family and no connections. So I've already told myself not to be heartbroken when I'm dismissed."

"Wow, you are *so* chilled." Her smile stretches wider. "This is great. I thought all the girls here would be ready to scratch their pointy fingernails down each other's faces and rip each other's fancy dresses to shreds." I cover my mouth as a snort of laughter attempts to escape. It seems Lina's imagination was a lot darker than mine when it came to picturing our interactions with the other contestants. "But maybe you and I can actually be friends," she continues. "That would make this all so much more fun."

"Definitely," I agree, deciding that whether her offer is genuine or has something to do with an ulterior motive, it's far better than the snide comments I was expecting about how I obviously don't belong here. "We can absolutely be friends. By the way, have you tasted any of the food? It looks amazing, but I don't see anyone—"

"OMG!" A loud voice interrupts me as someone stops at Lina's side. It's the larger-than-life Cadence. "You're related to Sofia Fernandez, right?" she says, beaming at Lina. "You look *just* like her."

I almost snap my fingers as I finally realize why my brain kept saying 'Spanish actress' earlier. Lina takes a breath before smiling in a way that doesn't seem natural. "Yep. She's my mom. The dazzling, famous Sofia Fernandez. She abandoned me for her second family years ago, though, so we haven't spoken in ages."

Before the words 'she abandoned me' can pierce my chest too deeply, someone calls out, "Attention, ladies!" I turn and find one of the many clipboard people standing in the doorway to the lounge. Her eyes are an unnatural green I can make out from across the room, and I wonder if she's fae or if she's a human who purchased a temporary illusion. "A few of the vehicles are late due to flight delays," she continues as the room grows quiet, "but we expect the last few contestants to arrive shortly. You can continue to chat among yourselves and get to know each other. Once everyone's here, Carwyn and Evanna will join us to formally welcome you to the Glittering Palace."

The low hum of conversation restarts, and I turn back to see that Cadence has left us. "Oh, will you excuse me for a minute?" Lina says, peering over my shoulder. "Someone's waving at me, and I think I've met her before. But I'll catch up with you later?" Her eyes are filled with such warmth as she refocuses on me for a moment that I can't help but believe she truly meant her offer of friendship.

"Yes, definitely," I tell her. She steps past me, and I let my gaze travel over the room, looking for somewhere to sit or for a girl standing on her own who might be open to a conversation. My gaze snags on a tall figure. Definitely *not* one of the female contestants of *The Princess Game*. He crosses the room with an easy confidence and—

My heart stops. All breath is sucked from my lungs. Because it's him. Mr. Arrogant Ass from the coffee shop.

Chapter Six

Half an hour in, and I'm already breaking the rules. I'm supposed to be sitting in a lounge drinking tea and making civilized conversation, but here I am hurrying along endless bright, sparkly passageways, peeking into lavishly furnished rooms, completely lost and positively terrified. I'm fairly certain I'm about three seconds away from being discovered and thrown out of this competition before it even begins.

I shouldn't have tried to follow Mr. Arrogant Ass. If I'd stopped to think about it for more than half a second, I would have realized it was a terrible idea. What was I even planning to say to him? *You owe me an apology, mister?!* Who knows. There was no plan in my head, only a single thought: *What the hell is he doing here?* He crossed the room, stepped neatly around a group of girls giggling about how hot the prince is, and slipped through a doorway I hadn't noticed when I first entered the lounge. And I, without another thought, slipped out after him.

Now all I can think is, *How the hell did he disappear so quickly?* And also ... *Please don't let anyone kill me on sight if they discover me running around their palace.* A tiny part of my brain is imagining the conversation I'll have with Quinn at some point—if I'm still alive—when I tell her that she was indeed right about Mr. Arrogant Ass. 'I told you he was fae!' she'll crow.

I peep around another corner and—nope. Still completely unfamiliar. I'm now staring across a large square space with decorative pillars on both sides and warm morning light streaming through arched glass doors. With a glance around to make sure I'm still alone, I hurry as quietly as my high-heeled shoes will allow toward the doors, drawn forward by the slice of garden I can see. I stop with my face pressed almost as close to the glass as it was inside the limo when we arrived here.

I see towering trees and bright flower beds bursting with color, marble statues and a fountain spurting arcs of water into the air. Between it all wander pathways that sparkle and gleam as if diamonds have been scattered among the paving stones. I know the palace grounds aren't in Faeworld, but for all their magic and beauty they may as well be. I stare in wonder, longing to slip outside and get lost among it all, forgetting the rest of the competition. But I manage to tear myself away and scurry back across the open hallway. I head for the same corridor, take the same turn, and—

"Oh!"

I jerk backward before I can smack face-first into ... *not* Mr. Arrogant Ass. The person who takes a hurried step away from me is a familiar girl with sheets of straight black hair rippling around her flawless face. Riya? Yes. Riya Patel. Ivy League Princess. British. Her family is involved with ... whatever. Doesn't matter right now. "Um—"

"Can you believe how big this place is?" she says, her expression relaxing as she laughs. "I can't even find a bathroom."

"Oh. I … I think I heard someone saying there's one next to that lounge we're all having tea in. Do you know—"

"Thanks! I'll find it. See you back there!" She swings around, but not before I see her friendly expression morph into something cold and hard. I almost take another step back before remembering she's my only way out of this maze.

"Wait, Riya." I follow after her, but she's walking so darn fast. She turns and heads through a doorway with the type of confidence that suggests she knows exactly where she's going. I start running because it seems that's the only way I'll catch up to her. I turn into the doorway, hurry forward—and she's nowhere to be seen.

There's a closed door on the far side of the room, so I aim for it. Where else could she have gone? But when I enter the next room—a little darker than the others; fewer windows, thicker curtains—I don't see her. How fast does this girl move?

With fear grasping its way up my throat again, I head for the next door. This one is standing ajar, and … Voices. Raised voices, terse and heated. I come to an abrupt halt, but before I can turn and flee, two figures move past the gap in the doorway. It's only a moment, but I see enough of their faces to know exactly who they are: Prince Kieren of the Autumn Court and his mother, Queen Erralee.

I duck sideways and flatten myself against the wall beside the doorway, heart slamming wildly against my ribcage. I wait for them to storm into this room and demand to know who's eavesdropping on their conversation. But they continue arguing in a language I don't recognize. Probably safe to assume it's one of the fae languages. It's beautiful. Melodic and fluid even when raised in argument. I wonder if it's one of the languages they've shared with us. Perhaps I'll get to learn some of it while I'm staying here at the—

I shake myself from my distracted thoughts before they can wander too far. I need to get out of here. Immediately. I take a deep breath and start tiptoeing away. And then: "It's an absurd charade, that's what it is!" the prince blurts out in English. I freeze again. "It makes me sick to have to play along with it."

"Would you prefer we do this the way the other courts do?" the queen snaps in return.

"Of course not."

"Then—" She launches back into their foreign tongue.

Absurd charade? It makes him *sick* to play along with it? Well. That's certainly not the way it seemed in the few interviews he's done leading up to—

The prince shouts something in a tone of finality, sounding a lot closer all of a sudden. The strip of light shining through the gap in the doorway widens abruptly. Without another thought, I dive—literally—behind the nearest couch. And of course, because I'm not made of feathers, I land with a loud thump and a barely muffled groan. Holy *flip*, that hurt!

"Who's there?" the prince demands.

Shitshitshitshitshit! I hold my breath and stare beneath the couch at the pair of shoes that's come to a halt on the other side. A single pair of shoes, which I hope means the queen stormed off in a different direction. Pain rockets up and down my right side, but I don't make a squeak. Maybe I'll get lucky and the prince will think the loud thump was just ... someone moving furniture around in the room above this one?

"I said," Prince Kieren utters in a voice deadly cold, *"who is there?"*

Right. Who am I kidding? I've never been lucky. "I—no one, sir," I stutter, still not moving an inch. "I mean, Your Majesty. Your Highness. *Crap.*" I smack my hand over my mouth before I can say anything else wrong.

"No one? I highly doubt that. Show yourself."

I can't very well disobey a prince. So I scramble to my feet, ignoring the ache throbbing along one side of my body, and pop up behind the couch. A quick sideways shuffle brings me out beside the couch and in front of Prince Kieren. I meet his gaze for barely a second, then sink awkwardly into a low curtsey, keeping my head bowed. He mutters something inaudible beneath his breath.

I wait. And wait. And wait. Then finally, I hear a single word: "Stand."

Straightening, I keep my eyes on the floor. All the names Quinn and I have ever used to describe the fae royals—superior, conceited, stuck-up—rush through my mind. I'm terrified he can somehow hear them. "I—I'm so sorry, Your—"

"What are you doing here?"

"I got lost. I—I only just arrived."

"I mean what are you doing in this palace?"

"Oh. I'm ... one of the contestants?" It's strange that he doesn't recognize me from all the media coverage about the show, but I suppose there are thirty of us, and I'm the least exciting, so perhaps I'm easily forgotten.

I hear a sound that might be the princely version of a snort. "You?"

Shame burns my cheeks. Is it so obvious that I don't belong here? Then again, I did just scramble out from behind a couch —after throwing myself on the floor—which is probably the least princess-like behavior in the entire world, so I don't blame him for doubting I'm a contender for the tiara. Still, I can't help feeling as if I'm ten years old again, standing in the playground at yet another new school, all the other kids eyeing my hand-me-down clothes and judging me. There's also a teeny part of me that wants to slap him for making me feel so small. A *very* teeny part.

"Y-yes, Your Highness," I stammer. "I'm Avery Evans. The, um, Girl Next Door?" Crapping crap, this is *so* awkward. Mary-Louise would be dying if she could see me now.

"Unbelievable," the prince mutters.

Yeah, I want to sigh. *I'm having a hard time believing this is happening too.*

"What did you overhear?" he demands.

I suck in a breath but pause before answering. I'm pretty sure I've never heard of fae having a specific magical ability to distinguish lies and truth, but I remember what Carwyn did in The Grumpy Bean, scrutinizing me before declaring my words to be true. I can't help wondering if Prince Kieren can do the same thing. "I overheard ... some words ... in a foreign language," I say hesitantly.

"And did you hear the part that was in *your* tongue?"

I can't help it. My eyes dart up, and I get my first proper look at Prince Kieren of the Autumn Court. He's taller in person than I imagined, broad shouldered and stiff in posture, but his face is just as perfect as it is in all the pictures. Strong jawline, angled cheekbones, lips not too thin and not too full. It takes only a few seconds to understand why his silvery blue eyes have been described as 'magnetic' so many times. I'm finding it almost impossible to look away. I do wonder, though, how much of what I'm seeing is a faerie illusion and how much is real.

"Well?" he demands, his tone harsh.

I flinch and look down again. "I—yes. I overheard that part. I'm sorry. I didn't mean to eavesdrop. On *any* of it. I was looking for someone and I ended up lost."

He breathes out sharply through his nose. "So. You now

know that I think this is all an absurd charade. And *I* know that you—" He cuts himself off, and I imagine all the ways he might finish that sentence.

Like to eavesdrop on private conversations.

Don't know how to address royalty.

Are incapable of judging a soft landing.

Are the furthest thing from princess material I've ever met.

"I know that you were sneaking around parts of the palace you do not belong in," he finishes. "If you can keep quiet about the former, I can keep quiet about the latter. I will send you home on Friday evening during the first dismissal dinner instead of throwing you out of the game immediately. No one need know about your behavior."

"I ..." I wilt at the thought of having to leave so soon. No two million from Carwyn for making it to the Top 10, though that was always a long shot. No enchanted jewelry gifted by the prince. Barely a few days for anyone to get to know musician Avery Evans and possibly check out her music. But I'm so relieved the prince isn't killing me on the spot with magical laser eyeballs that I say, "Of course, thank you, sir. I mean majesty. Highness." I squeeze my eyes shut and bite my tongue, then whisper, "Your Royal Highness."

More silence. I wonder if he's rolling his stupidly beautiful eyes. "You may go," he says eventually.

"Thank you." I'm about to scurry past him when I remember how I ended up in this awkward situation in the first place. "Oh. I ... um ... can't remember how to get back to the lounge where everyone's having tea."

His heavy sigh is almost a growl. "Fine. Follow me."

Chapter Seven

Prince Kieren leads me back across polished floors and past arched windows. At every turn, there's another ivy-wrapped sculpture or vase filled with flamboyant, otherworldly flowers. I'm pretty sure this isn't the way I came, but eventually I recognize the first passageway I hurried along. He stops before reaching the lounge where all the contestants are still chatting, gestures toward it, and then walks away without another word.

It appears no one noticed my absence, and soon I'm sitting on one of the couches, my hands folded neatly in my lap the way Mary-Louise taught me, my heart still racing as if I sprinted all the way back here. I try to ignore all the cameras that are suddenly crowding the edges of the room and tell myself to remain calm. Difficult when all I can focus on is the single thought blaring at the front of my mind: *I just met Freaking Prince Faerie Face! In the flesh!* I imagine telling Quinn when I finally get to talk to her that he's even worse than we imagined. Intimidatingly good-looking, which must surely be an illusion, and unbelievably condescending.

The clipboard lady claps her hands and calls for us to be quiet just as Riya slides into a chair on the other side of the room. She must have just returned. Now that I'm no longer lost and terrified, it occurs to me to wonder what *she* was doing wandering around. I highly doubt she was looking for a bathroom.

Before I can contemplate her motivations further, everyone around me is suddenly clapping, and I realize I've missed whatever the clipboard lady was saying. I join in with the applause, though, as every head in the room turns toward the main doorway and Carwyn Aster and Evanna Zynn come sashaying in. The clipboard lady scuttles out of the way, and Carwyn and Evanna take her place at the front of the room. Carwyn's suit is rose gold today, and Evanna's pink curls have been tamed into a perfectly smooth braid that's looped around her head like a crown.

"Welcome!" they cry out together, spreading their arms wide as they survey the room. "Tooooo ... *The Princess Game*!"

"Aren't you all looking *gorgeous* this fine morning?" Evanna says, beaming at us.

"Positively radiant!" Carwyn chimes in.

"Isn't it exciting," Evanna continues, clasping her hands together, "to think that one of the charming young ladies in this room will become the next princess of the Autumn Court?"

I can't help glancing around me, wondering who it might be. The Politician's Daughter? The Olympic Gymnast? The Ivy League Princess?

Carwyn turns to face one of the cameras. "For those of you at home who may have been living under a rock recently—" he pauses to share his loud, boisterous laugh "—here's how it works: Prince Kieren of Faeworld's Autumn Court will be choosing a bride from among thirty young women of the human world. There will be group activities and one-on-one time every week, giving the prince multiple chances to get to know our fine young ladies. At the end of every week, the prince will dismiss one or more contestants. He has up to eight weeks to dismiss the first twenty, leaving us with our Top 10, after which he can spend another three weeks selecting the Final Three. The show will then take a break for two weeks as Prince Kieren spends some private time with those three girls before making the decision of a lifetime: Who will be his princess?"

I press my lips together as the air around me positively hums with excitement. It sounds like the worst possible way in the world to find the one person you're supposed to spend the rest of your life with, but what do I know? I haven't been involved with anyone in years.

"Simple enough!" Evanna sings. She explains a few more things, all of which I'm already familiar with. Everything was spelled out in the contract. The camera crew will be around most days to capture candid moments and to interview all of us at least once every week. Dismissal dinners take place on a Friday night, and then—I assume—a massive scramble will take place over the weekend so that the latest episode will be ready to air on a Monday, showing everything that transpired over the previous week.

"Now that all of *that* is out of the way," Carwyn says, beaming at us, "here's what's in store for you today! You will separate into small groups and begin with a palace tour to get you better acquainted with your new home."

"The King of the Autumn Court," Evanna joins in, "has graciously allowed you unrestricted access to almost *all* of the Glittering Palace and its sprawling grounds. The North Tower, which houses the private quarters of the royal family, is the only section of the palace that is off limits. You're free to roam anywhere else during unstructured times."

"But remember!" Carwyn adds. "There's security everywhere, and the camera crew will be around most days, so don't do anything I wouldn't do." He gives us an exaggerated wink, and polite laughter fills the room.

"Following your tour," Evanna continues, "you will be shown to your rooms where you will each meet your retinue. This is your personal team, responsible for getting you ready for all formal events. Hair, makeup, dresses—the works! The various camera crews will be in and out of your rooms this afternoon, getting footage for the first episode—"

"The Makeover Episode," Carwyn adds with a wink.

"Then we'll take a few photos of you looking glam and gorgeous," Evanna says. "And *then*, this evening, the grand Opening Ball! You will each be formally introduced as you enter the ballroom. You will meet Prince Kieren for the first time, and each of you will dance with him."

I resist the urge to squirm in my seat. How much trouble would I be in if people found out I'd already met him? Then I refocus on the last part of that sentence—*each of you will dance with him*—and nerves tighten my insides. I think of the hours of dance classes I attended over the last several weeks in preparation for tonight's ball. I wasn't *terrible*, but I'm certainly not the most graceful of dancers. What if the entire world is forced to watch me tripping over Prince Kieren's feet?

"Off you go, and we'll see you all later!"

The cameras stop filming, and we're all ushered to our feet. I edge toward Lina, hoping to end up in a tour group with her. I'm right behind her, almost at the door, when I hear a booming voice. "Ah, Miss Girl Next Door!" Carwyn grips my arm and pulls me away from the sea of girls. "So lovely to see you here, and don't you look smashing when you're no longer covered up by an apron?"

"Um, thanks."

"Do enjoy yourself, darling." He leans closer and kisses the air beside my cheek. "And make us proud," he adds in a whisper before straightening. He releases my arm with a wink and a smile, and I turn away after a quick nod.

I manage to catch up to Lina in the foyer as we're all being separated into groups, and I end up with her, the redheaded whiskey heir Shay, and a girl named Ami. A man with an anxious tremor in his voice leads us out of the foyer, and I try not to look around every few moments for Mr. Arrogant Ass. I wonder if he's related to the royal family or if he's just some faerie noble who happens to live here.

But he soon moves to the back of my mind as we're led through the magnificent library, the grand ballroom, and then the throne room. I pass gigantic mirrors and striking arrangements of flowers and a chandelier the size of a small ship that's apparently constructed from over a million individual pieces. I admire an indoor swimming pool surrounded completely by glass and lush, exotic plants. It's all so unbelievably breathtaking that I almost forget about Mr. Arrogant Ass entirely. Who cares about one bad-mannered faerie when I'm standing in front of all this grandeur?

After a picnic lunch at the center of a rose bush maze, we're taken back inside and shown to our individual quarters. We follow our tour guide up a grand staircase and along several glittering passageways, and before I know it, he's stopping in front of a door, opening it for me, and announcing that this is my suite. My *suite*!

I almost fall over at the sight of the luxurious space, larger than the entire apartment Quinn and I share. A bed big enough for a giant, a sitting area with armchairs and a chaise lounge, a small desk, a vanity with little lights circling a round mirror, and another full-length mirror in one corner. Everything is white with subtle rose gold finishings, all elegant curving lines and delicate embellishments. An open door leads to what looks like a dressing room that came straight off the set of a princess makeover movie, while another door is open just enough for me to see the edge of a bath.

I step forward slowly, as if in a trance. I nudge my feet free of my shoes, and a sigh escapes my lips as my bare feet sink into the perfectly soft carpet. The door clicks shut behind me. When I'm certain I'm finally alone, I throw myself onto the enormous bed, bury my face between two of the pillows, and squeal until I'm breathless.

Holy freaking crap. Is this really my life?

"Miss Avery?"

I roll over and scramble up in a tangle of hair and eight million thread count pillowcases. "Hello, yes, hi?" I swipe the end of my ponytail out of my face and blink at the three people standing at the foot of my bed. My aide, Iris, plus another woman and a man. All looking the teeniest bit shocked.

"I did knock," Iris says hesitantly. "But you didn't answer, and then we heard you scream."

"Oh. Um ..." My face burns hotter than the sun. "I'm fine. Is there, uh, something I can do for you?"

Iris opens her mouth, but it's the young man who leans forward, presses both palms on the foot of my bed, and speaks. "We're here for *you*, love." He grins, and his eyes—vibrant purple surrounding pupils shaped like those of a cat—twinkle in his dark face. "It's makeover time."

Chapter Eight

Iris clears her throat. "We are your retinue, Miss Avery. This is Finneas." She takes the young man's arm and pulls him upright. "He designs all your outfits and is in charge of your overall look for any event. This is Mischa." Iris gestures to the woman beside her, so pale I wonder if perhaps she painted her face white. "She'll take care of your hair and makeup. And, as you already know, I'm Iris."

"Hi," I say, giving them all an awkward wave before scooting to the edge of the bed. "Um ... are you all fae? I'm sorry, is it rude to ask that? I've been wondering since I met you this morning," I add, looking at Iris. "It's just that it's impossible to tell by looking at you, and I don't want to assume one way or the other and then say the wrong thing like ..." *Like are all fae super stuck-up?* "Um, yeah."

"It's not rude, love," Finneas says with a smile. "I'm fae. So is Mischa. Iris is human."

"And ... you guys are all here just for me?"

"Yes," Iris confirms.

"And every contestant has a retinue?"

"Yes."

"Wow. That's a lot of people dedicated just to getting a bunch of girls ready for parties."

"Of course," Iris says, in a tone that suggests I should have expected nothing less. "The Glittering Palace and the studio have spared no expense. Now. I am the head of your retinue and in charge of your daily itinerary. I make sure you get to where you need to be on time. Social events, dates with the prince, interviews for the show, etc. I'm also your media manager, so I'm in charge of your social accounts and making sure appropriate content is shared across all your platforms throughout the week, leaving out key details, of course."

"Um, okay. Key details?" I'm assuming this includes moments when I'm naked or wearing nothing but the lacy underwear Mary-Louise picked out during our shopping spree. Surely that's not 'appropriate content.'

"Yes. With this makeover business, for example, I'll post a 'before' photo, maybe share some videos of you having your hair and makeup done, but obviously I *won't* share the 'after' photo. Your fans will have to tune in next Monday to watch the episode. Then, after it's been aired, we can share some snaps from this evening's photoshoot."

"Oh." Okay, so no mention of me in my underwear or half-naked while coming out of the bathroom. I'll take that as a good sign. "Wait, photoshoot?" I add as my brain backtracks and snags on that last word. I think I remember someone mentioning it earlier, but so much has already happened since I arrived here.

"Yes. Late afternoon, once you're dressed and ready, but before the ball begins. The photographers are getting things set up in the gardens somewhere with all their fancy lighting and whatnot. They'll take some photos of you on your own, and a few with some of the other girls."

"Oh. Cool."

"Anyway. This is your suite." Iris steps back and gestures around her. "Everything is pretty much self-explanatory, except for the digital piano you requested, which is hidden behind that panel over there." She points toward an empty section of wall beside the vanity, where I see a rectangular outline I hadn't previously noticed. "Press the panel with both hands," Iris explains, "and it will slide sideways behind the wall, revealing the piano."

"Wow," I whisper, a thrill dancing up my spine. I'm too excited to bother telling her that I didn't *request* anything. I asked if I could bring my battered old keyboard and headphones with me, and the short email I received in reply said not to worry. I believe the exact line was 'We'll take care of that.'

"I'll hand things over to Finneas now," Iris says, nodding at Finneas before moving to the sitting area where she lowers herself delicately to the edge of an armchair and scrutinizes something on her tablet.

"Wonderful!" Finneas exclaims. "Let me get a good look at you, love." He takes my arm and turns me around. "I have your pictures and measurements, of course. I've made several of your dresses already, including tonight's magnificent piece. But it's a delight to finally see you in the flesh." He steps back and tips his head to the side as his gaze sweeps up and down my form. "Yes, you are going to look *exquisite* tonight, love. But before all of *that* ..." He clasps his hands together. "Spa treatments."

"Spa treatments?"

"Yes. The unpleasant stuff first—"

"The what?"

"Waxing, of course. Nobody wants a hairy princess."

"I'm not—"

"Then a full-body scrub, a bit of a massage, mani, pedi, etc. Basically, everything to get you smooth, shiny and polished before tonight. All good?"

"But, um ..." My gaze darts back and forth between Finneas and Mischa as my cheeks warm. "The, uh, waxing already happened. A few days ago? The appointment was organized for me by someone involved with the show and the—"

"Yes, that was me," Iris pipes up. "Please stick to the clothing side of things, Finneas. I'm sure Mischa has the spa treatments under control."

"Oh, gosh." Finneas laughs as he claps a hand over his mouth. "Sorry, love! My bad."

With a small smile and a discreet roll of her eyes, Mischa steps closer. "Come with me," she says, her tone gentle as she guides me toward the bathroom door.

The bathroom is just as luxurious as everything else in this palace, with gleaming marble floors and walls, a freestanding bathtub, and a shower large enough to host a small party. Trailing plants hang from the ceiling and elegant ferns and orchids are positioned around the room. In the center of the space stands a raised bed with something that looks like a rigid doughnut-shaped pillow attached to one side. I've never set foot in a spa before, but I've seen enough movies and TV to know what I'm looking at: the kind of bed you lie on if you're getting a massage. And it's right here, in my own gigantic bathroom, which is attached to a penthouse-sized bedroom, which is inside a faerie palace. *How is any of this real?*

I take a deep breath and manage to contain my squeal. "So ... what exactly is about to happen?"

"No waxing," Mischa says with an amused smile. "You can

relax. We'll be doing a hair treatment, a full body scrub, and then a brief massage."

"Okay. That sounds ... nice?" It sounds like heaven.

Her laugh is quiet. "Yes, it is supposed to be. The Glittering Palace would like you to feel relaxed and pampered from the moment you arrive and for the duration of your stay. That is the life of a princess."

"Oh. Cool." I can't help thinking there must be another motive behind this pampering, but I'll enjoy it as long as I'm here—which, at this point, is roughly another four and a half days. I just have one remaining reservation. "None of this will be on camera, right?"

"No. As I understand it, a camera crew is scheduled to be here in about fifty minutes. We'll be done with the body and hair treatments, and you'll be back in your lounge area having your nails done. I think they may ask you a few questions for the interview sections of the show. Then they'll continue to some of the other girls, and then someone will be back a bit later to get some footage of your hair and makeup being done."

"Okay. Sounds good." After Mischa steps out of the room, I remove most of my clothing, climb onto the special massage bed thing, cover myself with a deliciously soft towel and then wait. I've just begun to feel awkward when Mischa returns, her voice almost a whisper as she says, "Let me just get the music started, and then we can begin."

"Okay, sure." I expect her to walk over to some hidden sound system in the walls, but instead she begins weaving her hands gently through the air, fingers rippling over invisible patterns, almost as if she's conducting an orchestra only she can see. It's exactly the kind of thing I do, hidden in my bedroom late at night with my headphones on and my eyes closed, my hands moving in a silent dance while I picture the music I've written as strands of color sliding and twisting through the air.

When Mischa does it, though, the music literally comes to life. The comforting *shh* of rain on leaves, the gentle twitter of birds, the distant chirp of insects, all accompanied by an other-worldly sort of hum. A shiver courses down my spine. "That's incredible," I breathe. "Can you—" I almost ask if she can teach me how to do it, but I catch myself as I realize what a ridiculous question that is. She's using *magic*. Of course she can't teach me how to do it.

She lifts her hands to shoulder height and slowly lowers them through the air, her lips moving silently. The room grows dimmer. "You can close your eyes," she tells me. "Relax."

And with the atmospheric sounds filling the air around me, I do relax. She massages something into my hair, and my mind starts to wander. My consciousness tiptoes lightly over the details of the day: meeting Lina, seeing the most magnificent parts of the palace, my terrifying accidental meeting with the prince, which honestly doesn't seem that bad now that I'm so relaxed.

I could stay like this forever, but the treatments are over all too soon, and suddenly the pace of everything speeds up dramatically. I'm in one of the armchairs, my wet hair wrapped in a towel, my hand splayed on a small table that appeared quite literally out of the air. Mischa is leaning over my nails, and a gigantic camera is intruding on our space. There are people and lights and a microphone on a long stick, and then Evanna herself is sitting on the armchair beside mine, firing a bunch of questions at me about my first impressions of the Glittering Palace and the other girls.

By the time my fingernails, toenails, hair and makeup are done, and I'm standing in front of the full-length mirror in a silk robe waiting for Finneas to bring my dress, I've had multiple cameras shoved in my face—including the one on my phone, handled by Iris—and I'm ready to shut myself away in the bathroom and hide for several hours. Sadly, this is not an option.

"Here it is, love!" Finneas calls to me, practically prancing out of my dressing room. A blue dress flutters through the air behind him. I'm too startled by the fact that my dress is *flying* to properly take in what it looks like until Finneas plucks it from the air and holds it out before me. A gasp catches in my throat as my gaze travels down the garment.

Layers of soft, floaty fabric make up the skirt, while the bodice is fitted with off-the-shoulder sleeves. Up close, I see the fabric isn't plain blue; it's covered in tiny specks of silver that glint like diamonds as the dress moves. More subtle, but no less beautiful, are the trailing leaf shapes made of delicate lace that extend down from the bodice over the upper part of the skirt.

"I know it's on the simpler side," Finneas rushes to say, "but in keeping with your image as the Girl Next Door, I decided not to go with anything huge or puffy or overly extravagant."

"No, no, it's *beautiful*. Finneas ..." I shake my head, struggling to find the right words. "Never in my life did I imagine I would wear something even *close* to this. It's gorgeous!"

He beams. "Well, I'm glad you like it."

"I just want to check ..." Something tightens in my stomach as I reach for the dress and turn it around. "Does the back ... okay, yes, it's quite high." I release the dress with an awkward laugh. "I just don't feel comfortable with anything too revealing."

"Oh, of course, of course. I'll go through all your dresses and make sure we're not showing too much of your back. The front, however ..." He winks, then laughs as my expression falls. "I'm kidding, love. You're the Girl Next Door. None of your outfits are too revealing."

"Have you made quite a few of them already?"

"Oh, only about a dozen or so. I was so excited, I wanted to make *hundreds*, but I managed to hold myself back."

A *dozen*? I don't have the heart to tell him I won't be needing most of them. How many more parties can there possibly be between now and the first dismissal dinner on Friday night? "That's amazing," I tell him instead, hoping he'll be able to find some other use for them.

"Okay, you can take that robe off, and then I'll help you into this."

"Oh, I'm sure I can do that myself."

He laughs again. "No, no, no, love. You don't dress yourself. What kind of princess does that?"

"I'm not a princess," I remind him with a wry smile. "Maybe you could just, uh, look away for a moment while I change, and then you can help me once I've got it on?" *Please, please, please don't make this a thing*, I plead silently.

After a moment's pause, he says, "Of course, love, certainly. Just hang on, there's a hidden zipper here on the side ..." He drags the zipper smoothly down, then hands me the dress and turns away. I change quickly. An easy task because—*obviously*—I've been dressing myself for as long as I can remember. Do the fae royals seriously not put their own clothes on? I almost roll my eyes. Yet another reason I don't belong here.

"Okay, you can turn around," I tell Finneas. He helps me with the zipper at my side, which is either hidden so well beneath the edges of the fabric that it's impossible to see, or it becomes *literally* invisible after he runs his finger along it. Probably the latter.

After a few finger snaps and twirls, the bodice tightens ever so slightly, perfectly encasing my form but still allowing me *just* enough room to breathe. Finneas moves to the sleeves then, sparkles drifting around his fingertips as he makes tiny adjustments so that the fabric falls in just the right way off my shoulders. Up close, his purple cat-like eyes are even more startling. "Is that an illusion?" I ask. "Your eyes."

He smiles, gaze still focused on my left sleeve as he runs a finger carefully along the edge of the fabric. "No. These are my real eyes. We fae generally use glamours to make ourselves look *more* like you humans, not the other way around. Helps us blend in while wandering through your world."

"Glamour, right. I always thought that was a bit of a strange word."

"You and the rest of the humans," he says with a chuckle as he steps back. "You all prefer the word 'illusion.'"

"But that's what it is, right?"

His smile curves a little higher on one side. "Mostly. All right, love, I think I'm done. Iris, Mischa, what do we think?"

Iris hurries over from the sitting area, and Mischa moves to my side as Finneas steps out of the way and gives me an unobstructed view of my reflection. I take a deep breath as someone I barely recognize stares back at me. The dress is like something out of a starlit dream, a look that is completed by the subtle silvery sheen on my bare skin from the powder Mischa dusted over my arms and chest earlier. My hair is pinned in a simple updo—no ponytail for an evening event—with tiny diamond-like flowers positioned here and there. They began as simple metal spheres on the ends of regular hairpins, but Mischa sang softly as she pushed them into my hair earlier, and I watched them morph into glittering flowers. My makeup isn't too heavy, but it's enough to make my eyes seem larger than usual and to define the angles I didn't even realize my face possessed.

Finneas claps his hands in delight, Mischa hugs herself and releases a muted squeal, and even Iris looks genuinely happy for the first time today. "You look *incredible*," Mischa says.

Iris nods. "Good job, team. You did well."

"What do *you* think, Miss Avery?" Mischa asks.

"I ... I'm not sure I even know who that is," I say, still staring at myself. "This must be what Cinderella felt like going to the ball."

"Is that a good thing?" Finneas asks.

I smile at him. "Yes, that's a good thing. Thank you for making something so beautiful for me."

His grin spreads wider. "This is just the beginning, love."

There's a knock at the door, and I let my gaze travel down the dress again as Iris hurries across the room to answer it. For a quiet moment, it feels as if all of this real. As if I'm about to walk into a ballroom hoping a prince will fall in love with me. As if I don't already know I'm going to be sent home in just a few days.

"Miss Avery?" Iris says, looking across the room at me. I meet her gaze in the mirror. "Time to go."

Chapter Nine

Standing in line outside the ballroom is almost as nerve-racking as driving up to the palace this morning. In fact, it might be worse. It's possible I feel more ill now than I did while almost hyperventilating climbing out of that limo. The cameras are rolling just as they were this morning, but at least tonight's ball isn't *live*. It will be edited and aired as part of the first episode. So if I trip and fall, they can cut it out. I squeeze my eyelids shut and force a slow breath out. Who am I kidding? If I trip and fall, they'll make *sure* to include it in the episode.

I shuffle forward, listening to the whispers around me and the occasional cough and stifled laughter. My attempt to focus on the many details of the antechamber we're assembled in—the high ceiling, the gold filigree-adorned pillars, the elegant drapes framing the windows—does little to calm my nerves. A few places ahead of me, Lina, in a gorgeous gown of deepest red, looks back and gives me a thumbs up and an encouraging smile. Then someone calls out her name and she disappears beyond the ornately carved double doors and into the ballroom.

All too soon, there's no one left in front of me, and I'm

trying to remember how to breathe. I try to swallow but my throat is suddenly impossibly dry. Two men in formal uniforms flank the doorway, and beyond them, stairs lead down into the ballroom, which means I can't see much of what's happening until I take a few more steps forward. Which I do. Somewhat mechanically.

"Avery Evans!" calls out one of the men in a rich baritone as I cross the threshold into the ballroom. *Do! Not! Faint!* I scream at myself. For one frozen moment, I take in the entire ballroom: a magnificent space with soaring vaulted arches, sparkling chandeliers, and a thousand tiny golden lights floating near the ceiling. Hundreds of faces stare up at me.

I descend the stairs, keeping my chin up and my smile in place while silently chanting *don't trip, don't trip, don't trip*. I ignore the cameras looming like giant predatory insects and the sea of people—probably a bunch of fancy fae nobles I would recognize if I kept up with the fae-obsessed blogs and websites—and keep my gaze focused on the raised dais on the far side of the room where King Eldyn, Queen Erralee and Prince Kieren are seated on their thrones.

Soft harp music drifts through the air as I cross the ballroom floor, but it isn't enough to mask the whispers and the rustle of fine fabrics all around me. Still, I keep my gaze pointed forward. I reach the other side of the room and stop in front of the royal family. My curtsey is low and graceful, thanks to the eleventy billion times Iris made me practice it in between the photoshoot and lining up outside the ballroom. Mary-Louise would be so proud.

I move to stand beside the row of girls who've already been announced, and then all eyes are on the next contestant walking down the stairs. I release a pent-up breath and try to keep my grin from taking over my entire face. Like this morning after successfully crossing the red carpet, I want to yell out, *I made it!*

I look around, taking in more of the ballroom—the towering columns adorned in fine scrollwork and delicate swirls, the flowing gowns and finely tailored suits—until my gaze accidentally lands on Prince Kieren's. Instead of looking at whoever's currently crossing the ballroom, he's frowning at me. I banish my smile with a sharp press of my lips and face forward again, a shiver darting up my spine.

When every contestant has been presented, Prince Kieren stands and walks off the dais. He moves to the start of the line, bows in front of the first girl, then offers her his hand. After a curtsey, she takes it, allowing him to lead her to the center of the ballroom as everyone shuffles backward to make more room for them. The prince, with tense shoulders and a strained smile, takes the girl in his arms. The harp music comes to an end and a lively waltz starts up, played by a string quartet I've just spotted on one side of the room. The couple begins dancing.

This is our cue to move out of line and start mingling around the edges of the ballroom. We were specifically instructed not to stand and gawk at the prince as he makes his way through thirty different dance partners. I catch Lina's eye and head toward her. "Guess what?" she says to me with a snicker as I reach her side. "I saw a woman's headpiece catch alight as I finished my walk across the ballroom."

"What? How?"

"I think it was one of those floating lights up there." She points up, then reaches over and grabs two champagne flutes from someone walking past with a silver tray balanced on his forearm. "It came down a little too low and got caught on the edge of her fancy flowery fascinator thing. I think I pulled a muscle I was trying so hard not to laugh while she flapped her hands around. She used magic to create some water, and then she ended up with this soggy thing dripping on top of her head."

I'm laughing as I take the glass Lina offers me. "I'm so glad I didn't see that. It was challenging enough not to trip without added distractions." I sniff the contents of the glass and add, "What is this?"

Lina shrugs. "Don't know." She takes a sip and makes a face. "Something non-alcoholic. I suppose they don't want us getting too tipsy and falling all over the prince or any of the other nobles."

"Yes, I imagine that wouldn't go down well." I take a sip as I look around for Prince Kieren and his partner. Most of the cameras are focused on him, while a few seem to be panning across the ballroom. Though stiff and formal, it appears the prince can dance well enough. He still doesn't look particularly happy, though.

The second he stops dancing with his current partner, a clipboard lady with a headset and simple black clothing like the rest of the camera crew darts forward and ushers a delicate-looking girl with a pixie cut toward him. With a strained almost-smile, he takes her hand, wraps an arm around her waist, and continues dancing. "I hope the editing team manages to cut away from his face each time he spins around," I comment as several other couples head for the dance floor at the direction of another person wearing a headset. "He looks like he'd rather be sitting in a dentist's chair having his teeth pulled out than dancing with any of us." Beside me, Lina snorts into her champagne glass. I decide I'm liking her more and more.

"Do you remember if anyone said anything about food at this ball?" she asks, craning her neck as she looks past me. "I'm starving."

"I hope so." I turn and look around. "They can't expect us to survive from lunchtime until tomorrow morning, can they?"

"I don't know, I've heard the fae have some strange eating habits." She loops her arm through mine, and we wander around the edge of the ballroom, hoping to find something to eat.

We haven't gone far when a commotion draws our attention back to the dance floor. The clipboard lady is trying to get the girl with the pixie cut—Alaska Adams, I think—to let go of Prince Kieren so she can push a tall blond girl into his arms. "No!" Alaska yells, shoving the clipboard lady so hard she falls over backwards, taking the blond contestant with her. "He's mine!" Alaska shrieks, apparently not so delicate after all. "You hear me? I'm not letting go!"

The prince's guards step in then, and Alaska is quickly removed, screaming 'Miiiiine!' the whole way out.

"Wow," Lina murmurs. "There's always one who's batshit crazy."

There's a brief huddle around the prince after that—probably some medical professionals making sure his flawless skin wasn't marred by a fingernail scratch. Never mind the two ladies who were knocked over. I don't see them anywhere. Soon enough, Prince Kieren is back on the dance floor, Cadence in his arms this time. She looks as though this is the happiest moment of her life.

"Lina? Lina Bezzler?"

The voice comes from behind us, and we both turn to find another woman dressed entirely in black and wearing a headset, though this one seems to be aware of what century we're in and is using a tablet instead of a clipboard.

"Yes?" Lina says.

"*There* you are! I couldn't find you. You were supposed to be next, but we grabbed Cadence instead."

"Oh. I'm sorry. Does it really—"

"Alphabetical order. We're just trying to keep things organized. Doesn't matter. You can go next."

"Oh, okay." Lina barely has time to shove her champagne glass at me before the woman tugs her away.

I stand there awkwardly for several moments, holding two glasses and looking around for someone to talk to. On the far side of the ballroom, at the base of the grand stairway, Carwyn and Evanna are chatting animatedly in front of one of the cameras. No doubt they have all sorts of opinions about our makeovers and our entrances into the ballroom. Or perhaps they're discussing Alaska Adams and her dramatic exist. I assume we won't be seeing her again.

My gaze continues to slide over the crowd, and then—

Him. *Him.* Mr. Arrogant Ass.

Just like this morning when I saw him in the lounge, he moves with an easy, laid-back confidence. It's clear he's far more at home here than he was in The Grumpy Bean. Without another thought, I move toward him. Heat pumps through my veins as my brain replays some of the things he said that morning.

I will not be dying *for anything in this place.*

There is nothing here but disappointment.

Your opinion of the food and drink in this place is as poor as your opinion of popular television.

I place both champagne glasses onto a tray carried by one of the waitstaff before planting myself in front of Mr. Arrogant Ass. He takes a surprised step backward but recovers quickly. A wide grin spreads across his face. "Good evening. Would you like to dance?"

"Dance?" I repeat in disbelief. "After what happened in the coffee shop?"

He feigns confusion. "The coffee shop?"

"You're going to pretend you don't remember?"

His frown deepens. The confused look he gives me is so convincing I almost believe him. Damn these fae and their deceptions. Whoever came up with the old stories about fae being unable to lie was sadly misinformed. "I'm sorry," he says. "It seems my memory fails me. Could you elaborate?"

"The coffee shop. The Grumpy Bean. You were so rude, and then—okay, admittedly, I was rude too, but only because you started it. Then you left your coffee behind and walked out. And now, by some strange coincidence, you're here. Are you fae? I assume so, since you seemed offended by what I said."

He blinks, mouth half open. Then he shakes his head as if to clear it. "I'm a close friend of Prince Kieren's. My name is Rhylan. I'm residing at the Glittering Palace for the duration of the competition. Moral support. And, forgive me. Back to the coffee shop incident. That certainly wasn't me. I would remember meeting you, I can assure you of that, Miss ..." He raises a brow in question, and I assume he's asking for my name.

"Avery," I answer before I can stop myself. Though I'm pretty sure he knows that already. I remember the way my name left his lips on a cold, threatening breath before he leaned right into my space and told me to be careful what I say.

"Miss Avery," he repeats, a curve to his lips and a charming glint in his eyes. Damn, this guy can act. He's nothing like the uptight ass who got me so riled up that morning.

"Just Avery," I correct. "And you really expect me to believe that I was arguing with someone who looks exactly like you? Do you have a twin or something?"

A crease forms between his brows. He glances away for a

moment before returning his gaze to me. This time, his smile is the tiniest bit strained. "It appears I may indeed have a twin."

"It *appears*?"

"I'm afraid I must excuse myself."

"Oh, wonderful," I mutter as he walks away. Of course I can't get a straight answer out of a faerie. My gaze darts across the ballroom until I find Lina on the far side, chatting with an older gentleman. Her brief time with the prince is over, and he's dancing with someone else now. I make my way toward her, smiling politely at anyone who catches my gaze as I go.

"Ah, you're the hosts' choice, correct?" a woman asks, stepping into my path. Her bare arms are covered in leafy vine markings that seem to twist around each other.

"Uh, yes, ma'am. My lady." I blink and tear my gaze away from the moving tattoos, then try to remember if I'm supposed to curtsey.

"Lovely," she says before I can come to a decision about the curtsey. She presses her thin lips together as she assesses me. "You must have made quite an impression on them. We're all *so* looking forward to learning more about you as the show goes on. Oh, and there's Miss Riya Patel! Excuse me, dear. I'm hoping to meet all the contestants before the night is up." And with that, she moves on.

I exhale and continue around the side of the ballroom, relieved I escaped that conversation before I could embarrass myself too much. I reach Lina just as the man she was speaking with walks away. "I think that was one of the king's cousins," she whispers to me. "I hope I didn't say anything horribly offensive."

"Oh, I'm sure you were great," I tell her. "But speaking of offensive, there's a guy here who ..." But my words trail off as I see who's striding toward us: Prince Kieren, an embellished crystal glass in his hand, his gaze pinned on me. My heart lodges itself in my throat.

"Uh, Your Royal Highness," one of the black-clad, headset-adorned people say, hurrying at the prince's side, "according to the schedule, you're supposed to take a short break now before continuing. That's why someone handed you a drink. So you can—"

"I don't need a break."

"Uh, okay, if you're—"

"I'm sure." He stops in front of me, and the camera crew person melts away into the crowd. "I'm told it's your turn next," Prince Kieren says to me, his cold eyes lacking all expression. "If you'd be so kind," he adds, handing his glass to Lina without even looking at her.

Rude, I think to myself. But when Prince Kieren holds his hand out toward me, I pause for only the briefest moment before taking it. I'm not an idiot. A shiver dances up my arm from the point of contact as we head for the center of the ballroom. I'm holding a prince's hand. This is so weird. So freaking weird. *Not as weird as when he puts his other arm around you*, my brain very helpfully reminds me, a mere moment before we stop and turn to face each other. *Yes, this is definitely weirder*, I think as his other hand settles just below my left shoulder blade.

And then we're moving, Prince Kieren leading us confidently through the steps of the autumn sunset waltz, a dance similar to a ballroom waltz from our world—according to Mary-Louise—but with a few differences. Since I wasn't exactly familiar with a ballroom waltz to begin with—i.e. never attempted a waltz in my life—I didn't have to worry about unlearning one version to make space in my brain for another.

"So," he says, startling me because I assumed we would be

enduring this dance in silence. "Everyone has a label, and you are Miss Girl Next Door."

"Uh, yes. Correct. Your Highness." I hate this whole label business, but it's not as though I have to deal with it for much longer. My gaze darts up for a moment, but he's looking over my shoulder, his jaw tight. I return my eyes to the scene around us, taking in nothing as my brain focuses on the invisible pattern of the dance.

"Are you enjoying yourself so far?" he asks after I've managed several more steps without treading on his shoes.

"It's ... incredible. Completely breathtaking."

"And yet you don't even want to be here."

"I—" Have no idea what to say to that. Was that a patronizing *clearly you don't want to be here if you threw away the opportunity by breaking the rules within the first few minutes of your arrival*? "I reviewed some footage," he continues before I can find my voice. "Carwyn and Evanna's announcement. You looked quite startled. Almost as if you didn't know they were about to name you a contestant."

"I'm just not used to ... crowds. It was very overwhelming."

I sense his eyes on me now, and I can't help shifting my gaze to meet his. "So it was no surprise to you, then?" he says. "They must have contacted you some time before that morning, after they reviewed your ... application."

There's something purposeful about the way he hesitates over that word. My *application*. Which never existed, of course. Does he know? I'm not supposed to publicly admit that I was a desperate, last-second choice, but is this conversation considered public? The cameras can *see* us, but are there any microphones close enough to record our conversation? I end up humming a vague "Mm hmm" that I hope could be interpreted either way.

With that same growl-sigh I remember from earlier, he stares past me again. "I'd like you to explain your actions earlier. What were you doing hiding outside the queen's Lavender Lounge earlier?"

The queen's Lavender Lounge? I'm not sure if I'm supposed to know what that is, but now is not the time to ask. "I saw someone I thought I recognized," I tell him. "I didn't think. It was wrong, of course, *completely* wrong, but I followed him because I wanted to, um, confront him. But then I couldn't find him. I ended up lost. You know this place is like a maze, right? Or is it magic that makes it so confusing? I swear I turned back at one point and the corridor looked completely different to the one I'd just walked down."

"Who?"

"I—" My thoughts slam up against one another. "I'm sorry? Who what? What are you ..."

"Who did you see that you wanted to confront?"

"Oh." I pause, wondering exactly how much of the truth I should give. But if Rhylan truly is the prince's friend, he'll find out about The Grumpy Bean incident soon enough. "Your friend. Rhylan. We've met before. He was ... rude."

"Ah. *Ah.* It makes sense now."

"It does? Because I tried to talk to him a few minutes ago and he kept denying it. I mean, he doesn't *have* to apologize if he doesn't think he needs to. Though he does. He really does. But why is he *lying* about the whole encounter? He and I both know he was there."

"Perhaps you are the one who should be apologizing."

My eyes shoot to his face. "Oh. No, no. Definitely not. I mean ... perhaps, yes, but only after he apologizes first. He definitely started it. And I know that sounds petty and childish, but you should have heard him. He was so *arrogant*! As bad as—" I clamp my mouth shut before the word 'you' can slip out. *Shit, Avery, are you* trying *to get yourself beheaded?*

"As bad as?" Prince Kieren enquires, one eyebrow quirked and a cold hardness in his gaze.

"Nothing. No one. Your Highness," I add quickly, swallowing as I stare over his shoulder again. Why hasn't someone come over to push another contestant into Prince's Kieren's arms yet? It feels as though we've been dancing for ages.

"Why are you really here, Miss Girl Next Door?"

I smile in a way that I hope seems graceful and natural. "Same reason as everyone else." I force the words past my tongue, though I can barely manage the lie: "I'm hoping I may be your princess."

His laugh is humorless. "The girl who thinks this competition is *trash* is certainly not here to marry 'Prince Faerie Face.'"

Prince Faerie Face.

Trash.

You don't even want to be here.

My gaze is on him again, my heart pounding as I search his face. I have not uttered any of those words within this palace. I wouldn't dare. There are cameras everywhere, ready to catch every second of drama, every scandal. The only person I've said any of this to is Quinn. And the only conversation Prince Kieren could possibly know about is the one Quinn and I were having in The Grumpy Bean just as his friend Rhylan walked in.

I realize I'm no longer dancing. "He told you. Your friend. He told you what I ..." My words die on my tongue as I attempt to make sense of the expression on Prince Kieren's face. Is it ... guilt? Two images overlay in my head: the stiff, arrogant young man standing on the other side of the counter in The Grumpy Bean, and the formal, frowning prince in front of me. "No," I murmur. "It was *you*."

Suddenly I'm reeling. His posture, his attitude, the way he speaks. It made little sense that the seemingly easygoing Rhylan was the same man who seemed so out of place in The Grumpy Bean. But Prince Kieren is exactly that man. "You ... you wore his face." It's a guess, mostly, but the prince's answering expression—a flicker of genuine fear in his eyes—confirms it immediately. "It *is* possible. You've all been lying to us, swearing you can't take on someone else's appearance."

"I did not say—"

"*That's* why you were so startled to see me earlier. Not because you couldn't believe that such an ordinary-looking girl could possibly be one of the contestants in *The Princess Game*, but because the girl you insulted in a random coffee shop in the human world was suddenly inside your palace. I'm still confused as to why this was a surprise to you, though. Carwyn and Evanna did that huge announcement not even half an hour after you stormed out of The Grumpy Bean, and I've been in the media just like the rest of the—"

"I haven't had the time to scrutinize every single contestant," he hisses, head lowered toward mine now. "Is it so hard to believe that a prince might have other, more important matters to—"

A piercing scream cuts him off. I look around, my first thought that there must be another fight going on somewhere. Another crazy contestant. But the crowd parts quickly, everyone stepping away from ... a body? Someone in a red dress, twitching on the floor. There are gasps and murmurs and a few more screams as some people rush to move away from the girl while others try to get closer.

She goes still.

An unnatural hush falls over the ballroom.

My pulse beats faster, because that dress, that deep red gown

... I know exactly who was wearing it. I push past Prince Kieren, past women and men with their hands over their mouths in shock, past Carwyn and Evanna whispering in horrified tones to each other. My feet come to a halt when I finally see her face. Eyes closed, deathly still, blood staining her lips.

It's Lina.

Chapter Ten

"Up, up!" The voice rouses me from a deep sleep.

"Hmmwhat?" I mumble, my brain traveling sluggishly through the events of last night as I attempt to orient myself. I only got to sleep some time after three this morning. I was in Lina's room, huddled in one of the armchairs beside her aide, our hands clasped together as a human doctor and a fae healer attended to Lina. She wasn't the only girl who collapsed; there were six of them. Based on the murmurs and whispers as people hurried in and out of Lina's room, someone in the kitchen screwed up. An ingredient from Faeworld unfit for human consumption ended up in some of the drinks. "A potentially fatal mistake," the healer whispered at some point. "But I think she will recover."

I was planning to spend all night in Lina's room—emotional support for her devastated aide, who seemed to think she was somehow at fault and should have been able to prevent this from happening—until someone noticed my presence and realized I wasn't part of Lina's retinue. I was quickly ushered out and sent to my own room.

"Prince Kieren is here!" Iris hisses in my ear.

That gets my attention. I sit up straight in bed. "What?"

"He wants to speak to you. Right now."

"But ... in here? In *this*?" I clutch the nightgown I'm wearing, one of the many items Mary-Louise chose for me during our shopping spree. It's miles better than the ratty old T-shirts I usually sleep in—and surprisingly comfortable—but nowhere near appropriate for an audience with a prince.

"He said I had thirty seconds to wake you up, and then he'd be in here." She drags me out of bed and shoves a silky, floral-print robe at me. "This will have to do. At least it covers you down to your knees."

I push my arms into the sleeves and just manage to finish tying the gown around my waist when the door opens. Prince Kieren walks in with zero hesitation. Iris curtsies, and I follow a moment later, my sleep-deprived body almost falling over.

"Leave us," Prince Kieren says, and Iris disappears without another word. The door closes behind her with a barely audible click. Now that my mind is no longer focused entirely on Lina, I remember the conversation that came just before she collapsed. The revelation that it was Prince Kieren who was in The Grumpy Bean. The discovery that the fae can, in fact, glamour themselves to look like other people.

He moves a step closer. Another step. Though nothing else has changed, I imagine the room darkening around me, shadows drawing closer. I know what's coming next. There's only one way this can end. I know a truth I should not know, and he can't allow me to tell anyone. The easiest way to ensure my silence is to get rid of me. And though part of me is terrified of death and ready to beg for him to reconsider, another part of me is furious. I hate, *hate* that the fae have this kind of power over us. And that's what has me blurting out my true feelings at him instead of begging for my life.

"This is why we hate you all," I hiss, rising from my shaky curtsey and daring to lift my eyes to his. "Because you can do whatever you please and get away with it. No repercussions. Those in power like to pretend there are rules and laws that protect us from your kind, your spells and your illusions, but we all know the truth. Our world is just a playground for the fae, and this competition is no different. And even though a large part of my world is completely enraptured by all things fae, there are those of us who see you for the monsters you truly are. Getting rid of me isn't going to change that."

I reach the end of my tirade, breathing heavily. Prince Kieren continues to watch me with a deep frown. "You were a lot friendlier at the coffee shop," he comments. "That is, until you started going on about a stick being wedged into a certain part of my body."

My face burns even hotter. "I *am* usually friendly, but you're condescending and rude and you're about to kill me, so what do I have to lose?"

"Kill you? Where did you get that idea?"

"Because ... I know something about you—about all the fae—that you can't have me sharing with anyone else. It was bad enough that I overheard what you really think of *The Princess Game*, but now I also know you can all glamour yourselves to look like other people, which you always swore was impossible."

"First of all, you don't actually know that. The truth is that most fae can*not* do what I did in your coffee shop that day. And secondly, you think I'm going to *kill* you to keep you quiet? What kind of brute do you think I am?"

"Uh ... do you want me to answer that?"

It's his turn to pause. Then: "No. I suppose you've shared

enough of your honest opinions already." He sighs. "Despite what you believe, I am not here to *kill* you, Miss Girl Next Door. I came to propose a deal instead."

I blink. My brain is still catching up with the fact that I'm not about to die. My body, too, if my shaking hands are anything to go by. "A deal?"

"Yes. But first, answer this: What are you really doing here? It's clear that you are not, as you put it last night, hoping to become my princess. So what was your true goal in coming to the Glittering Palace to take part in *The Princess Game*? Sabotage? Assassination?"

My mouth falls open. "Assassination? Are you—are you *serious*?"

"You seem preoccupied with the idea of killing."

"Um, the idea of *being* killed, perhaps. I certainly didn't come here with the intention of *doing* any killing."

"Good. So your intention was?"

I bite my lip. Crap, crap, crap. If he's asking me this, then he obviously doesn't know why Carwyn and Evanna ended up choosing me. I don't want to get them fired, but I can't lie. Not to the prince. "The two hosts of the show, Carwyn and Evanna, asked me to take on the role of Girl Next Door. It happened right after I met you. The contestant they chose turned out to be ... unsuitable, and they only discovered this at the last minute. They were in my coffee shop, a whole load of media professionals were about to descend on us, they were desperate, and I was right there. Being *friendly and helpful*, which is my default setting, by the way."

"So you agreed, despite your feelings about the competition and fae in general. Out of the pure *helpfulness* of your heart."

"Well, okay, I was definitely swayed by the possibility of being gifted rare, expensive jewels—"

His eyebrows jerk upward at that, and I can't help rolling my eyes. "Yes, I know, extremely unlikely that you would have chosen to gift me *anything* after I made the stupid decision to wander off on my own around your palace, ended up unintentionally eavesdropping, and then embarrassed myself further by crashing onto the floor behind a piece of furniture. But *before* all of that, the gifts were still a possibility. And even without that part, the idea of spending time in a palace, even for a short while, was kind of appealing. You know, living in luxury, eating amazing food, and the bonus of maybe getting some exposure for my music. I figured it would be worth it, even if I had to put up with being around stuck-up fae royalty for a bit."

Plus the two million bucks Carwyn promised me, but if I mention that part, Carwyn will no doubt be in far more trouble than he might already be in after my confession. Oh, and I just said 'stuck-up fae royalty' out loud. In front of a fae prince. Crud. I lower my gaze and rush on. "Um, will Carwyn and Evanna get into trouble for this?"

"Not if I don't tell anyone."

I hesitate, hoping my next words will come out sounding like a polite request rather than begging. I do *not* want to beg this man for anything. "Please don't, Your Highness. I don't want to cause trouble for anyone."

"Really?" I peek up, and he's looking confused again. "You want to protect them? You're aware that they are not particularly nice people?"

It's on the tip of my tongue to say something about the pot calling the kettle black, but I manage to keep the words to myself. He probably wouldn't get it anyway. "I'd still rather not get them into any trouble, if possible."

He considers this for a moment, then says, "Fine. I suppose

your answer to my question is sufficient. I will, of course, confirm with Carwyn and Evanna."

"Of course," I mumble. I assume this means that he *can't* automatically discern whether my answer is the truth. If that is some kind of fae special ability, they don't all possess it.

"This brings me to the deal I would like to propose." He moves a few paces away, clasps his hands behind his back, and regards me. "You and I both know that this competition is not about me finding my true love. Rather, I must find the best match for the future of my court."

I nod slowly. "Right. The best political match."

He pauses, turning slightly and staring out of one of the windows. "Call it what you will." Another pause, and then a sigh. "This television show. I hated the idea when it was first presented. I did not want to agree to it. But after careful consideration, my parents and I decided that due to the nature of the type of match I am required to make, this would be the best way to narrow down the options."

I'm not sure that's true, but I'm also not about to argue with him.

"Though I am not looking for true love, I would like to end up with someone who has ... specific qualities. What I need, in order to find this person, is someone on the inside."

"I see," I say slowly.

"I want to know what each contestant is really like. They are sure to act differently when I'm not around. As far as I know, you are the only one who isn't here to win, so I'm hoping I can rely on you to truthfully report the other contestants' personalities and motivations without any concern for your own position in the game."

"Without any concern for my position," I repeat. "What exactly are you proposing?"

"The following: I will not dismiss you at the end of this week, as I originally decided after discovering your indiscretion yesterday. I will keep you around for as long as possible. I will name you as one of my Favorites each week and gift you rare and valuable items. By the time I dismiss you, you will have amassed a small fortune in priceless fae pieces. You can do with them whatever you see fit. In exchange, you will not tell anyone of my true feelings about *The Princess Game*, nor will you mention the fact that I or anyone else might have the ability to take on another person's appearance. In addition, you will assist me in narrowing down the contestants to the best possible options by answering my questions regarding each of them and sharing any information you gather while they are not in my presence. Do you agree to these terms?"

"Wow. It all sounds so romantic when you put it that way."

His eyes narrow. "Do you agree to these terms?" he repeats, his tone icier this time.

"So essentially, you're buying my silence with enchanted jewelry."

"Yes. Essentially. Your silence *and* your assistance."

"What if no one wants to share anything with me? If I'm a Favorite, they'll see me as competition. No one will trust me."

He doesn't pause before answering. "People are aware of your backstory. No one expects me to choose you. No one sees you as genuine competition."

Ouch. I know this is true, of course—Carwyn said the same thing; I even said it myself—but it still stings to hear the prince dismiss me so easily.

"But if you think it will make you seem less of a threat," he continues, "you will be at the bottom of my list of Favorites, and I won't name you *every* week. Do you agree to these terms?"

I don't tell him just how ludicrous it is that I'm the one he's enlisting to help him narrow down his romantic options. My love life has been nonexistent for years. I've had zero interest in anyone since—

Don't go there, I remind myself, forcing my thoughts to veer sharply away from the darkness lurking at the back of my mind. This deal Prince Kieren is proposing is the best possible thing I could have hoped for after my disastrous first day here. I don't have to worry about being kicked out for at least a few weeks, and I'm guaranteed to walk away with *something* by the time I leave. There must be a ton of collectors around the world who would pay a fortune for any item of jewelry gifted to me by Prince Kieren of Faeworld's Autumn Court.

"Can I make a counter offer?" I ask.

He looks shocked. Clearly this possibility didn't occur to him. But eventually he says, "I suppose you can."

"Keep me here until the Top 10. I'll happily leave after that." *With my two million from Carwyn* and *all the jewels I've just been promised.*

"Done."

"And you're *definitely* not planning to kill me at some point?"

He appears genuinely confused. "Do you think I go around killing people all the time?"

"Well, not *you*. But ... your guards or soldiers or whatever."

A muscle in his jaw twitches, and he inhales deeply before responding. "Neither I nor my guards nor soldiers nor *whatever* are planning to kill you."

A whoosh of breath escapes my lips. "Well, that's a huge relief. When you first walked in here, I figured I was either dead or about to disappear into some dungeon, never to see the light of day again. Although, in a place this beautiful, your dungeons are probably gorgeous too. View of the gardens, croissants for breakfast. It's probably a whole wing on the side of the palace, not buried underground. Wait—" I hesitate, frowning. "Is it still called a dungeon if it's not below ground?"

He stares at me for another few moments, his expression barely changing. Then: "I will leave you now."

"Wait," I say as he begins to turn. "Can I ask you something?"

He pauses, then turns back. "If you feel you must."

"What were you doing in The Grumpy Bean that morning? Why were you pretending to be one of your friends?"

I don't really expect him to answer, but he doesn't turn away. His gaze shifts past me. "I ... should not have been there. But I was curious."

"Curious? About The Grumpy Bean?"

His eyes flick back to mine. "No. About your world. I have not been there much. I evaded my security so that I could walk around on my own. My face is well known in your world, but Rhylan's is not, so I glamoured myself to look like him. A difficult feat that most cannot accomplish, so you needn't panic about the possibility of every second faerie taking on someone else's face. It requires a great deal of power and focus, but I decided it was worth the effort given how desperately I needed some—" He breaks off then, as if rethinking whatever he was about to say. "Anyway. That is what happened." He turns away before I can say another word and heads for the door.

Then he's gone and I'm left alone and holy *freak*! Did that seriously just happen? The prince himself was in my *bedroom*? I take a deep breath as feeling starts to return to my fingertips. I hadn't even realized they were numb.

"Ohmyfreaking*goodness*!" Iris races back into the bedroom, shoves the door shut, and falls back against it. "What just happened? Are you okay? Is he dismissing you? What's going on? The only thing he said to me was that I mustn't tell anyone he was here, and I can't work out if that's a good thing or a bad thing."

"Hey, calm down, it's okay." I cross the room, grab her hand, and tug her toward the sitting area. "We're not in trouble. He's definitely not dismissing me. He, uh ..." I push her gently onto the nearest armchair and decide there's no harm in admitting a small part of the truth. "I think he may even name me as one of his Favorites this week."

She presses her hands over her mouth and squeals. It's by far the most emotion I've seen from her since we met yesterday morning, and I can't help laughing. "Ohthankgoodness," she breathes. "I'm so scared of doing a terrible job, of proving that I don't belong here with all these super cool fae like Finneas and Mischa and their incredible magic. I'm scared of messing up your chances of—"

"Hey, stop." Her aloof attitude is starting to make sense. She isn't antisocial, she's just anxious about fitting in. She's the human in charge of my retinue, and yet she's probably worried that the 'super cool' Finneas and Mischa don't think she should be here. "You're doing an amazing job so far," I assure you. "Look at what just happened: A private audience with the prince himself! And he didn't even care that I was dressed in my pajamas."

She laughs. "I suppose things could be worse—"

"Avery?"

I look up and see my door cracked open, someone peeping around it. Or, more accurately, clinging tightly to it. "Lina! What are you doing here? You should be in bed!"

Iris jumps up, and we both hurry across the room to help Lina toward one of the chairs. "I'm ... I'm fine."

"You're not *fine*. You're—"

"At least I'm still here. My aide told me there were five other girls who also got sick from the drinks, and two of them ended up in hospital last night."

"What?"

"I think they're okay now, but ..." Lina looks up at me, her face pale, dark shadows beneath her eyes. Then her gaze bounces to Iris before returning to me. "Can I speak to you alone?"

"Of course, yes," Iris says before I can answer, all business-like again. "Please excuse me." She bobs her head forward in a brief half-bow before hurrying out of the room and pulling the door closed behind her

"I need to tell you something," Lina says in a low tone. "I'm not supposed to know ... I heard two of the healers whispering early this morning when they thought I was still asleep ... they were talking about the king forbidding them from sharing the truth ..."

"About what?"

"The other girls got sick because it was a faerie drink or something. Some ingredient humans aren't supposed to consume. But my symptoms ... my drink ..." She grips my hand. "It was poison."

A chill courses through my veins. "What?"

"And Avery, it wasn't just some random glass. It was the one Prince Kieren handed to me when he came to dance with you. I was so preoccupied watching the two of you that I forgot it wasn't my own glass, and I took a sip. I think ..." She swallows, her eyes darting across my face. "I think someone tried to poison the prince."

Chapter Eleven

Iris points through the doorway, and Lina and I hurry onto the lawn to join the other girls. It's been two days since the disastrous Opening Ball and Lina's accidental poisoning. Two days of carrying the knowledge that it was Prince Kieren who should have been poisoned and telling no one. Two days of rest for Lina, who decided at the last moment that she was well enough to join us for this morning's group activity. I decided to wait for her, which put me about three and a half minutes outside of Iris's carefully planned schedule. She was chewing her fingernails with anxiety by the time Lina and I hurried down the stairs with her, Lina's aide trying to keep up.

I'm comfortable today in a spaghetti strap sundress that hits just above the knee, a ponytail—of course—and open-toe flats. Jeans would be preferable, but Finneas told me he would burn any pair of jeans he found in my wardrobe. I quickly hid the pair I brought with me after he left my room this morning.

Lina and I quietly join the back of the group of girls assembled near a pretty pond as someone from the camera crew whispers to Carwyn and Evanna. Carwyn delicately pats his voluminous hair as if to check it's still there, while Evanna adjusts the tiny microphone attached to the front of her blouse. Then they step up onto the low wall surrounding the pond and smile down at us.

"Welcome to another glorious morning at the Glittering Palace!" Carwyn calls out.

"We last saw you on Monday night at the Opening Ball," Evanna says, "and that was quite an event, wasn't it?" They both chuckle, which I think might be a little inappropriate, given that six girls almost died. "Plenty of rumors have been flying around since then," Evanna continues, "but we would like to assure you that all the girls who accidentally consumed a drink of faerie origin at the Opening Ball are *totally* fine. Most of them were treated right here in the Glittering Palace, and one of those lovely young ladies is already well enough to join us this morning." She smiles at Lina, and almost every head swivels in our direction.

"The other three contestants who were treated here at the palace are still resting in their rooms," Carwyn says. "However, it saddens us to inform you that Yindi and Inessa, the two unfortunate young ladies who were treated in human hospitals due to their conditions being slightly more serious, have chosen not to return. And, of course, there was the particularly fiery Alaska Adams who was asked to leave after assaulting a fellow contestant and a member of the TV crew at the Opening Ball."

"Three down, and we haven't even got to the first dismissal yet," Lina murmurs.

"Moving on!" Evanna exclaims with a clap of her hands. "This morning, you'll be taking a boat ride along the Elledin River, which flows through the forested area of the palace grounds and passes very close to the Shimmer."

"It actually flows just *beyond* the Shimmer, Evanna,"

Carwyn adds, flashing a grin in her direction, "before turning and winding back through the palace grounds on this side. Which means our contestants will have a brief view into the Autumn Court of Faeworld. Isn't that exciting?"

"Indeed!" Evanna exclaims. "Each boat will seat six of you, and you'll find a picnic basket with snacks and drinks inside each one. All confirmed safe for human consumption," she adds with a high-pitched laugh. "Prince Kieren will move from boat to boat throughout the morning, which will give him a chance to chat to all of you. As always, there will be cameras around, and there are microphones in each boat, so don't say anything *too* naughty." She winks at us.

"Or *do*," Carwyn adds with a waggle of his brows, "but be aware that it will almost certainly show up in the next episode."

"All right then! Let's head to the boats!"

It feels a little like a school tour group, all thirty of us shuffling forward and following Carwyn and Evanna. But my attention is soon captured by our surroundings. The trees are alive with birdsong, their branches heavy with lush green leaves and hanging bunches of white blossoms. Tiny insects with wings that shimmer like emeralds in the morning light flit around them, along with butterflies of vibrant purple-blue. No, not butterflies, I realize as one darts closer and lands on the shoulder of the girl in front of me. The body of the winged creature looks more like a tiny *person*.

"Here we are!" Evanna calls out from the front of the group. We spread out along the riverbank, and I almost sigh out loud at the complete perfection of the scene laid out before me. A tranquil river, soft light streaming through the trees, and a collection of boats that look like oversized white gondolas with elegant carvings and gold embellishments decorating the sides. A glance up reveals cameras rigged discreetly on a system of wires running through the trees alongside the river. My smile slips a little. It wasn't as though I didn't know we would be watched at all times, but it still leaves me feeling a little uncomfortable.

TV crew people move among us, checking lists of names on their tablets and dividing us into small groups. A cameraman steps in front of Evanna, and with a polished smile and a *snap-snap* of her fingers, walkways appear out of thin air, connecting the side of each boat to the riverbank.

I find myself in a boat with Lina—thank goodness—Cadence, Shay, Natalya and Annemarie, who is an actual princess of some European country. "But please just call me Annemarie," she tells us after Lina asks how we're supposed to address her. "I don't want to be any different from anyone else here."

Natalya Petrova, Miss Olympic Gymnast, rolls her ice blue eyes at that. "Well that's a stupid strategy," she murmurs in her accented English, just loud enough for all of us to hear.

Here we go, I think with a glance at Lina, who sighs and shakes her head. No doubt she's thinking the same thing.

Either by magic or some hidden mechanism, the boats move away from the bank and begin gliding smoothly down the center of the river. And it's probably silly because it's just a boat, but I can't help the thrill that dances through me. I've never been on a boat before, so this is yet another experience I most likely would never have had if not for *The Princess Game.*

I peer over the side of the boat and look down into the water, and from this angle, without the sunlight glinting off its surface, I realize the water is *literally* glittering with bright specks of silver. "Look!" I whisper to Lina, pointing. "Isn't it pretty?"

"It's from the starlight opal fish," Cadence tells us before Lina can say anything. "Their scales have the ability to capture starlight at night, and then tiny bits of their scales flake off into the water and look like glowing glitter."

"Oh, cool," I say, wondering if this is actually true but not daring to question her when I'm aware of the microphones hidden in the boat and the cameras watching us. I'm not going to be the one to start an argument, and if Cadence is wrong, someone else will no doubt correct her at some point. I look at Lina, but she merely shrugs.

"If you need to know anything, you can just ask me, by the way," Cadence adds. "I've interviewed several fae who work for the Glittering Palace on my YouTube channel."

"That must fit so well with your brand," Natalya comments with a fake smile. "Are the fae also interested in makeup tutorials and room tours?"

Cadence's smile is equally fake. "They are. We discussed makeup illusions at length. It's one of my most popular videos."

"I, uh, wonder how long Prince Kieren will take to reach our boat," Annemarie says loudly, clearly trying to diffuse the situation. She makes a show of craning her neck to look past Natalya at the boats ahead of us. "Ah, I don't think it will be too long."

I follow her gaze and spot Prince Kieren with several girls practically draping themselves across his lap they're trying to get so close. He looks as though he'd like to drown himself in the river. I should probably tell him he's doing a terrible job of hiding his true feelings about this whole thing.

"Well then," Natalya says, flipping her platinum hair over her shoulder, "we still have a little time to get to know each other." She surveys us. "Okay. You." She points at Cadence. "No. You're famous on social media. So what? You." She points at me. "No. You come from *literally* nothing. I don't even know why you're here. You." She's moved on to Lina before I even have a chance to feel offended. "Your father started what is now one of the largest e-commerce platforms in the world. So I suppose that makes you a threat of some sort. But there is no *class* in e-commerce. You were not bred for a life of royalty. And you." She looks at Shay. "Your family does whiskey? Who cares? And you." Her eyes fall on Annemarie. "The only contestant who is already a princess. If you were not such a pushover, you might be the biggest threat here. Although ... what does your country really have to offer in terms of an alliance?"

"And we're supposed to be threatened by you because you're an Olympic gymnast who didn't win anything?" Cadence snaps back, venom in her tone. "If you couldn't win something you're actually good at, there's no way you're going to win this."

Natalya leans back and crosses one leg over the other. "As if I would disclose my secret weapon to any of you."

A snort of laughter escapes Lina, and Natalya's eyes land on her. She cocks her head and smiles. "You think this is funny, Retail Heiress."

"I'm sorry. I'm still trying to figure out if you're actually for real," Lina says. "Or did the studio put you up to this? I mean, you're trying to *create* drama, right? That's what this is?"

"I'm trying to determine who the real competition is. Anyone who can be scared off this early in the game does not deserve to be here."

"And as you can see, we're all positively shivering," Shay says, staring past all of us with a small frown.

"You're not going to fight back?" Natalya asks her, a playful glint in her eyes. I'm starting to wonder if Lina is right. Maybe someone did plant this girl here to create drama. I can say with absolute certainty that at least some of this conversation, if not all of it, is going to end up in the first episode.

Shay focuses on Natalya with mild irritation in her gaze. "Does it look like I'm interested in playing your games?"

Natalya shifts her attention to me. "And you? The Girl Next Door with literally nothing to offer aside from a silly dream of a music career? Don't you have anything to say in your defense?"

I smile at her. If only she knew that of all of us sitting in this boat, I'm the one with the most power. *I want to know what they're really like,* Prince Kieren said. And as much as I dislike him, I'm pretty sure I like Natalya even less. "Nope," I say, holding both hands up. "I have nothing to say."

Her smile creeps a little higher. "Like I said. I don't know what you're even doing here."

"Hosts' choice," I say with a shrug. "I guess you'll have to take it up with them if you don't agree with their opinions."

Her gaze hardens, but she isn't stupid enough to say a word against Carwyn and Evanna. Her painted lips remain frozen in a smile. Beside me, Lina leans forward with a smirk. "You only *wish* you could say that the wildly popular Carwyn Aster and Evanna Zynn personally chose you."

"No, Miss Retail Heiress. There is only one person who needs to choose me, and that is Prince Kieren." Natalya's confidence has returned to her smile. "I will make sure of it."

"Wow," Cadence says. "Game on, bitch."

Annemarie coughs delicately, and Lina stifles more laughter. We continue down the river in awkward silence for the next several minutes, until our boat is brought to a stop and Prince Kieren climbs up another magically appearing walkway and steps into the boat. I sense everyone sitting straighter, pulling on their best smiles, fluttering their eyelashes. Well, okay, perhaps not everyone. I'm certainly not doing any eyelash-fluttering, and Shay looks like she's trying to curl in on herself and get as far away from all of us as possible.

"Good morning, ladies," Prince Kieren says, attempting a smile that looks like a grimace as he sits in the empty space Natalya is patting beside her. Cadence immediately moves to his other side. Poor guy. I almost feel sorry for him. He looks around at all of us, his gaze moving swiftly away from mine as if he's afraid a normal amount of eye contact might give away our deal. "Miss Natalya, Miss Shay, Princess Annemarie," he says. "I'm sorry I did not get a chance to dance with you the other night."

"Don't worry about it," Annemarie says, sounding genuine. "There was a lot going on after those poor girls collapsed. I'm just relieved everyone is all right."

There's the tiniest twitch in the prince's jaw. "Yes. So am I." He takes a breath, then turns to Natalya. "Miss Natalya, I believe I met your father a year or two ago at the opening ceremony of an international sporting event in your world."

"Yes, you did!" Natalya looks positively radiant that he's brought this up. "He'll be so pleased you remembered. We're very close, the two of us, so I'll be sure to tell him. We speak almost every day. It will be difficult here to have such limited contact with our loved ones. But worth it, of course," she adds with a laugh, placing her hand on his arm, "to get to know you."

He nods, looking even more awkward now. "Yes, of course. I'm glad to hear you're close to your family. That's important." He takes another deep breath and looks around, probably deciding which of us to engage in stilted conversation next. "Miss—"

"What about you?" Natalya asks, drawing his attention back to her. "Are you close to your parents?"

"I—yes. I am. We would ... do anything for each other."

"Ah, a family man," Natalya croons. "I love that."

"Me too," Cadence says, snuggling against Prince Kieren's

other side. "I have a huge family, and it's the absolute best. You're never alone, you know? All the noise and chatter around the dinner table when everyone's gathered together. It used to annoy me, but I already miss it."

Something tightens in my chest as I listen to her. A slow, squeezing pain.

"What do you think, Avery?"

I blink, caught off guard, and find Natalya's piercing gaze on me. I swallow and force a smile. "About?"

"Family. Are you close to yours?" She allows a beat of silence to pass before placing a hand delicately over her mouth. "Oh, I'm so sorry. I forgot. You don't have a family."

And that single comment right there slices sharper than a blade ever could. I meet Prince Kieren's eyes for a second before looking away. Natalya didn't need to remind him of my lack of family. He already knows I'm entirely unsuitable. "I ... think ... family is what you make it," I say hesitantly. "It isn't always about blood. It's the people you love. The people you would do anything for. Like Quinn. We met when we were in a foster home together, but she's as close to me as a real sister."

Natalya smiles sweetly at me, but I see the masked condescension in her eyes. "That's precious."

"Oh look!" Lina says, leaning past me and looking forward. "You can see into Faeworld from here!"

I turn, my face hot, blood still pounding heavily in my ears. But the tension in my limbs begins to melt away as I lay eyes on the tranquil autumn scene we're drifting toward. I glance up and see the rippling, opalescent part of the sky directly above us. Holy shit. We're going *through* the Shimmer. *We're in freaking Faeworld!*

Lina and I scramble to our feet and move to the front of the boat, balancing as close to the edge as we dare. Shay is at Lina's other side a moment later. “Incredible,” she breathes, sounding more surprised than anything else.

The trees that now line the riverbank are bursting with brilliant reds, oranges and yellows. The birds fluttering from branch to branch have tail feathers of shimmering bronze, and the insects darting through the air look like specks of glowing gold. The air is different here too. Crisper, cooler, and something else I can’t quite define. Something distinctly different. Is this was *magic* feels like? I’m surprised by the strange ‘rightness’ of it.

“Oh my goodness, isn’t it *beautiful*?” Natalya exclaims. I sense movement behind me, and I know she’s trying to clamber forward too. “I’ve never seen anything so—Oh *shit*!”

I turn just in time to see her falling toward me, and I know it’s already too late. My heart flies into my throat as she shoves hard into me, falling to her knees while I topple backwards right over the edge of the boat.

Chapter Twelve

I plunge beneath the water, bubbles streaming around me. It isn't deep, and there's barely a current, but it still takes a few moments of what probably looks like desperate flailing before my head breaks the surface of the water and I gulp in a deep breath of air. The girls are all leaning over the side of the boat, gasping and pointing and asking if I'm okay. "I am *so* sorry!" Natalya calls out, her pretty face stricken. She and I both know that wasn't an accident, but the only thing the cameras will see is the award-winning act she's putting on.

"I'm fine!" I call out, treading water and lifting one hand to wave awkwardly at everyone. I grit my teeth into a forced smile. This is going to be a meme. I can already tell. Slow-motion Avery, landing backside-first in a river. It'll probably go viral.

But before I can turn toward the riverbank, a dark figure launches over the side of the boat, and the next thing I know, Prince Kieren is in the water beside me. He rises swiftly, flicking his wet hair back in that way guys do that makes me want to simultaneously roll my eyes and maybe, *maybe* sigh just the tiniest bit.

"Are you all right?" he asks, reaching for me.

"I know how to swim," I inform him, turning toward the bank and swimming away from him. He catches up to me with swift, strong strokes, then slows so he doesn't swim ahead of me. We climb out of the water together, and when he offers his hand to help me up the bank, I decide not to refuse. There are probably still at least a few cameras on us, and I'm supposed to be a swooning princess-in-training. It wouldn't make sense for me to scramble awkwardly up the slippery bank when I could gratefully take Prince Kieren's hand instead.

I heave a breath when we finally reach flat ground. I drop his hand and look around, realizing two things in the same instant: One, the boats have continued their journey along the river and are now almost out of sight. Two, I'm surrounded by autumn. "Crap," I say. "We're on the wrong side of the Shimmer."

Prince Kieren is quiet a moment before answering. "We are on the *Faeworld* side of the Shimmer, if that's what you mean."

"Yes. It's ..." I trail off as my eyes travel the riot of rich colors. The birds with the shimmering bronze feathers are even more beautiful up close, and the glowing gold specks I thought were insects seem to be more like minuscule burning embers dancing on the breeze. I lift my hand to catch some, and they disintegrate on my palm, vanishing into nothing like the magical autumn version of snowflakes. A strange thrill dances through me. "I mean, it's beautiful," I finish, "but it isn't safe. I'm not supposed to be here."

"You will be fine," he says dismissively. "Magic cannot kill you in only a few minutes. There is a bridge a little further back that way. We can return to the Glittering Palace grounds there."

I frown as I turn and follow his gaze back up the river. "We didn't go under any bridges. Your Highness."

"It's there. I assure you."

I decide now is probably not the time to argue. "Okay then." I reach behind my head with both hands, squeeze the excess water out of my dripping wet ponytail, and start walking. Prince Kieren joins me. Leaves crunch beneath my wet shoes, the rich scent of damp earth fills my nose, and I wonder if I should be attempting to make conversation or if he's happy with silence. A breeze stirs up a flurry of leaves, which dance across the ground with a soft shushing noise. I shiver and wrap my arms around my wet body.

"Are you—"

"I'm fine," I answer, then hurriedly add, "Your Highness." I don't need Prince Faerie Face pretending to be all chivalrous and producing a warm, cozy blanket out of thin air, as wonderful as the idea might sound right now. "Do you think there are any cameras still watching us?"

"No. They cannot see through the Shimmer. It ... distorts something. There would have to be cameras on this side, and I know for a fact that there are not."

"Okay. Oh!" I jump back as a small, furry creature darts across our path. Something that looks like a fox, except ... it has wings?

"It's harmless," Prince Kieren says, stopping and looking back at me.

"Okay, it just ... startled me." I peer between the trees, trying to see where the creature went, but it's either hidden or well camouflaged among the autumn colors of the forest. I force my gaze forward again and continue walking. "Is the bridge close?" I ask as another breeze curls past, raising goosebumps on my bare arms.

Instead of answering, he says, "Would you please allow me to dry you?"

"What? No, that sounds weird. Thank you, but I'm fine.

Your Highness. We'll be back on the other side of the Shimmer soon, right? And it's a lot warmer there."

"You're shivering."

"I'm really not."

"Why are you being so stubborn? Are you hoping to end up ill? I know how fragile you humans are."

"Wow." I look sideways and meet his silvery gaze. "You sure know how to compliment a girl." He stares at me, and I realize I've said this last part out loud instead of just inside my head. "Um ... can you pretend you didn't hear that last bit?"

He sighs that quiet grumble-sigh of his, the one I'm starting to recognize after only a few meetings with him. The one that's like a low growl in the back of his throat. He looks away and says, "Yes, the bridge is just there, beside that twisted tree."

My eyes find the twisted tree he's referring to, a gnarled crescent shape of intertwined branches right on the edge of the riverbank, but I see no bridge. I'm about to ask if I'm missing something—like, hello, the *bridge*—when Prince Kieren walks forward and presses one of the knots on the side of the tree.

Something springs into existence from the ground at the base of the tree and unfurls itself over the water. It touches the bank on the other side of the river and within seconds, I'm staring at a perfectly formed bridge of gleaming gold and burnished bronze leaves, intricately intertwined to create a delicate filigree pattern.

"Okay," I breathe. "So that's why I didn't see it earlier."

We walk in silence across the bridge, and I'm half expecting it to vanish when we're partway across and drop us into the water, like most other faerie illusions that have no lasting power. I reach out and carefully touch one of the solid bronze leaves curling around the railing, marveling at how real it feels. How long until it disintegrates into nothing?

The air is noticeably warmer on the other side of the river, the trees lush and green, the sweet fragrance of flowers hanging in the air. It's still unpleasant to be walking around dripping wet, but at least I'm no longer covered in goosebumps.

"Well," I say, turning to face Prince Kieren. "Thanks for jumping into the water after me, Your Royal Highness. The palace is that way, right?" I gesture through the trees.

"Yes."

"Okay, then I'll head back that way—" I start walking "—and I'm sure you can return to the boats. They're probably waiting for you further downstream."

"Yes, probably. But I'll accompany you back to the palace," he says, falling into step beside me.

"Oh, don't worry, that's not necessary. I'm sure I can find my own way back."

"I'm sure you could, but it's still better you don't walk alone."

I manage to keep my annoyed sigh to myself. I was hoping to enjoy my beautiful surroundings in comfortable silence, but now I have a royal bodyguard making sure I don't sneak into places I don't belong. Which, fair enough. He did discover me eavesdropping in a part of the palace I shouldn't have been in just a few days ago.

I decide to try one last time. "Don't you think you need to get back to the boats? I'm pretty sure they're still filming, and you just so happen to be the star of the show."

He sighs, an almost-growl that sounds like disapproval. "It is my sincere hope that they will find a selection of contestants to become the stars of the show instead."

"Well, keep looking like you want to strangle yourself in our presence, and I'm sure they'll do their best to give you minimal screen time."

He comes to an abrupt halt and, once again, I realize I've uttered my thoughts out loud instead of keeping them locked in my head. I spin around to face him, clapping my hand over my mouth. "I ... um ..." Slowly, I lower my hand. "Sometimes I don't think before speaking. My thoughts just kind of ... tumble out."

"I've noticed. You never would have made it onto this show if you'd been through the proper application and interview process."

"That is one hundred percent correct. I'll try to keep my thoughts to myself."

"Don't."

I hesitate. "Your Highness?"

He continues walking, and I turn to follow him. "Part of our deal is that you are honest with me," he says. "I did not realize back there on the boats that my true feelings were so obvious in my expression. I'll try to mask them better next time."

"Oh. I thought everything—" I silence myself before the rest of that sentence can leave my tongue. He might want honesty from me, but there's definitely a line and I don't want to step beyond it. "Never mind."

"It has quite literally been less than a minute since I asked you *not* to keep your thoughts to yourself."

Well, shoot. "I ... I was going to say ... I thought everything was already a mask with you guys. You know, just with all ... the illusions. The glamours. Who knows what's real and what isn't?" I gesture toward him. "We don't even know what you really look like."

He blinks at me, confusion written in every line of his face. "What do you mean? This is what I really look like."

I open my mouth to reply, but I'm not entirely sure what to

say, so in the end, nothing comes out. *Guess what, Quinn? He* is *that stupidly handsome.* "Um ... right. Cool." I give him a double thumbs up.

I look forward again just as a branch snaps loudly nearby, followed by a quick rustle of leaves. Just like with the winged fox creature, I'm startled into taking a step back. I search the trees and catch movement—a dark shape—but it's gone a second later, and my eyes can't make out anything beyond the trailing leaves and bunches of blossoms. But there's a prickle along the back of my neck as I stare between the trees. I get the distinct feeling we're being watched.

"My guards," Prince Kieren says before I can ask. "There are four of them, positioned in the trees around us."

"Oh." My pounding heart slows and the tension in my shoulders releases. "Of course."

"They will keep their distance, but they won't let me out of their sight."

"Right." I look at him. "You're the prince. Can't risk leaving you alone with a stranger, especially not one as dangerous as me. What if I tried to stab you or something?"

His expression doesn't change. "I believe I would probably be able to defend myself."

I tilt my head. "Do you even *have* a sense of humor?"

He sighs and looks forward again.

"I'll take that as a 'no,'" I whisper as we continue walking.

"I can still hear you."

"I thought you *wanted* to hear all my thoughts, Your Highness."

"Perhaps not all of them."

The trees thin out as we reach the edge of the forest, and soon we join up with a glittering pathway winding between manicured bushes and artfully positioned sculptures. We end up near a white pavilion surrounded by magnificent white rose bushes, and I see part of the palace not far beyond it.

"We're near the greenhouse end of the palace," Prince Kieren says, coming to a stop. "I don't believe you and the other contestants have spent much time in this area yet, so you may not be familiar with it. I will send one of my guards inside with you. He can show you back to your quarters so you can change." He looks behind him, raises one hand, and signals with two fingers.

"Well, thank you for walking back with me," I tell him, since that seems the polite thing to say, "and good job jumping into the water after me. That'll make you look fabulously galant."

A small frown creases his brow. "Yes, I suppose it will." He takes a deep breath and throws another glance over his shoulder. "One of them should be—"

"Wait," I say quickly, "before your guard gets here. I need to tell you something." He looks at me. I've been debating bringing this up the entire walk through the forest, and there's something in me that just can't keep quiet about it. "You probably know this already because you must have at least a hundred people trying to protect your life at all times, but in case someone's keeping this from you ..." He raises an eyebrow in question. "I think someone tried to poison you."

He's silent for a long moment, his expression giving nothing away. "Why do you think that?"

I explain what happened with Lina and what she overheard. "Clearly this isn't meant to be public knowledge," I add, "since no one seems to be talking about it. But I thought you should know."

He nods slowly. "Interesting. I would have thought you might be pleased if there was one less stuck-up fae royal to worry about."

Embarrassment heats my face as I realize he's repeating my words from our last meeting. "Look, I may not *like* you, but that doesn't mean I want you poisoned." I pause, then add, "Who's going to name me a Favorite and give me rare faerie gifts if you're not around?"

The corners of his mouth turn up in what might almost, *almost* be considered a smile. "Well, thank you for telling me," he says, still not revealing whether he already knew about the poison. "I appreciate it, Miss Girl Next Door."

I open my mouth to remind him that I have a name, but a shadow darts across the pavilion in my periphery, distracting me. I look toward it, but there's nothing there. Only dappled light dancing across the pavilion steps. "What was that?" I ask, sensing that same prickle at the back of my neck. "That wasn't one of your guards." The movement was too quick. Too ... unnatural.

But instead of looking around, Prince Kieren is watching me. "Nothing to be concerned about. There are dozens of small, harmless creatures roaming the grounds. Ah, this is Illiam." He steps to the side as a young man in uniform joins us. "He'll show you back to your quarters."

"Um, hi, thanks." He seems vaguely familiar, and after a moment of searching my brain, I place him as the guard who was instructed to carry Lina out of the ballroom after she collapsed.

"Thank you for providing an excuse for me to get away from the boats this morning," Prince Kieren says. "While it was a pleasant reprieve, I should probably return to the river and speak with the remainder of the contestants. I will see you on Friday evening at the first dismissal dinner." With a brief nod, he turns and strides away.

Chapter Thirteen

"Holy shit, Aves," Quinn says, her eyes enormous as she shoves her face right in front of her phone's camera. "Talk about starting with a bang. That first episode was crazy! Girls collapsing at the Opening Ball, a contestant dragged away by guards for trying to assault another contestant, *six* girls already gone from the show, *and* you went flying into a river!"

"Ugh, how bad was it?" I've finished showing Quinn my spectacular bedroom, so I seat myself at the digital piano in the alcove beside the vanity. "Did I flash my underwear at the entire world? Are there shocking boomerang gifs all over the internet?"

"Wait, you haven't seen the episode?" Quinn scrunches her nose. "I was imagining you all sitting together last night in some fancy palace cinema with gourmet popcorn and champagne, gasping in horror as you discover all the scandalous things everyone says about each other when they're interviewed in private."

"Nope." I place my phone on the music rack and rest my right hand on the keys. "We're not allowed to see any of the episodes while we're still part of the competition. That's why

I'm only allowed to call you once a week on a Tuesday, the day *after* the previous week's episode has aired. So I can't share details with you before an episode comes out. And they don't let us make calls in *private*, just so you know." I send a glance over my shoulder at Iris, who's tapping away on her tablet in my sitting area. She looks up.

"Sorry," she whispers with a grimace. "*Princess Game* rules."

"Again, it's to make sure I don't tell you anything I'm not allowed to tell you," I continue with a sigh, turning back to the piano and letting my fingers travel idly through a random melody. *Like the fact that one of the contestants was poisoned, and it was meant for the prince*, I add silently. I wish I could tell Quinn that part, but Iris doesn't know, and even if she did, there's no way I would be allowed to spread that bit of scandal beyond the Glittering Palace walls.

"Oh." Quinn scratches the tip of her nose before pushing her glasses back up. "You told me about only having your phone during approved times, but I didn't realize you don't get to see the show. I guess that makes sense though. Wait, but surely I can sit here and tell you exactly what was aired. Like, if that Russian girl called you a gold-digging tart behind your back, I could tell you."

My hands go still on the keyboard. "Natalya called me a gold-digging tart?"

"No, but she called someone else a gold-digging tart, and she said that all the girls who collapsed during the Opening Ball are obviously too weak to be there. 'Aren't they taking their vitamins?'" she says in a terrible imitation of Natalya's accent, which I can't help laughing at.

"What kind of person are they portraying her to be on screen?" I ask. "Because in real life, she's truly awful." I shoot another glance over my shoulder, wondering if I'm about to wind up in trouble for saying that, but Iris doesn't even look up.

"Oh, yeah, she seems like a conniving witch. She totally pushed you out of that boat, even though she denied it multiple times. But joke's on her because Prince Faerie Face chose to jump in after *you*, and then—*eeeek!*—he named you one of his Favorites at the end of the episode!" Quinn squeals and everything goes blurry on screen as she bounces up and down. "Not that you or I would ever want to be legitimately favored by that fake-ass prince," she adds as she flops back down onto her bed, "but flip, he gave you the prettiest bracelet!"

I smile as my eyes move to my left arm where the delicate diamond bracelet encircles my wrist. We sat in our pretty dresses in an opulent lounge while Prince Kieren politely dismissed three girls before calling out five names as his Favorites for the first week. As promised, I was last on the list. I did an excellent job of crossing the room with a huge fake grin on my face. If I could have made myself blush, I would have, but since that wasn't possible, I fluttered my eyelids and pressed my right hand delicately to my lips as Prince Kieren fastened the bracelet around my wrist.

Then I almost tripped over the edge of a rug as I returned to my seat, which was nearly as embarrassing as falling out of a boat, but hopefully added to the whole *I'm so overwhelmed he chose me that I can't even walk straight* vibe I was going for.

"You did well, Aves," Quinn says, drawing me back to the present. "Excellent acting. Almost as good as the fae," she adds with a laugh. "Although someone needs to teach Prince Faerie Face how to act. He comes across so snobby and condescending. Like ... super standoffish."

"Yeah, he's ... not the best at social interactions."

"Understatement. Though it seems the world is even more

in love with him after that first episode. They made him look like the super hot hero when he jumped into the water after you."

I smile at that. "He did look like the super hot hero."

"Um, Miss Avery?"

I look around at Iris. A week later, and she's still calling me Miss. So are Finneas and Mischa. I can't get them to stop, no matter how many times I tell them *just Avery*. "Yes?"

"Five more minutes," she whispers.

"Really? We only just started chatting."

"I know, I'm sorry, but you were allowed one hour, and that time's almost up. We need to be downstairs for lunch and then lessons."

"Did someone say *lessons*?" Quinn demands.

"Yeah. Just Faeworld history and geography and stuff like that. The future princess has to be at least a little bit educated, blah blah blah. So yeah. I have to go soon."

"But we've only been talking for like two seconds! I *miss* you!"

"I know, but I have an allotted period of time during which I'm allowed to use my phone, and since you were finishing a shift, I spent most of that time scrolling through the insane number of comments from my insane number of followers on all the pictures and videos my aide has been posting for me."

"Well, thank goodness you finally have someone doing your social media," Quinn says, twirling a strand of hair around one finger. "You were *so* bad at that."

I stick my tongue out at her as I swing my legs over the piano bench and stand. "Okay, tell me quickly: How are *you*? How's everything going?"

"Ugh, everything sucks without you."

"I'm sure that's not true."

"It's *so* true. I still haven't found something to replace my tutoring hours, and The Grumpy Bean is really busy these days now that we're 'famous' because *The Princess Game* hosts did their announcement here and the Girl Next Door used to work here." She rolls her eyes.

"But that's good, right? More money coming in? More tips?"

"Yeah, I suppose. It's just super tiring, and the new girl they hired isn't nearly as nice as you, and Nigel's always moaning about—"

"Quinn?" I interrupt as I look around for the sandals I was wearing earlier. "Remember you were going to try to be a glass-half-full person?"

"Ugh, no," she moans. "It requires too much energy."

"Hey." I refocus on the screen and point a finger at her. "Don't make me do the elbow dance."

"You know it's not called the—"

"Stop being such a grouch, or I'll do it."

"You wouldn't. There's someone else in the room with you."

"I *so* would. I don't care what Iris thinks of me."

"Here, Miss Avery," Iris says quietly, handing me the sandals I was searching for. Sometimes it's like she's inside my head.

"Okay, I'm just getting my shoes on, and then I'm doing the dance," I warn Quinn as I prop the phone up against a stack of music notebooks on my bed.

"Please, *no*," Quinn groans as I slip my feet into the sandals. "I'll try to be positive, I promise. And if I'm really down and I need a pick-me-up, I'll just find that video of you dancing on the counter of The Grumpy Bean."

I throw myself onto my bed and grab the phone. "Quinn!

You told me you deleted that. Do *not* let Nigel see that video. Ever!"

She laughs. "You don't even work here anymore. What's the big deal?"

"It's not a *big deal*. I'm just looking out for Nigel's health, that's all. He'd probably have heart failure if he saw that video."

Quinn's laugh is a wicked cackle now, and I suddenly miss her so much it causes a physical ache in my chest. "I wish I could give you a giant, squishy hug," I tell her. "Prepare to be knocked over by my enthusiastic embrace when I ..." I trail off, squinting at the wall behind one of my couches where I swear a strange shadow just flickered across the ivory colored space.

"Aves? Avery?"

"Hmm, yeah?" I tear my gaze from the wall and look at Quinn again.

"What happened? Seems like you froze for a bit."

"Oh, sorry. No. Just ... distracted by something." I look at the wall again, but it's still blank, pristine, no suspicious, crawling shapes in sight. Maybe it was just some strange fae creature that cast a shadow as it went flying past my window. "Um ... you said you're going to try and be positive. That's great. You can let me know how that's going next week."

"Fiiiiine," she groans, sounding anything but happy.

Iris signals to me, and I nod. "Okay, I have to go. Any parting words of wisdom for me?"

"Yes." Quinn sits up, her expression turning serious. "Be careful what you eat and drink there. I totally don't believe that Opening Ball incident was an accident."

I bite back the answer I wish I could give her—*I know for a fact that one of those glasses* wasn't *an accident*—and nod instead. "Yeah. I will be. Love you, Quinn."

Chapter Fourteen

"So you're saying that Faeworld is like ... prehistoric?" Ami asks as we sit at our desks in a sunny room in the West Tower with notebooks open in front of us. Tall windows allow a fragrant flower-scented breeze to drift inside, and, as always, there are an uncomfortable number of cameras squished into the room with us.

Our instructor, a fae woman named Madrigal, sighs through her nose. "What do you mean, Miss ...?"

"Ami Mariko," Ami answers. "I mean because their world is one whole continent." She tilts her head sideways while staring at the map currently being projected onto the wall—by magic, as far as I can tell. There's no projector in sight. "You know, like ours was millions of years ago."

"That's an interesting comparison, Ami," Madrigal says in a patient tone, looking at the oddly shaped continent that's divided into four territories, "but no, I wouldn't call Faeworld prehistoric."

"The season thing is strange," a girl at the front of the room says. "The fact that it's only ever one season in each court. How is that sustainable? In the Autumn Court, I assume all the leaves fall off the trees—because that's what happens in autumn—and then ... what? How do they get back on the trees?"

The smallest frown mars Madrigal's flawless face. "Well, by magic, of course. The magic that exists in all things in our world, the magic that is an innate part of all nature, is what sustains each court and keeps it cycling through the same season at all times. This is not *strange* for us. It's the way it's always been."

"Honestly, where have half these girls been for the past five years?" Cadence whispers from the chair on my right. "Living under a rock? How do they not know these things?"

I refrain from pointing out that most of the population in our world hasn't spent the past five years interviewing fae for their YouTube channels and digging up information about their world.

"Doesn't that have major agricultural consequences?" Shay asks. One row ahead of me, she's leaning back in her chair, arms folded, her notebook closed on the desk in front of her. "I mean, in the Winter Court, for example, how does anything grow? Where do they get their food from?"

Madrigal's perfect smile doesn't falter. "There are trade agreements between the—"

"But you just said the courts hate each other."

"I did not use the word *hate*."

"You may as well have," Lina mutters.

"There is a tenuous alliance between the courts," Madrigal explains. "It has been this way forever. We all understand that we need each other if we are to survive."

"Is there a reason you didn't mention the Summer Court?" someone else pipes up.

Madrigal looks confused. "I did."

"Okay, you *mentioned* it, and you've got it there on the map with the other countries. I mean territories. Courts. But then you described autumn, winter and spring, but you didn't say anything about summer."

"Are they the ones who hate us the most?" Lina asks with a knowing smile. "Is that why you don't want to tell us anything about them?"

"That's—no one *hates* you."

"The Summer, Spring and Winter Courts have still refused to have anything to do with our world," a quiet voice points out from Cadence's other side. I lean forward slightly and see that it's Riya. "That's the official line, at least," she adds. "We all know there are probably fae from all the courts who have found their way into our world, and there is that story of a Winter princess and the human she had the audacity to fall in love with. But the only court that has any *official* dealings with us remains the Autumn Court."

"What story about a Winter princess?" Cadence asks, clearly upset that there is some juicy bit of gossip she's somehow missed out on.

Riya's gaze falls on her. "It happened within our lifetime, I believe. One of the daughters of the current Winter King. I've heard she had a human companion who grew up in their court. A plaything for the royal children."

"How is that even possible?" Cadence demands. "Humans die on that side of the Shimmer from the magic toxicity."

Riya gives her a quelling look. "If you really believe it isn't possible for them to come up with ways to keep us alive on that side of the Shimmer, you're sillier than I thought."

Cadence protests loudly while Madrigal interrupts with, "How *ridiculous*."

Riya looks at her. "Is it? Anyway, the story I heard is that she fell in love with her human friend and the two of them ran away together. The court said that if they were found, the human would be killed and the princess banished forever. *That's* how the Winter Court truly feels about humans."

"Such nonsense," Madrigal scoffs. "I don't know where you girls hear these stories. Yes, it's true that the Summer, Spring and Winter Courts will not have any dealings with your world, but no one *hates* humans. The other courts are simply indifferent to your world and its inhabitants and don't feel they need to get involved in any way. And you all know what summer is, so I'm sure you can imagine the beauty of the Summer Court without me having to go into great detail about it. Now. Moving on!" She claps her hands. "We're done with this lesson, so—"

"Wait, is that it?" Cadence asks. "I feel like we've learned hardly anything about Faeworld. I think I already knew just about everything you've told us today."

"That's all you need to know for now." Madrigal's smile is becoming more strained.

"So ... there will be more lessons at a later point in the competition?"

"A few, yes." Madrigal manages to say this in a way that leaves me entirely unconvinced.

"But ... I'm sorry," Cadence says, "it just seems strange that the person who will become a princess of the Autumn Court will know so little of the world she's becoming part of. Of the court she may one day rule over beside the prince, when he's king."

Madrigal's smile remains fixed in place. "She will learn everything she needs to know after she marries the prince and becomes part of the royal family."

Cadence hesitates before finally saying, "Okay."

"Good. Now then—"

"Can I ask something?" I blurt out, finally plucking up the

courage to voice a question that's been on my mind since the beginning of this lesson. After the entire world watched me fall backwards out of a boat, I didn't want to bring unnecessary attention to myself, but I'm starting to wonder why no one else has asked this question.

Madrigal sighs. "Yes, Miss ..."

"Uh, Avery Evans. I just wanted to ask ... what do the rest of the fae of the Autumn Court think about having a human for a princess?"

"Oh. Uh ..."

"I mean, they would traditionally have had a fae princess, right? Whether it was someone noble or—"

"Traditionally, heirs of the Autumn Court have always married someone of noble blood," Cadence chimes in. "Based on everything I've read and all the fae I've spoken to," she adds.

"Right, okay." My eyes move from her back to Madrigal. "My point is, the royals have always been fae, so what does everyone on that side of the Shimmer think about having a *human* princess?"

Madrigal's eyes dart behind me, and I turn in my seat to find ... oh, shoot. Queen Erralee herself is standing in the doorway. There's a collective shuffle around the room as everyone sits straighter, instantly alert. Madrigal clears her throat and curtsies. "Welcome, Your Majesty. Ladies, I will now hand over to Queen Erralee."

The queen sweeps past us toward the front of the room. In an ankle length dress of mint green and with her dark hair falling in perfect waves over one shoulder, she looks flawlessly elegant without being overdressed. "Girls," she says with a warm smile, clasping her hands together. "How lovely to see you all again. We will soon have tea together so that I can get to know you all a little bit better, but before that, we thought it might be fun for you to play with some magic."

The atmosphere in the room changes instantly. Something almost electric pulses between us as those few simple words hang in the air: *Play with some magic*. No one ever promised this, or even suggested it, but I did wonder vaguely in the back of my mind if we might have some lessons that involved magic. After all, the winner of this competition will become a princess of a faerie court. Her 'vitamin' regimen will be adjusted to the point where it begins to lengthen her life—the average fae lifespan is about two hundred years—and create enough changes in her body to make it safe for her to live in Faeworld for extended periods of time. It's only natural to wonder if that girl might, at some point, be able to use magic too.

With a graceful movement of her hand, Queen Erralee gestures for us to stand. "Please follow my aide, Marlissa. She will lead you to the Opal Lounge."

We file out of the lesson room, excited whispers passed back and forth between us as we follow the petite, blue-haired Marlissa down the curved stairway to the bottom of the West Tower. I keep my lips sealed as a tug of war plays out inside me. I want to be as excited as everyone else, but I can't help the trepidation that gnaws at the edges of my mind.

Marlissa leads us into a lounge, exquisite with finely detailed velvety curtains sweeping the windows and sparkling lights hanging from the ceiling. There is, however, a conspicuous lack of furniture. "Everyone here?" Queen Erralee asks, walking in after us. "Wonderful." She looks up, and with another elegant gesture of her hand, it's as if an invisible layer is peeled away from the ceiling, revealing dozens of shimmering ribbons in pastel shades of pink, blue, purple and yellow. They twirl and curl around each other, dipping and spinning around the light fittings and then darting away as if they're playing some sort of game.

"As you can no doubt tell," Queen Erralee says, "the ribbons are magical. But the fun part is that there is also additional magic present in this room, which means it should be possible for you all to manipulate and move the ribbons." She looks around with a smile. "Who would like to try first?"

Natalya steps forward before anyone else can utter a word. "Your Majesty, I would *love* to."

"Go ahead then, dear. All you have to do is raise your hands and move them about, directing your intention toward specific ribbons."

Natalya does as instructed, clearly not worried about embarrassing herself. There's a breathless moment as we all wait, and it seems as if nothing is happening. But then three of the ribbons glide toward Natalya and spin in the same direction her fingers are twirling. I'm not the only one who sucks in a breath of surprise. "No freaking way," Lina murmurs beside me.

"Right?" I whisper.

Cadence and Lina both hurry forward, clearly eager to experiment for themselves. They've barely raised their hands when several other girls move to join them, their faces turned upward in delight. A small part of me is caught up in the excitement and wonder, longing to rush forward and try this out for myself. But the memory of the last time I was so close to magic —the pain, the fear—

No. Stop it.

I blink and shake my head. That memory doesn't belong here in this moment of light and color and fun. Besides, there are cameras around—*obviously*—and if I don't join in I'll find myself on a couch later being interviewed by Carwyn or Evanna, having to explain why I was too scared to play with a little magic.

The episode that goes out next week will show everyone else giggling and smiling while Avery Evans shivers in a corner. Besides, they're just *ribbons*. Probably the tamest thing Queen Erralee could have allowed us to play with.

So I take a breath and step forward. I lift one hand, focus on a pastel blue ribbon not too far above my head, and point at the far side of the room. The ribbon darts away obediently, curling back on itself before it can bump into the wall. Laughter bursts from me without my permission. Did I seriously just do something with *magic*? I look at another ribbon and curl my fingers back toward myself. The ribbon dances toward me. It wraps lightly around my arm, but before I can panic, it's tickling my shoulder and then darting away, for all the world as if it's playing with me.

Soon we're all laughing and shouting, sending ribbons flying through the air at each other in what is likely a far rowdier gathering than Queen Erralee probably had in mind. At some point I look across the room and realize that Prince Kieren is standing in the doorway, watching our antics. He isn't smiling—that would probably cause some sort of allergic reaction for him—but there's definitely amusement in his eyes. Probably wondering how he's going to choose a wife from this ridiculous bunch of humans. I almost dare to send a ribbon shooting his way, but a loud squeal draws my attention back to the group.

There's a cry of pain, then another and another. Confused, I try to see through the mass of girls and ribbons to what's going on. The laughter is dying down, and there are more shouts of "Ow!" and "Shit, that hurt!" Girls start to stumble away from the center of the room, and I finally see what's happening.

The ribbons are no longer twirling playfully about. They're lashing out, striking arms and hands and faces, leaving angry red welts wherever they meet bare skin. I lurch backward, fear shooting through me, and a thought darts unbidden across my mind: *I* knew *we couldn't trust magic.*

Some girls are looking around in confusion, saying the ribbons' touch barely stings at all, while others are crying out in apparent agony. Annemarie is on her knees, her face screwed up in pain as she clutches her arm. More ribbons are flicking their way toward her, and there's one sneaking over her shoulder and around her neck and—*Shit, shit, shit.* I race forward as the ribbon wraps tighter. Her hands are clawing at it, her fingers blistering from the contact, her neck already red and raw and —"Let me help!" I gasp as I reach her, trying to hook my fingers beneath the ribbon's edge. My heart slams in my chest. I'm terrified of pain, terrified of the ribbons snapping above my head, but I can't let it *strangle* her!

"Here—" Prince Kieren is suddenly beside us, his hands moving deftly at her neck, and the ribbon is gone, and he's scooping her hastily into his arms, and I'm stumbling beside him as he carries her to the doorway, and—

A tangle of yellow and pink flies at me. I flinch sideways, knocking into the doorframe as the ribbons graze past my neck. I tense against the expected pain, but all I feel is a soft caress. Prince Kieren has handed Annemarie over to someone else, and his hand is on my arm now. "Are you okay?"

"I ... I think I'm fine."

"Good." He steps swiftly away, heading across the room as he shouts, "Mother! Stop this *now*!" He continues calling out in a foreign tongue, his words becoming more urgent as he sends the rogue ribbons back up to the ceiling with quick hand motions while girls continue scrambling toward the edges of the room. But the queen is busy hissing furious instructions at her aide, Marlissa, who seems to be apologizing profusely as she makes the same hand gestures as Prince

Kieren, gathering up all the ribbons and banishing them to the ceiling.

"I *told* you not to use too much magic for this!" The queen's voice filters through the commotion of the room.

"Holy crap, are you okay?" Lina gasps as she catches herself against the wall beside me. "This is insane. I think I was only mildly stung, though," she adds, examining the faint red lines on her left arm.

"Yeah, I think I'm okay," I answer, rubbing my arm where I knocked it against the doorframe. I can't stop seeing that ribbon pulling tighter and tighter around Annemarie's neck. Her blistering skin, her desperate fingers, her—

"This is brilliant," someone snickers nearby, interrupting my thought spiral. I know the voice well enough by now to identify it as Natalya's. She's standing a little apart from the rest of us, her right hand raised and a purple ribbon twirling lazily around her fingers. I see no red marks anywhere on her skin. "First they make half the girls sick at the Opening Ball," she says, "and now their pretty magical ribbons are leaving welts on their precious contestants' skin. The media is going to pounce all over this."

"That isn't a good thing, you maniac," Lina mutters.

Natalya shrugs. "More drama, more attention for the show."

"You are such a *nutcase*!" Cadence shouts, leaping out of the way as a stray ribbon escapes Prince Kieren's commands and shoots straight for her. The end of the ribbon catches her cheek, instantly raising an angry red mark on her perfect skin, just as she collides with Natalya. The two of them go sprawling across the floor.

They continue to push each other down repeatedly while at least half the girls are escorted from the room by healers to deal with the painful, swollen welts. Those remaining are either perfectly unharmed or bear little more than a few faint red marks they seem to barely feel. As far as I can tell, I'm uninjured. Cadence finally scrambles after the last few girls who are leaving the room, and Natalya attempts to straighten her dress and smooth her hair down as she joins the rest of us, looking a lot less smug than before she was knocked over.

"Well then," Queen Erralee says, smiling at us as if nothing strange just happened. "Shall we move on to tea now?"

I have to clamp my jaw shut to keep from blurting out, *Are you kidding?* A glance around the room reveals that pretty much everyone else feels the same way, but she's the queen, so of course no one's about to say, *Um, are you sure that's appropriate after we were just attacked by bits of enchanted fabric?* It sounds so ridiculous in my head.

"You're all right?" The deep voice is close to my ear, and I realize Prince Kieren is standing beside me. "You weren't harmed?"

"I don't think so," I answer as we all head out of the room in a subdued shuffle. "What the hell just happened?"

"An accident," he says quickly. "Some of the ribbons clearly had too much magic in them. The other contestants will be fine, I assure you. This is not serious. Our healers will fix them quickly."

I glance sideways at him and see his jaw tight, his shoulders tense. "Not serious? A girl was almost *strangled*."

"She was never in any real danger. *None* of you were in any real danger. It looked worse than it was. There is nothing to worry about."

But his expression says otherwise, and as I watch him hurry toward the guard who's carrying Annemarie and offer to take her to her room himself, the same words play on repeat in my brain: *I knew we couldn't trust magic. I knew we couldn't trust magic. I knew it, I knew it, I knew it.*

Chapter Fifteen

Strong hands are on me, pinning me down, and I'm powerless, so powerless. His knee is between my legs, forcing them apart, and this isn't happening, this isn't happening, and then a scream—*"Get off her!"*—and he falls sideways, and I'm struggling, scrambling, turning over, clawing at the bed, and then something tears across my back and the pain, the *pain*—

I jolt awake, terror fluttering like a trapped bird in my chest. I blink at the ceiling above my bed. Sitting up, I force breath into my lungs, telling myself over and over that it wasn't real. When I'm a little calmer, I move to the edge of the bed and swing my legs over the side, letting my feet sink into the soft carpet. My hands are still shaking. The nightmare doesn't come for me often anymore, but when it does, it can leave me on edge for hours afterwards.

I stand and walk slowly around my room. I consider sitting at the piano, plugging the headphones in, and playing something. Music would soothe me, I know it would, but I feel to jittery to even begin playing. I sweep a curtain aside, open the balcony doors, and step outside. The air outside is fresh, fragrant, cool against my hot skin. The moon is large, the stars twinkle happily, and the garden is alive with glowing color and chirping insects and the trickling sound of water. It's all so much brighter and happier than the nightmare in my head.

It doesn't take long for me to pull my silky robe on, walk silently through the palace, find an unlocked door to the garden, and step outside. At first I move quickly, putting some distance between me and the palace before someone wandering around inside can see me through a window. But I slow down after several minutes when no one calls my name. I tread softly over the grass, enjoying the damp coolness between my toes. My fingers trail over the delicate feathery fronds of ferns that seem to be lit from within by their own faint light. "Be happy," I whisper to myself. "Be happy." It's easier out here, the memory of the nightmare becoming more distant with every step. It becomes easier still when some of the tiny emerald-like insects I noticed last week before the boat ride land in my open palm and tickle my skin before flying away.

I reach the pavilion surrounded by white rose bushes and continue past it, discovering that there's a lake on the other side. I stop near the edge of the water beside a huge tree with clusters of pink blossoms. Some kind of nest-like chair of interwoven branches and tiny blue flowers hangs from one of the enormous branches.

I stare across the lake, so still with barely a breeze to ripple its surface, and wonder how much of this beauty is real and how much is illusion. I wish I could trust my eyes, but I know I can't. I can't trust any of this, as I was so abruptly reminded by the whole ribbon incident two days ago.

Everyone was perfectly fine, just as Prince Kieren promised. The fae occupants of the palace brushed it off as if it was nothing, and the girls who were hurt began to wonder if they were really in that much pain to start with. Even I wondered if perhaps we'd overreacted. Was that ribbon really wrapped so tightly around Annemarie's neck, or was it just that we were trying so desperately to get it off her? But I can't get rid of the voice at the back of my head that keeps saying, *I knew we couldn't trust magic.*

"Who's there?"

"Holy *shit*!" I lurch at the sound of the unexpected voice so near, tripping over my own feet and almost plunging headfirst into the water. "Crap, crap, *crap*," I hiss, grabbing hold of the edge of the hanging chair, which of course swings away from me. I let go before I can topple forward with it, but then it swings back with just enough force to knock me off balance. "Seriously?" I gasp as my backside hits the ground. And in that same instant, I remember one of the many rules Iris gave me: *The palace gardens are out of bounds after sundown.*

"Are you all right?"

There's a hand reaching for me, but I'm already scrambling up. "I'm sorry!" I say, hurriedly brushing twigs and leaves off myself as I stare at a pair of shoes belonging to His Royal Highness, Prince Kieren.

"Who—oh. Miss Girl Next Door. Are you all right?"

"Yes! I'm so sorry Your, uh, Highness. I'm going back inside right now. I was just—" I stop myself before explaining that I'm out here because of a nightmare. It would sound so childish. "I couldn't sleep," I say instead. "I thought about playing my piano, but I needed ... air. I needed to walk. Space, you know? Not that the suites aren't spacious. They're enormous. But I just needed to get *out*. But now I've just remembered the rule about not coming out here after dark. I'll head straight back inside." I try to hurry past him.

"Stop."

I do.

"You don't have to leave. We may as well speak, since you're here and there are no cameras around."

I think of the nightmare I just escaped, and the fact that we're alone, and for a moment I think, *He could do whatever he wants with me. No one would know.*

"Are you cold?" he asks, interrupting my racing thoughts.

"Um, what? No, I'm ... I'm fine." I realize I've wrapped my arms around my body though, and my breaths are coming a little too quickly.

"Ah, yes, that's right. I forgot you are particularly stubborn when it comes to the cold. But ... are you sure you're okay?"

I peek up at him. He seems genuinely concerned, and he's made no move to come any closer. In fact, I think he's taken a step or two back since we began speaking. And didn't we walk through the forest alone the other day? He didn't try anything then. "I'm fine," I repeat. I stand taller and force my arms to my sides. I clear my throat. "I'm fine." And I am fine. This is Prince Faerie Face, condescending snob, not the monster from my nightmares.

Prince Kieren turns toward the lake and looks out over the still water. "The rule about not coming outside after dark is for your own safety. There are certain fae creatures that live in the trees here. Creatures that have crossed through the Shimmer but don't venture further than the palace grounds because they require the magic of their own world to stay alive. They sleep during the day and roam around at night, and at times they can be a little ... vicious. They most likely wouldn't hurt you, but we can't guarantee it. Hence the rule. But they won't approach if I'm with you."

"Oh. Right. Good thing you turned up then." I feel silly for being afraid of him when I should have been afraid of what may be lurking in the darkness instead.

"I'm sorry if I sounded harsh at first. I didn't recognize you. You ... look different."

"Oh! Shoot." I suddenly remember the robe I'm wearing over my nightgown and pull it tighter around myself. "I thought the robe was long enough to be considered decent, but you're right. I should have put on a jacket or—"

"No, not the clothing. Your ..." He gestures toward my head. "You look different without the ponytail."

"Oh. Right." I roll my eyes and run a hand self-consciously through my sleep-tangled tresses. "I've been told I have to wear my hair like that every day. Part of my 'image.' I told my retinue that my image should include a pair of jeans, but they weren't buying that. Apparently jeans aren't allowed in the Glittering Palace. Not considered princessy enough."

Prince Kieren's brows pinch together a fraction. "Princessy?"

"Okay, I don't think that was the *exact* word used, but you know what I mean. So then I told them that there are plenty of princesses in *my* world who wear jeans all the time when they're not parading around in fancy dresses and uncomfortable pants at formal events."

"And you know this ... how?"

"Oh. Well, I suppose I don't know for sure, but I'd be very surprised if I'm wrong. Jeans are one of the most comfortable items of clothing in the world. Aside from pajamas, of course."

"Of course." He nods, his gaze traveling my face as he appears to consider something. "Do you think we should introduce a Pajama Day here at the Glittering Palace? Perhaps feature it on the next episode of the show?"

"Ooh! Yes! That would be so much fun! Although I'm sure

some of the girls would ruin it by taking things too far and wearing something completely inappropriate like lacy, see-through lingerie, so there would probably need to be some rules about ..." I trail off as I notice the way he's looking at me with something like amused disbelief. "Oh. You were joking." My cheeks flush. Of course he was joking. "Never mind then." I look out at the lake again. "You, uh, said you needed to talk to me about something?"

"Yes." He clears his throat and looks away. "Tomorrow is Friday. Second dismissal dinner. I'm considering ... quite a few names. I wanted to ask you about Natalya. I've had two dates with her and she is, of course, charming in my presence. But I sense that perhaps there is ..." He glances at me, then looks back out at the water. "More to her," he finishes. "Can you shed any light on this?"

"There's certainly more to her than 'charming,'" I mutter.

"Elaborate please," Prince Kieren says.

I think of Natalya standing calmly by while girls screamed and ran from the enchanted ribbons stinging them. She saw Annemarie almost strangled and said nothing but, "This is brilliant." I have to work hard not to blurt out that she's a malicious bitch. "I've had limited interactions with her, but she, uh, seems like the kind of person who's willing to trample all over everyone else in order to get to the top," I say instead. "I don't think she cares who she takes down on her way up."

"I see. Thank you. That's helpful."

I nod, secretly hoping this means we'll be saying goodbye to Natalya tomorrow night. Prince Kieren says nothing else, and after a while I start to wonder if I can ask to leave or if I'm supposed to wait until I'm dismissed. I lean forward and peer past him, realizing I can just make out the edge of the Shimmer from here. "It's cool," I say to him. "The Shimmer. Seeing it in real life. I didn't realize it was so big." He nods but doesn't say anything, which I suppose is fair considering I didn't ask a question. "It, uh, has another name in your language, right? Something that means 'shimmering light'?"

"Yes."

"Nice. I like it. Very descriptive. Way better than the word *Faeworld*, which honestly sounds like the name of a theme park." *Ugh, Avery, you should really just keep your mouth shut.*

"Well, again," Prince Kieren says slowly, "we have a different name for it."

"I know, I'm sorry."

"But you're not wrong about the theme park aspect. There are people from your world who have made genuine attempts to turn it into something like that. We've had numerous proposals over the years from various entities promising we could make a fortune by allowing tour groups of humans to go on short guided trips into our world. And now, with these ... vitamins you're taking every day, helping your body to acclimate to the magic, the proposals have restarted." He shakes his head. "People don't seem to know how to accept the word 'no' as an answer." He sighs, then looks at me, brows drawn together. "Did you mention a piano earlier in the midst of all your rambling?"

"Oh. Um ... yeah, I probably did. That's kind of my thing," I explain. "I know the Glittering Palace wants me to play the part of the average 'girl next door,' representing every ordinary person who wishes they could have been chosen for a spectacular makeover, and a glamorous palace life, and a shot at becoming a real princess. But ... none of that is actually my thing. I make music. I ..." My gaze skims the lake again. "I hear it in my head. I play it on this battered old keyboard someone gave me years ago. I write it down. I use free or cheap software and a way-too-old laptop to produce it. I obviously don't have a full orchestra at my disposal, so all the instrument sounds are synthesized. And then it gets distributed via streaming services and I earn literal pennies from it and continue daydreaming about the day I might be able to make an actual living from it."

"Pennies? For all that hard work?"

"Actually, that's not entirely true. I got a ton of social media followers after Carwyn and Evanna made me a contestant, and because of that I've had a lot more people checking out my music. Nothing to retire on, but it's more than pennies, so that's really cool."

"This ... social media," he says slowly. "I admit I don't know much about it."

"Me neither, to be honest. I suck at it. Some of the other girls have been complaining about having to hand their phones over and having someone else post on their behalf, but I'm just relieved. I'm sure Iris is doing a far better job than I ever did."

"Iris?"

"My aide."

He nods. "And this ... battered old keyboard you mentioned. You brought it with you?"

"Oh, no, the Glittering Palace built this cool hidden recess into my bedroom wall and put this *amazing* digital piano in there. It's honestly the best thing I've ever played on in my entire life."

"Digital? It isn't real?"

"Well, the structure is real, but the sound it produces is synthesized. Or maybe a recorded sample from an acoustic piano? I'm not sure. But it sounds so real, and it *feels* so real. It might possibly be the best part about this whole *Princess Game* thing."

He nods again and makes a noncommittal *hmm* sound.

"So ... if there isn't anything else you want to talk about ..."

"Oh. Of course. If you'd like to return to your suite, you may. I realize it's quite late."

"Cool, thanks. Um, good night, I guess." I cringe internally as I start walking away. *Good night, I guess?* Mary-Louise would be wailing at that.

"Miss Girl Next Door," Prince Kieren calls after me.

I stop and look back. "Yes?"

"I'm sorry. About that morning in your coffee shop. I've been over it in my head, and the things I said ... I did not originally intend to give offense, but I realize now that there was, of course, no other way my words could have been interpreted. And then, after you spoke back to me, I couldn't help retaliating. I should not have, and I apologize."

I'm so surprised that for several moments I can't say a word. Then I manage to stutter, "I, uh, thank you. I'm sorry too. I definitely overreacted in the moment."

"With good reason."

"I ... suppose. Yes."

"Well. Good night, then."

"You said that everything there disappointed you," I blurt out before I can think better of it. "Why? What were you expecting?"

His sigh his heavy. He looks down at the ground. "I was not looking forward to this. The contest. The *game*. I grew up hearing mostly unpleasant things about your world and its people, but I had little firsthand experience. The time I've spent here has been passed mostly at the Glittering Palace, with occasional brief meetings in other parts of your world. Rhylan, ever the positive one, told me to go and walk around on my own for a while. He promised that it would not be as bad as I expected."

"Well, you probably came to one of the worst possible

places," I say with a laugh. "I mean, there's nothing thrilling about the small town I ended up in. You should have gone to ... I don't know, Paris or the Grand Canyon or the Great Barrier Reef."

"Yes. Perhaps. But your town is the one we were in because we were following Carwyn and Evanna. I was initially meant to make a surprise appearance after they announced the show's final contestant. But then ..." Something resembling a smirk crosses his face. "Well, I gave my guards the slip and decided to take on Rhylan's appearance. I ended up in your coffee shop, not knowing that that's precisely where Carwyn and Evanna were headed. I was hoping to be dazzled by something, but as you clearly remember, I said something about finding only disappointment. I was not in a particularly good frame of mind at the time. I'm not sure if I even intended to say it out loud, but I did, and it was obviously hurtful to you. Hence my apology."

I blink a few times before I'm able to answer. "Thank you," I say quietly. "I wasn't expecting such an honest answer."

His lips twitch in a way that makes me think there's probably a smile trying to fight past his usually grim expression. "I don't think I was entirely expecting it either."

I grin, wide enough for both of us. "Well. Good night, then, Prince Kieren."

"Good night, Miss Girl Next Door."

Chapter Sixteen

Last night was a bit of a shock. Prince Kieren got rid of seven contestants at the second dismissal dinner—*not* Natalya, for some reason I can't fathom—and most girls began the morning in low spirits. I don't think anyone expected the numbers to go down so quickly. At this rate, it'll take far less than the planned eight weeks to go from thirty girls to the Top 10. Possibly a good thing, considering this game hasn't turned out to be as safe for humans as everyone initially promised.

Everyone mopes around at breakfast until Carwyn and Evanna waltz—literally—into the dining room to announce we'll be taking our first trip into Faeworld this evening. "Thanks to roughly two weeks of vitamins," Evanna says, "the palace experts estimate you can safely remain in Faeworld for about six hours. To be on the safe side, we'll limit your visit to four hours, which is still far longer than any human has ever spent in our world." She beams and rubs her hands together.

"The cameras will film us heading off through the Shimmer," Carwyn says, "and then King Eldyn has allowed several photographers to accompany us to document the remainder of the outing through still images.

"And what is this outing, you must be asking yourselves," Evanna says. "We will be going to see an opera! Oh, it will be *spectacular*! We'll leave here just before sunset to give you a chance to see the magnificence of Faeworld on the other side of the Shimmer before the sun goes down. Then we'll spend the evening at the Royal Autumn Opera House."

Despite my reservations about this being 'safe' for us, given the accidental drinks and the dangerous enchanted ribbons, I'll admit to being just the tiniest bit ecstatic. If operas in Faeworld are anything like those in our world—and, admittedly, they might not be at all—a live orchestra will be involved. I can close my eyes, forget the rest of it, and simply enjoy the music.

A little before sunset, we all parade downstairs in the glamorous gowns our retinues have chosen for us. A line of golden carriages each pulled by what looks like a solid gold horse greets us in the driveway. I'm not the only one wondering how these seemingly inanimate creatures are supposed to pull the carriages—and I'm not the only one startled when one of them *moves*. We all take a collective step back, and the ever-present cameras move in to get close-ups of the magical creatures. Or are they enchanted metal structures? I can't tell if they're actually alive.

The carriages themselves are round, highly embellished with gold filigree, and big enough to fit only three people. Sadly, I'm separated from Lina this time and directed into a carriage with Shay and Natalya. Wonderful. I'm sandwiched on a velvet seat between a girl with a permanent scowl on her face and a girl who would throw me under this carriage if she thought she could get away with it. This should be fun.

Miraculously, Natalya says nothing once we're seated.

Perhaps, like me, she's too busy looking around. Large spaces between the decorative metalwork of the carriage give us a wide view of everything happening outside: The three girls in the carriage in front of ours arguing over who should sit where, the strange gilded horses, the palace employees moving along the line of carriages as they whisper into the golden ears of these strange creatures.

With the smallest lurch, we begin moving. The carriage glides forward, following the one in front of ours and heading around the side of the palace. We gradually pick up speed until —*holyshitshitshit!*—we're suddenly in the air. We're freaking *flying*! Natalya shrieks, and Shay, the most disinterested and distant of all the contestants here, is suddenly gripping my hand tightly and gasping, "Shit, why don't they *warn* us about these things?" Her eyes are wide and she's squeezing my hand so hard it hurts.

"Are you afraid of heights?" I ask.

"Maybe," she whispers.

"You should probably close your eyes."

"I ... I can't look away ..." She shakes her head. "It's all so—"

"Close your eyes," I repeat, my tone firmer, and this time she obeys. "Now just pretend we're ... in an airplane. There's a gigantic structure around you, and we're perfectly safe." I manage to say this with a confidence I don't feel. I have no idea if we're perfectly safe. Accidents seem to happen all too easily when humans come too close to magic.

Shay hangs onto my hand, and I don't try to pull it away as I look around. We're soaring above the palace grounds, over the river, and then through the Shimmer. *We're in another world.* Prickles dance along my skin. My brain tells me I should be wary —scared, even—but there's a very real thrill of excitement coursing through me. The sky is painted with the glorious oranges, pinks and purples of sunset, while the forest below is a sea of gold, bronze and red.

It takes me another few moments to notice that our hair isn't blowing around and that the air is a comfortable temperature instead of the crisp, cool breeze I remember from my walk on the wrong side of the river with Prince Kieren. We must be protected somehow inside the carriage, despite the fact that there's no glass covering any of the gaps between the metalwork. Curious, I reach forward and stick my free hand through one of the spaces. It's like pushing my hand through a layer of warm water—if water was dry and invisible. On the other side, a chilly wind whips across my skin.

"What are you *doing*?" Natalya hisses. "I swear, if you break the enchantment on this thing and we go crashing down—"

"We're not *crashing* anywhere," I interrupt hastily, my eyes on Shay again as I pull my hand back.

She keeps her eyelids squeezed shut and mumbles between gritted teeth, "Tell Natalya to keep her damn twelve-year-old, mean-girl mouth shut. And please let me know when it's safe to open my eyes."

I smother my smile at the 'damn twelve-year-old, mean-girl mouth' comment and look forward again. And that's when I get my first glimpse of one of the fae cities. Glittering in the distance like a multifaceted jewel, the city is all gleaming glass and golden spires, graceful curves and elegantly pointed arches. Towering trees stand as tall as the buildings, bursting with the same rich colors we're currently flying over.

"Wow," I breathe. There's no other word for it. The Golden City has been photographed from a distance, and there are paintings of it that exist in our world, but none of the two dimensional renderings I've seen come close to capturing what I can now appreciate with my own eyes. "Shay," I say, squeezing her hand with what little feeling I have left in my own fingers. "Open your eyes and look straight ahead. You don't want to miss this."

She peeks through one eye, then opens the other. She blinks. "Holy ... wow," she murmurs.

"Right?"

"That view almost makes this whole charade worth it," she whispers. She shuts her eyes again, and it takes me another moment to process her words. *This whole charade.* She's been moody and distant since the day we all got here, but I thought she was just wary of the rest of us. Unwilling to make friends with the competition. But now I wonder if perhaps, like me, she doesn't believe in any of this *Princess Game* nonsense. Which then makes me wonder how she ended up here.

We begin our descent as we approach the city, soon dropping down below the forest canopy. Our enchanted horse dodges and turns, guiding the carriage expertly between the trees. I barely have time to be afraid we're going to crash into something before the trees thin out and the carriage wheels bump against the ground. We're on a paved road now, the trees bowing over us on either side. "Safe to open your eyes," I tell Shay.

She releases my hand with a somewhat embarrassed expression. "Um, thanks."

I lean forward and peer out of the carriage as the trees slide past. Dressed in autumn hues, they're as beautiful as everything else I've seen of the Autumn Court so far, though there's something a little strange about the ends of the branches. Perhaps it's a trick of the light at this time of day, but they seem to fade away at the edges and disappear into the shadows.

The trees give way to the edge of the city, and soon there are tall glass structures rising all around us, gleaming like diamonds in the waning light. My eyes catch on gold embellishments: swirls and latticework and graceful archways between the buildings and trees. There's something distinctly fae in the delicate, elegant design of everything. Though again, I think as I peer a little more closely at the buildings we're passing, the very edges of things seem to almost disintegrate. The top of a spire, the highest point of an arch. I can squint and see particles drifting away on a breeze. An autumn thing, perhaps. It's a season of decay and decline, after all. Magic probably keeps the buildings intact the same way it returns falling leaves to the trees.

The carriages come to a stop in front of a building that looks like a giant pearl with a huge pointed arch as its entrance and a grand, curved stairway leading up to it. The carriage door closest to the steps opens of its own accord. After a moment's hesitation, we climb out. I spot Carwyn and Evanna on the steps already, their smiles wide as they look down at us. "Welcome," they call out, "to the Golden City and the Royal Autumn Opera House!"

They beckon us forward, and we ascend the shimmering, pearlescent stairs. People are lined up on either side, some waving and smiling, some watching with mild interest. A few look on with something more like suspicion. I guess this is my answer to the question of what those in Faeworld think about having a human princess: Most seem excited, but there are definitely those who aren't.

I look past the unfriendly expressions, and my attention catches on some of the distinctly non-human features of these people. Delicately curved horns, pointed teeth, large eyes with oddly shaped pupils. My first thought is that I'm seeing a collection of illusions, glamours, because the fae look just like us, don't they? But then I recall what Finneas told me, about fae using glamours to make themselves look *more* like us, not the other way around. Is everything I'm seeing real?

My gaze lands on Lina just ahead of me, and I quicken my pace to catch up to her. "This is so weird," I whisper as we climb the stairs side by side. "It's like we're celebrities or something. And wasn't that carriage ride incredible?"

"It was until Gigi What's-Her-Name threw up all over our carriage floor."

I look at Lina to see if she's joking. "Seriously?"

"Seriously. I don't think any of it splashed onto me or Annemarie, but I still feel gross. I'm going to find a restroom as soon as we get into this place." She pauses. "Assuming the fae *have* restrooms in their public buildings like we do."

"Well ... they need to pee like everyone else, right?"

Lina laughs loudly. "Good point."

I look around as we climb the steps, trying to see past all the people. "Isn't the Autumn Palace somewhere not too far from here? Where the royal family normally resides when they're not at the Glittering Palace in our world? I think Madrigal mentioned it during the lesson."

"Oh yes. Didn't she say it's a little further beyond the Golden City? I don't think we can see it from here."

We walk beneath the arched doorway and find a grand foyer with a high ceiling and a wide staircase on either side. "We'll take our seats in about fifteen minutes," Carwyn calls out to us. "You can mingle out here until then. Take in the atmosphere, enjoy the setting."

"But please don't wander off," Evanna adds. "If you get lost and we can't find you, you'll be left behind later when we return. And, well, you know what happens to humans who linger in Faeworld for too long." Her high-pitched tinkling laughter carries over the murmurs of the girls around me.

"Yeah, we end up *dead*," someone mutters just behind me. Shay, I think.

As Carwyn and Evanna wander off, Lina looks around. "Okay, I think I need to go and find a—"

"Hey, Lina." Cadence saunters toward us, a smug expression on her face. I'm immediately suspicious, and so, it seems, is Lina.

"Why do you look so pleased with yourself, Miss Social Media Personality?" she asks. "Did you get some extra time with your phone or something?"

"As a matter of fact, I did, Miss Retail Heiress. You might remember that I answered the most questions correctly at our first lesson the other day, and I was rewarded with an hour of phone time."

"Wow. Thrilling."

"It was thrilling. The internet has all kinds of juicy secrets if you know where to look, *Evangeline*."

The words 'internet' and 'juicy secrets' send a shot of anxiety shooting through me, despite the fact that Cadence's attention is on Lina. Lina rolls her eyes. "Like my full name? That's not a secret, Cadence."

"But the fact that you ran away from home a few years ago might be. The fact that you and your bazillionaire dad don't get along. *At all.* The fact that you only started talking to him again after *The Princess Game* was announced."

Lina regards Cadence with a blank expression. "I'm still not seeing the big secret here, Cay."

"You used him to get on the show. Used his influence. He went around official channels—*outside* of the official selection process—to get you chosen."

Lina lets out a long sigh. "Well. That's a nice story."

"A nice story that could get you immediately disqualified if it's true."

"Don't you remember the rules, Cay-Cay? Now that we're here, only Prince Kieren can dismiss us."

"Well. I guess I can whisper a few things in his ear that might help him make the right choice about you."

Lina shrugs. "Go right ahead."

"I will." Cadence sticks her nose in the air and spins around before marching away. I can't help remembering Shay's 'twelve-year-old, mean-girl mouth' comment about Natalya. I think she and Cadence are the two youngest contestants, which probably has something to do with their lack of maturity.

I look at Lina. "Is that true?"

Her gaze, sharper than usual, shoots to me. "What, that my dad went outside official channels to get me onto this show? That I basically broke the rules to get here?"

"No, I know you entered because of a dare. You already told me that. I mean the part about you running away. About ... not getting along with your dad."

"Oh." She looks away, pressing her lips together. "Maybe," she says quietly. "But my dad never said anything about it publicly, and I don't generally tell people about it. I don't know how Cadence found out."

"Okay," I answer, just as quietly. "I'm ... sorry. I know a little bit about just wanting to have a normal family. Obviously," I add with a roll of my eyes. "Since I never had any family at all. So ... yeah. That sucks."

Her expression softens as she returns her eyes to me. "Thanks. I'm sorry too. I can only imagine how rough it was for you, growing up like that."

I nod, silently adding, *You have* no *idea.*

"Anyway, I still need to find a restroom. Are you okay here?"

"Yes." I smile at her. "I'll 'mingle' as I've been instructed." I look around, hoping to spot Shay so I can ask her if she's recovered from the carriage ride. I find her hiding in the shadows beneath the staircase on the right hand side of the foyer. "Are you okay?" I ask as I reach her side.

She glances at me before looking away. "Uh, yeah. Just trying not to think about the journey home, I guess."

"If you need to squeeze the life out of my hand again, you're welcome to."

Her lips twitch into a small smile. "Thanks." She takes a deep breath. "You know what's funny? My sister—my twin—is the total opposite. Completely fine with heights. She would have loved that carriage ride."

I smile. "If only you could have swapped places just for that, right?"

Her eyes shoot to mine before darting away again. "Yeah. If only."

"You must miss her a lot," I add, thinking of how much I miss Quinn. "What's her name?"

"Uh, Sadie," Shay says. "Her name is Sadie."

I nod. "Um ... so how did you come to be on the show? What made you decide to enter?"

Her expression shutters immediately. "I don't think that's—"

"Good evening, ladies," a cheerful voice says. I look around as Prince Kieren's friend Rhylan stops beside us. We haven't spoken since I confronted him at the Opening Ball, but he must know by now why I thought it was him in my coffee shop. "Miss Avery," he says to me. "Miss Sunshine," he says to Shay, grinning widely now. "You look as happy to be alive as always."

"Bite me," Shay answers.

"I'm just saying you could smile once in a while."

"And I'm just saying you could mind your own business once in a while."

My gaze bounces back and forth between the two of them. There's something about this exchange that makes me think it isn't the first time they've spoken.

"Oh, you know what?" Shay says. "I forgot something. I need to go and rip my fingernails out. Please excuse me." She gathers her skirt in her fists and strides away before I can think of anything to say.

"Please stop provoking the contestants," another voice says, and Prince Kieren stops beside his friend. "Miss Girl Next Door," he adds with a nod in my direction.

"Hey, I'm just trying to get her to smile," Rhylan says before I can greet the prince.

"Not everyone wants to smile all the time."

"Yes, you'd know *all* about that, my friend," Rhylan says, a grin still in place as he claps a hand on the prince's shoulder.

Prince Kieren releases a long-suffering sigh. "Weren't you looking for someone?"

"Ah, yes, I was. Good evening," he says to me with a brief bow before walking away.

Prince Kieren looks at me. Then he looks down. "Why are you doing that?"

"Why am I doing—Oh." I hadn't realized I was tapping my foot along to the music playing in the background. I stop.

"Thank you," he says with a sigh.

I tilt my head to the side. "Are you always in a bad mood, or am I unlucky enough that it's only when I'm around?"

His expression darkens in a way that's almost comical. "I'm not in a bad mood."

"You're always frowning and grumpy. Okay, I suppose you weren't exactly *grumpy* the other night in the garden, but you weren't happy either."

"I am not in a bad mood," he repeats, his frown still stuck to his face.

"Okay. What would you call it then, Your Highness?"

"I'm ... guarded."

"Guarded? What do you have to guard yourself against? I'm harmless. Well, unless you're a piece of furniture, in which case I might accidentally throw myself at you."

He stares at me, and I suddenly realize how that may have sounded. "That was a joke," I add quickly.

"Yes. I know." He looks away. "I'm sorry if I appear to be in a bad mood. I have a meeting tomorrow that's causing me some ... anxiety."

"Oh. Well," I say with a smile, "I can distract you, if you want."

His eyes shoot to mine and I realize that, once again, that came out the wrong way. "Whatever you're thinking," I add quickly, holding both hands up, "it's not what I meant."

"I have no doubt."

"It's actually a dance."

His eyes narrow.

"Again," I rush to add, "not what you're thinking. *Not* a seductive kind of dance. At all. It's this silly thing that went viral on social media a few years ago, and every time my best friend Quinn gets super low, I dance around our place. She's one of the grouchiest people alive, and I can get her to laugh every time."

Prince Kieren's expression doesn't change. "Just because I don't have a permanent smile on my face doesn't mean I'm a *grouch*. You sound just like Rhylan."

"Look, all I'm saying is that I could do the dance for you, if you want. It works for Quinn."

"I don't think that's—"

"Not properly. I mean, we're in a semi-public area. I can't go all out like I would in the privacy of my own bedroom. Although ..." I look around. "We're kind of hidden here under the stairs. Oh, and there's no video footage of this outing! I just remembered."

"That doesn't mean you need to—"

"So it's got a little bit of shoulder shimmy like this." I bob on the spot, shifting my shoulders up and down. "And then this side-to-side elbow thing that looks really stupid." I move my elbows from left to right, continuing the shoulder shimmy thing and trying not to bump into him. "And then the hip wiggle that Quinn rolls her eyes at *every* single time because I'm so bad at it." I lean forward, press my palms against my knees, and do a brief hip rotation, aware that this probably looks even sillier than usual because I'm wearing a ball gown while doing it. "And then you just repeat," I say, straightening. A pained expression I'm hoping is stifled laughter has worked its way onto Prince Kieren's face. "See? It works, right? You're trying not to laugh."

"I ... have no words."

"That's a good thing!"

"I don't think it is."

"Of course it is. It means—" My gaze slips over his shoulder and follows a tall, broad-shouldered figure on the other side of the foyer. The rest of my words end up strangled in the back of my throat. *It's him. It's HIM.* My pulse rockets out of control. I'm suddenly breathing so quickly it's making me lightheaded. *It can't be. It can't be him it can't be him it can't be—*

"Miss Avery?"

My heart is beating too fast. The air around me is too thin, and my lungs aren't working, and it can't be him, it can't be—

"Miss Avery!"

Prince Kieren is right in front of me now, blocking my view, his hands on my arms as he steadies me. I push him away, equal parts desperate and terrified to see past him. I stagger forward, eyes searching. My darting gaze finds the man on the other side of the vast space and—

It isn't him.

I sag backward against a wall, relief weakening my knees. Of course it isn't him. There's no possible way it could be. Why did I think otherwise?

"Miss Avery?"

"Oh, shoot, sorry!" I lurch forward and turn around as I realize the surface I fell back against was not, in fact, a wall. It was Prince Kieren.

"What happened? Are you all right?"

"I'm ... yes. I'm fine."

"You weren't a moment ago."

I swallow. "I ... just ... thought I saw someone I recognized." A moment later, I realize this is the same excuse I gave him the first time we met. "Not your friend Rhylan this time. Obviously. Someone ... else." An involuntary shiver skitters across my skin.

"Are you sure you're all right?" His eyes search my face. "Do you need me to ..." He hesitates, looks past me, sighs, then asks, "Do you need me to dance?"

I blink at him. Then again. "I'm sorry, was that—did you just make a joke?"

His eyes narrow a fraction. I can't be certain, but I think there may be some color in his cheeks. "That was my attempt, yes. I don't intend to do the actual dance, by the way. The joke itself is the part that was meant to cheer you up."

I start laughing. "This is brilliant. I'm imagining you doing the elbow dance now."

"Please don't."

"I can never unsee it."

"You never saw it to begin with," he reminds me.

"It's all up here," I say, tapping the side of my head with one finger.

He sighs. "If you agree to *stop* imagining it, I have something else in mind that might cheer you up even more."

I pause, watching him "Okay. What is it?"

"I thought you might like to ..." He hesitates, then shakes his head. "Forgive me if this is silly. If it doesn't appeal to you in any way, you can feel free to say so. But I wondered if you might want to sit with the orchestra when the performance begins. It's nothing fancy down there, not like the plush seating in the royal box, and you wouldn't be able to see much of what's happening on stage, but if you'd like the opportunity to feel as if you are one of the—"

"Yes!" I blurt out before he can finish. "Yesyesyes! Please can I do that?"

He almost smiles. Almost. "I'll arrange it now," he says with a nod.

"Thank you, thank you!" I realize a moment too late that I'm gripping his arm with both hands. I'm also *genuinely* grateful. To someone who is *fae*. This is very strange. I drop his arm and take a step back. "Um, thank you."

Over his shoulder, I see Lina walking toward us. "Prince Kieren," she says, curtseying when she reaches us.

"Miss E—uh, Lina." With a curt bow of his head, he adds, "It was nice speaking with you, Miss Avery. I hope you both enjoy the opera." With that, he walks away.

I give Lina a questioning look. "Miss E?"

She rolls her eyes. "I think he was going to say Evangeline. Clearly Cadence isn't the only one who knows my full name." She shivers. "Ugh. Never liked it. But hey, what's up? You look like an overexcited kid at Christmas who just got handed the puppy they begged Santa for."

I grip her hands and squeal. "I'm going to sit with the orchestra!"

Chapter Seventeen

"Ooh, this one," Lina says, handing me the midnight blue bottle.

"Yes, blue is definitely your color," Iris agrees.

"Because of your baby blue *eeeeeyes*," Lina sing-songs.

"Shut up," I say with a laugh, pushing her with one hand and grabbing the nail polish bottle with the other.

A group of us are gathered in my sitting area on Sunday afternoon, sifting through bottles of nail polish. Sundays are our days off. We can hang out in groups, wander around the palace, sit in the various lounges, or remain on our own in our bedrooms. Essentially, there are no planned activities, lessons, or dates. Last Sunday, our first Sunday here, Lina and I explored parts of the vast palace gardens.

Today, I spent the morning at my piano, still basking in the magic of being surrounded by a real live orchestra. The kind of magic that has nothing to do with fae and everything to do with music. Some of the instruments looked exactly like those I'd expect to see in a human orchestra, while others had a distinctly fae influence. I couldn't tear my eyes away from any of them all night.

But eventually I grew tired of sitting in one place, and somehow, after inviting Lina in and asking Iris to stay, and then leaving my door open and welcoming anyone who happened to walk past, I've ended up with a bunch of girls doing mani-pedis in my suite this afternoon. I won't admit to any of them how much fun I'm actually having. How much I wish I could have done this with a group of girlfriends when I was in high school. If I'd *had* girlfriends and a normal high school experience.

"What about this one for you?" I say to Riya, offering her a shimmery blue-green bottle called *Peacock*. "I've seen you in a few dresses this color."

"Actually," she says slowly, "I really like yellow and orange."

"Ooh, okay. Bright and sunshiney. I like that." She nods as she reaches for a yellow gold bottle. "Why don't you wear those colors more often?" I ask, trying to coax her to join the conversation. I was surprised she accepted my invitation when I called out to her as she passed by. Almost as quiet and distant as Shay, I don't often see her hanging out with any of the other girls.

She pauses before saying, "My mother doesn't really like those colors."

"Oh, okay."

"I don't know if this is strange to say," Annemarie comments in her usual gentle manner, "but I love your hair today, Riya. I wanted to mention it at breakfast but I thought you might think me a bit strange. Is it naturally curly?"

Riya smiles and runs a hand through her wild curls. I almost didn't recognize her when she first walked past my door. I think I've only ever seen her with perfectly straight glossy hair. "Yes, it is. But my—" She cuts herself off, then sighs. She pushes her shoulders back, her posture as perfect as a dancer's. "My mother prefers it straight."

I sense this is a touchy subject, the issue of her mother, and decide it's probably good to shift our focus elsewhere. "Gigi," I say, turning to the girl who threw up in Lina's carriage last night. She's busy painting a pearly pink color onto her toenails. "How are you feeling since—"

"You know you guys are all enemies, right?"

I look toward the source of the loud accented voice in my doorway, already knowing who I'll see there. "Stop stirring, Natalya," I tell her in a bored tone. "We're actually having a good time in here."

"Are you, though? Or are you all just pretending? There isn't any world in which you could all possibly be *real* friends."

"Speak for yourself," Lina says, holding up a bottle of silvery gray polish to examine the color more closely.

"Wait, is that your *aide*?" Natalya's voice is laced with genuine shock. I glance up to see her push away from the doorframe, her face contorted into an expression of revulsion. "Are you kidding me? You are so desperate for friends, you've even roped in the help?"

"She's right, you know," Iris mumbles. She lowers her feet to the floor and stands. "I really shouldn't be—"

"Sit down," I say, my words coming out harsher than I intended. Iris drops back down without a word. I rise and cross the room, blue nail polish bottle gripped tightly in my hand. "Her name is *Iris* not 'the help' and she's here in *my* room at *my* invitation just like the other girls sitting in my lounge. I might have invited you too if you didn't insist on being so immature and bitchy all the time. Now please leave before you say anything else offensive to one of my *friends*."

Instead of moving, Natalya's painted lips pull into a wide smile. "Ooh, Miss Girl Next Door has *claws*. Being one of the prince's Favorites has made you bold, Avery Evans."

Something hot and bitter erupts inside me, the kind of rage I haven't allowed near the surface in years. "Get out." Then I slam the door in her face. I turn back and find everyone in the room staring at me.

"Wow," Lina says quietly. "You okay?"

"Do you think that was *acceptable*?" I demand. "What Natalya was saying?"

"No, of course not. I was more than ready to toss a few nail polish bottles at her head. I'm just surprised at the way you reacted. You're usually so good at ignoring her."

"Yes, well, I don't really care if she constantly digs at me, but what she said about Iris? Implying that she's *lesser* in some way?" I inhale deeply and look at Iris. "I'm sorry, but you have every right to be here. I mean, if you *want* to go, that's totally fine, but don't leave just because someone thinks you're not, like, our equal or something stupid like that."

Iris shifts uncomfortably in her seat. "Avery ..." she says slowly. "The thing is ... in our world, of course we're all equals. But here? In this palace that's basically an extension of *their* world? There's a hierarchy, and I'm *not* on the same level as the rest of you. I appreciate you sticking up for me. I can't tell you how much I appreciate it. But—"

"Can you smell something burning?" Lina interrupts, wrinkling her nose.

I stare at her, assuming for a moment that she's making a stupid joke about my anger. But then the scent of smoke reaches my nose, and a second later my gaze catches on the small flame rising from an arm of one of the couches.

"Holy *shit*!" Lina gasps before I can even take a step forward, just as Iris shrieks something similar and grabs her bunched-up sweater to smother the flame. Moments later, all the girls are on their feet, staring at the smoking patch on the side of the couch.

"Well," Iris says in a shaky tone. "That was ... unexpected."

"What the heck was that?" I ask, though I don't expect anyone to actually have an answer.

"You should ask your designer if he's incorporated any spontaneously combustible materials into any of your clothing," Gigi says matter-of-factly, turning to look at me. "My bra caught fire the other day and it was apparently because of some special magical beads."

A beat of silence passes between us, and then laughter bursts forth from almost everyone in the room. "I'm sorry, your *bra* caught fire?" Lina repeats.

"Oh my goodness, did you get burned?" Annemarie asks.

"No, no, I chucked a glass of water at myself, so it went out pretty quickly."

At that, Lina starts snort-laughing and covers her mouth with her hand. Even Riya seems amused. "Um, I'll be sure to check with Finneas," I say through my laughter as I head back toward the sitting area.

"Look on the bright side," Lina says. "At least it was your bra and not your—"

A knock at my door cuts her off. I swing around and glare at it. "Natalya wouldn't come back, would she?"

"She wouldn't knock," Riya says.

"True," I mutter. I tug the door open—and on the other side is one of Prince Kieren's guards. The man who escorted me back to my quarters the other day. His eyes dart past me for a second before returning to my face. "Shit," I whisper. "Am I in trouble?"

Confusion flickers across his face. "Why would you be in trouble, Miss Avery?"

"I, uh ... no reason."

"I've been asked to escort you somewhere."

I blink. "Somewhere?"

"Don't ask questions," Iris hisses from across the room.

"I, uh, okay. But I'm wearing—" I look down and gesture to my jeans and T-shirt. I figured today was a safe day to wear jeans without having to worry that Finneas might burn them.

"Your clothing is fine," says the guard whose name I can't remember. "You don't need to change."

"Uh, okay." I look over my shoulder at the five faces turned toward me. "If you never hear from me again, please tell my best friend Quinn I love her. She can have my stuffed rabbit."

Lina grabs a small decorative cushion off the chaise lounge and throws it at my head. "Shut up, smartass, and just go with the nice guard."

I duck before the pillow can hit me, which means it smacks the guard square in the face. "Oh, crap, sorry!" I press a hand over my mouth. He blinks and takes a step backward. "Sorry, sorry, sorry," I mutter as I slip around the door and pull it shut.

Out in the corridor, my smile disappears and apprehension starts to pool in my stomach. *Don't ask questions*, Iris instructed, but I'm itching to ask at least a dozen, starting with *Where the heck are you taking me?* And then *Is something bad about to happen?* But I manage to keep my mouth shut until we cross a glass-covered atrium and the guard opens a door on the other side.

"Wait." I stop walking. "This is the door to the North Tower. I'm *definitely* not allowed in there."

"You are if the prince requests it." He steps back and gestures to the open doorway, but still I hesitate. What if this is some sort of setup? "Please, Miss Avery," the guard says, gesturing again. "It isn't anything horrible, I assure you."

I suppose Prince Kieren has had multiple chances to kick me out of this game and he hasn't done so yet. Why would he try to get me into trouble now? With a final glance over my shoulder to see if someone's waiting to jump out and yell 'Caught you breaking the rules!'—there isn't—I step through the doorway into the forbidden North Tower.

Don't ask questions. Iris's instruction keeps playing through my mind as we ascend a spiral staircase, but I can't keep quiet any longer. I clear my throat. "I'm so sorry, I've forgotten your name. My brain keeps calling you 'Mr. Guard Sir,' which I'm pretty sure is not the correct way to address you."

He chuckles. "No, not quite. My name is Illiam. No need for formalities like 'Mr. Guard Sir.'"

"In that case, there's no need to call me *Miss* Avery."

From the corner of my eye, I catch his smile. "It doesn't work that way, Miss Avery."

It's all I can do to keep from heaving a sigh. "Yeah, I've gathered as much. I've tried repeatedly to get my retinue to drop the 'Miss,' but they seem determined not to. Actually, I did get my aide Iris to call me just *Avery* this afternoon, but I could tell she wasn't comfortable with it."

We reach the next floor, a large space with open windows and arrangements of fresh flowers, and several doors leading to other rooms. We head for a door that stands ajar, and Illiam stops in front of it. "Here we are," he says, gesturing for me to walk in ahead of him.

It's a sitting room. Another opulent space with plush furniture, intricate patterns adorning the walls, and warm afternoon light filtering through tall windows. But I'm only vaguely aware of these details because on the other side of the room, occupying a good third of the space, is a grand piano.

"The prince thought you might like to play it," Illiam says.

He thought ... he thought I might ...

I can't speak. I'm not sure I can breathe either. The instrument is too breathtaking for words. The lid is propped open, not a speck of dust on its glossy black surface, polished keys gleaming in the afternoon light. It is absolute perfection, and Prince Kieren thought *I*, a complete *nobody*, might want to play it?

I'm jolted from my stunned thoughts as Illiam turns and makes for the door. "Wait!" I call after him. "Are you sure I'm allowed to be in here? Prince Kieren specifically said I could play this piano?"

"Yes. He told me to wait outside the door, to inform anyone who comes by that you have his permission to be here." He tips his head forward in a brief bow. "You have an hour."

An hour. An *entire hour*. With the most magnificent piano I've ever laid eyes on. I'm almost giddy with wonder and awe. The door closes behind Illiam, and I turn back toward the instrument. I force myself to take a breath. The scent of old wood and leather lingers in the air, along with the sweet perfume of fresh flowers. My heart drums heavily against my ribcage.

I cross the room on tiptoe. After another moment of hesitation, I seat myself carefully on the edge of the cushioned piano bench and slide across to the middle. I place both hands on the polished keys, as carefully as if I might break them. Then I press a single key. The sound, rich and warm, resonates through every corner of the room. Warmth blooms in my chest. I'm holding my breath again. Then my fingers are moving, improvising a slow, soothing melody, and the sound drifts around me, washes over me. I shut my eyes and exhale, giving myself over to the music. Prince Kieren has no idea that this, beyond any precious stone or item of jewelry, is the most treasured gift he could give me.

Chapter Eighteen

Monday passes without too much excitement, followed by a fancy group date in enchanted hot air balloons on Tuesday morning and another unnecessary—in my opinion—photoshoot in the afternoon. Mischa and Finneas fuss around me for at least an hour, and then I have to try and look mysterious and sultry while draping myself across the front steps of the Glittering Palace in a shimmery pink dress covered in hundreds of tiny flowers. I get told off multiple times for smiling—not allowed, apparently—before being allowed to escape for early evening drinks with a group of the queen's friends.

All of this means that our Tuesday phone time with loved ones is moved to the evening after yet another formal dinner in which I'm terrified to eat half the things placed in front of me in case I drop something on my magnificent dress.

I collapse onto my bed after dinner, the many layers of fabric momentarily puffing up around my legs before settling around me. The bodice is a little more sheer than I would like—my skin is definitely visible through parts of it—but Finneas made sure to cover up *just* enough to be respectable, including the lower half of my back, and at least it's comfortable enough to breathe in. Lina's gown was laced up so tight she spent most of the evening taking small sips of air and almost passing out. Someone had to help her to her room before dinner was over.

"Hello? Are you still there, or did you get strangled by your own dress?" The voice belongs to Quinn, and it's coming from the phone I'm clutching in my left hand.

"Yeah, still here." I lift the phone and hold it above me so she can see my face again. "Sorry, just had to take a moment to get horizontal. I'm so tired."

She laughs. "Yeah, playing dress-up is exhausting, I'm sure."

"It sounds ridiculous, I know." I sit up to take my shoes off while Quinn details some of the things that were in the latest episode.

"But that Natalya girl?" she says as I lie back on the bed. "I honestly think she's being *told* to stir things up all the time. And it's not just her. Seriously, the contrived drama never ends. It's always 'Oh my gosh someone tore my dress and *sabotaged* my date' and 'Oh my gosh my heel broke and my whole night is *ruined*' and 'Oh my gosh she said this *terrible* thing about me *behind my back* so now I'm going to sob my eyes out while the other contestants gather around me to find out what's wrong.'"

I raise both eyebrows. "I have no idea what you're talking about. Pretty sure I missed all of that."

"You missed nothing, trust me." Quinn rolls onto her side and hugs a pillow. "Half the time I'm like, 'I can't believe I'm watching this trash,' and then the other half of the time I'm like, 'That's Avery! She's *so* beautiful!'

My cheeks flush as I smile. "Thanks."

"Going into Faeworld must have been quite cool."

"Oh! The opera!" I sit up straight. "I got to sit with the orchestra. It was *amazing*!"

"That's cool. I wish we could have seen more of that. They weren't allowed to video anything, so they just showed a bunch of photos on the episode. Oh, and there was this photo of you and the prince standing under a stairway, and you're looking up at him with this huge smile on your face, positively *beaming*. I have to hand it to you, Aves. You're acting the part of the sweet, blushing contestant *so* well."

My face heats again as I remember accidentally grabbing Prince Kieren's arm. "I think he had just told me about the orchestra, so at that point I probably would have beamed at anything. Oh, and Quinn—" I press a hand to my heart, which still goes all fluttery every time I think of this. "He let me play his grand piano."

Quinn sits up, a frown creasing her brow. "Is that a euphemism for something?"

"What?" I blink. "Ew, no. I'm talking about an actual grand piano."

"Oh. What's his play there? Did someone tell him to do it? Are they going to put it in the next episode?"

"No, I don't think so. There were no cameras around. It was in a private part of the palace. I think he genuinely thought I might like to play it."

Her glasses shift up her nose as she wrinkles it. "Why, though? Is he trying to like ... seduce you?"

"No, I think he was just being nice."

Her eyebrows climb even higher, and her tone is heavy with doubt as she says, "Sure, okay."

"Quinn. Just ... never mind." I hate that she's tainting this perfect, beautiful memory in her hunt for ulterior motives. "Tell me what's happening your side. Are you okay with the bills and food and everything?"

"Yes, everything's been covered by the palace. I have more

than enough. But things at The Grumpy Bean are still crazy. I hardly sit down at all during my shifts these days." She fills me in on everything I've been missing while I try to whisper to Iris that she really doesn't need to pick up my shoes and move them to the dressing room. She waves me off, moves my silk robe from the back of one of the armchairs to my bed, and sits down again.

Quinn tells me more about the ongoing drama at The Grumpy Bean, including all the people who come in only to take selfies and then hang around without actually ordering anything. The remainder of our conversation is taken up by her sharing a blow-by-blow account of her ongoing feud with Holly, the girl who replaced me at The Grumpy Bean.

"Time's up, Miss Avery," Iris eventually whispers.

"Okay. Sorry, Quinn." I scoot to the edge of my bed and stand. "My phone time is up. But at least we got to talk for longer this time."

"Yeah, okay," Quinn grumbles. "Until next week then. Have fun with Fake Prince Faerie Face!"

"Um, yeah." Her words grate at me in a way I don't expect. I force a smile and give her a small wave. "Night." I cross to the sitting area and hand my phone to Iris. "Thank you."

She nods and bends to slip the phone into the pink leather laptop bag she often carries around. She hesitates, then straightens abruptly and says, "Can I ask you something?"

A little surprised, I say, "Yes, of course."

She pulls her shoulders straighter and keeps her eyes on the armchair that stands between us. "Do you actually want to be here? It's just that I overheard part of what your friend was saying. I'm sorry, I didn't mean to, but it's kind of impossible not to hear everything. And she was calling the prince fake, and telling you that you're acting really well."

"Oh, I ... um ..." I was so careful tonight and last week not to tell Quinn all the things *she* isn't supposed to know that I wasn't paying attention to all the things Quinn was saying that *Iris* shouldn't know.

"It's just that this job means a great deal to me," Iris says, and she's reverted to that tone she used when I first met her. Detached, businesslike, unfeeling. "I know there are some who don't like the fae. Many people, probably. But ... there are reasons to respect and admire them. *I* have my reasons."

"I'm sure, Iris, I'm sorry—"

"And the three of us—Finneas, Mischa and I—are doing everything we can to give you the best chance at succeeding, but if you don't actually want to be here, then ... it all feels pointless. *I* feel like a fraud, and I'm sure Finneas and Mischa would too if they knew, dressing you up for a prince you don't even like. He came here to speak to you in private in our first week here, and he's chosen you as a Favorite twice, and it seems as though he honestly likes you, but you're just *pretending* you like him too, which—"

"Which makes *me* seem like the one who's fake," I finish quietly, my face burning. She's absolutely right. I'm in no position to judge anyone else if I'm putting on a mask every day and pretending to be something I'm not.

"Well, I wasn't going to put it like *that*," Iris says, still staring determinedly at the armchair. "I suppose I just want to know where we all stand. I don't know if I should put my heart and soul into this job if you're not as committed as Finneas, Mischa and I are."

Her heart and soul? Now I really feel guilty. "I'm sorry, I ... I don't ..." I pace away from her and drop onto the edge of the bed. "Okay. Can I tell you the truth? Can I trust you? I mean, you're on my side, right?"

Her eyes meet mine, and I see the first flicker of emotion

since she began speaking. "Of course I'm on your side. My one and only purpose here is *you*."

"Right." That makes me feel even more awkward. I'll never get used to having people serve me and dress me and run around after me. "So ..." I run my hands up and down my arms, take a breath, and then let the truth spill out. "It was all an accident. Me ending up here as part of *The Princess Game*. Wrong place, wrong time. Or ... right place, right time, I suppose. Depending on your perspective."

"Okay," she says slowly, following what I'm saying with a frown.

"My point is, I don't even like the fae. I ... have my reasons. Just as you have yours for respecting them. So it didn't even cross my mind to apply to be on *The Princess Game*. I was a last-minute replacement for someone else. But since arriving here ... I don't know. I guess I've come to realize that I've been unfair in judging them. Obviously they're not all the same, just like humans aren't all the same. Finneas and Mischa are totally awesome, and they're fae. And Prince Kieren ..." My eyes move to my lap, and I realize I'm picking at the edge of my manicured nails. I force my hands to be still.

"Prince Kieren?" Iris prompts gently.

"He isn't exactly what I thought. He's ..." I think of him jumping into the river after me. I think of the way he's opened up a little when it's just the two of us and he doesn't have the pressure of the cameras and a dozen other people watching him. He personally escorted Princess Annemarie back to her room after that strange ribbon attack and checked on her multiple times that afternoon. He even attempted a joke when he saw how shaken I was at the opera house. And then there was the orchestra, and the grand piano ... that glorious grand piano. It wasn't an ostentatious gift in front of all the cameras. He sent his guard to quietly accompany me to a private space so I could play in peace.

"He isn't at all what I thought," I finish quietly. I lift my eyes and find a soft smile on Iris's lips.

"So you *do* want to be here now?"

I take the time to properly consider her question. To properly examine my own feelings. "I do," I say, almost in surprise. When did this change? "I mean, not to *marry* him. Which is a good thing, because he obviously can't choose me. But ... I do want to be here. And I don't think he's a huge fake. Not at all."

Iris nods, but her expression is still a bit strained as she says, "But all the things your friend was saying ... you didn't disagree with her."

I bite my lip. "I know. I should have. It was starting to make me feel uncomfortable." I groan and rub my hands over my face. "I need to tell her next time. I want her to know what he's really like. He isn't selfish or aloof or superior. I think he comes across that way because he doesn't say much in a group setting, and he's kind of stiff and formal, but that's just because he's ... well, I'm pretty sure he's just shy. But he's always listening, paying attention. He's observant. He's kind, even."

I glance up and find Iris giving me a knowing look. "Okay, do *not* give me that look," I say immediately, pointing at her.

"What look?" She spreads her hands wide, her face a mask of innocence.

"You think I'm falling for him."

"I didn't say that."

"You were thinking it. And I'm *not* falling for him. I think I've figured him out, that's all."

"Well, I'm glad. We'll continue to do our absolute best to present you as the perfect choice for Prince Kieren, and maybe at some point you'll believe it too."

"Hey! That's not—"

She's laughing as we both hear a knock on the door. I cross the room and open it to find Illiam on the other side. "Oh, hi."

"Good evening, Miss Avery. Prince Kieren asked if you would like to come to the music room again tonight to play the piano."

A shiver of pleasure zings its way up my spine. I smile. "I would love that."

"He also asked me to inform you that he will be present this evening, should this influence your decision."

"I ... oh."

He hesitates, then adds, "I believe he asked me to tell you this in case it might make you uncomfortable to play the instrument while he's in the room."

"Right, I see." I shake my head, my smile back in place. "My decision is the same. I would love to play again."

Chapter Nineteen

"So there were no pillow fights?" Prince Kieren asks.

My answer to him is a bark of laughter. We're in the music room on the evening of my fourth Friday here, me at the piano and the prince on one of the uncomfortable-looking couches with a stack of papers on his lap. In the twelve days since I first sat at this magnificent instrument, I've been here almost every evening. Illiam comes to collect me after dinner, and sometimes Kieren is here, reading something or asking me questions about the other girls, and sometimes I have the space to myself. "No, there were no *pillow fights*," I tell him through my laughter. "Have you been watching terrible movies again?"

He sighs. "Rhylan forced a few of them on me. He found them most amusing."

"Well, just to reiterate," I continue, turning back to face the piano keys, "when I invited a bunch of girls to hang out in my suite for the evening, we did not attack each other with pillows. We did facials."

I can hear the frown in his tone. "Don't you have someone in your retinue for things like that?"

"Yes, but that's not the point." My fingers travel slowly across the notes of a minor key, exploring the haunting melody that's been on a continuous loop in my head over the past few days.

"What is the point?"

"It was *fun*! I think I've managed to convince almost everyone that you can't possibly choose me as your princess, so most people don't think of me as a threat anymore. Parties in my room are becoming a bit of a thing."

When he doesn't respond, I stop playing and look over my shoulder at him again. A difficult maneuver, given the constricting corset top of the dress Finneas made for tonight's dismissal dinner. Kieren is frowning at the floor, lost in thought. His gaze rises to mine. "Why did you stop playing?"

"Why did you stop talking?"

He hesitates. "I was merely ... thinking."

"About?"

He tips his head to the side. "Parties in your room."

I arch a brow. "Pretty sure that's not what you were thinking about."

"What if it was?"

My lips curve up on one side. "Would you like an invitation next time? I'll invite the TV crew too. I think it would make the best episode yet. Pajama party in Avery's room, everyone!" I call out in my best imitation of Evanna. "Prince Kieren will be attending in his fanciest pair of PJs."

A smile spreads across his face, and I laugh out loud in surprise. "Oh my goodness. You just *smiled*. Like a genuine smile."

His face falls instantly, as if being caught smiling is the worst thing in the world. "So?"

"So you *never* smile."

His expression twists into something that can only be described as a scowl. "I *smile.*"

I'm laughing harder now. "You do not. You do this like ... lip twitch thing that could *maybe* be described as a fraction of a smile."

"A *lip twitch thing*?"

"Like your mouth *wants* to smile, but it's so out of practice it can't remember how."

He shakes his head. "Ridiculous," he mutters, turning back to the pages in his hand. "Please continue. With the piano, I mean, not that nonsense about lip twitches. I like whatever it is you've been playing this evening."

"You do?" I pick up the half-formed piece of music from where I left it hanging and let my fingers follow it along a melancholic path. "I think it sounds quite sad."

"It does, yes."

I hesitate, my hands pausing over a pivot chord before modulating into a different minor key. "And you like sad music?"

"I ... like to feel something."

I smile down at the keys and continue playing. My music makes the cold-hearted prince *feel* something. Now that's an accomplishment. Or it would be if he were truly cold-hearted. I'm aware now that he is something quite different.

Quinn, however, is still entirely *un*aware of this. I squirm internally at the reminder. I should have told her by now just how wrong she and I have always been about the crown prince of the Autumn Court, but I chickened out during our third call last week. I steered the conversation deftly away from 'Fake

Prince Faerie Face,' and Iris was decent enough not to call me out on it afterward. Instead, the call focused on all the drama of the dancing lesson featured in episode three, plus the latest major fight Quinn had with Holly, my replacement at The Grumpy Bean.

I'll tell her in person, I kept thinking to myself. Next week Tuesday, instead of getting an hour of phone time to contact loved ones, our loved ones have been invited *here*, to the Glittering Palace, to spend the evening with us. My excitement at finally seeing Quinn again and getting to show her the Glittering Palace *far* outweighs any anxiety I may feel over attempting to explain that I feel something almost like friendship for the prince I once thought was a shallow nitwit.

"Do you also play?" I ask him. "The piano, I mean." In all the evenings we've sat here together, I've never seen him anywhere near the instrument, but it's strange that he would have one if he doesn't know how to play it. Then again, perhaps it's merely another decoration among the vast array of magnificent items that adorn the Glittering Palace.

"I used to," he says.

"Why did you stop?"

"I ... no longer enjoyed it. There was ... someone I was very close to who also played the piano, and after she was ... gone, I found it no longer held the same appeal for me."

"Oh." There is an odd twinge in my chest at the thought of what this woman must have meant to him. And when he says 'gone,' does he mean ...

He clears his throat. "What is your favorite of the works you've composed?" he asks before I can probe further.

My gaze slides up, and I continue playing as I stare out of one of the windows into the dark night. "I don't think I could choose. Different pieces are my favorites for different reasons.

Some are more complex and I love them because they feel like more of an achievement, and then there are others that are simple, but they mean a lot to me because of what was going on in my life when I wrote them."

"That makes sense."

"Oh, but there is something I'm quite proud of that I would *love* a real orchestra to play one day. I mean, if I end up famous enough from being a contestant on *The Princess Game*, which I guess isn't something to hinge one's career on. But hey, I can dream."

"Tell me about it. What is it called?"

"It's, um ..." All of a sudden, I wish I hadn't brought it up. Even admitting just the name of this piece of music feels like revealing some inner part of my soul. "Well it's ..." I wriggle a little in my uncomfortable dress, looking down at the keyboard again. "I attempted to write an orchestral piece. Not just something for the piano or for a few instruments. And the name ... I mean, it's just a working title. Likely to change. Kind of just a placeholder really ..."

"Tell me. Please."

I'm glad I don't have to look at him as I share the name of my most ambitious work. "I called it ... *A Dream Triumphant*. See? It's silly. I even put the word 'dream' in it. And half the time while I was writing it, I had no idea what I was doing. It's not as though I have any formal training. Everything I know—which probably isn't much—I've taught myself. All based on whatever free resources I've been able to get my hands on over the years. So I just wrote down what I heard in my head and put all the parts together until they sounded right. I moved things around and rewrote sections, and then ... yeah. I ended up with *A Dream Triumphant*."

A pause follows the avalanche of words that just tumbled

awkwardly from my mouth. Then: "I like it."

A short breath of laugh escapes me. "You don't even know what it sounds like."

"Well, I like the title," Kieren says, "and if it's anything like what I've heard so far, I'm sure it's magnificent."

I attempt to sit straighter on the piano bench and take a deep breath. "Um, thanks. Hey, can you loosen this thing?" I toss another look over my shoulder as I reach back with my left hand and fumble across the ribbons lacing up my corset. "I feel like it's trying to strangle me."

He looks up with a startled expression. "Uh ..."

"Oh, sorry, never mind." I realize my mistake almost as soon as the request is out of my mouth. In his world, loosening corset strings is a job for one's servants. "That's *way* below your pay grade. You've probably had personal attendants or manservants or whatever to dress you since the day you were born." I laugh as I face the piano again. "I doubt you have any idea how to remove your *own* clothes, never mind someone else's."

"I know how to remove clothing," he says, and his voice is suddenly closer than it was before. I turn my head and find him crossing the room. He stops behind me, bends slightly, and I hastily face forward again. I sense his fingers moving along the base of the criss-cross pattern as he searches for the knot. He finds it, and what little breath I have left catches in my throat as he slowly pulls the end of the ribbon to undo it.

Heat pools unexpectedly in my lower belly, and the atmosphere is suddenly charged, as if electricity pulses in the space between us. His fingers hook in the laced-up ribbons, pulling gently to loosen them bit by bit, and ... okay. Yeah. I should not have asked him to do this.

"Better?" he asks eventually, his lips closer to my ear than I expected. And suddenly, for some utterly *insane* reason, my imagination pictures him moving close enough to brush those perfect lips against my neck. I swallow.

"Yes. Thanks," I manage to whisper. Though now I'm breathless for an entirely different reason. He steps away, and I force a deep breath of air into my lungs and out again. I rest my fingers on the piano keys. I clear my throat. *Play, Avery. Just play. Something. Anything.* My fingers begin moving, purely by instinct it seems because I have no idea what I'm playing. I can barely hear a single note over the rushing sound of my pulse in my ears.

Was it just me? Was I the only one who noticed that weird, tension-filled moment? A quick glance over my shoulder reveals that Kieren is back on the couch, seemingly absorbed in his papers once more. I don't think he noticed anything strange at all.

Stop being weird, Avery. He was just doing exactly as you asked. Keeping your dress from squeezing the life out of you so you don't keel over onto his grand piano.

I breathe again. Air in, air out. Oxygen seems to finally reach my brain, allowing me to focus on what I'm playing. Something soothing, calming. I'm fine. Everything is fine. It isn't weird that he's saying nothing. He often says nothing. This is *fine*!

But the part of my brain that lacks a filter clearly doesn't believe me, and before I know it, my mouth is open and words are spilling out. "You know, as odd as it sounds, this is almost exactly how my days used to end in my normal life."

A pause. "Is that so?" Kieren asks. "Your day job ended with a gentleman loosening your corset while you sat at a grand piano?"

Shit, Avery, you're just making this worse. I force a laugh and continue babbling. "No, I mean this feeling of relief. I obviously didn't wear a corset to work in a coffee shop or tutor kids, but do you know how uncomfortable a pair of high-rise skinny jeans is? That feeling when you get to the end of the day, collapse onto the couch, and finally, *finally* undo the top button and just breathe? It's amazing."

"I see."

"A feeling you will never appreciate," I continue, my fingers starting to move with increasing speed across the keys, "because you'll probably never wear a pair of jeans. And now that I think about it, men's jeans aren't super tight like women's jeans, or super high, so you'd never know the kind of discomfort I'm talking about. Although I guess they're tight enough that your ass would look totally hot in them."

Silence crashes over me as my fingers come to an abrupt halt. My brain replays the words that just fell out of my mouth. Face burning, I look around and meet Kieren's gaze across the room. "You can pretend I didn't say that last bit."

He presses his lips together, eyes alight with humor. "I don't think I can."

"You can."

"You seem to be contradicting yourself, Miss Girl Next Door."

"Oh yeah?" I turn away, my face still hot, and resume my playing.

"Yes. You previously told me jeans are the most comfortable thing in the world, next to pajamas."

"Oh. That's true. I did say that. I was talking about low-rise jeans then."

"Low rise."

"The kind that sit on your hips."

"Your hips."

I look over my shoulder yet again—someone really needs to turn this piano around before I get a repetitive stress injury in my neck—and find his gaze darting back up from wherever it was a second ago. My blush intensifies. "If you were trying to see my hips, Sir Prince," I say, attempting a scolding sort of tone, "I'm afraid you'll have to try a lot harder given the number of layers of fabric they're currently hidden beneath."

He tilts his head a fraction. Gives me the smallest smile. Says absolutely nothing.

"What, no comeback?" I ask.

"Unlike you," he says, "I think before I speak. And I've decided, on this occasion, that my thoughts are better left unspoken."

I roll my eyes because that's the classiest response I can come up with. "Fine."

"Fine."

"Fine."

He almost smiles. "You can wear jeans tomorrow night, if that would make you happy."

"To the Opal Ball?"

"Oh." He blinks and looks across the room. "I forgot about that." He sighs. "I suppose my mother would be speechless with horror if you wore a pair of jeans to the ball she's been planning for weeks."

"So would my designer, trust me," I say, thinking of Finneas's reaction if I dared to do such a thing. "He's threatened to burn any jeans he happens to find in my suite."

"Well, we can't have that. Not before I've—" He slices off the end of his words, and I have a single moment in which to wonder what he was about to say before a dark shape separates itself from the shadows and leaps at him.

Chapter Twenty

The creature tackles Kieren to the floor, and I'm up in an instant, shoving clumsily away from the piano as I shout his name. It's a writhing mass of shadows, swirling and separating and snapping back together, smothering him as he tries to fight it off. I fall to my knees beside him. "No, Avery—" he grunts, but I'm already trying to grab hold of the shadowy thing to pull it off him. My hands are useless though, sinking right through it.

"Sir—Kieren—what the hell is—"

And then the shadow-beast-creature-thing rears back and dives straight down at Kieren's chest. He arches backward, crying out in agony as it somehow goes through his clothing and into his skin. "Shitshitshit!" I gasp, my eyes darting back and forth, following the horrifying, unnatural shadows flickering across his arms, his neck, his face. They're in his eyes too, blotting out the whites and making them roll back in a way that freaks me the hell out.

"What do I do, what do I *do*? Help!" I shout toward the door. "Someone—"

"No, my—my ring—" Kieren gasps. He's still twisting and twitching in pain, but I see his left hand fumble across his right. There's a ring on his second finger, silver with tiny markings etched into it. I push his fumbling hand out of the way and tug the ring free.

"Holy—" I fall back with a gasp as a blade flashes into existence, and suddenly I'm holding a long crystal-like knife instead of a ring. I scramble forward and press the knife into his outstretched hand. He raises it, hand shaking, deadly tip pointed down. "How are you going to—No, no, *no*!" A blinding flash of confusion-fear-horror rips through me as he plunges the knife downward. But it's too late. He's already stabbed the blade straight into his abdomen.

He goes still. I'm frozen too, barely breathing, unable to comprehend what's just happened. And then the shadows begin bleeding out of him. His mouth, his eyes, his skin. It's as if he's covered in black blood until the dark substance starts to disintegrate and rise away from him like wisps of smoke. Within a few moments, all traces of the horrifying creature are gone. His hand, still wrapped around the knife, tugs the blade free. It comes away clean. I see no evidence of a wound through the hole in his shirt.

"Holy *shit*," I gasp. My hands are on his face now, gently tilting it toward me as I examine his skin, his eyes, his lips. "Are you okay?" His blinking gaze comes to rest on me. I watch the way his eyes finally focus on my face. He lifts one hand and presses it gently over mine.

"Yes. Are you ... you tried to touch it, but ..."

"My hands just went straight through it. I'm fine."

"You're fine," he murmurs.

I suddenly realize I'm far too close to him. I pull my hands away from his face and shift backward slightly. "What the hell *was* that?"

"A ... a ..." He coughs, then shakes his head. "I can't say."

"Do we need to alert someone? Evacuate the palace? What if there are—"

"No. It was only here for me. Any others will also be here only for me."

I hesitate. "Are you sure?"

"Yes. They want ... they want ..." Again he shakes his head and groans. "I cannot explain." He pushes himself into an upright position and leans back against the couch.

At that moment, the door bangs open and Illiam and another one of Kieren's guards rush in. "Sir! Prince Kieren! I'm so sorry—"

"It's fine. I'm fine."

"We heard a cry for help, but—"

"But you were at the bottom of the tower. I know. I'm the one who instructed you to wait there tonight."

Illiam's eyes finally shift to me. "Is she—"

"I'm fine," I assure him. "It didn't touch me."

He nods. "Good. Very good. The effects are ..."

"Unpleasant," the other guard fills in quietly. "Sir, if there are more—"

"Unlikely," Kieren says. "And if there are, we will deal with them in the usual manner. You may return to your normal posts on this floor. Thank you."

The two guards hesitate. "If you're sure, Your Highness."

"I am."

They both bow before leaving the room and pulling the door closed. I look at Kieren. He returns my gaze. "You stabbed yourself," I say quietly.

"Not the first time."

"Really? You've had to stab yourself multiple times? Because of the same type of creature?"

"Yes."

"Is this what you meant when you said there are creatures roaming the grounds at night that are a little ... vicious?"

"No. This is something entirely different. These shadows ... they are not supposed to come through the Shimmer."

I'm quiet a moment before saying, "I think I saw one in the gardens. That day I fell into the river and you walked back with me through the trees. It moved the same way."

He sighs. "I suspected as much. I saw no need to tell you, though. It was there for me, not you."

"But creatures like this have attacked your guards as well?"

"Yes. Though the shadows do not want them, my guards have felt the effects while helping me fight them off."

I hesitate, biting my lip. "Can I ask ... what do they do to you?"

"They ..." He shuts his eyes. "They pull out everything that's dark within me. Every painful memory, every insidious thought, every nightmare, every hopeless moment. They bring everything to the surface, wrap it all into a single mass of despair that consumes me until that's all I feel. That's all I know. And I fear I will drown in it." He opens his eyes, letting them settle on mine. "The first time it happened, I almost did drown in it. I saw no hope left in anything, only misery and despair. Fortunately, I know better now."

I nod slowly. "I'm somewhat familiar with that kind of hopelessness."

"You?" He lets out a humorless breath of a laugh. "You of the eternal optimism and the ever-present sweet smiles and that light in your eyes that never seems to dim?" His voice is gentle as he adds, "I don't think it's possible for you to know anything about that kind of hopelessness."

It would be easy enough to say nothing. To brush off his comment and move on from this line of conversation. But I decide not to. "You're fae," I say quietly. "A master of illusions. You should know that with everyone there is always more than meets the eye."

He frowns, leaning forward slightly. "Then what is it that I am not seeing about you, Avery?"

My breath catches in the back of my throat. I don't want to admit that I like the way he says my name. Not Miss Avery. Not Miss Girl Next Door. Just ... *Avery*. "You mentioned my optimism and ever-present smiles. And apparently there's *light* in my eyes," I add with a small roll of said eyes. "But did it occur to you that perhaps the amount of light I need in my life is directly related to the amount of darkness I'm constantly trying to obliterate?"

He's silent for several moments, watching me closely. "No," he says eventually. "I'm ashamed to say it did not. What darkness are you trying to obliterate?"

My eyes slide away from his. It feels too personal, too intimate, to say any of this while holding his gaze. "Evanna and Carwyn got it wrong when they chose me to fill the role of Girl Next Door. Perhaps I look it, but my life in no way resembles it. The girl next door is the one whose family is perfect and happy, whose mom cooks meals for other people and bakes for school events. She's the girl who's reliable, helpful, always ready with a smile. Liked by her peers and teachers and other parents.

"But that was never me. I was the girl who was abandoned as a baby. The girl who grew up knowing no one wanted her. The girl who always lived in some dodgy house in some rundown street that everyone else's parents warned them not to go down. The girl whose clothes always looked a little shabby and who never had sleepovers at her own house because she would never dare to invite anyone to any of those ... less than friendly homes she lived in." A shiver creeps along my arms as I skirt a little too close to the truth I've tried so hard to run from.

I catch a glimpse of Kieren's jaw clenching before I look away again. "What precisely do you mean by 'less than friendly'?" he asks in a tone that is suddenly icy cold.

"It doesn't matter. My point is—"

"It does matter."

I place my hand over his and give him a genuine smile. "It really doesn't. Not anymore."

"It matters to *me*."

Something tightens in my belly. Something ... not exactly unpleasant. We're both quiet for several moments as my eyes search his and he continues to stare back. My skin heats beneath his gaze, but I don't look away. "Kieren, it's—I mean, sir—Prince—"

"Forget the titles. You're terrible at them."

"I know, I'm so sorry. I really don't mean to be disrespectful or—"

"I know you don't. Please tell me what you mean. What happened while you were growing up?"

I take a deep breath. "My point ... Kieren," I say hesitantly, trying out the name on purpose rather than by accident. He turns his hand over beneath mine and threads our fingers together. A shiver dances along my skin and something flutters in my stomach. "My point is that I know something about darkness trying to pull you under," I say gently but firmly, hoping he'll understand that I don't want to share any more details. "But I've never been able to stay in that space. I *can't*. I would die. There's something in me that has to reach for the light, no matter how difficult."

Another few moments pass as his eyes travel my face. "And is the darkness still there? Underneath it all?"

I consider lying to him, but he'll probably see right through me. Besides, I don't *want* to lie to him. Something has shifted between us, and I find myself wanting to share things I've never shared with anyone except Quinn. "Yes," I say quietly, holding his gaze. "It's still there. Far beneath the surface. My life is happier now. Things are better."

He's quiet for a long time. Then: "You accuse us of being fake," he says gently, "of hiding behind illusions. But you wear a mask too."

I bite down my immediate reaction—defensiveness—and instead take a moment to consider his words. "I don't think of it as a mask," I say eventually. "I *am* a positive person. It's just that some days it comes easily and other days I have to try a lot harder."

"Have you considered that some days it's okay if you don't try at all?"

"Yes." My voice is barely more than a whisper now. "But then I think ... what if I don't try today and then I never feel like trying again?"

He nods slowly, then rubs his free hand over his face and lets out a long sigh. "Avery," he says, and again there's that flutter in my stomach. "I think you may be the only thing about this blasted game that's truly real."

"Well, I know I'm not a real contender, which means I have nothing to hide." *Not true*, a quiet voice reminds me. *You will always have something to hide.* I look away. "I think I should probably go, Your ... Kieren." I shake my head and allow myself a small laugh. "As much as I stumble over the titles, it feels even stranger to call you just Kieren." What I don't admit is that I've already been thinking of him as just *Kieren* in my head. I don't know exactly when it happened, but my brain dropped the title a while ago.

"It shouldn't," he says. "We have the sort of relationship where fancy titles feel as though they're simply in the way."

"We, um ... we do?"

"Yes. Rhylan doesn't address me as 'prince' or 'your highness.' Neither do my other friends."

"So we're ... friends?" For some reason, I think of his hands on the back of my corset. I think of the achingly slow way he pulled the end of the ribbon. I think of the way I held his face after the shadows left his body. None of that felt like ... *friends.* There's also the fact that our fingers are still interlaced and my pulse is doing a strange sort of giddy rush through my veins.

"Something like friends, yes," he says, which isn't really an answer at all.

"Well ... if you're sure you're fine then, I should probably return to my room." I force myself to pull my hand away from his. I may have been allowed to drop the fancy titles, but he's still a fae prince and I'm still a nobody and there's still never going to be anything between us except 'something like friends.'

"I'm definitely fine," he says, standing and extending a hand to pull me to my feet. "And please don't worry about these shadow creatures. It's unlikely there are any more on this side of the Shimmer, and if there are, they will not go near you or any of the other contestants. I cannot give you more details, but know that they are only here for me."

I think he's saying this to reassure me, to put my mind at ease, but it only makes me more concerned for him. I have a dozen questions about these strange creatures and why they're after him, but it's clear he won't answer any of them. So I leave the room reminding myself that he has multiple guards, that they've faced these strange shadows before, and that everything will be fine. *And soon*, a quiet voice reminds me, *you'll be gone and none of this will be your concern any longer.*

Chapter Twenty-One

"Oh you both look *stunning*!" Gigi exclaims as she walks up to Lina and me in the ballroom on Saturday night. For the queen's opal-themed ball, our designers have dressed us all in gowns of the same silvery white hue with subtle shimmering highlights of blue-green and pinky peach. The designs are all different, though, and I enjoy looking around at the varying styles while we wait for the evening's proceedings to begin.

"Thank you," I say with a smile, looking down as I turn gently from side to side. I love the deliciously soft feel of the cool fabric swishing around my ankles and across my legs. "I thought at first it might be too revealing, but I think it's okay."

Finneas was more daring with the front of the dress than I usually allow him to be, designing a neckline that plunges in a narrow V all the way down to my waist. A piece of sheer fabric holds the two sides together. I was mildly horrified when he presented it to me, but he told me to reserve my judgment until the dress was on. As usual, he was right. And he at least followed my usual instructions regarding the back of the dress, keeping it at a fairly decent height.

"No way, it's gorgeous," Gigi says. "Did you see what Natalya wore last weekend for the golden unicorn cocktail event? That dress was almost transparent and she was *not* wearing underwear. I'm surprised she wasn't asked to change."

Lina laughs. "And my designer went in the opposite direction tonight and made me look like a Disney princess."

"I keep telling you that's not a bad thing," I say to her. "Your dress is literally magical. Look at how it sparkles!"

"Avery's right," Gigi agrees. "You look gorgeous, Lina."

"Well, thank you. So do you, Gigi."

They smile politely at each other. Then Gigi smiles politely at me. A moment of awkward silence passes. Then we all look around, still saying nothing. Things are fine between Lina and me—we both know we're not here to win—but when anyone else is around, the atmosphere is a little ... tense. After four dismissal dinners, there are only twelve of us left. Only two to go until we reach the Top 10. It's gone a lot faster than anyone expected. I imagine the producers of *The Princess Game* aren't pleased. There was never any guarantee of a particular number of episodes, but I'm sure they hoped Kieren would use the maximum amount of time offered to him, thereby providing material for the maximum number of episodes.

"My goodness, isn't everyone looking lovely tonight."

I almost roll my eyes at the sound of Natalya's voice behind me. *Here comes the drama*, I think as I turn toward her, imagining every camera in the room zooming in on us. "Good evening to you too, Na—" My words end on a startled gasp as Natalya and her glass of pink punch walk straight into me.

"Oh!" Her eyes are wide, her lips a perfect, painted ring as I stand there completely frozen, not wanting to look down. "Oh wow. That was *totally* an accident. I'm so sorry, Avery. What a mess! I did *not* mean to ruin your gorgeous—"

"Are you kidding?" I demand.

Natalya hesitates, still feigning innocence. "What?"

"I'm continually astounded by how petty you are. Are you ever going to grow up?"

She shrugs and smiles. "I'll do whatever growing up I need to do *after* I become princess."

"Like that's ever going to happen," Lina says as Natalya sashays past us. "Can I push her into the chocolate fountain?" she asks. "I know it's pearly white chocolate so it won't be nearly as spectacular as shoving her into something brown and gloopy, but I still think it would make for some excellent TV."

Jaw clenched, I turn my face away from the nearest camera. "I'm going to change into something else," I mutter. "I'll be quick."

"Do you want me to go with—"

"No, it's okay, don't worry." I'm trying to bite down my anger, and my response is sharper than I intended. "Thanks, Lina," I add quietly, not looking around at her. The last thing I want is all these cameras seeing how mad I am over a silly dress. "No point in us both winding up in trouble if I end up being late."

I hastily exit the ballroom through one of the smaller side doors. I've only ever used the main door at the top of the stairs, but I don't want to draw more attention to myself by leaving that way, and I'm sure I can figure out how to get back to my suite.

Taking a steadying breath once I'm out of sight of the crowd and the cameras, I look a little closer at the large pink stain that stretches from my right hip all the way to the bottom of the skirt. It's just a dress. I *know* it's just a dress. I didn't care about such things before I arrived at the Glittering Palace, and it's not as though I care a great deal about them now. More than anything, I'm angry on Finneas's behalf. He works so hard and puts so much care and attention into the outfits he creates for me, and Natalya's childish spitefulness has ruined it.

Movement up ahead catches my attention, and I look up. *Kieren.* My heart does a happy little flip, which is, of course, an entirely normal way to react when one sees a friend. He strides toward me, right hand fastening a button on his left cuff, eyes on the floor and a deep frown etched into his face. It's stupid, but I like watching the way he walks. He has a quiet confidence, a way of commanding an entire room without saying a word. I'd be swooning if I was one of the girls who's here to win his heart. Okay, maybe I'm swooning a little bit. I'm not *totally* immune to his good looks.

He glances up and comes to a stop. Something lights up in his eyes, and there's that *almost*-smile on his lips. "Avery, you—" His gaze halts near the bottom of my dress. "What happened?"

I sigh, roll my eyes, and say one word: "Natalya."

"Ah. An 'accident,' I presume."

"Definitely an 'accident,' yes. I was on my way back to my room to change into something else."

"Hmm." His eyes are still tracing over me in a way that causes my blood to pump a little faster, and *darn it*, why do I like the way he does that deep growl-sigh so much? "It would be a shame to waste a gown so … lovely. Perhaps I can fix it and save you from having to return to your suite."

I blink at him. "You can fix stains?"

"Well, no, I'm not sure how to *remove* it. But I am adept with glamours. *Illusions*, as you always like to call them." He steps closer. "May I?"

"Oh. Uh ... sure. That's a better option than being late to your mother's ball."

"Definitely." He lowers himself onto one knee. He is *kneeling*. The crown prince of the Autumn Court *is on his knees before me*, and surely there is something fundamentally wrong about this? I glance about, hoping no one finds us in this position because I'm sure I would somehow wind up in trouble for it, even though I'm pretty sure I've done nothing wrong.

He raises one hand, holds it several inches above the fabric, and slowly moves it downward. I watch as the stain vanishes bit by bit from my hip all the way down to my toes. "See? Easy enough." He looks up at me with those silvery blue eyes and I suddenly feel as if I could fall into them. "It isn't permanent, but it should last the evening."

Speak, Avery. Use words. "Um, thanks. Thank you." I clear my throat as he stands. Thank *goodness*. It's a lot easier to think when he isn't kneeling at my feet. "So, um, what's wrong? You look extra worried about something tonight. Is it those weird shadowy creatures? Have there been more?"

"No. I told you there is no need to worry about that. It's ..." He sighs. "They've told me I need to kiss someone tonight. Apparently the audience has been expecting it since the first episode, and now that three episodes have passed and there's been no ... *action* ..." He just about growls the word out before taking a deep, steadying breath. "Well, something about ratings dropping. I don't know. I stop listening when they talk about that side of things."

"Okay." I ignore the weird feeling I get in the pit of my stomach at the thought of him kissing someone. "I guess they're right. In the human version of this show, there would have been way more, uh ... *action* by now."

"Well. The bottom line is this: Cadence, Natalya, Lina, or

Shay. They're apparently the top four favorites according to ..." He waves a dismissive hand and shrugs. "Something."

"Natalya? Really?" I almost physically shrink away from the idea. "But she's horrible."

"The producers don't seem to care whether anyone is *nice* or not. They care about how many people are watching the show each week. I'm not sure if anyone actually *likes* Natalya, but they seem to like the drama she insists on creating. Cadence had millions of fans before she even came on the show. Lina is one of the friendliest and most likable, and Shay is apparently appealing because she's mysterious. Though from the limited time I've spent with her, I'm beginning to get the feeling she doesn't actually want to be here." He looks away, shakes his head, and I see him clench his fist briefly before releasing it. "So," he says without looking at me. "Those are my options. What are your thoughts?"

"Um ... wow, this is so romantic," I deadpan. He quiets me with a single look. "Right. Sorry. Okay, obviously I'm going to say Lina. She's the most genuine of the four. Natalya is out, obviously, and Cadence is *so* committed to winning the tiara. Like, scarily so. She definitely cares more about the position than about you. I can't say much about Shay because I don't really know her. Although you both walk around with near-permanent scowls, so I guess maybe you have grumpiness in common. So ... yeah. Lina's probably your best option." As I say this, though, there's something inside me that squirms at the thought of Kieren kissing Lina. Perhaps because I know she only entered on a dare and not because she has any real feelings for him.

His jaw clenches. "I can't kiss Lina."

"Oh." I'm annoyed by the amount of relief I feel at his words. I should *want* my friend to possibly win this thing, shouldn't I? It isn't going to be me, so why not her? "Um, why?"

Kieren exhales slowly, gaze focused somewhere beyond me, expression unreadable as usual. "I feel nothing in her presence."

I can't help rolling my eyes. "You know just what to say to make a girl swoon."

"It's the truth."

"Well have you even *tried*?"

His eyes snap to mine. "I shouldn't have to *try*. If she's the one for me, shouldn't things come naturally?"

"I'm sorry, but if you were hoping to find true love *naturally*, you shouldn't have agreed to *The Princess Game*."

"You make it sound as if I had a choice," he murmurs, looking away again. "As if my parents don't remind me daily of my *responsibility*." He shakes his head. "Never mind. This is a pointless discussion. It's not as though I'm even looking for ..." He trails off.

"For true love?" I nod slowly. "Yeah. I know. You're looking for the best alliance or something like that."

He inhales deeply and pulls his shoulders a little straighter. "I should go. Thank you for sharing your thoughts." He's striding past me before I can say another word, and I'm left wondering what I've done to upset him. Because I must have done something. Things have become so easy between us over the past couple of weeks, and now suddenly he's distant again.

I wait a few moments, giving him time to enter the ballroom alone, then follow slowly. Lina spots me as soon as I walk back in and hurries over to ask how I managed to save my dress. "It's just an illusion," I tell her. "It'll probably only last a few hours." I don't mention *who* created the illusion. Lina knows I've spent some time in private with the prince, but she thinks it's mainly because he's allowed me to play the piano that happens to be housed in the private North Tower. She doesn't know how much we've spoken. She doesn't know we've grown ... close. *No, you're not* close *to him, Avery, don't be silly. He's a prince and you're a nobody and you're using each other until your agreement comes to an end and you return to your normal life.*

I shrug off this internal reminder and try to focus on the evening's proceedings. The queen welcomes her honored guests. We, the twelve remaining contestants, parade in front of them with curtseys and smiles. The lights dim, darkening the room just enough for us to notice the pretty opalescent sheen brightening the walls, moving in shifting patterns like sunlight on water. The music starts back up, and we drink and chat and laugh and dance, and I try to pretend I'm not following Kieren's every move, waiting for the moment he chooses someone to kiss. But I *am* watching him, which means I don't miss it when he strides across the ballroom and heads for one of the side doors. He pauses, looks back, and when his eyes land on mine, he tilts his head slightly, as if indicating I should follow him.

Shoot. I hope no one else saw that.

I allow myself approximately five seconds before excusing myself from a conversation with Lina, Riya and the queen's great aunt. *Walk slowly, normally, calmly*, I tell myself, hoping not to draw any attention.

Out in the hallway, I find Kieren pacing. "What's happening?" I ask. "Are you—"

"I'm calling of this entire thing."

I blink at him. "Calling off—what, the whole game?"

"Yes. It's completely absurd. I should never have agreed to this. I'm sending everyone home."

"What? No! No, no, no, you can't do that."

"I'm the crown prince of the—"

"—of the whole freaking fancy pants world, yes, I know.

But that doesn't mean you can just call off this whole thing. Your parents will be furious. You told me at the beginning of all this that they think *The Princess Game* is the best way to narrow down your options to the most appropriate match. You think they're going to be okay with you messing it all up now?"

He stops. Heaves a heavy breath. "I don't care. None of this is right. It needs to end."

I manage to stop myself from rolling my eyes through the ceiling. "Well of course none of this is *right*. No one chooses their life partner in this way."

"That isn't—"

"But it's happening now, and I'm trying to help you choose the best option, so just go with it."

He stares at me. "Why are you so intent on keeping all of this going? You think it's as ridiculous as I do."

"Because if the game is over then I have to leave—" The truth smacks me so suddenly in the face that I almost reel backwards. If the game is over, then I have to leave *him*. And somehow, over the past few weeks, he's become someone I care about.

"Yes, if the game is over, you have to leave. No more jewels every week."

"No, that's—"

"I'll give you more, if that's what you need. But this competition ... I cannot do this anymore."

"No, I don't need more gifts." I shake my head, annoyed now. "It isn't that. It's ... you told me you have a responsibility. That you have to do this, whether you like it or not. But now you're freaking out because of one kiss? What's the big deal? Just pick someone and do it."

"The big deal? *The big deal?*" He swings away from me, shoving his hands through his hair. The perfect prince who's always perfectly in control. I've never seen him so agitated. "The big deal is that I've come to realize ... things."

"Things?"

"Things I ... didn't know before. About your world and its people. And now ..."

He's still facing away from me, so I can't see his expression. I can't figure out if he's implying that we humans are even worse than he expected and he can't bear to bind himself to one of us, or if it's something else entirely.

"Look," I say quietly. "It's just a kiss. Just do it, get tonight over with, and then take a day to think this all through. If you decide you need to end the competition, then wait until Friday night and dismiss us all. Say that you've realized you can't marry any of us. A great many people will still be furious with you, but at least it'll come across a little less ... rash."

He looks at me. "And you want me to believe this isn't about the gifts?"

It's about you! I want to shout. "You can have the silly gifts back if you want. I mean they're not *silly*," I add quickly at the sight of something that might possibly be hurt flickering across his face. "They're beautiful. Thoughtful. But I'd be helping you whether you'd given them to me or not."

"No, you would not. You couldn't stand the sight of me when you first got here."

"Okay, sure," I admit. "But maybe I was wrong about you."

"Maybe?"

"Fine. I was *definitely* wrong. You're not as bad as I thought."

"Such high praise from you, Miss Girl Next Door."

"My point is that my opinion of you has changed. Kind of ... dramatically. So yes, I'm helping you now regardless of what I get in return. That's what I do for friends. I help them."

Something shifts in his expression. He pauses for too long. "Yes," he says eventually. "We are ... something like friends."

"Yes, of course, not *friends* friends," I hurriedly correct. "Not like you and Rhylan, who—"

"Definitely not like me and Rhylan."

"—who would *also* tell you that you're insane for thinking about calling off this whole thing. So can we get back in there now? People are probably already wondering where you are. Some poor clipboard person is probably frantic with worry."

He does that growl-sigh I like a little too much. "Fine." He pauses, breathes, says nothing. Then: "Perhaps you're right. I am being a little ... rash. It is, after all, just a kiss. All I need to do is decide *who*."

And there it is again, that feeling of wrongness that comes with the thought of him kissing someone. "Yes." I clear my throat, because somehow that word didn't come out sounding normal. "Yes, it's just a kiss."

We turn toward the ballroom, and when I try to hang back to let him enter alone, he looks over his shoulder at me. "Why aren't you walking in with me?"

"Oh, because, um ... people might think ..."

"Might think what?"

"They might think that ... you know ..."

"That I had a private conversation with you? So? Isn't that the entire point of this game? This show? That I get to know all of the contestants and form relationships with each of you?"

With each of you. His words punch a hole clear through my chest. I've answered so many questions about the other girls, heard little details about all the dates he's been on, and yet for some reason it didn't occur to me that he might have grown as close to them as he's grown to me. That he might have *relationships* with all of us, instead of merely a collection of outings involving stilted, awkward conversation. I also can't figure out why this bothers me so much. As he said, this is the entire point of the show. Of *course* he's supposed to form relationships with all of us until he determines which contestant is his best match. "Um ... yes, that's true. That's very true."

So I walk in beside him. The music and conversation continue. The magical opalescent sheen still sparkles on the walls. The heady scent of perfumes fills the air. "Dance with me," Kieren says, catching my hand just as I'm about to excuse myself.

"Oh, okay." I turn to face him. "You can't put off this silly kiss forever," I add in a quieter tone.

"No. But I can put it off for one more dance." He lifts my hand, steps closer, and fits his other arm around me. And then we're moving across the ballroom floor, perfectly in time to the music. It's perhaps the third or fourth time I'm dancing with him, and it's so much easier now than that first night at the Opening Ball. I suppose I've had more practice, and I'm used to him, used to this place, used to the cameras. This glittering world that was so strange to me a few weeks ago feels like a new kind of normal.

I stare over his shoulder, and as he sweeps me across the ballroom again and again, I realize I'm enjoying this too much. The press of his hand against my back. His fingers wrapped around mine. The dance has already gone on too long—I know he's stalling—and yet I don't want it to end. Finally, he twirls me beneath his arm one last time and we come to a stop. I look up and find his eyes. "So. Have you decided?"

He smiles. He *smiles*. It's only the second time I've seen it and I like it far, *far* too much. It touches something deep inside me, snatches my breath away and leaves fluttering wings in its place. "Yes," he answers before I can find that stolen breath. Then he leans forward and presses his lips to mine.

For a moment, I don't respond. I *can't* respond. Shock has wiped my mind blank. Then ... my eyelids slide closed. Kieren's hands rise to gently cup my face, and his lips are so soft against mine, and how is it possible that our mouths fit so perfectly together? All remaining air evaporates from my lungs, and every nerve in my body sings. My heart hammers faster, pounding out a wild beat in my chest, and as our lips part further and his tongue nudges against mine, something inside me is suddenly, desperately, achingly *awake*. It's that something that shut down years ago. The thing I've had no desire to fix it. Desire itself, for another person. I thought I had lost the ability to feel that way for anyone, but it's as if a switch has flipped and a light is now on and my entire body is humming, waiting, wanting. *Wanting*. That's the part I thought I would never experience again.

But I realize, as the kiss ends and I stand in this frozen moment with his lips barely a breath away from mine, that I've felt this before, very recently. Last night in the music room when he stood close behind me and gently hooked his fingers into the ribbons of my corset. I paid the moment little attention once it passed, but it was *this*. This aching need pooling low in my center. This desire for *more*, for *him*. How long have I wanted him without even realizing it?

Kieren finally steps back, breaking the moment, and though my gaze is ensnared by his captivating eyes, I sense the stares of every other person in the ballroom. The whispers, the disapproving glares. I am *not* the girl he was supposed to kiss tonight.

"You're in trouble now," I whisper, a little breathlessly.

His expression is heavy with something I can't define. "You have no idea."

Chapter Twenty-Two

I fall asleep with my fingers tracing my own lips, replaying the sensation of Kieren's kiss. It's stupid. So stupid. I know I can't get attached. I know there will never be anything more between us than the deal we struck at the start of this game. But the kiss follows me into my dreams, sparking the desire for things I haven't wanted in years. I dream of his arms tight around me, his fingers twisting in my hair and liquid heat curling low in my belly. I dream of kissing him until I'm breathless and straining against him, needing more, more—

I'm startled awake by a scream.

I sit up straight. Everything is silent. Did I dream that sound? No. My skin flushes as I remember precisely what I was dreaming. I wait, listening, breathing quietly and—

Another blood-curdling scream shatters the silence, and I'm out of bed before I can even process that my limbs are moving. Adrenaline pounds in my veins. I rush to my door and tug it open. Through the near darkness, I see doors opening, girls emerging, a shadowy figure running along the corridor toward us screaming, "Get back in your rooms!" She throws herself through an open doorway and slams the door shut.

The shadows. That's my first thought. There are more shadow creatures and Kieren was wrong and they *are* attacking other people. Most of the other girls vanish into their rooms with gasps and cries, but I hesitate. Should I go to Kieren? To his guards? They can fight these things. We—

I barely have time to form another thought before a gasping cry echoes down the corridor, and someone else comes racing toward me. There's a dark shape behind her, huge and hulking, heavy enough that I feel the floor vibrate with every thud of its feet. This is no shadow, I realize. It's *real*.

I should move. I should hide. But someone—Riya—is running, and I can't leave her out here on her own. Her bedroom is on another floor, and every door in this corridor is closed now except mine. "Riya!" I shout at her. "Here!"

But it's too late, because the *thing* behind her swipes out with what appears to be a black feathery wing and knocks her off her feet. She rolls across the floor in a way that only body doubles in movies should be able to roll and lands in a crouch, facing the thing. But I don't have time to be startled by this because I finally see the monster for what it is: Huge, grotesque, with dripping fangs and overly large eyes and tattered wings that fill the corridor. Its four powerful limbs end in talons. It's like nothing I've ever seen before, and nothing I've ever imagined. And Riya is ... she's fighting it. She's dodging, spinning around, swiping at it with a knife and then leaping out of its reach. "Avery, get back!" she yells. "And get ready!"

I stumble backward into my room. With a final swipe of her blade, Riya launches herself after me. I slam the door shut and turn the key. "Okay, that door is *not* going to hold against that thing," I gasp.

"No. And there's—" A loud thump and an inhuman screech interrupt her. Then silence. "We'll have to climb over the balcony and down the wall," she continues, already hurrying across my room. "There's nothing tall enough or heavy enough to push against the door."

"Climb over the *balcony*?"

She looks back at me as she shoves my curtains aside. "Do you want to get eaten by that thing?"

"Of course not, but we're like three floors up! Maybe you're some kind of parkour champion, but I'm just a regular person."

"I'm sure you can manage." She tugs my balcony doors open.

"Wait. Listen."

She hesitates. "Don't tell me you think it's *gone*," she scoffs. "That silence means nothing. It's still out there."

"No, listen." I tiptoe back to the door and press my ear against it.

"Are you *insane*?" she hisses.

"There's someone crying out there," I whisper. "In the corridor where that monster—" A screech reaches my ears, followed closely by a second piercing cry. I jump away from the door. "Shit, I think there are two of them. And—"

"Get *off* me!" The words are muffled, followed by a gasp. Then bumps, flapping, another stifled scream.

"Riya, there's someone out there. I think it's Shay."

"Do *not* tell me you're thinking about opening that door," Riya says, backing away onto the balcony.

"We can't just leave her!"

"Of course we can. It's every girl for herself in this damn place."

"No it isn't!"

She hesitates, her lips pressed tightly together. Then,

muttering beneath her breath, she darts back inside, still gripping a knife. "Fine. I'll distract it—or them—and you grab her and pull her in here." I nod, and we both huddle beside the door. "Open it very slowly," she whispers, "so they don't notice us."

I nod, my hand already twisting the doorknob. I crack the door open ever so slowly, painfully aware of Shay's cries out in the corridor. When it's finally open enough to see what's happening, I discover I was right. There are two of them, one a little smaller than the other. Shay is cornered at the end of the corridor, fighting off the two beasts with what looks like the broken leg of a chair.

Riya darts out, dancing away in the other direction. "Hey, arseholes!" she shouts in her perfect, posh accent. The two monsters whirl around. One leaps immediately after her, while the smaller one hesitates, looking back at Shay. With an angry cry, she swings her chair leg at it again. It takes a step away from her, turns, and lunges after Riya.

I race out of my room and grab Shay's hand. The chair leg falls from her other hand and hits the carpeted floor. Blood streaks her arms, and tears streak her face. A kind of furious fear is etched into her expression. "Holy fuck! *Fuck!* I did *not* sign up for this!"

"Come on!" I bend and grab the fallen chair leg, then tug her toward my room. Further down the corridor, Riya is dodging beneath an enormous flapping wing. The monster shrieks as she slashes at it with her knife. We dive through my doorway, and barely moments later, Riya hurries in after us, limping slightly. I drop Shay's hand and turn for the door—

But the monstrous creature is already in the doorway, tattered wings rising, mouth spitting saliva as it snaps its jaws together. It swipes a wing at me. The chair leg is still in my hand,

and I swing it, striking the edge of the wing and making the monster shriek. I raise the piece of wood again, but before I can deliver another blow, the monster lashes out and rakes a taloned foot down my left arm.

Pain blazes through every inch of my body. My cry is a strangled gasp in my throat. The chair leg slips from my hand. I stagger backward just as something—the stool from my vanity? —comes flying past me. It strikes the monster's head, forcing it a few steps back. Riya lunges past me and sinks her knife into the monster's chest. Then she kicks the creature the final distance out of my room and shoves the door shut. "Okay," she says, somewhat breathless as she faces us. She grips the top of her right leg, and blood seeps through her fingers. "Now for the balcony."

"I ... I don't think ..." I'm trying to tell her I don't think I can do that, but my breath is coming too fast and my head is starting to spin. Blood drips down my arm. I stumble sideways, one hand reaching for the edge of my bed, but it's further away than I thought and I end up landing on the floor on my knees.

"*Now* what?" Riya mutters.

The pain is gone from my arm, and all I can feel is a kind of prickly numbness. There are shouts and thumps and screeches, and Shay is cursing loudly, and I can't tell if Riya has left us to fend for ourselves, and ... are the monsters back? I think I'm lying down. The world is tilting dangerously. My hands grasp to hold onto something, to keep myself from sliding off the edge of everything.

Rhylan. Rhylan? Why is he ... And Kieren. *Kieren.* I think I sigh his name. "What happened?" he demands. *"What happened?"* His words are strangely distant, as if reaching me through a tunnel.

Then the world tips completely and drops me into darkness.

❧

I'm aware of people arguing. One voice I recognize, the other is older, gruff, unfamiliar. They're speaking in that foreign tongue. The beautiful lilting one. I'm wandering the periphery of a nightmare, trying to find a way out, trying to follow the sound of their voices.

"But not like this!" the familiar voice explodes, in English now. I twist toward Kieren's voice, trying to drag my heavy eyelids open. A hand takes mine. Grips it tightly. "This is different," Kieren says, voice quieter but just as tense.

"Your Highness, we always knew this would be one of the more dangerous—"

"I know! But there were only supposed to be two possible outcomes. Either it—" He continues in that foreign tongue, leaving me lost once more. It's not a feeling I enjoy. Someone needs to unravel this confusion for me.

I make another attempt at forcing my eyelids open. I struggle to push myself up before collapsing back onto the bed. "What's ... going on?"

"Hush, you'll be fine. Don't try to get up." Through the blurry haze, I manage to make out Kieren's face, closer to mine now.

"But ... what ..." The question is there, on the edge of my tongue, but I can't seem to form the words. It's as impossible as keeping my eyes open.

"It would not be wise to return her to her own quarters." The other voice now. The one that was quietly arguing with Kieren. "If the other contestants see her like this, or the cameras ... even if you forbid them from showing this to the world, it would still get out. Perhaps find a different room for her, out of the way, until she is well enough to—"

"She will stay here. In my quarters. "

"Wow," I breathe out with intense difficulty. "That's ... not necessary."

"It is."

"Must be ... more suitable ..." I argue faintly. Even amid this confused jumble of thoughts and blurry images, I'm aware enough to know that sleeping in a prince's bed is *not* appropriate for me. "A ... a couch or ..."

"You will not lie on a *couch*."

The effort it took to force those few words from my tongue was clearly too much. I let go and succumb to the pull of the swirling darkness at the edge of my thoughts. The nightmare pulls me under again. I wade through it for an eternity while monsters snarl at me from the shadows.

Darkness.

Confusion.

Nothingness.

When I finally find myself rising to the surface again, I feel slightly more alert than last time. My thoughts are still muddled, my head still stuffed with cotton wool, but I can at least open my eyes. I blink a few times before forcing myself to sit up. I don't recognize the sheets, the bed, the room. The furniture is dark wood, the walls are navy with golden ornate accents, and almost one entire wall is open to a balcony where a circular pool shines silver with barely a ripple.

Part of me wonders if I'm still dreaming.

I push myself to the edge of the bed, trying to remember what happened and why I'm here. Do I even know where *here* is? There's an answer whispering at the back of my mind—it's *his* room, Prince Kieren's—but I'm not sure where that answer came from. My feet touch the cool floor. I stand. My head swims, and I grip the edge of the bed with a shaking hand as I stagger forward. I can't pass out. I can't pass out. I need to know where I ...

"Avery!"

Strong arms catch me before I hit the floor. Time loses meaning again. Images blur together. Patterns across the ceiling, endless puffy clouds of duvet trying to smother me. I think I'm trapped in a nightmare again, though there's no monstrous creature in this one. Just a bed and my shivering body and arms around me. Soft lips against my temple, and a deep voice so close I *feel* it rather than hear it. "You're okay. You're going to be okay." And eventually I drop off the edge and into oblivion.

Chapter Twenty-Three

I WAKE SLOWLY, MY EYES STILL CLOSED, MY LEGS sliding down over the deliciously cool sheets as I stretch and then roll over to snuggle further into my princess-perfect pillows. Wisps of memory begin rising to the surface. The Opal Ball, the kiss, my own fingers trailing over my lips as I fell asleep. I sigh into my pillow, hoping to return to my dreams of Kieren, trying to remember where they left off.

Then there's a jolt in my mind, and my stomach drops. I remember what came next. The monster. Everyone screaming, running, hiding. Trying to fight it off. Teeth and talons and deep gouges in my arm, and tossing deliriously in a bed that wasn't mine. Kieren's bed.

My eyes fly open and I sit up in a rush.

But I'm not in his bed. I'm in my own. All my furniture is in its usual place, and there is no blood on the carpet. I flinch as I remember the slicing, bone-deep pain, and my gaze drops immediately to my left arm. But there's nothing there. No wounds, no scars, not even a scratch. I run my hand over the perfect, unmarred skin. "What the actual hell?" I whisper.

I climb out of bed and dress hastily, not waiting for Iris to come in and tell me what I'm supposed to be wearing today. With my hand on the doorknob, I look around my room once more. Completely normal. *How?* I catch sight of the time on the little clock beside my bed and realize it's later than I thought. Strange that Iris hasn't come in yet. I pull the door open and hurry out in search of answers.

Downstairs, I find most of the remaining contestants gathered in the hallway outside the dining room. Evanna and Carwyn are there. No sign of any cameras, which is strange. The hosts don't generally show up unless something needs to be filmed.

"Yes, my aide was there, but she left quickly," Annemarie is saying to Lina. "Yours didn't wake you this morning?"

Lina shakes her head. "Oh, there you are," she says to me as I stop beside them.

"What's going on?" I ask.

"No idea. People are talking about some kind of—"

"My dears," Evanna calls out. She smiles widely. "Are we all here now? Ah ... yes, Shay, dear. Hurry up, hurry up."

I look around and see Shay shuffling toward us, a look of deep suspicion on her face. My eyes go to her arms immediately —they were definitely covered in blood last night—but they're as unmarred as my own. I look around for Riya and spot her on Annemarie's other side. Standing in a pretty ankle-length dress with her hands clasped demurely in front of her, it's difficult to picture her as the girl who wielded a knife and fought off monsters.

"The palace has asked us to address you this morning," Carwyn says, "because some of you are concerned about an incident that you believe took place during the night. An incident involving several ferocious fae beasts. We would like to assure you that this was nothing more than a complex illusion that—"

"Excuse me?" A few heads turn in my direction, and I realize I've spoken out loud.

"That was no illusion," Riya mutters, just loud enough for me to hear.

"Right?" I whisper in return. "There's no way that wasn't real."

"Honestly?" Lina murmurs, leaning closer to me. "I thought it was a dream when I woke up. Like, with super hazy details that started to slip away almost immediately."

"Really?" I look at her. Everything that happened in Kieren's room is hazy—as if I was drugged or half asleep when I was in there—but the details of everything that came before it are still painfully clear in my mind.

"... young daughter of one of our visiting noble families," Carwyn is busy saying. "She was playing around in the middle of the night, experimenting with her sister. They were trying to outdo one another with fearsome illusions, as young children are prone to do at times." He laughs his loud, boisterous laugh. "They pushed things a little too far, that's all. Sent their illusions racing around the palace instead of confining them to their own suite."

"Such bullshit," Shay mutters behind me.

"It seems," whispers that voice I've come to hate, "we finally agree on something." Natalya, standing just in front of me, peeks over her shoulder. "Not that I'm stupid enough to publicly argue about it. I almost *died* last night, but you don't see me complaining about it."

"Now there is another matter we need to address," Evanna says as I pull my head back. "A few girls have requested to leave, and we need to remind you that you are contractually bound to remain at the Glittering Palace until Prince Kieren dismisses you."

"Seriously?" Shay says. "We can't *choose* to leave?"

"Correct. But you are already aware of this, since you signed a contract that stipulated as such."

But Shay is shaking her head. "What about those two girls at the beginning? The ones who ended up in hospital after drinking that faerie wine or whatever it was? We were told they *chose* not to return."

"It is correct that they had no desire to return, but Prince Kieren had already decided to dismiss them. If he had wanted to keep them around, they would have been politely reminded—as you are being reminded right now—that they could not choose to leave the game."

"But—"

"Their names were read out at the first dismissal, thus formally releasing them from their contracts."

"Well, you're going to be hearing from my family's team of lawyers," Gigi says, arms crossed tightly over her chest. "They'll find a way to get me out of—"

"They will not," Evanna politely corrects. "The contract is magical."

"The contract is ... *magical*?" Gigi whispers in response.

Voices erupt across the space as everyone starts speaking over everyone else. "What are you all going on about?" Cadence demands, a panicked look crossing her face. "Did I miss out because I was asleep? I was so tired after the ball, I didn't wake once."

"Me neither," Annemarie says, her uncertain gaze darting around. "I don't think it's anything to be concerned about. I've spoken to two other girls who also slept through the whole thing."

"Shay's right," I mutter to Lina. "This is bullshit."

"Why, what happened?"

I shake my head and start backing away from the group. "I'll tell you later. I'm going to find someone who can give me a real answer."

I walk away before she can protest, determined to find Kieren. Something isn't right about all of this. Either I'm losing my mind, or it definitely happened. It was *so real*. That pain. There's no way I—

"Miss Avery!" Iris says as I almost walk into her.

"Iris—"

"I'm so, so sorry I wasn't there this morning to wake you! I was a little bit late, but I was *just* about to come to your suite when all the aides were summoned for a meeting."

"That's okay, it's fine. I know how to get myself out of bed. But—your meeting. Were they telling you the same thing? That the attack last night wasn't real?"

"The illusion of monsters roaming the corridors? Yes, they said it was just children playing around with their magic. I didn't know anything about it—I don't think any of the aides did. We couldn't hear anything from our rooms, but apparently some of the contestants were very upset over it. Did you see something last night?"

"Did I—Iris, I was attacked. So were Riya and Shay. The creature ripped through my arm."

She blinks at me. I watch as her gaze shifts to my bare arms, then back to my face. "But your arms are fine. None of it was real."

"It was definitely real. Someone must have healed me. With magic, obviously. And then put me back into my bed." I leave out the part about spending some time in Prince Kieren's room during the night.

"But ... okay. If that's true, then why are they lying about the whole thing?"

"Come on, Iris. Because they don't want it getting out that this place is legitimately *dangerous*!" I pace away from her, my hands on my hips, then look back over my shoulder. "Are you still posting on all my social media platforms?"

"Of course. It's a requirement for the show. You know I'm always snapping photos of you when—"

"Okay, yes." I turn to face her again. "So have you seen anything today about this incident? Is anyone outside of the palace talking about it?"

"I did do a quick skim through some of your feeds this morning before I was about to come to your suite, but I didn't see anything. I've been keeping an eye on some of the hater accounts, just to—"

"Hater accounts?"

"Sorry, that's just what I call them in my head. The accounts that are publicly against *The Princess Game*. They're hypercritical, they don't believe anything the fae say. They like to pick apart what they think the Autumn Court's true agenda is."

"Huh. Okay." Kinda sounds like Quinn and me before I got here.

"There was a lot of discussion after the first episode about the girls who got sick from the fae drinks. There was some mainstream media backlash about that as well, people talking about how it isn't actually safe for humans to be at the Glittering Palace. But some palace representatives made a few public announcements about it being accidental and about upping their precautionary measures, so that mostly died down. Then there was some public discourse after those weird ribbons turned on all of you while you were playing with magic. A bunch of people said that you were almost all strangled and that *The Princess Game* should be called off immediately."

"Okay. So you're saying that even if it isn't public yet, someone will most likely get wind of last night's incident as well, and they'll probably try to turn it into a huge deal. Which it *was*. And then the Glittering Palace will explain it away, and most people will believe it really was just a harmless illusion, and the game will continue."

"Well ... you can see why people would believe that, right?" Iris says carefully. "You all woke up fine this morning in your own beds."

I shake my head, staring past her, my thoughts racing. "Last night wasn't the illusion, Iris. This—our perfectly healed skin and untouched bedrooms—is the illusion." I drop my hands to my sides and head past her.

"Wait, Avery—Miss Avery—where are you—"

"To find someone who knows the answer to all of this," I call without looking back. I make my way to the North Tower, not stopping to question whether I'm about to land myself in enormous trouble. My feet are fueled by the knowledge that we're all being lied to and that *something* else is going on here. But my indignation begins to waver when I'm about halfway up the tower stairs. Fear whispers at the edge of my mind. I'm not supposed to be here. It's still forbidden, and this time I don't have the prince's permission.

But I don't turn back. I reach the floor where the music room is and start to cautiously look around. Kieren has mentioned more than once that his quarters are close by, which makes me think they're on the same floor. I peek around two other doors and find smaller sitting areas. A third open doorway leads to a corridor that curves around the outer edge of the tower. I follow it, my heart climbing into my throat and fluttering rapidly. There's nowhere to hide if I hear someone coming. No crevices or furniture.

I follow the curve of the corridor until it opens abruptly to a large space. There's no door to peek around, no small antechamber in which to take a deep breath and gather my thoughts. I'm just suddenly there, standing at the edge of the bedroom I recognize from my hazy memories of last night. And he's there too, standing near the open wardrobe, doing up the buttons of a shirt. My silly brain chooses this moment to remind me of the words I so casually tossed over my shoulder at him the other night: *I doubt you have any idea how to remove your* own *clothes, never mind someone else's.* Of course I was wrong. I've been wrong about pretty much everything when it comes to him.

"Did I dream you?" I ask quietly. Words, as always, fall from my tongue before I can decide if they're the right ones.

Kieren startles as he looks up. "Avery." He breathes my name in a way that sends a shiver dancing along my skin as a dozen emotions flicker in rapid succession across his normally impassive face. Then he shakes his head, confusion clouding his expression. "What did you say?"

"We were attacked last night. I passed out because of a horrible wound from a very real, very deadly monster. Now my wounds are gone, and I'm being told the entire thing was nothing more than an illusion gone wrong. So please answer this: The part where I tossed and turned in your bed, where you held my hand and argued with someone, where you caught me before I passed out once again—did I dream all of that?" He doesn't answer, but I know at once from his expression that I'm right. It was all real. "Tell me!" I insist, moving further into the room. "My arm was almost *shredded*! Don't you think I have a right to know the truth about that?"

"You should not remember the truth," he says, his words so quiet they're almost a whisper.

"What?"

"There are things I cannot—" He stops, eyes darting past me. I hear footsteps and—

"Kieren?" The queen's voice.

Kieren grabs my arm and tugs me around the side of his wardrobe. From the entrance to his bedroom, we're now hidden from view. His body is pressed right against mine, and holy freaking shit we're invisible. We're *invisible.* My heart sends blood pounding through my veins, a rapid staccato against my eardrums.

"Mela nís alleneah adar—" Queen Erralee breaks off, presumably because she's been met by an empty room. I hear her sigh of frustration. She mutters something beneath her breath, but I don't hear her leave.

Kieren's hand on my arm squeezes a little tighter. Though I can't see him, I can feel how close he is, and suddenly my body doesn't care all that much about the attack last night. Instead, I'm remembering the dreams that came before it. The fevered way I kissed him. The desperate need for—

Footsteps recede. Silence. "I think she's gone," Kieren whispers. We both reappear. He steps past me and leans forward to press his hands against his knees. Then he straightens, breathing heavily. "I apologize. That kind of glamour is ... difficult. Blending completely into one's background. It requires a great deal of focus."

"I ... um ... thank you for hiding me." It terrifies me to imagine what kind of trouble I would be in if the queen discovered me in here. Then again, given the type of game we're playing and the nature of the relationship Kieren is meant to be in search of, perhaps it wouldn't surprise his mother to find one of the contestants in his bedroom. Perhaps he's already had—

I stop that thought before it can go further. I don't need to picture that. I'm not the girl he's going to end up with, and I don't need to know if he's been intimate with any of—

Stop, stop, stop.

"Um ..." I blink and shake my head. "Last night—"

"I have to go. I'm so sorry. I think my father wants to see me."

"Kieren—"

"But I will speak to you tonight. No, tomorrow night." He lets out a frustrated sigh. "I already have something on tonight. I'll send you an official invitation for a date. A private one. Word will spread, of course, and I'm sure someone will mention it on the show, but that's fine. After the ... the kiss last night, people will wonder why we haven't been out more together." He doesn't look at me as he stumbles over this mention of 'the kiss' neither of us planned on. "But the date itself will be private," he continues. "No cameras. We can discuss ... last night."

I suddenly wonder if he means the attack or the kiss. I came looking for him wanting answers for the former, but I'm just as curious about the latter. Why did he kiss *me*? Was it simply the easiest decision in the moment? Kiss the girl who was already in his arms instead of having to decide on one of the others?

I exhale and bite back all my questions. "Okay. Tomorrow night then."

So I leave the North Tower and return to the dining room where everything seems back to normal. Well, 'normal' with an undercurrent of tension. Natalya is unusually quiet, and Shay and Riya don't seem to be eating. But no one says anything about canceling the show. No one suggests we may be in terrible danger here. The food is delicious as always and the morning sunlight is warm and no one is demanding to be sent home. At least half the girls, including Lina, are now chattering happily away as if they've already forgotten last night. Perhaps they have. I dish up a plate of food for myself and try to pretend I have an appetite.

Chapter Twenty-Four

"No," I say to Finneas as he turns me to face the mirror. "Absolutely not. This is basically lingerie."

"It is *not*," he says with a horrified gasp, placing one hand against his chest. We both stare at the pale blue dress he's put together for my date with Prince Kieren, a piece that's little more than sheer, floaty fabric covered in twisting flowers and leaves. The skirt seems to have enough layers that I can't see through to my underwear, thank goodness, but the top part is essentially two triangles of sheer fabric covered in strategically positioned flowers and leaves.

"I don't know why you're so shocked," Finneas says. "This isn't all that different from the last few dresses you've worn. I've slowly been moving you toward more traditional faerie wear, so I thought you'd be okay with something like this by now."

"*This* is traditional faerie wear? You must be joking. I thought the fae were all prim and prissy about these kinds of things."

He lets out a hoot of laughter. "You got a lot of things wrong about the fae, love."

I blink at him. "What did I—"

"For example, you had the wrong idea about *us* when you first got here."

"What do you mean?"

"You think we couldn't tell how uncomfortable you were around us when you first got here? That you didn't trust us? Simply because we're fae?"

Behind me, pinning tiny sparkling stones into my loose curls, Mischa chuckles in a way that makes me think she agrees with him.

"It wasn't *you* I was uncomfortable around," I protest, though I know there's some truth to his words. "It was all of ... this." I gesture broadly at my magnificent suite.

"Okay, sure. Let's say it was everything. Including us."

"I ... Finneas ..."

"But you like us now. You know we're spectacularly awesome. You realize you were wrong. So it shouldn't be too difficult to accept that other ideas you hold about the fae are also wrong."

"But ... didn't my contract for *The Princess Game* have specific stipulations about what's considered appropriate clothing?"

"Yes. Because the whole thing is being televised. Not because *we* care about such things."

"But the royal fae ... whenever they make public appearances in our world ..."

"Because you lot were already uncomfortable with the idea of magical beings that supposedly sprang straight out of myth. The royals didn't want to make things worse by parading around in sheer flowery creations as if they'd just stepped out of some ancient ritual from one of the many strange tales you humans have concocted over the years. Didn't you notice the clothing when you were at the opera?"

"Um ... not really?" I attempt to cast my mind back to that evening. "I suppose some of it was on the more revealing side."

"Exactly."

"But ..." I'm still fumbling for evidence to back up my theories about the fae. "Prince Kieren. He's ... I mean he's the epitome of stiff and formal."

"Oh, that's just his personality, love," Finneas says with a dismissive wave of his hand. "The man is reserved, withdrawn, slow to warm up. That has absolutely nothing to do with the style of clothing traditionally favored by the majority of the fae population."

I pause. "Oh."

"Now please tell me why you're panicking about this dress." He stands beside me while Mischa moves to my other side and they both admire my reflection. "It's stunning! I wouldn't dress you in this for the ballroom, of course. I know you wouldn't be comfortable with that. But you have a private date tonight. No cameras. The prince won't be able to keep his eyes off you."

"I guess, maybe," I mumble. Finneas doesn't know that the real reason for tonight's date is so Kieren can explain what the other night's attack was really about. That's beside the point, though. I can tell I'm not going to win this argument about the dress. I sigh, peering over my shoulder at my reflection. "Fine. I suppose as long as it doesn't go too low at the back—"

"The back is fine, love. It's positively prudish."

"That is so not true," I mutter. "Do you have a coat or something I can put over it? For when I walk through the palace."

"A *coat*," Finneas scoffs. "No, love, I have the most delightful cape for you to wear. I assumed you wouldn't want anyone seeing this magnificent work of art—"

"This lingerie?"

"—while you're walking downstairs and across the main foyer," he finishes, ignoring my interruption. "Here you go." He beckons with curled fingers, and something silvery flies out of my dressing room. Finneas catches it from the air and places it carefully over my shoulders. The soft fabric falls like liquid over my arms. I resist the urge to rub it between my fingers, to lift an edge and press it to my cheek. *Don't be weird, Avery.* Finneas stands in front of me and fastens the cape with a glittering brooch at the hollow of my neck.

"So ... are these glass crystals or something like that?" I ask, touching the brooch.

He makes a noise in the back of his throat. "Haven't I told you already that I only use real materials?"

"Well, yes, but that means you used real glass, doesn't it? This isn't some imaginary illusion holding my cape together?"

He laughs. "You still think that's all our magic boils down to? Impermanent illusions? Love, those are real diamonds at your throat. And those tiny sparkles among the flowers and leaves all over your dress? Diamonds. And the itty bitty ones in your hair? Diamonds."

I pause, my mouth half open. "They ... but ..."

"Didn't you believe me," Iris says from my sitting area, "when I said the Glittering Palace has spared no expense for this competition?"

"Well, I ..."

"And you look completely amazing, by the way."

I lower my hand, staring at my reflection, mesmerized by the way the diamonds catch the light. I haven't forgotten that there's something else going on beneath all this glitter and opulence, but for a moment all I can do is wonder at the sheer fairytale-ness of it all. I'm in a palace, surrounded by fae nobility and magic beyond my comprehension, my body glittering with diamonds and a prince waiting to spend the evening with me. It's all just a little bit crazy.

When I'm ready to leave, Lina meets me at the end of our corridor, already in her pajamas. "Ooh, off to your fancy date with Prince Charming?"

I roll my eyes. "You know that's not what this is. I'm just trying to find answers about what really happened the other night."

She reaches for the edge of my cape, and I don't move away as she lifts it just enough to get a peek at the dress beneath. She arches a brow. "Well, your retinue clearly doesn't know that's all tonight is about."

"No, they don't."

Her expression becomes more serious. "Look, I know I didn't have the same experience as you the other night, but if you say there's something else going on here, I believe you. Just let me know what it is when you find out."

I nod as I step past her onto the stairs. "I will." I pass a few other girls on my way down to the main foyer, keeping my gaze averted. I'm sure they can all guess I'm off to spend an evening with the prince, and I don't want to see the looks they're sending my way.

I'm almost at the bottom of the grand staircase when someone calls out loudly from behind me. "So. Is that your secret weapon then? *Sex?*"

I'm so startled I stop walking. The voice belongs to Cadence, but she can't possibly have been speaking to me, can she? I turn and look back up the stairs. She's a few steps above me, and her gaze, instead of being pinned on me, is directed somewhere behind me. I look back down the stairs and find Natalya at the bottom. I see a flicker of surprise, possibly even fear, but both are wiped away an instant later as a satisfied smirk curves her lips. "Should I bother trying to deny it?" she says, placing one foot on the first step.

"No," Cadence answers. "Annemarie saw you coming out of the North Tower early this morning looking all disheveled and far too pleased with yourself, and we know you had a date with him last night. Easy to put the pieces together."

A hole opens up inside me and my stomach drops clean through it. *The North Tower.* The royal family's private quarters. Kieren's private quarters. *I already have something on tonight.* That's what he said yesterday morning, though he failed to add that that 'something' was a date with Natalya. My head is suddenly spinning, my body as numb and tingly as if I've been plunged into ice.

"Well, I guess I've been caught then," Natalya says with a careless shrug.

"You really are low," Cadence snaps. "This has been your plan from the beginning? Your 'secret weapon'? Get him into bed, and you think that's all it will take to convince him to choose you?"

Natalya's sultry smile spreads wider. "If you heard the way he gasped my name, you wouldn't doubt it."

I grip the handrail so tightly my fingers ache. I'm sick, numb, dizzy. I want to hurt her. I want to hurt *him*. But I force myself to move, jerky motions down the last few steps, my eyes pointed determinedly past her. I'm desperate to get away from her, to get *out*, to be alone. I think she snickers something as I move past her, but the pounding in my ears is too loud for me to make out her words. My reaction is ridiculous. I know it is. Kieren owes me nothing. He isn't *mine*. I'm not supposed to care this much about him. I'm not supposed to care *at all*.

I blink the tears away with vicious force as I descend the front steps outside the palace. The cool night air caresses my skin. I stand still, close my eyes, and instruct myself to breathe. "Be happy, be happy," I whisper out of habit. But the words fall from shaking lips, and happiness seems an impossibility right now. I take another deep breath and remind myself that he's fae. That I don't like the fae. That so many of them are conniving and false, that all they do is *use* humans, and do I really want to bind myself to one of them?

Of course not. I've never wanted that.

Feeling a little calmer, I open my eyes and look around. One of those golden carriages with the magically animated golden horse is waiting in the driveway beside the fountain, but I don't see Kieren anywhere. His invitation definitely requested I meet him here, though, so I wait.

My thoughts turn to this week's episode of *The Princess Game*, probably airing right now. Will the supposed attack 'illusion' come up, or will the palace have ensured that all mention of it has been removed? Most likely the latter. The kiss will certainly be included, though. The kiss at the Opal Ball. It'll probably be the climax of the episode. What will Quinn think when she sees it? Will she notice the way I was completely captivated by the moment, by Kieren's lips on mine and the way his hands so gently cupped my face?

Worse still, were there any cameras around when Natalya snuck out of the North Tower this morning looking, as Cadence put it, all disheveled and far too pleased with herself? If so, I have no doubt that someone will have squeezed it into the episode at the last minute. It'll probably be the cliffhanger right at the end. Oh, the drama! Prince Kieren kisses Miss Girl Next Door and then goes on to sleep with Miss Olympic Gymnast. Tune in next week for the fallout!

I squeeze my eyes shut as another crack fractures my heart. I know I have to tell Quinn the truth about all of this, about the fact that I haven't been acting and that I've stupidly allowed myself to fall for the prince. And perhaps I shouldn't be so scared of her reaction. She is my best friend, after all. Hopefully she'll understand after I explain—

"Miss Avery?"

I look around at the sound of Illiam's voice. He hurries down the stairs and stops in front of me with a bow. "Good evening, Miss Avery. There has been a slight change of plan. Prince Kieren will meet us there."

"Okay. Um, where? I don't actually know where we're going."

"Faeworld. To the Royal Autumn Opera House."

Despite the ache that's settled at the core of my being, a shiver of delight courses through me. This is followed by the thought, *He noticed how much I loved it there*. And then: *But one can't exactly have an in-depth conversation while watching an opera. Is he trying to distract me?* And finally: *Don't forget he slept with Natalya.*

My emotions play a tug of war inside me as we soar through the Shimmer and across the early evening sky. The last traces of sunset still color the horizon, while stars twinkle higher up against the dark velvety blue. I can't help wishing Kieren was sitting beside me, taking in this breathtaking view with me. And then I remember he's the reason my heart is sore, and I'm relieved he isn't here.

This is what the game is supposed to be like, I realize. Falling for him while knowing that he's pursuing other options at the same time. There must be other girls who genuinely care about him who feel the same way whenever they see him spending time with someone else. But they came into this game expecting it, while I'm the idiot who's been blindsided by my own foolish heart.

I focus on the glittering details of the tall glass structures and the graceful, otherworldly trees as the carriage heads through the Golden City. There's something about this world that seems vibrant and alive in a way my own world has never felt to me, even with the strange way things seem to disintegrate at the edges. As I stare out of the carriage, I can't deny the almost physical tug in my chest. The longing to climb out of the carriage, to walk the golden tree-lined streets, to immerse myself in this world and learn more of its people, its cultures, its traditions, its magic. I know so little. The fae have *allowed* us to know so little.

We arrive at the opera house where there is far less activity tonight than the first time I was here. I assume, as Illiam leads me through the arched doorway and I see only two or three people standing around in the foyer, that we must be late. We ascend the stairs to the upper part of the theatre—no orchestra pit for me this time, I think with some sadness—and head for one of the closed doors. Illiam heaves it open for me, and ... the vast space on the other side is entirely empty.

"Oh, wait," I say, stopping in the doorway. "I think we're in the wrong place. There's no one here."

"No, I believe this is correct, Miss Avery. Prince Kieren specifically said he would meet you here. He mentioned hiring the entire space for the evening."

"The entire ..." I look back into the enormous space. Does he want to have our private conversation in an empty opera theatre? Except, now that I'm paying attention, I can hear the sounds of instruments being tuned and musicians warming up. There's definitely *something* happening here tonight.

Illiam directs me to a seat in the front center of the balcony area. "Would you like me to take your cape, Miss Avery?"

"Oh, uh ... yes, I suppose I'm not supposed to be wearing it now that I'm inside." Not that there's anyone else around to judge me for what I'm supposed to or not supposed to be wearing. I undo the clasp at my neck and hand Illiam the cape. He disappears, and I sit. The musicians continue to warm up, time ticks by, and I begin to feel awkward. I try not to pick at my nails —Mischa would be so upset if I ruined the pretty blue polish with tiny silver leaf patterns painted onto each nail—and instead start to count the seats.

I'm not sure how much time has passed when Illiam finally returns to my row, but it feels like far too much. "Is he here?" I ask quietly as Illiam bends to speak to me.

"No, Miss Avery." He hesitates, then adds, "The conductor is asking whether he should begin."

"I ... I don't know? What would Kieren—um, the prince— what would he tell you to do?"

"It's entirely up to you, Miss Avery."

"Then, um ..." I'm torn. It would be rude to begin whatever this is without waiting for the man who organized it all, but I'm mindful of the orchestra and the performers, no doubt growing restless, and I feel bad for them. If we still have to get through an entire opera, we should probably start now. And whatever it is, Kieren has probably seen it before. "Okay. Tell the conductor he can begin. Thank you."

Illiam nods and straightens.

"Wait, Illiam." I catch his arm before he can leave, then immediately let go. He bends again and waits patiently for me to speak. "Is this ... is it normal for the prince to be so late? I mean, do you think he's okay?"

"I'm sure he's perfectly fine, Miss Avery. Sometimes things come up that keep him busy for longer than expected."

I nod. Of course he has plenty of other things going on, many of them likely more important than an opera performance. *Like Natalya*, my traitorous brain whispers. I stamp the thought down immediately, take a deep breath, and settle further back into my seat. The lights dim, and I wait for the curtain on stage to go up, but nothing happens.

Then the music begins. The opening notes from a single violin soar through the air and snatch my breath away. A shiver raises every hair on my body. It's my piece. It's *my music*. The rest of the strings join in, and everything swims before me as a sheen of moisture coats my eyes. I'm lightheaded and my hands are sweating and it's so beautiful I think I'm crying. They're playing *my music*.

I shut my eyes and feel my mind transported away from this auditorium as the sound encompasses me. I step across clouds and drift beyond stars and my arms sweep out around me as I reach out and touch every color of every instrument as the sound lights up an imaginary sky like an aurora.

In reality, the piece isn't all that long. Around eight minutes in total. But I remember what a gigantic accomplishment it felt like to write something of that length for so many instruments. I remember sitting on my bed listening to it through my headphones. It didn't sound half bad when I used synthesized sounds for all the instruments and put everything together. But that was nothing, *nothing* compared to the glorious sound filling this magnificent space. Surely I was not the one who wrote this. This couldn't have come from *my head*, could it?

My cheeks are wet with tears when the music comes to an end. This is more than anything I could ever have dreamed of, and I don't understand how Kieren could do this beautiful, perfect thing for me after he spent the night with Natalya. It makes no sense.

And he still isn't here.

On the return trip, I lean my head against the side of the carriage, unable to keep the smile from my lips despite the edge of concern I feel for Kieren and the painful tug in my chest every time I think of him with Natalya. I stare into the night as the music continues to play in my head. I'm floating as high as the clouds we're soaring past.

Illiam escorts me to the music room once we're back inside the Glittering Palace. "You can wait here. I'm sure Prince Kieren will join you shortly."

"Thank you." I examine Illiam's face before he turns, searching for any hint of concern, but his expression betrays nothing. I don't know if that means I have nothing to worry about or if he's simply well trained.

I sit on one of the uncomfortable couches, but when Kieren doesn't appear within the first few minutes, I move to the piano. My fingers position themselves automatically on the opening notes of tonight's orchestral piece and begin playing through the main melody. It's a pattern my hands know so well I could probably play it in my sleep. The world around me falls away, and I sink into that trance-like state where all that exists is the music.

But it doesn't last forever. The music ends, and I blink and look around, and the room is still empty. A jolt of anxiety shoots through me as I'm gripped by the certainty that *something isn't right*. Kieren has never left me waiting like this. On any evening that we've agreed to meet, he's always been on time.

I slide off the piano seat and move to the doorway. I peep out, but Illiam isn't there. The landing is empty save for the ever-present arrangements of exotic fresh flowers. I slip my shoes off and tiptoe toward the curving passageway that leads to

Kieren's quarters. With one last look over my shoulder, I keep going. My heart pounds faster with every step I take. I tell myself it's unlikely I'll find answers there. The room will be empty. Of course Kieren won't be there, because if he was so close by, then why wouldn't he come to the music room?

But I reach his room and my searching eyes dart across the space and *there he is*. One hand pressed against a wall, his face screwed up in pain, and multiple bloody gashes across his chest and arms.

Chapter Twenty-Five

"Kieren! What happened?"

He jerks around, shoving away from the wall. "Avery. I'm so sorry." He struggles to remove his torn shirt, grimacing as he attempts to pull it down over one bloodied arm. "I realize I'm late. Terribly late. I was on my way to you."

"Like *this*?" I rush to his side, reaching for the edge of the shirt to help him.

"Well, I was planning to clean up first." He clenches his teeth as I peel the fabric away from his wounded skin and down over his right arm.

"Should I call someone? Illiam or—"

"No, no. I'll be fine shortly. I just—" He winces again as I slowly pull the other sleeve down over his left arm. Some of the wounds are straight slashes, while others have a strange spiral pattern to them. I drop the shredded piece of fabric onto the floor.

"Fine?" I repeat. "I don't think you'll be *fine shortly*."

"I will be. I just need to get into the pool."

"The pool?" I release a short bark of a laugh. "You think now is a good time for a swim?"

"Healing magic," he says as he limps past me onto the balcony. "In the water." I hurry to his side again, hovering in a protective manner even though I have no idea how I would help him if he suddenly collapsed. He stops at the pool's edge and lowers himself carefully, shakily until he's sitting. Up close, I see that the water is silver, like liquid mercury. Kieren eases forward and slides in, sinking low until only his head and neck are above the surface. He exhales slowly and looks up at me. "You were in here the night before last."

"I—I was?" Now *that* I have no memory of.

"Well, your arm was. I brought you here immediately, knowing the pool would help. Your arm healed quickly, but it seemed it was more than a mere wound. You woke, delirious, and I realized there was something else going on. You did eventually recover—clearly—but I still don't understand what caused your fevered delirium."

I lower myself to the floor beside the pool and cross my legs beneath the layers of my dress. "That creature. Perhaps it had some kind of venom. It could have poisoned my blood when it bit me."

Kieren shakes his head. "That creature is not venomous. A bite from its teeth should not have had that kind of effect on you. I'm so sorry."

"What happened to *you*?" I ask again. "Was it the same thing? The same animal?"

"No. It was ... I was trying to deal with something."

Again with the evasive answers. "*Deal* with something?"

"Yes."

"And does this something happen often?" My eyes catch on a spiral wound at the top of his neck, just above the level of the water. "Seeing as how you have a magic healing pool right next to your bedroom?"

This time, he doesn't answer at all. I figure that's probably a 'yes.' So there are strange shadow creatures that attack without leaving a trace, there are ferocious winged, fanged beasts that can send a person into a delirious haze, and there's something else that leaves deep gashes and strange spiral wounds. The Autumn Court would have us believe that the Glittering Palace is a fairy-tale come to life. A perfect, sparkling dream filled with magical wonders beyond our imaginations. But all fairytales have monsters, and this place is no different.

Kieren straightens, his shoulders and upper arms rising above the water. I'm startled to see that the wounds are already gone. Blood, however, still stains his skin. I shift forward until I'm sitting right at the edge of the pool, then bunch my dress up around my knees and lower my feet into the water. "Come closer," I tell him, not allowing myself to stop and consider whether this is a good idea. He remains still for another moment, eyes trained on my face. Then he moves closer. I gesture for him to turn around. His back brushes against one of my knees for just a moment, but it's enough to send an electric jolt through my body and a shiver across my skin. Then there is space between us again, and I remember how to breathe. I tell myself to stop being so ridiculously stupid. *He's just a friend and I'm helping him.*

I reach forward and scoop water onto his skin before gently rubbing across his shoulders and upper back, removing all traces of blood. It vanishes in the water, leaving the ripples as pristinely silver as when he slid into the pool. *How nice*, I think in some distracted recess of my mind, *to have a pool that keeps itself clean.*

"What really happened the other night?" I ask quietly, forcing myself to remember the main reason we agreed to meet tonight. "I know those beasts were real and not an illusion. What were they doing here? Were they only in our part—the contestants' part—of the palace? Or did they attack some of the other guests and the staff? Did they come here, to the North Tower?"

He shakes his head. "They were not here. They got into your section of the palace first and we stopped them before they could go further." He pauses, and though I can't see his expression, I can see enough of the side of his face to watch the way he clenches his jaw. "These creatures are not normally found anywhere near the Shimmer. We caught them recently. They were in a highly guarded part of the palace, below ground, far from any staff or guests. They ... got loose." He turns to face me. "I'm so sorry, Avery. When I found you—"

"It wasn't your fault," I remind him.

"It—" He squeezes his eyes shut, jaw tense again. After a deep breath, he says, "Please tell me what happened."

I bite my lip, then nod. "I ... I woke up because of the screams." Kieren winces and mutters something in his own language. "I found girls out in the corridor," I continue, "and then someone yelled at us to all get back inside our rooms. Someone who must have seen the monster coming. Everyone hid. Well, except me. I could see Riya coming, with that *thing* chasing behind her, and I didn't want to leave her out there on her own. But she had a knife and she was fighting back, and ..." I frown and look past him, remembering the way Riya moved. "I forgot about that part, but she seemed unusually good. Both with the knife and the way she darted around the creature. Like she knew what she was doing. Then she raced into my room, and I slammed the door."

Kieren is watching me closely. "But Shay was also in your room when Rhylan and I got there. And you were all injured."

"We heard Shay out in the corridor, trying to fight it off. Well, trying to fight off two of them by that point. The second one must have chased her into our corridor after I shut my door. So we went back out and Riya distracted them while I got Shay into my room, and that's when I got hurt."

"So the two beasts weren't attacking *you* specifically," Kieren says. "They were after Riya and Shay, and you were helping them, and that's how you ended up so badly hurt. And you—shit, it should *not* have happened, Avery. I'm so, so—"

"We were *all* hurt," I interrupt. "And yeah, I'm pretty sure they were attacked more than I was, but you don't seem to be all that concerned about *them*."

His frown deepens. "Of course I was concerned about them. I made sure they were taken to their rooms immediately where their injuries were treated. But you were the one who collapsed and became unresponsive and—" He shakes his head, eyes never leaving mine. "You are right. My concern for them was nothing in comparison to what I feel for you. You have come to mean far more to me than anyone else in this ridiculous game, and I could hardly bear to see you like that."

My breath is snatched away at the back of my throat. I forget how to form words, how to swallow, how to inhale oxygen. He has come to mean far more to *me* than he was ever supposed to, but I am the least of all the girls selected for this competition, and he is *not supposed to care about me more than the others.*

I force myself to look away. At the water, at the glint of moonlight catching on the ripples. What were we talking about again? The monsters. Right. The fact that we're all being lied to. "So, um ..." I clear my throat. "It was all a horrible accident. Nothing more than that? No one specifically trying to get the game called off? And the palace tried to make us all forget because of course this would be terrible publicity if it got out?"

"Yes. And more than that, I did not want any of you traumatized by the memory of it. We knew the spell would not be one hundred percent effective, but at most, you should have remembered the incident as little more than a dream. A collection of hazy moments easily brushed aside."

"Well ..." I let out a long sigh and look over my shoulder, back into his room and toward the bed. I remember puffy clouds of duvet all around me and the patterns of the ceiling sliding in and out of focus. "Some moments are definitely hazy," I murmur. I look back around and meet his eyes. "Dream or reality: I was in your bed."

"Reality."

"Dream or reality," I say again, my voice softer now. "You held me as you whispered that I would be okay."

His beautiful silver-blue eyes trace my features before he answers. "Reality."

He glides closer through the water, but I look away and force my next question from my lips before any of this—whatever *this* is—can go further. "Did you sleep with Natalya last night?"

He stops. My gaze shifts back to him in time to see the intense confusion on his face. "No," he answers. "Why would you think that?"

I hesitate, my eyes searching his, my heart not ready to trust that he's telling the truth in case it might be crushed again. But as far as I can see, there is no lie in his eyes. "Because she told us she did. And someone saw her coming out of the North Tower early this morning looking ... well, looking like she'd just spent the night with someone. And she had a date with you last night, didn't she? So it seemed plausible."

His frown deepens, his eyes focusing somewhere beyond

me. "We had a date, yes, but it certainly did not end that way. Whoever she was with, it was not me."

I let my eyes slide shut for several moments. I know I shouldn't feel this relief. He isn't *mine*. He can't choose me. We both know this. Still, whoever he ends up with, it shouldn't be Natalya. She'll only make his life miserable once she's won that tiara and a place within the Autumn Court. I open my eyes and ask, "Why is she still here? I've told you what she's really like. Don't you believe me?"

"I believe you. She acts differently in my presence, of course, but I can read enough between the lines to see what she's really like, even if you hadn't shared her true nature with me."

"So then ... why haven't you dismissed her yet?"

"I wish I could explain to you. There are reasons. Important reasons. That's all I can say."

My eyes are narrowed. I can't imagine what any of those reasons might be. Is there something about Natalya's family that I'm not aware of? Are they powerful in some way? "As long as none of those reasons have anything to do with you actually *liking* her."

He moves closer. Closer still. His chest brushes against my knees. "I can assure you they do not." Heat rushes through my body from the point of contact, but I don't move away. "Avery." His voice is husky. "Come into the water."

I swallow. "Why?"

"Because you want to. Because *I* want you to."

My blood pumps faster through my veins. My chest rises and falls with shallow breaths. Part of me is terrified of what will happen if I get into this pool with him, but another part of me hums with desperate, aching anticipation. He's right that I want this. That I want *him*. And that's a very good reason *not* to get in: because I can never have him.

He lifts his hands out of the water and places them on my thighs, just above my knees. For a moment I freeze. My brain pictures what comes next—him shoving my legs apart, forcing me down onto my back—and everything inside me threatens to shut down once more. But his hands make no further move, and my panic eases away before it can take hold of me. I remind myself, as I did the night he came across me in the palace gardens, that he is not the monster from my nightmares.

"If I'm wrong," he says, eyes never leaving mine, "if you don't want to get in, then tell me. I hope you know I would not force anything on you."

I don't trust myself to speak—I'm pretty sure my voice would come out all breathy and weird and embarrassing—so instead I answer by shifting myself forward and sliding into the water. I don't know what I'm doing. Being stupid, most likely. Putting my heart out there to be crushed. *You can't choose me*, I keep thinking, but I can't seem to force the words past my lips. I can't pull my gaze away from his either.

His hands settle at my waist, pulling me a little closer through the deliciously cool water. "I think I forgot to mention how beautiful you look tonight," he says.

"I think you were preoccupied with other things," I say with a wry smile, "like being horribly injured."

"Not too preoccupied to notice. Everything about you ... your sparkling eyes, your warm smile, this dress that is so very ... fae. You are magnificent."

My skin heats beneath his words. There was a time when I would have hated the idea of being dressed in something considered to be 'fae' in design, but I find that I don't mind now. In fact, with the way Kieren is looking at me, I like it very much.

"I know I was unable to meet you as planned earlier this

evening," he adds, "but I am very glad you came looking for me. I did not want to miss seeing you tonight."

I'm reminded abruptly of how this evening began. "Oh. The opera house. The orchestra." A giddy rush of joy floods my veins. "They played my music. *My* music."

He takes a breath, his brow wrinkling. "I hope that was okay. I hope I did not ... overstep."

"You hope it was *okay*?" I laugh. "It was the most incredible thing anyone's ever done for me."

He gives me a tentative smile, and I want to lift my hand to trace his lips with my fingers. "I asked your aide, Iris, to look for the music among your things," he says. "It was a risk, a violation of your privacy that you would have every right to be angry about, but you spoke of it being a dream of yours. To hear this specific piece of music played by a real orchestra. And I wanted to give you that."

I nod, a wide smile still stretching my lips and emotion tightening my throat. "Thank you," I manage to whisper. "So much."

His hands slide up the sides of my body. One hand rises out of the water to gently cup my face. He drags his thumb across my cheek, leaving a cool, wet streak across my burning skin. He is so close now. So close that there is barely a breath between us.

"You should not have kissed me," I whisper. "At the Opal Ball."

"I would kiss you again. Over and over." He lowers his head, angling it slightly until his lips graze over my cheekbone. "Everywhere," he murmurs.

My blood is liquid fire. My breath is a pair of quivering wings, trapped in my chest. My eyelids slide shut.

"You consume my thoughts," he says, lips whispering against my skin as he drags them down over my jaw. "My dreams." His mouth continues down the side of my neck. His fingers slide the sheer strip of fabric over the edge of my shoulder. Beneath the silvery water, I feel the fabric drift down, uncovering the part of my body it was already doing a poor job of concealing. A delicious shiver courses through me at the gentle caress of cool water against my bare breast.

Kieren presses a kiss against the curve of my neck, his hand still at my shoulder. "I would be lying," he murmurs, "if I said I had not replayed that evening in the music room over and over in my mind, wishing I could have unlaced the ribbons of that corset entirely."

My body ignites. There is an inferno rushing through my veins. Were I not in the water, I think I would be consumed by this fire.

"I did not think I could tell you these things," he says, lips gliding up the side of my neck again. "You were very clear in your opinion of me when you first arrived here. You hated me. And though my feelings for you have changed as the weeks have passed, I did not believe myself lucky enough that yours might have changed too. I believed you were only agreeable because of our bargain." He pauses when his lips reach the corner of my mouth. He pulls back a few inches. "But then the kiss ..." he murmurs. "The kiss I could not imagine giving anyone else. The kiss you say should not have happened. You returned that kiss. And I dared to hope that you may no longer hate me."

My eyes open, and my gaze rests on his. I swallow, trying to find my voice. "I ... don't hate you," I manage to whisper. "I really, *really* ... don't hate you."

All the fire consuming me is reflected in his silver-blue gaze. He dips his head, presses his mouth to mine, and my eyes glide shut again. His lips move with tantalizing slowness, deepening the kiss as his hand skims over my other shoulder, sliding the fabric down over my arm to expose my other breast. His hand cups it, thumb brushing over the erect peak, and I suck in a breath against his mouth as the sensation radiates all the way down to my core.

Like a spark that ignites me to life, I remember that I have use of my limbs. I free my arms entirely from the flimsy excuse for sleeves and press my palms against Kieren's chest before sliding them upward. My fingers curl around the back of his neck and pull him closer to me, deepening the kiss further. We are skin to skin, heartbeat to heartbeat, breath to breath, and there is a groan at the back of his throat as he lifts me and wraps my legs around his waist.

Then his hands are at my lower back, pressing into my skin, pulling me tight against him, and I wish the silly dress wasn't tangled between us. Even so, the thin layers of fabric don't prevent me from feeling his hard length pressed between my legs. My heart pounds wildly, recklessly. Part terror, part pure exhilaration. I have never done this, never gone this far, but I want it, I want *more*, I want—

"What is this?" Kieren pulls away, breaking the kiss. Breathless, I blink at him. My thoughts are still tangled up in the heady rush of it all, and I have no idea what he's talking about. Then his hands skim across my lower back, his fingers following the ridges of skin, and everything comes to a frozen halt.

I am instantly ice cold.

"Avery?" Kieren prompts.

"Nothing," I answer automatically.

He pulls back a further few inches, frowning. "This is not *nothing*."

"They're just ... scars."

"From what?" He hesitates, gaze darkening. "*Who?*"

"It doesn't matter."

"I will say this again, because clearly it did not sink in the first time: it matters to *me*." His hand brushes gently over my skin again, but my legs slip down and I pull free of his grasp. I fumble with the tangled dress floating around my waist, trying to find the sleeves so I can pull them back on. I should never have got into this pool. Should never have let things go this far.

"Avery, please. Talk to me."

I shake my head, staring determinedly into the water despite the fact that I can see nothing below its surface. I force my hands to slow down, to feel properly, and I finally find the two insubstantial pieces of fabric that are meant to run up each side of my torso and over my shoulders. I pull them on, hoping the small flowers and leaves are still positioned correctly. I move to one side of the pool, intending to hoist myself up. Kieren follows me.

"Wait. Please don't leave."

"I have to," I mutter. "I shouldn't be here." The scars are a cold reminder of what men with power—what *fae* with power—can do. A reminder of why I never planned to get close to someone like Kieren in the first place. I allowed myself to be swept away in the magic and romance of this place, the allure of the faerie world, but reality has dumped a bucket of ice over my head, tugging me firmly back into my own world.

"That isn't true," Kieren says. "There is no reason you shouldn't be here."

I turn to face him. "You can't choose me. *You can't choose me.* We both know that. You should be focusing your attention on someone you can form a genuine alliance with. Someone that has something to offer you and your court. Isn't that the real point of this game?"

He doesn't answer. Instead he moves closer through the water. Slow, unthreatening. He stops in front of me, eyes searching my face, then leans down to press the gentlest kiss against my brow. “I do not want anyone else,” he whispers.

My throat is tight and my skin is hot. No one has ever *chosen* me before. No one has ever wanted me like this. There is an odd ache behind my eyes. I squeeze them shut before tears can fall. Whether I want this or not, whether he means his words or not, it doesn’t change the truth of our circumstances. I swallow and turn away from him, reaching for the edge of the pool.

“Let me help you,” he says quietly. Then his hands are at my waist, lifting me effortlessly from the water. I scramble away from the pool on my knees and push myself to my feet, clumsy and inelegant in my soaking wet dress. “Wait,” he adds. I almost ignore him, then look back as he extends one hand toward the edge of my dress. Warm air tickles my ankles, seeming to originate from his fingertips. Within moments, my dress is almost dry. For some stupid reason, this simple thing makes tears threaten behind my eyes again.

I swallow and clear my throat. “Thank you,” I manage to say, then turn away and hurry from his suite.

Chapter Twenty-Six

Tuesday dawns, and instead of the excitement I once thought I would feel at the thought of having my best friend visit me *here*, at the Glittering Palace, all I feel is dread. The day is a quiet one for most of us. Kieren has a date with Riya in the morning and Shay in the afternoon—the thought makes me sick—and the rest of us are free to spend our time as we wish.

After avoiding Lina so I don't have to answer any questions about last night, I hide out in my suite, alternating between moments of elation and heartache. It's impossible to forget the things Kieren said to me last night, but daylight has brought no change to our situation. He's still a prince in search of a strategic match, and I'm still a nobody.

I would kiss you again. Over and over. Everywhere.

You consume my thoughts. My dreams.

I smile every time I remember his words, my skin flushed, and then I try to force the words from my brain all over again. I spend most of the day at my piano, vaguely aware of Iris hovering behind me with a phone or tablet. Possibly filming me, possibly uploading things to social media, possibly checking her endless schedule. I lose myself in the music and forget that she's there.

In the evening, my retinue prepares me for the ballroom where our loved ones will be waiting for us, ready to hug and gush over us as the cameras capture every emotional moment. We'll drink sparkling drinks and eat exotic canapés, we'll have dinner together and dance the night away, and—hopefully—there will be a chance for the kind of private conversations we can't normally have during our weekly calls when our aides are listening in.

Finneas and Mischa ask a dozen questions about last night, and I answer as vaguely as possible. I certainly don't admit that I ended up half naked in a pool in the prince's private quarters.

"Time for tonight's dress!" Finneas announces after they've finished interrogating me. "I've been saving this one, and I think tonight's event is perfect." He disappears into my dressing room, then returns to reveal his latest creation with a flourish: a dress covered almost entirely in leaves of dazzling gold, burnt orange, bronze-brown, and deepest red. A train made of the same leaves and dozens of tiny white flowers trails across the floor.

"Exquisite," I whisper. "Perfect for the Autumn Court."

"Isn't it?" Finneas grins, turning the gown this way and that. "I want every person in that ballroom," he says, "every contestant and their loved ones, every member of the court in attendance, to look at you and know beyond a doubt that *you* would make the perfect Autumn princess."

"So ... you want to paint a giant target on my back?" I ask wryly.

"Love," he says with a smirk, "Prince Kieren already did that when he kissed you in front of a ballroom full of people. Half the world thinks he's chosen you already."

A shiver dances up my spine. "Really?" I whisper.

"Yes. Honestly, doesn't Iris tell you anything about what's going on out there on all the socials?" He throws a glance over his shoulder toward my sitting area. "All the viral videos and trending what's-its and popularity charts?"

"I'm not supposed to, remember?" Iris calls back. I can almost hear the eye-roll in her voice.

"Oh, come now, I'm sure you could share *some* details," Finneas replies with a mischievous glint in his eyes. "Don't you want Avery to know how popular she is?"

"Avery's told me repeatedly how little interest she has in social media," Iris says, putting her tablet down and standing. "She's also told me she's enjoying the break from having to check her streams and downloads and things like that."

"One hundred percent true," I say. "Though I recognize that I'm going to have to make a lot more of an effort once I leave this game if I hope to continue whatever small amount of success you've managed to build for me." Finneas laughs, and Iris smiles at him in a way that makes me think they're sharing some kind of inside joke. "What?" I ask.

"Nothing," Iris says, still smiling as she comes to stand beside me. "This dress is magnificent, Finneas. Truly incredible." She reaches for my hand and squeezes it lightly, quietly adding, "Hopefully we can convince *you* along with everyone else that you would make the perfect Autumn princess."

An hour later, I'm standing outside the ballroom, still thinking about her words. *Would* I make the perfect Autumn princess? I have nothing at all to offer the Autumn Court and its prince—other than the fact that I care deeply for him. But perhaps that would be enough. Do the fae really need anything from our world? Surely they're powerful enough without the influence, technology or wealth any human might be able to offer them. Perhaps I *could* be enough for him.

No, an insidious voice whispers. *Not with a past like yours.*

I shrug the voice away and focus on the open ballroom doors as Lina walks in ahead of me. We've been instructed to enter separately, making a grand entrance down the main stairway in a manner reminiscent of our first entrance on the night of the Opening Ball four weeks ago. Like then, someone in a formal uniform calls out my name in a voice so deep and loud I wonder if it's been magically enhanced.

I walk forward and begin descending the stairs. I've entered this ballroom enough times by now that I'm no longer in awe of the magnificent details. The glittering chandeliers, the golden light that bathes everything in a magical glow, the gleaming floors and vaulted arches. Instead, my eyes scan the people already gathered, seeking out the one person I've been longing to see since the moment I got here. Gone is my earlier trepidation. My fears about speaking to her seem silly now. I've missed her *so much*, and she's finally here in person!

My gaze passes over Lina—giving her father an awkward hug —and then Shay, who has one arm wrapped around someone who is essentially her double. She and her twin sister wear almost identical smiles. A refreshing look for Shay, whose face is normally pulled into a scowl. Annemarie stands beside a tall man, a short woman, and a young boy I assume are her family. And there, in a soft pink dress more beautiful than anything I've ever seen her in, with her hands clasped tightly in front of her and a wide smile on her lips, is my best friend in the whole world.

I have to refrain from running down the stairs and across the space between us. I'm still a couple of steps away when I launch myself at Quinn with a delighted laugh. The motion almost sends us both to the floor. This is most certainly *not* the way we were instructed to greet our loved ones, but I don't care. "You're *here*!" I whisper into her ear as I wrap her in a tight hug. She clings to me until I reluctantly pull away, and as I turn to face forward, I catch Kieren's eye. He's seated on the raised dais with his parents. The moment lasts barely a second, but it's long enough for me to see the corner of his mouth lifted in one of his almost-smiles. I look away quickly, gripping Quinn's hand as the last contestant descends the stairs.

I wait with mounting impatience as Gigi hugs two older women and as Carwyn and Evanna step forward to say a few completely unnecessary words of welcome. And then finally, *finally* they tell us with a sweeping gesture of their hands to have fun catching up with our loved ones. I turn to face my best friend.

"Ho. Ly. *Shiiiiit!*" she squeals in a pitch so high it's almost beyond human hearing. "I can't believe I'm here! I still can't believe *you're* here! And you kissed the freaking *prince*! Aves, you're going viral on like every social media platform out there. *Everyone* is using your music. It's insane!"

"What?" My skin heats up and goosebumps prickle along my arms. "Seriously?"

"Seriously! People are using it in all their emo, heartfelt videos. You know how your music is like ... really moving? Like it touches something deep inside a person? Your assistant lady has been posting videos of you just playing quietly in your room here at the palace, and I guess the sound has really resonated with people. You were already getting a lot of views, but they've *skyrocketed* in the last twenty-four hours."

"I ... that's ..." I start laughing, not quite able to comprehend this, even though it's what I hoped for in the moments when I dared to dream as wild as possible. "That's amazing!"

"I know! And obviously it's translating over to the music streaming platforms too. Loads of people searching for your stuff and listening to it. It's *so* cool."

My smile is so wide now it's starting to hurt. "This is crazy!"

"Right? I mean, it's gross that you had to kiss a fae prince in order to gain this kind of popularity," she adds with an eye roll, "but look at how it's paid off already!"

I glance around to make sure the cameras aren't too close by. "Quinn, you—"

"This is *all* just so insane!" she exclaims. "This dress they gave me? And the plane ride here? And this *palace*? Avery, I've had to pinch myself multiple times. It's like ... unreal."

"I know," I agree with a laugh. "I thought the same thing over and over when I first got here. And oh my gosh, Quinn, there are *so* many things I have to tell you. Things I couldn't say over the phone." I set aside my thrill over the sudden success of my music, which feels like it's almost too much to process right now. I don't want to miss out on any of the things I need to tell Quinn. "Like—oh, hang on." I stop one of the waitrons passing nearby and grab two tall, slim glasses of a sparkling golden drink. I hand one to Quinn, who eyes it with deep suspicion. "Like, okay," I continue. "Remember that day Carwyn and Evanna came into The Grumpy Bean? Remember there was that really rude guy who came in just before them, and you said he was probably fae?"

"Yeah?" She sniffs the drink but doesn't taste it.

"That was—" I cut myself off as I look around again, checking for the locations of the various cameras. Evanna is standing in front of one, interviewing Riya and her mother. Carwyn is interviewing Cadence and her family. Another two cameras glide across the far side of the ballroom. There don't seem to be any nearby. I turn back to Quinn. "That was *him*," I say in a low voice. "Prince Kieren. But he was glamoured to look like his friend."

"Wait, what?" She lowers her glass. "*What?* Holy *shit*. That's like ... that's huge. That's a huge deal. I *knew* they were lying to us about that! Aves, we have to tell someone. Like, I don't know. The police or something. I mean, it's a major security issue if they can glamour themselves to look like other people."

"Oh, no, it sounded like it's a really difficult kind of glamour, so most fae can't do it. And I kind of agreed not to tell anyone about it because of a deal I made with Kieren." I realize as these words fall from my lips that I've broken our agreement by telling Quinn. But she doesn't count, does she? She's my closest friend. She's like an extension of me.

"Kieren?" Quinn repeats in an incredulous tone. "One kiss and you're on a first-name basis with the stiff-as-a-wooden-plank prince? And why are you making *deals* with him, Avery? That sounds super dodge. And it is *not* reassuring to hear that only some fae can glamour themselves to look like other people. That's still really dangerous, and it's probably not even true. He was probably lying to you. I bet they can all—"

"Ah, Miss Girl Next Door!" Carwyn is suddenly beside us, a camera and several members of the TV crew crowding behind him. Despite my aversion to the cameras, I find that I'm grateful for the interruption. "And your sweet friend from that darling little coffee shop," he continues. "Quinn, is it? A foster sister who is as close to you as a real sister, if I recall?" I nod, and Carwyn slides an arm around Quinn to draw her closer to the camera. "Delightful to have you here, my dear. Do tell us, what has life been like for you since your best friend became a contestant in *The Princess Game*?"

Quinn stumbles her way through a few answers, helped

along by Carwyn's cheerful and easygoing nature. When he reaches the end of his questions and sweeps himself and the camera crew away, Quinn and I barely have a few seconds to look at each other with expressions of *thank goodness that's over* before someone announces dinner.

We're ushered to one of a ring of opulently decorated tables encircling the outer edge of the ballroom. Gigi and her moms and Annemarie and her family soon join us. At the table beside ours, Lina sits with her father while shooting *please rescue me* glances my way. I meet her eyes and mouth *sorry* when her father is looking the other way.

Though Quinn is initially skeptical about the food—she probably thinks we may all be poisoned by it—she soon relaxes and starts to enjoy it. We converse comfortably with the other people at our table, and I gather from all the chatter about the latest episode that it seems as if Natalya may have an inappropriate relationship with one of the guards. "There weren't any specifically incriminating shots," Quinn says, "but the episode showed her giggling with a blond guard on multiple occasions, putting her hand on his arm and his shoulder. And once she was whispering something to him and then she hurried away when she realized there was a camera nearby. So it definitely seems as though something's going on."

I nod, thinking of Cadence's accusation after Natalya was seen leaving the North Tower early in the morning a few days ago. Natalya was quick to agree that she'd been with Kieren, but after he denied it, I didn't spare much thought for what she must have actually been doing there. Perhaps she was with this blond guard Quinn is talking about.

"Wouldn't that violate her contract, if it were true?" Annemarie's mother asks.

"I think so," Quinn says, looking at me for confirmation.

I nod. "We're not allowed to be in a relationship with anyone else while we're still part of the game. I think the contract said something about 'severe repercussions,' but I think it was pretty vague on what those repercussions would actually be. I don't know. I didn't make an effort to remember that part."

"And there would have to be actual proof," Gigi says. "Sounds like that isn't the case yet."

"Ugh, I hope someone finds something," Quinn says. "She's awful. She really needs to go."

I lower my head to hide my smirk. I strongly agree with her, but now that I might possibly be considered everyone's number one competition—which is so ridiculous I don't even know where to start—I'd rather keep my mouth shut when it comes to my opinions on the other contestants.

"Good evening, everyone."

I sit up straight, my heart rocketing into my throat at the sound of Kieren's voice. Crap, crap, *crap*. I had noticed him moving from table to table to meet everyone's loved ones, but some silly, illogical part of my brain was hoping he might somehow forget to come to ours. He greets everyone at the table by name, holding my gaze for a moment longer than anyone else's. Then his eyes move to Quinn. "I am so pleased to meet you, Quinn. Avery speaks of you often. She must be overjoyed to have you here."

Quinn opens her mouth, a barely veiled glare directed at him, then presses her lips together. I'm fairly certain she's remembering the heated conversation he and I had in The Grumpy Bean. I half expect her to blurt out that she's met him before. I wait, hardly breathing, but she doesn't say a word. I'm hoping everyone at the table will put her reaction down to shyness, but I know Kieren isn't so easily fooled. He's too perceptive not to detect her hostility.

There is a question in his eyes as his gaze shifts back to mine for a moment, but then he's turning to Annemarie's family, asking them how their flight was and telling her younger brother that he's heard what a big tennis fan he is.

"I need to talk to you," Quinn murmurs beside me, pushing her chair back. Before I can ask what's wrong, she's standing and hurrying away from the tables. I rise quickly and follow her. She heads through one of the side doors and into a wide corridor. A memory comes instantly to mind: Kieren kneeling at my feet, casting a glamour to hide the stain on my dress.

I blink the thought away and face Quinn, now pacing agitatedly from one side of the corridor to the other. "How does he ... what have you been telling him about me? Why does he know anything about me at all?"

"Because ... I talk to him."

"About me?" She's looking confused.

"About everything." I take a breath. Here it is. The conversation I've been dreading. "We ... we have an agreement that has resulted in me spending a lot more time with him than I originally thought I would. So we've spoken a lot. We've grown ... closer."

Her lip curls as if she can smell something bad. "Closer? To Fake Prince Faerie Face? And what *agreement* is this?" She spits the word out as if it's dirty. Whatever she's imagining probably *is* dirty.

"Whatever you're thinking, no. It's *not* like that. I'm offended you would even think that of me!"

"You don't know what I'm thinking!" she protests.

"I do. It's written all over your fae. And the agreement was basically information in exchange for him not throwing me out of the game right at the start. He caught me eavesdropping—a stupid accident—and was going to dismiss me at the end of the first week. Then I discovered it was *him* that day in the coffee shop and that it is possible for some fae to make themselves look like others. So then he agreed to keep me here if I would share everything I learned about the other girls, to help him decide who the best options would be."

"Right, because he can't just spend the time with them himself to figure it out."

I roll my eyes. "No, because half of them aren't genuine with him. He wanted to know what everyone's *really* like."

"What a hypocrite," she mutters.

"Yes, I thought so too, but then I got to know him better."

"Did you? Because it seems like instead of seeing how truly awful he really is, he's tricked you into falling in love with him."

"He isn't *truly awful*!" I exclaim. "You don't know him at all! He isn't stuck-up and arrogant. He's ... he's shy and introverted. He isn't comfortable with large crowds or people he doesn't know well. That's why comes across so formal and—"

"He's rude, Avery. Downright rude. I was there that morning in the coffee shop, remember? I heard the way he spoke to you."

"That was just ..." I shut my eyes and groan. "A bad day. A misunderstanding. We've both apologized for that conversation and moved on. I'm telling you he's a *decent guy*." I open my eyes and look at her. "Why won't you—"

"I can't believe this is happening," she says, not even listening to me now. She spins away from me again, hands pressed to her cheeks. "Shit, shit, shit. I was so scared it would, but then I told myself you've always been super sensible, but now—"

"Scared of what?"

"You've *changed*!" she blurts out, hands falling to her sides, eyes wide and fearful. "This place has changed you. I could tell during our video calls, but I was hoping it was just ... I don't know. The fact that your PA was hanging around and you couldn't be yourself. But now, speaking to you in person, just the two of us, you're ... I don't know. It's like you've bought into all of this crap. The charade. The lie."

"I definitely have not *bought into* all of this. I know there's something else going on beneath this polished, perfect exterior. There are dangers, secrets, cover-ups. They're lying to us about so much, and I don't—"

"Exactly! You can't trust any of these people!"

"No, I can't, but I can trust *him*!"

She's looking at me like she doesn't know me. "That kiss," she says quietly. "On the episode last night. I thought it was all an act for you, but it was real."

Heat is crawling up my neck now. For the briefest moment, I consider lying to her. But that would make me the worst friend in the world. "It wasn't, at first," I admit, "and then it was."

"And what else has happened before and since then? I mean, I assume there must be more. Things no camera managed to capture."

"There's been ... nothing too big a deal," I stammer, a blush flooding my cheeks.

She nods. "I see. And you didn't tell me about any of this."

"Things only just changed between us, and it's not the kind of thing I wanted to talk about over the phone—"

"You know he can't choose you, right? He would never choose you." Her words contain an edge of spite, but I see the fear in her eyes. I wonder if she's trying to convince me or herself.

"I know that," I respond hotly, the reminder like a knife twisting in my chest. "Of course I know he can't choose me."

"This is just ... you're just ... who *are* you that you've become the kind of person who would even *want* someone like him?"

There are tears pricking behind my eyes now. "Clearly I'm someone more open to admitting I was wrong than you are."

"Oh, sure, you're *open-minded*. That's what this is about." She shakes her head. "You've *changed*, Avery. Just admit it."

"Maybe I have! And maybe you're scared that you're the one getting left behind!"

She takes a step back, her jaw slack. "I don't have to listen to this shit," she mutters, then turns and starts marching away.

"Where are you going?" I call after her.

"I don't know!" she yells back.

"You can't just—"

"Leave me alone!"

Chapter Twenty-Seven

It's on the tip of my tongue to yell after Quinn that she's being as overly dramatic as the contestants she so dearly loves to make fun of, but I manage to keep that petty thought to myself. Instead of following—which I probably *should* do, given that she's about to get lost inside a faerie palace—I give in to my anger and spin the other way.

I'm blinking fiercely as I aim for the doorway to the ballroom, attempting to banish tears while silently chanting *Be happy, be happy*. The camera crews are on the lookout for any sign of drama, and I don't need the whole world speculating as to why I might be teary at tonight's joyful event. With a deep breath, I walk back into the ballroom.

Dinner is drawing to an end, and at least half the room's occupants are now at the center of the magnificent space, twirling in time to a fae version of a lively waltz. Human guests who have no idea what they're doing laugh riotously and try to keep from tripping over one another. Petals drift down like confetti from some unknown source near the ceiling, and sparks of light that may or may not be tiny creatures dart about over everyone's heads. The ballroom fills up as other palace residents and fae of the Autumn Court join us.

"Tonight's event will be the biggest party we've had so far!" Evanna told us this morning. "Let us show our guests what a real faerie revel is!"

I'm not sure *we*—the contestants who've been here for weeks—know what a real faerie revel is. From what Finneas said, the fae have been keeping their true nature from us. That, and numerous other secrets.

I stand at the edge of the room for a while, looking for Lina, but I fail to spot her among the many dancers. Perhaps she's managed to escape her father and is hiding somewhere. I move forward, wondering if I might find her in one of the small sitting rooms adjacent to the ballroom—and that's when Queen Erralee herself steps into my path.

"Miss Avery." She inclines her head in greeting as I jerk to a halt.

"Y-your Majesty." I curtsey as low as I dare.

"Rise," Queen Erralee says, so I do. "I will admit I paid you little attention until the night my son decided to kiss *you* instead of one of the more suitable options." Her gaze—not threatening, though not exactly warm—travels my face. I try to ignore the sting her words cause me. I've always known I am not the 'suitable' option. Nothing has changed there. "So now," she continues, "I have to wonder ..."

I swallow, waiting for her to continue. When she doesn't, I dare to ask a question. "Wonder what, Your Majesty?"

"What he sees in you." Her words hold no judgement. More ... curiosity. "Your dress," she continues, her eyes moving down the length of my body. "Spectacular. We have not yet seen something quite so perfectly autumn in the weeks since this game began. If you were hoping for us all to imagine what it might be like to see you on a throne beside my son, congratulations. You have achieved this. What remains to be seen, however," she adds as she moves to step past me, "is whether or not that is a good thing for you."

She walks away, and I exhale a trembling breath. That figurative target I mentioned to Finneas—the one I joked about him painting on my back—suddenly feels a whole lot like a real one. I keep my head down as I skirt the edge of the ballroom, aiming for the other side where the doorways lead to small sitting areas. It's not as though I can hide my dress though. Besides, everyone seems to be having too much fun to pay any attention to me.

At least, *almost* everyone is having fun. I glance up as I pass Riya and her mother standing beside one of the tall, arched windows. " ... and this *hair*?" her mother is saying, an expression of disgust on her face. "You look as though you've been rolling around in a bush."

"Perhaps I like it this—"

"Oh, indeed. Next thing you'll be telling me you *like* the color yellow and that you didn't wear it simply to irritate me."

"Is it irritating you?" Riya asks calmly. "I can't tell."

"Have you *forgotten* ..."

Their voices trail away as I move out of earshot, but I feel a pang of sympathy for Riya. I'm guessing she was probably as excited about tonight as Lina was.

I reach the other side of the ballroom and walk through an open doorway into one of the dimly lit sitting rooms, this one decorated in earthy tones with gold embellishments. I stop just inside the room when I realize it isn't empty. Lamplight bathes two identical redheads, one dressed in green and the other in blue, hugging each other fiercely. "Thank you a thousand times over, Sades," the one in blue says. "I'm so, so, *so* grateful."

"You'd better—Oh." The green twin spots me and pulls away from her sister.

"Hi, sorry," I say, taking a step backward. "I didn't realize anyone was in here." For a moment, I can't tell them apart, but then the twin in green gives me that wary glare I've come to recognize as Shay's. Except ... didn't the blue twin just call the green twin 'Sades'? As in ... *Sadie*? No. I must have heard wrong. She must have said *Shay*. They wouldn't ... no way. I remember joking about it—making a comment in passing—but they wouldn't *actually* swap places, would they?

None of my business, I remind myself. "Uh, have you seen Lina?"

"Oh, yeah, she slipped into one of the other rooms," Shay—Sadie?—says. "The green one with all the plants. Hiding from her dad, I think."

"Thanks." I head back out, pass another group of laughing, chatting people, and find the doorway that leads to a sitting room almost overflowing with plants. I don't see Lina, but there's an exit on the far side of the room, so perhaps she's hiding somewhere a little further away from the ballroom.

My conscience pricks at me, telling me I should be looking for Quinn instead. I don't want her to wind up in the kind of trouble I almost landed in the first day I got here. Then again, the palace probably expects to find humans wandering all over the place, poking their noses into everything. They did knowingly invite a whole bunch of them here tonight.

I cross the lush space, deciding to look into just one more room or corridor before heading back to search for Quinn. I twist the polished bronze doorknob and push the door open just wide enough to look around it. I find a darkened room filled with books—and a man and woman entwined in each other's arms, kissing passionately. They break apart immediately, before I can pull my head back, and—

"Lina?" Surprise flares in my chest, though that's nothing compared to the shock that takes its place when my eyes land on the man she's with. "Illiam?"

Lina curses beneath her breath as Illiam grips her hand in a reassuring manner.

"What ..." I shake my head. First Natalya, and now Lina? Doesn't she realize how dangerous this is? "I—um—I'm sorry," I stutter, deciding to back away and pretend I never saw this.

"Wait, Avery," Lina says quickly. "Wait, wait, wait." Illiam murmurs something, and she adds, "Yes, it's fine, go. I'll talk to her."

He nods to me as he slips past, but doesn't meet my eyes. "Miss Avery," he says, and then he's gone.

I step into the room, pulling the door hastily shut behind me. "Okay, *what*?"

"Please don't tell anyone!" she begs.

"Lina!" I hope my expression conveys how horrified I am that she thinks I would do that to her. "Why would I *tell* anyone?"

"Because ... I don't know. Because I wasn't truthful with you?"

My gaze drops as I think of all the ways in which I haven't been truthful with her. She knows nothing of the deal I struck with Kieren at the start of this game, or the feelings I've developed for him, or even how I came to be a contestant. "Of course I won't tell anyone. You could wind up in loads of trouble for this. The contract was pretty clear."

"Yeah, I know. I *know*. The guilt when I signed that contract was pretty intense."

"Wait. You were with Illiam before the show even started? I just assumed you'd met him now, while living at the palace."

"I wasn't *with* him, but I already knew him. And I knew that *this* ... the two of us growing closer ... was a possibility. I mean, I wanted it to happen. Kind of. I sort of hated him, but I also really loved him."

"You're not making a lot of sense."

"I know, I'm sorry." With a groan, she tugs both hands through her dark, wavy hair. She steps back and sits on the edge of a couch. "I mean that I entered this game with zero intention of falling for the prince I'm supposed to be here for and knowing full well that something could develop with someone else. That's where the guilt came in."

I sit opposite her, my hands pressed to my knees. "And then something did develop with him."

"Yes. I know it's a stupid risk. Illiam knows too."

"Well, you could probably make it less of a risk by *not* making out barely two rooms away from the main ballroom."

"Ugh, I know."

"I mean, what if Kieren walked in here?"

"Actually ..." Lina takes a deep breath. "He already knows."

I blink at her before answering. "What?"

"He didn't at first, of course. But then after it happened, after Illiam and I became ... something very definitely *more* than friends, Illiam felt that we should tell him. He's bound to Prince Kieren by an oath that contains actual magic, if I understand correctly, and he felt that he couldn't serve the prince with complete loyalty and honesty if he didn't tell him what had happened between us."

I nod. "Sounds like an honorable guy. And I guess Kieren didn't kick you out or fire Illiam, since you're both still here."

"Yes, *Kieren*—" she gives me a knowing look, acknowledging

with a curve of her lips that she hasn't missed the way I've dropped his title when speaking of him "—actually agreed to try and help us. He said ... well, he *hinted* that there are ways—other ways the fae have never told us about—of making it possible for a human to live in their world. He didn't say anything explicit. Nothing I could go and tell the media about if I wanted to be stupid enough to betray his trust. But enough to give me hope. He plans to keep me here a little longer, for Illiam's sake, and for ..." Her smile softens as she watches me. "And for you."

"For me?"

"He knows we're friends. That you're closer to me than to the other girls. He thought you might get lonely if he dismissed me."

There's a flutter in my chest at this small revelation. At the reminder that he notices, that he cares. I try to shrug it off. I've been reminded too many times this evening that he can't choose me. "But, I mean, he obviously has to dismiss me soon too."

She hesitates, that smile still on her lips. "Does he?"

"Of course. He can't choose me."

She nods slowly, though she doesn't look as though she agrees with me. "Well. Anyway. I'm sorry for not being honest with you. That story about entering *The Princess Game* on a dare was obviously a lie. I thought I was going to be stuck with a bunch of backstabbing bitches all trying to sabotage each other, and I wanted to make it seem like I wasn't a huge threat to anyone, so that's where that story came from. And I spoke to you first because it seemed as though, of all the girls, you'd probably be the most normal and down to earth. And you were. Are. So yeah. I apologize for the dishonesty."

I sigh and roll my eyes. "I guess this is the part where I apologize for *my* lack of honesty and admit that I've spent far more time with Kieren than anyone knows and that I may have possibly, um, fallen for him."

Her lips spread into a wide grin. "I knew it."

"Oh, whatever. There's no way you could have known anything. Wait." A thought occurs to me. "Did Illiam say something to you? Does he know something? About, um, Kieren and me?"

Lina feigns a look of innocence. "I mean ... he may have some *suspicions* about how the prince feels—"

The door flies open and we both look around. Iris is standing there, looking far more flustered than I've ever seen her. "Oh shit, oh shit," she gasps. "I'm *so*, so sorry. I wouldn't normally do this. I know I'm not supposed to show my face at any of these events, but it's urgent—she sounds terrified, like life-and-death terrified—and I honestly don't care if I get fired over—"

"Iris, slow down," I tell her, getting to my feet. "Who's terrified? What are you talking about?"

"Your phone. It kept ringing and ringing, and I wouldn't normally answer it, but I saw that it was your friend Quinn, and I know she's supposed to be *here* tonight, so eventually I answered, and ... I mean ... she wasn't even making sense. Completely freaking out. All I could gather is that she needs you *right now*. I said I would find you, and I think she's going to call back—"

My phone starts buzzing in Iris's hand. She shoves it at me as if it's literally burning her fingers. My heart is in my throat as I answer, racing a million miles an hour. "Hello? Quinn? Are you okay?"

"Hello, Avery. This is Maddox."

All the blood drains from my face. My body. I'm ice-cold,

numb, frozen. For several moments, I can't force a single word past my lips. "W-what do you want?" I stammer eventually.

"I have Quinn. We're in the South Tower. If you don't want me to hurt her any further, you should probably come and get her."

"What—what are you doing to her? How did you—What do you want?"

"Come and have a chat. I'll lay out precisely what I want from you. And Avery? Dare to bring anyone with you, and the whole world will find out what you did."

Chapter Twenty-Eight

I RACE THROUGH THE GLITTERING PALACE TOWARD the South Tower. All I know of it is that it isn't off-limits and not much happens there, which means it's generally the quietest part of the palace. *How does he know this? How does he know anything? How is he* here?

I managed to remain calm enough to convince Iris and Lina that Quinn was only freaking out because she got lost and she's afraid of fae. "I'll find her," I told them with a smile that felt all too fake. "I know where she is."

"Are you sure?" Iris asked. "She did *not* sound okay."

"Yeah, I'm—I'm so sorry she made you panic. Thank you for coming to find me."

I can barely think as I run past endless chandeliers, portraits, and gold-threaded tapestries, the skirt of my dress clutched in my fists. The beautiful train Finneas fashioned drags behind me, keeping me from running as fast as I'd like. Though I know my way around far better than when I first got here, I turn the wrong way twice and have to retrace my steps until I recognize something. Finally, after traversing corridors that grow dimmer and dimmer, I find myself in a darkened atrium on the other side of which is the enormous door leading into the South Tower.

With shaking fingers, I twist the doorknob and tug the heavy door open. I find a circular space with doorways leading off it. A staircase winds upward on my left. How many rooms will I have to search before I find Quinn?

I don't have to wonder for long, because in the first room I step into—a simple space sparsely decorated with a few pieces of dark wooden furniture—there she is. Moonlight streaming in through a window illuminates her sitting in a chair, her wrists bound to the armrests and a scarf tied tightly over her mouth, eyes wider than I've ever seen them. Maddox has a gun pressed against the back of her head.

A gun.

A *gun*.

I'm suddenly so weak with terror I have to grip the doorframe to keep myself up. "Maddox," I whisper, his name a trembling whisper on my lips. "H-how did you get in here?"

He looks as sloppy as he always did in faded jeans and a T-shirt several sizes too large. His hair is different, though. He always used to keep it short, but now it's long enough to hang in his eyes. "Security doesn't seem to be so fantastic tonight," he tells me. "Too many people going in and out. Nobody checking the staff too thoroughly. Wasn't actually that difficult."

"Whatever this is about, I'm sure you don't need to involve Quinn."

"Yeah, well, you might not be as cooperative if she wasn't here, so I think I'll keep her where she is." He steps around her, tapping her ear lightly with the end of the gun as he goes. Quinn and I both flinch. "Looks like you're close to getting everything, Aves. Wealth, magic, a *prince* for fuck's sake." He laughs. "Who would have thought Little Miss Nobody could rise so high?"

"I haven't even made it to the Top 10," I remind him in a shaking voice. "Everyone knows he isn't going to choose me."

"Well, he certainly won't choose you if he knows the truth about you."

"What truth?" I ask through trembling lips, though I know exactly what he's referring to.

"Don't play dumb." He takes a step closer. "You think I don't know what really happened with Caz? You think I couldn't put the pieces together? I may never have said it out loud, but I know what you did. And I know it was *you*, not her." He gestures over his shoulder at Quinn with the gun. "I could see it on your face when the two of you came to me for help that night."

I see it in my head: my hands covered in blood, my clothes covered in blood, my whole body trembling as Quinn dragged me up the back steps to Maddox's kitchen door and banged against it with a bloodied fist. I blink and blink again, refusing to be sucked under by the memory. I lift my chin. "So what do you want then?"

He cocks his head. "Everything you've been given so far. Don't leave out a single piece. I'm an avid follower of the show, you see, so I know exactly what you've been gifted so far."

An avid follower of the show, my ass. He probably spotted me on screen once, recognized me, and immediately started scheming as to how he could twist this situation to his advantage. "Once upon a time, you helped us," I remind him. "We came to you because you were our *friend*. And now you're doing this?"

"Everyone's gotta eat, Aves. Life sucks out there. I'm just making the best of the situation I'm in."

I almost let out a disgusted laugh. He was never *in* this situation. He created it. "Fine. You can have everything. But what's to stop you threatening me again?"

His lips twist into a smirk. "You mean if the pretty prince doesn't kick you out in the next week or so? If you make it closer and closer to the end? If—shock of all shocks—he actually *chooses you*? Well." He shrugs. "I guess you may have to buy my silence over and over if that's the life you wanna keep." He steps back, waving the gun idly at Quinn, who whimpers and tugs at her bonds again. "Run along to your fancy room, Aves. We don't have all night. And if *anyone* comes back with you, Quinn is dead."

"Of course I'm not going to come back with someone, you worthless piece of—"

He's across the room, his hand raised, before I can even think to move. He strikes me so hard I stumble sideways and catch myself against the edge of a table, pain exploding across one side of my face. "Think you're better than me now?" he snarls, leaning over me. "Think you can talk to me like that? A few weeks with these fancy fucking faeries and you're as high and mighty as they are. Don't forget what you came from, Avery. *Nothing.* You—"

A dark figure slams hard into Maddox. In little more than the blink of an eye, he's pressed up against the wall, a large hand clamped around his throat and his own gun shoved hard against his temple. "Touch her again," Kieren says in a tone brittle with ice, "and you will know the kind of pain that leaves you begging for death."

"I—I wasn't going to—" Maddox stammers.

Kieren throws him to the floor and squeezes the gun until it bursts into a cloud of dry leaves. He's at my side in the next second, gently pulling my hand away from my cheek. "Are you okay?"

"Yeah, I'm—it's fine. I'll be fine." My voice is trembling and my cheek is throbbing. The pain brings tears to my eyes, but I blink them away, my gaze going to Quinn. I hurry toward her as Maddox scrambles across the floor.

"I'm trying to *help* you, man!" he says to Kieren. "Don't you know what she is? What she's done? She killed someone! She's a murderer!"

My hands freeze on the scarf securing Quinn's left arm to the chair. *Murderer. Murderer.*

Kieren leans down, grips Maddox by the neck, and pulls him up high enough to hiss in his ear. "Shall I let her kill you too? If she doesn't feel up to it, I'd be happy to do it for her."

"You can't—"

"I can. I will. If you think you can touch anyone in the manner in which you touched her, you do not deserve to take another breath." He shoves Maddox down again, then turns to the doorway where two of his guards have just come running in. "You know where to take him," Kieren says.

He crosses the room to where I'm struggling with the knots of the scarves, my heart still pounding and my fingers shaking. Quinn is almost hysterical, tugging, tugging, tugging, and the stupid scarves are so slippery, and I can't make my fingers work, and—

Kieren slices right through them—presumably with magic—before turning back toward the doorway to answer someone's question. Quinn just about leaps from her chair as Kieren crosses back to the door. "No, there's no need," he says to whoever's standing there. "It's under control. No need to bother them."

Quinn scrabbles desperately at the scarf covering her mouth, finally managing to pull it down. "Holy shit, Quinn, are you okay?" I reach for her arm, but instead of letting me pull her closer, she shoves me away.

"I told you," she gasps. "I told you! I said at the beginning that this was a huge risk. Drawing so much attention to yourself when Maddox *knew* what happened. And you said something stupid about guesses not counting, and then here we are with me tied to a chair and a freaking *gun shoved at my head*!"

"Hey, calm down. You're okay. You're—"

"I'm not okay!" she shrieks.

"Okay, okay, I'm sorry." I stand back, my hands raised.

"And you had to come here with *him*?" She throws a glare over my shoulder at Kieren. "Maddox specifically said to come alone. Did you seriously not care if he *killed* me?"

"I did come alone!" I insist. "But you spoke to my aide, remember? She heard how completely freaked out you were. She probably went to tell someone else after I—"

"We handled *everything* on our own for years," she hisses at me, "but now you can't do a thing without a prince at your side?"

"Quinn, let's just—can we just sit down? Let's go outside. Get some air. Let's just *talk*—"

"Talk? About how instead of immediately jumping to get what Maddox demanded, you stood there arguing with him, risking him getting irritated enough to *shoot* me?"

"Quinn—"

"You were more worried about the possibility of having to give up extra money in the future than about the life of your so-called best friend."

I'm staring at her in disbelief. My hands are still trembling, and the memory of what happened years ago is *far* too close to the surface, and I need *air*, I need to *sit*, but now I have to convince my best friend that of course I care about her more than the rest of this crap. "I was worried about *our* future safety. If Maddox comes after me again, he'll come after you too. And —what do you mean my *so-called* best friend? How can you say that?"

"Because you've changed! You're becoming just like *them*!" She thrusts an angry hand in Kieren's direction. He's standing just behind me now, finished with whoever was at the door. He takes a step closer, placing a reassuring hand against the small of my back. Quinn doesn't miss the gesture, her eyes growing narrower and her lips pressing tightly together.

"Quinn, I am so sorry for what happened here tonight," Kieren says, ignoring her insult. "I don't doubt that what you just went through was incredibly traumatic. Please be assured that that man will never bother either of you ever again."

"Oh, wow, thanks. Now I'm indebted to you. Brilliant."

"Quinn," I murmur.

Kieren takes a breath, but his voice is still patient and gentle when he speaks. "You are understandably upset—"

"Don't tell me what I am." She swallows, then takes a shuddery breath. "I know I'm supposed to be scared of you. You could kill me just like that." She snaps her fingers. "You've probably killed Maddox already. You fae are all the same, just doing whatever the hell you please with zero concern for consequences because there aren't any for you."

"We are not all like that," Kieren says quietly, "just as all humans are not—"

"Oh, so you *didn't* come into our coffee shop pretending to be someone else entirely, perpetuating a lie the fae have been telling us since the day they stepped into our world? "

"Quinn, please," I say, taking a step in front of Kieren so she'll focus on me instead of him. "Can we sit down and talk?

Just the two of us. I want you to understand where I'm coming from. There are lots of fae here who are actually really cool—"

"Oh just *stop it*, Avery! Stop defending them! They make bargains for enchantments that backfire, deliberately confuse us with their illusions, and it's oh so easy for them to forge documents, pretend to be human, and take the jobs that are supposed to be *ours*. Then they disappear into their world for a while, come back, and do it all over again."

"They are *not* all like that," I insist. "Please just *listen* to me. I know we haven't had a chance to properly talk about things like we usually do the last few weeks, but now you're here and I want to talk, but you're so *angry* with me for some—"

"Yes I'm angry with you!" she yells. "I'm the one who's out there, dealing with real-life shit, while you get to prance around in pretty dresses in a magical palace, basically living the perfect life. Why are *you* always the one who gets everything good?"

I reel back as if she slapped me, bumping into Kieren. "What?"

"I guess it's because you're the beautiful one. The outgoing one. The one who'll suck up to anybody for anything."

"*Excuse me?* You mean the part where I'm a decent, friendly human being?"

"Oh please." She shoves her glasses up her nose with a hand that's still shaking. "Nobody's that nice for the sake of being nice. Especially not after the shit we've lived through. You figured out a while ago that your looks would get you further than anything else, and you've been using them ever since. You think you always got the biggest tips because you were *friendly*? And *chatty*? We all know it was because of your pretty smile and your baby blue eyes and your stupid, bouncy ponytail. I guess it pays off to have zero self respect, right? Look at you now. Not only do you have jewels and servants and a fancy palace to live in and tons of fans of your music, you're also fucking a damn *prince*!"

I'm so stunned I can't think of a single thing to say. Not one single thing. The girl I've been through the absolute worst with, the girl I pulled myself out of the darkness with, the girl who has never in her life spoken to *anyone* like this because she's usually so terrified of confrontation—that's the girl who's standing in front of me, driving a knife straight through my heart and spitting acid in my face.

"This is how you speak to your closest friend?" Kieren asks, his voice low and dangerous.

"Oh, and he fights your battles for you too. How romantic. Total knight in shining armor. Until he gets to the end of the competition, remembers he can't choose a *nobody* for a wife, and dumps you back on your ass in the real world. But I guess you'll have your thousands of fans and your two million bucks from Carwyn Aster by then, so you'll be fine."

"Two million what?" Kieren asks quietly.

"I—" I want to spin around to face him, to explain Carwyn's offer, but I can't tear my attention from Quinn. She'll hate me even more if I choose Kieren over her in this moment. "Quinn, I did all of this for *us*, remember? We're *both* going to be better off when this is over."

"You did not do this for *us*. At their core, everyone is selfish. *That's* the world we live in. *That's* the lesson we learned. If you don't look out for yourself, nobody will."

"*I* look out for you!" I shout. "I came to find you as soon as Maddox told me where you were!"

"You were looking out for *yourself* when you came here! So that asshole wouldn't tell everyone what happened with Caz!"

"I came here because he was hurting you!"

"Okay. Sure." She folds her arms over her chest, expression

closing off. "You came here for me. Thanks. Is this conversation over yet? Can I go now?"

I shake my head in disbelief. The words she flung at me are still ringing in my ears. *Stupid, bouncy ponytail. Zero self-respect. Fucking a damn prince.* I didn't know she had the capacity to be so cruel.

But I see past her fierce expression to the way her jaw trembles. I see the sheen of tears she's blinking away. She's trying to shut me out to protect herself. I know she's hurt by all of this. She's bitter about the hand life has dealt her, and she's taking it out on me, and it's *so* unfair and part of me hates her for it, but another part of me remembers everything we've been through.

So I take a deep breath and bite back every angry retort I can think of. I step closer and hold her gaze. "I'm sorry, Quinn. I'm sorry for the shitty life we had. I'm sorry everything has always been so hard. But I swear, I'm still *me*. I haven't changed. I haven't abandoned you. I still believe that we can get through anything life throws at—"

"Stop doing that!" she screeches. "I *hate* when you do that! Do you know that it makes you just as fake as them?" She gestures harshly over my shoulder at Kieren. "For some people, life is *never* going to be okay, no matter how many times you lie to yourself. I just want you to be *real* with me!"

"When have I not been *real* with you?"

"All the time! Your stupid, fake sunshininess! Pretending everything's fine when I know it's not. When I know *you're* not fine."

"The sunshininess isn't *fake*. That's how I cope with life! You choose to be miserable and pessimistic, and I choose the opposite. How would life ever have got any better for either of us if *I* didn't hope for it?"

"Fine, okay, so you have *hope*. That's great. Thank you. But some days life sucks and everything feels like shit and I just want you to *be in that space with me*. I want you to let me *feel* it! I want *you* to let yourself feel it! Don't always push it away and pretend that everything's fine. Sometimes that's not helpful."

I'm shaking my head over and over, refusing to believe what she's saying about me. She's got this all wrong. "I'm not trying to pretend. I *know* things aren't fine. I'm not stupid. I … I just …" Doesn't she realize what she's asking? Doesn't she know that letting the darkness in, even for a short while, means the light may vanish forever?

"You see?" she says. "I'm not the only one with issues here. You have shit to deal with but you keep hiding behind your sunny—"

"Stop. I'm not *hiding*. I just—"

"I think I need to go now." Her arms tighten around her middle as she looks past me. "Your assistant's been pacing around out there. She can show me where to go." The fire is gone from her voice, from her expression. I feel the same coldness as the dying embers of my anger settle in a pit in my stomach.

"Fine," I say quietly. Her eyes dart back to me once more before she walks past, saying nothing. No apology, no goodbye. I say nothing else either. Then she's gone, and I'm lifting both hands to cover my face as a sob wrenches itself from my throat and tears spill from my eyes.

Chapter Twenty-Nine

I'm ugly-crying as Kieren pulls me gently against his side and leads me across the room. My shoulders shudder, and the tears keep falling, and I can't bear to remove my hands from my face. I hear the sound of a door opening. "Fresh air," he says as a cool breeze drifts across my bare arms. "It will help." He directs my steps outside before urging me down onto a hard surface. I finally lower my hands and realize we're sitting on a bench.

My fingers swipe beneath my eyes. I press my hands flat on my knees as I stare up at the starry sky, blinking the remaining tears away and letting out a shaky breath. My brain almost whispers *Be happy, be happy* like it usually does, but the thought is so ridiculous, so far out of reach, that the words drift away before they can take shape in my mind. "I'm sorry," I say, my chest tight, my words barely audible.

"Don't be."

I exhale another long, shuddery breath and wait a few moments before attempting to speak again. "How did you know to come?"

"Lina came to find me. Both she and your aide Iris were worried that something wasn't right. I found you by—Well. It was a magical method. One I probably should not have used without your consent. Quinn is right that we have power that can easily be abused. But—"

"Whatever you did, I'm grateful. Thank you for coming. And I'm sorry Quinn was so ..." I trail off, unable to pick one word from the many I could use. Ungrateful, rude, cruel.

"You do not have to apologize for her." He pauses, then gently adds, "If my memory serves me correctly, you had a lot of the same opinions about me when you first got here."

I let out a sniffly half-laugh. "Yeah. I guess I did. And I eventually had to admit I was wrong. I just assumed she would listen to me—that she would trust I wasn't lying to her—but she's being so stubborn. And ..." I shake my head, staring down at my hands. "I had no idea she's always thought those things about me. That I ... that I use my *looks* to get me further, and that all the good things in life happen to me." I twist my hands tightly together. She *knows* what happened with Caz. She's the only one who knows, despite what Maddox may go around telling people. There's no way she thinks that was a *good* thing.

"It is likely she said things she did not mean in the heat of the moment," Kieren says.

"Maybe." And yet ... where would those words have come from if they were not already buried somewhere inside her? "And she—oh, shoot, the two million. She threw that in there as well, didn't she." I cover my face with my hands again, knowing this is going to look terrible for me, but also knowing I can't lie about it. "Carwyn promised me two million dollars if I made it to the Top 10. I'm so sorry I never told you about that. In the beginning, it was one of the main reasons I said yes to this whole thing, but it doesn't matter to me now, I swear." I lower my hands and turn my gaze to him, hoping he'll see the truth in my eyes. "That isn't the reason I still want to be here. I know you probably think that's why I was trying to convince you not to call off the whole competition—"

"I don't think that. And I don't care what Carwyn offered you or what caused you to agree to all of this. I care that you are here. I care about what happened tonight. I care that you are hurting."

My eyes trace his beautiful face, and I see only a deep and heartfelt sincerity. I lower my gaze to my hands, once again twisting in my lap. "I'm not the only one who's hurting," I say quietly. "I know Quinn is hurting too. But that was still ..." I shake my head. "It was a huge shock, hearing her say all those things. It never crossed my mind that I might make her feel ... I don't know, like I was lying to her by being *happy*. I thought it was helpful to always try and push away the negative stuff and look on the bright side, to forget the stuff from our past and hope that life could be better for us."

"This 'stuff' from your past," Kieren says slowly. "You spoke before of darkness you're constantly trying to obliterate. Is this part of it? This ... accusation that young man threw at you?"

My hands are clasped so tightly together now that my fingers are beginning to ache. "Yes," I whisper.

After another moment of quiet, he says, "Do you want to talk about what happened?"

I bite my lip until the urge to start crying again passes. "He already told you."

"I'm sure there is far more to it than the few words he shouted."

I nod. "There is ... a bit."

"Perhaps it will help you to speak of it."

"Um ... I don't know about that."

You have shit to deal with but you keep hiding.

I don't want to entertain the idea that Quinn may have been right, but it's there, nudging at the edge of my mind.

"You do not have to, of course," Kieren says, "but I will listen if you want to talk."

I'm surprised to find that there's a small part of me that *does* want to talk about this. With Kieren, at least, who has made it so easy these past weeks for me to speak of anything and everything. There's a part of me that wonders if I may feel lighter. Burying the past has certainly never helped. It's still there, lurking at the back of my mind, ready to take shape in my nightmares. Quinn is the only one who knows what happened, and she was there. I didn't have to speak any words to her. So, in truth, I have never told anyone.

But I wonder if Kieren will look at me differently once he knows exactly what I did. This part of my history will confirm for him that I'm the least suitable choice of princess. But I suppose that's always been the case, whether he knew I killed someone or not.

"It happened at the house where Quinn and I met," I say softly. "I had been moved around through various foster homes over the years. So had Quinn. We were almost seventeen when we were both placed with Alice. She was nice. I mean, no one's perfect, but she was cool, younger than most of my other foster moms, and she did her best. But she had ..." My fingers are twisting in my lap again. I look down at them. "She had this boyfriend. Caz. He was ... also nice, I guess. Young and good-looking. Liked to make us laugh. But I was never totally comfortable around him. And then it turned out ... well, we slowly came to realize that he was abusing her."

Kieren sucks in a hiss of breath. I wonder if he'll say something, but he remains silent.

"We should have told someone. I know we should have. But we were too scared. The way he looked at us sometimes, like he was threatening us through his smile." I shiver at the memory. "And Alice never said a thing. She always pretended everything was normal. And her bruises seemed to miraculously disappear. We thought she was great with makeup. We didn't realize it was more than that." I take another deep breath. "We didn't realize Caz was fae."

"Fuck," Kieren breathes, and I'm startled at the sound of this profanity coming from his lips. I don't think I've heard him use the word before.

"Yeah. We were even more scared when we discovered that. Like it gave him more power over us than we had realized and there was nothing we could do to stop him. But I guess the neighbors heard stuff. The arguments and Alice crying. Some of them must have reported something. Suspicions of domestic violence. I don't know. A social worker visited a few times. We could tell she was worried about us, but Alice never said a word against Caz, and neither did we. He told us he would hurt us too if we did. 'Try me,' he said. 'You know I can get away with it.'"

Kieren mutters a few more choice curse words.

"We lived like that for almost a year. We were so close to aging out. And then one night I left the library Quinn and I used to study at a little early because I wasn't feeling well," I continue, trying to keep my voice steady, "and I heard them upstairs when I got home. It sounded like ... I don't know, like he was forcing himself on her and she kept saying no. They were fighting, both shouting at each other, and then there was a loud thump and suddenly I couldn't hear her anymore. I was hit with this terror, like I just *knew* that he'd done something to her. I ran upstairs without thinking, and—" I'm shaking my head now, my breaths coming faster, tears threatening behind my eyes again. "I shouldn't have gone in. I mean, I had to, because I had to help her, but I shouldn't have."

I squeeze my eyes shut, but instead of banishing the memory, I find myself reliving it: Alice's normally tidy bedroom with the contents of her vanity strewn across the floor. Creams and bottles of makeup and little glass ornaments shattered. Alice on the floor, half dressed, completely limp, with Caz leaning over her in only his boxer briefs, his hands wrapped around her throat. Squeezing tighter and tighter.

I run at him without thinking, beating his back with my fists. He shoves me away so hard I fall backward and sprawl across the bed. He stands and turns to face me. "Well," he says breathlessly, stalking closer, pushing his messy blond hair back with one hand. "I should have guessed it was you coming to interrupt us. You have what you want now."

"W-what?"

"Me." He gestures to himself in all his near-naked glory. "All to yourself. No Alice in the way."

I'm shaking my head fervently, trying to scramble to the edge of the bed. "No. That isn't—"

"I see the way you look at me, dirty little girl. Always eye fucking me when you think Alice isn't watching."

"I didn't. I haven't—"

"Yes you do." He shoves me back down on the bed. "I know you want this."

"No!" I say more forcefully this time, trying to kick him away.

Then he pushes me down again, and it's all happening too quickly. His hands ripping my jeans down, his knees forcing my legs apart, and I'm clawing at him, screaming, writhing, and—

"Get off her!"

I suck in a breath, blinking away the memory and coming

back to the present. There are trees and stars and tiny white lights glowing at the centers of little blue flowers. There is cool air and the sound of water tripping over pebbles. I breathe out slowly.

"Are you okay?" Kieren asks.

I nod, though I'm not sure if I am. I tell him what happened in that bedroom in as detached a manner as possible. "Quinn got home before things could go too far. Turned out she wasn't feeling well either. She heard me screaming and came upstairs. She yelled at him to get off me and then struck his head with a flowerpot Alice kept on top of the dresser. He fell away from me, and I rolled over and tried to scramble away, and then ... my back." I reach instinctively behind me, pressing my palm against the leaves stitched across my dress. "It wasn't just his hands or his nails. It was magic. He was trying to drag me back with some kind of magic, and the pain ..." I shake my head again. "It was unimaginable. It sliced right into my skin."

Kieren's hands are balled into fists in his lap, shaking with the same kind of pent-up rage I've buried deep inside me for years.

"Quinn attacked him again, so he went for her instead. He had her pinned against the wall. Strangling her like he strangled Alice. I managed to get myself off the bed despite the pain. Alice had this weird metal sculpture on her bookshelf, like half a face. I grabbed it." I swallow, running my hands agitatedly up and down my legs, ruffling the leaves of my dress. "I hit him. Again and again. Until he stopped moving. And then I just stood there, staring at him, staring at all the blood, until it finally sank in. The knowledge of what I'd done." I shake my head. "Realizing that I'd *killed* him. I was shaking so much I could hardly stand.

"Quinn checked Alice and she was ... she was ..." I take

another hiccup of breath. "She was also dead. He killed her. If I had just got to that room a few moments earlier ..." There are tears on my cheeks again, and I press one hand over my trembling lips. "I hated him so much. *So* much. And then his body suddenly burst into flames and it was all we could do to get out of the room before the fire spread to the bed and the curtains. I'd heard of fae bodies sometimes disintegrating into leaves or dirt or petals, but I didn't know about the flames. I was glad of it, though. I *wanted* what was left of him to be burned up forever.

"Quinn dragged me out of the house, and we went to Maddox. He lived nearby, and we'd been friends since Quinn and I both moved in with Alice. He helped us get cleaned up, helped us dispose of our clothes and find something to wear from his sister's closet. He asked only a few questions, and we didn't give much in the way of answers. By the time we got back to Alice's, her little house had almost burned to the ground."

I swipe at my cheeks again, inhaling deeply and deciding I've told as much as I need to tell. Nothing that came afterwards was ever as bad as that night. We aged out, lived for a few months with a friend who'd left school a year before us, took whatever work we could get, and eventually figured out how to survive on our own. I decided I could still be happy and bright and positive and that that dark period of our lives would stay where it belonged—in the past.

"Thank you for sharing this with me," Kieren says eventually, releasing his curled fists and carefully flexing his fingers. "I'm so sorry it happened. So very sorry." He shifts as if to move closer, one hand almost lifting, but then he goes still. Perhaps he wants to hug me, or place his hand on mine, but it's clear he's unsure of touching me right now. In this moment when everything from that night feels so near, so raw, I appreciate him maintaining that small distance between us.

"It makes a lot of sense now," he adds, "the feelings you had for me when you first got here. The feelings Quinn still has. And that man ... that worthless fae specimen ..." There is a low growl in the back of Kieren's throat. "If he was not dead already, I would kill him myself."

I let out another long breath, relieved to note that it no longer sounds as shaky. "Most of the time, I don't really think about it anymore. I feel like I've moved on. It comes up in my dreams, my nightmares, or if I happen to see someone who looks like him. But other than that, it doesn't really affect me now.

"Well, actually, I suppose that's not entirely true," I correct. "There is the fact that I ... well, since it happened ... I haven't been romantically involved with anyone. I haven't wanted to do ... *that*." A slow flush creeps into my face. I feel as though I'm thirteen again, unable to speak about physical intimacy without blushing furiously. "I mean, I've *never* actually done that, even before Caz, but since then, I haven't wanted it at all. I would just freeze up at the idea. I thought maybe something inside me was broken and I might never want anyone again, but then ... then you kissed me—"

"I'm sorry. I'm so sorry. I had no idea—"

"No, it's okay. I didn't realize it until it happened, but ... I wanted that kiss. The night before, in the music room—"

"I'm sorry."

"No, it was me. I'm the one who asked you to loosen the corset. You were standing so close to me, and something kind of ... woke up inside me. Something I didn't know was there."

"But then the pool." Kieren leans forward, head in his hands, and groans. "I'm an insensitive bastard. I'm so sorry. I urged you into the water, and I started undressing you, and the way I was touching you—"

"I wanted it," I interrupt. I pull his hands away from his face and wait for him to look at me. "I wanted it," I say again. "In fact," I add, my blush intensifying, "even though you could probably tell that I had *no* idea what I was doing, I wanted us to keep going."

He shakes his head. "You were perfect."

"You mean perfectly clumsy and inexperienced?"

"No. Just perfect. And then I ruined it."

"It wasn't you. It was the memory. It was my body shutting down when you discovered my scars and everything from that night came rushing back to me. But you are nothing like him. *Nothing.* Please don't be sorry for what happened between us. I'm not. Even though I know there's no future for us and it's unlikely anything like that will happen again."

"Avery ..." he murmurs, eyes closing as he trails off.

"Don't pretend you might actually choose me," I say gently. "We both know Quinn was right: you can't have a nobody for a wife."

"You are not nobody to me." He leans close enough to touch his brow to mine. His eyes close. "I want you," he whispers. *"I want you."*

A shiver raises the tiny hairs across my body. The traumatic memories are receding, a tide going out, losing their grip on me with each passing moment. And in their wake, my body begins to remember what it feels for the prince who sits beside me. "I want you too," I admit to him in a whisper. "I want you to choose me. I want a life with you. I want to belong in your world, with all its strange, glorious, disintegrating beauty. But please don't allow me to believe it's actually a possibility unless it really is."

He moves back a few inches. "Wait." A frown pulls at his brow. "What did you say? About something disintegrating?"

"Oh. I mean ... I remember seeing it when we had our first trip into Faeworld, and then again when I was supposed to meet you there. The way the edges of things seem to sort of disappear into the shadows, or like particles drifting away on ..." I trail off, wondering why he's looking at me so strangely. "What's wrong?"

"You could see that?" he asks.

"Um ... yes? Was I not supposed to?"

He stands and paces away from me, pushing one hand through his hair. "Tell me," he says, that frown still creasing his brow, "how exactly did Carwyn and Evanna end up choosing you?"

I blink at him. "I told you, didn't I? That it was by chance? They needed someone at the last minute, and I happened to be there."

"Yes, I know. Please tell me again what happened."

I stand, apprehension building in my chest. "What's wrong?"

"I'm just trying to understand something. Please, Avery. Tell me again what happened."

"Okay. Uh ... they came rushing in. The coffee shop was quiet, no one else was there besides Quinn and me, and you know Carwyn and Evanna are kind of ... loud and dramatic. So I heard what they were talking about. Complaining about how the other girl—the one they chose as their original Girl Next Door—had turned out to be unsuitable at the last minute."

"What was unsuitable about her? Contestants were narrowed down to a short-list through a special ... selection process. She would have been on that list for a reason."

"It sounded like there was a video of some, uh, inappropriate content." Kieren stares at me, his expression unchanging. "Of a very *intimate* nature," I add. "With another person."

"Ah." He draws his head back. "Yes. I see how the Glittering Palace would not have appreciated one of the contestants being linked to something like that."

"Yeah. I actually knew her. Suzanna. Not that that's weird. It's a small town. Everyone knows everyone. I helped her with her application."

He looks at me sharply. "You helped her? How?"

"I just ... gave her some ideas for what to write."

"You gave her ideas? That was all?"

I sigh and roll my eyes. "I mean, okay, I sat there with a pen in my hand, giving her ideas and then writing down the stuff she agreed with. Her handwriting's terrible. She spends *way* too much time on her phone. Probably hasn't picked up a pen in ... Why are you looking at me like that?" I can't figure out his expression. Disbelief? Fear?

"It was you," he murmurs. "They shouldn't have chosen her, they should have chosen *you*. And then they *did* choose you, purely by accident."

"Wait, because *I* was the one who physically wrote her answers on the application form? What did that have to do with anything?"

He swipes a hand over his face as he turns away from me again, muttering something in his own language. "Did anything else happen? Anything else that prompted them to choose you?"

"Uh ... they liked my music?" I suggest with a shrug. "It was playing in the background and they commented on it, and then Quinn told them it was one of my pieces. They paid more attention to me after that, as if ... I don't know, like maybe they thought I was cultured enough to be a princess if I could write music. I don't know."

He nods slowly, looking past me. "The music. I should have known when I first heard you play. I *did* suspect, but I didn't think ..."

"Did suspect *what*?"

"Your Highness?" We both look around at the sound of a breathless call and hurried footsteps across the pathway. "Prince Kieren." Illiam comes to a stop. "Forgive the interruption, but you need to come immediately. To the ballroom. They came through the Shimmer, unannounced and—"

"Who?" Kieren demands.

Illiam answers with one word: "Winter."

Chapter Thirty

I'm right behind Kieren as we reach the ballroom, breathless from running all the way here. We enter through one of the side doors. He takes my hand as he begins crossing the room, eyes peeled for someone or something. Evanna, leaning on Carwyn's arm as she laughs, spots the two of us and attempts to wave us over. Kieren ignores her. "Stay close to me," he says.

"What's going on? What did Illiam mean by—"

There's a shout across the room and the music comes to an abrupt end halfway through a dance. Rowdy laughter and animated conversation die down until all that remains is a low hush of murmurs as everyone's attention moves toward the grand staircase and the entrance at the top. A moment later, I see why.

A young man stands there, skin fair and hair so blond it's almost white. He's dressed in formal fae clothing, velvety black with silver embellishments, and a crown that glitters crystal blue like shards of ice sits atop his head. His perfect features are twisted into a cruel smile.

"Fuck," Kieren breathes, surprising me for the second time tonight. There is something about this word he so rarely utters that tells me how bad this situation is. I just don't understand why.

"A revel!" the newcomer cries out. "And we were not invited." He gestures to the entourage behind him, a group of men and women dressed in unfamiliar uniforms.

"You have made your position clear." It is King Eldyn's voice that rings out. My gaze darts about until I find him climbing the steps onto the raised dais, Queen Erralee beside him. "The Winter Court will have nothing to do with the human world. We assumed its prince held the same view."

A prince of the Winter Court. That's who he is.

"Yes," the prince answers. "That remains our position. But I heard about your lovely little game. Your *princess* game." He descends the steps with lazy confidence, his guards remaining a few paces behind him. "And I wanted to come and ... play." His wicked grin curves higher.

"Stay here," Kieren whispers to me, moving hastily away from my side and heading for the stairs. The Winter Prince stops one step up from the ballroom floor and surveys us with ice-blue eyes. "So many pretty little humans." His lip curls. "Disgusting creatures. Don't you find it tedious that we need them? Hmm, Autumn Prince?" His gaze alights on Kieren who has come to a halt a few feet away from the stairs. Then his eyes move on, searching the crowd. "And Spring Prince? You are here somewhere too, are you not?"

Spring Prince? Who is he talking to?

"You should leave," Kieren says, his voice low and deadly. "We wouldn't want you to remain in a world you find so disgusting any longer than necessary."

I notice movement from the corner of my eye. Kieren's guards and soldiers of the Autumn Court edging closer to him. The Winter Prince's glittering eyes follow them, missing nothing. "How thoughtful of you to look out for me," he says in his lazy, condescending manner. "I suppose I should be on my way before tainting myself further. However," he adds with a slight tilt of his head, "I have heard of a tradition in this world. Something known as a ... *party favor*. A gift given to guests at a party. It would be a shame to leave here without such a memento."

"You are not a *guest*," Kieren all but snarls.

The Winter Prince bares his teeth in another threatening smile. Then his piercing gaze shifts beyond Kieren again and settles on someone else. I turn my head to follow his line of sight. The queen. He has locked eyes with Queen Erralee. She is furious, breathing heavily, eyes narrowed. And then suddenly she is looking at ... *me*. My breath catches. I swing my head back around and find the Winter Prince's hungry gaze on me too. My eyes dart to Kieren. And now it's his turn to look back and forth between the prince, his mother and me as something indefinable crosses his expression. Then he spins around to face the ballroom.

"The game is over!" he shouts out, drawing everyone's attention back to him. "I have chosen my bride."

Wait, what? *What?* Quiet gasps fill the room. TV crews huddle closer around cameras. Carwyn whispers to Evanna, his eyes trained on me. My heart slams against my ribcage. Kieren can't possibly mean *me*, can he?

You consume my thoughts. My dreams.

I do not want anyone else.

I want you.

For a moment, I allow myself to believe that he meant everything he said. That a world exists in which he *can* choose me. A world in which politics and alliances don't matter.

But then he turns his back to me, facing in an entirely different direction, and utters the words that shatter my heart: "Natalya Petrova."

Chapter Thirty-One

Gasps travel through the crowd as Natalya's name rings over and over in my ears. I'm numb. Numb and cold and motionless. My heart is a heavy thud, thud, thud in my chest. He chose her. He chose *her*. I think I'm supposed to clap or pretend to be happy for her, but my brain can't seem to communicate with the rest of my body. Is this really happening?

"The other contestants and their loved ones are dismissed from the Glittering Palace with immediate effect," Kieren says. "Our guards will escort them out."

He isn't looking at me. Why isn't he looking at me?

Why is he ending the game now?

A scream like the battle cry of a warrior jolts me from my reverie. I blink and look around, my heart suddenly beating wildly again. It's Riya. Running full-speed at the Winter Prince. A knife—*a knife?*—flashing in her grip. She slashes wide, and he spins out of the way at the last second. His guards move quickly, but he is faster. Within seconds, he has Riya clamped against his chest, facing away from him, one arm tight around her neck and the other pinning her arms to her sides. "I think we'll take this one," he says through a vicious grin. "And perhaps a few of the others. The Autumn Court has been so kind to narrow down the options for us."

"You will do no such thing," Queen Erralee shouts. I whip around in time to see her fling her arms out, fingers spread wide.

"No!" Kieren yells, but a ripple of power is already shooting away from his mother and—

I'm thrown backward clear off my feet. I tense, expecting to hit the floor, but I'm still flying through the air, the golden hue of the ballroom consumed by silvery white light shimmering with blue-green-pink. It blots everything else out for a strange, weightless moment before I sense my body hurtling into darkness.

I strike a hard surface and roll across something that smells like dirt and feels like the crunch of leaves. My body comes to a halt, and I lie there for several shocked moments, gasping for breath, blinking up at the dark shapes of trees towering above me and the night sky beyond, trying to figure out what the freaking hell just happened. Is this even real?

A distant howl reaches my ears, and the cold from the ground seeps through my dress into my back. I scramble up, sharp stones and broken twigs digging into my palms. This has to be real. No nightmare has ever felt like this.

He chose her. He chose her.

I try to push the reminder aside, my legs shaking as I stand. I squint into the darkness, but all I can see are the trees. This is not the lush, flower-scented forest of the Glittering Palace, nor is it the autumn wonderland just on the other side of the Shimmer, bursting with brilliant reds and golds and yellows. But there's that feeling in the air. That *something* indefinable that I'm fairly certain is magic. I think of the queen throwing her arms out and that rush of power that radiated across the ballroom. Somehow, she pushed me into Faeworld. A part of it I've never seen before.

He chose her.

Stop it, I tell myself. But I can't unsee that moment when Kieren turned his back to me. I can't forget the way my heart dropped through my body when he uttered her name. I've been hurled into an unknown part of a dangerous world, and I should be thinking *which way do I go? How do I get back? Why was I sent here? How long do I have before all the magic in this world kills me?* But all I can focus on is that moment in the ballroom when Kieren chose Natalya Petrova to be his bride. And there has to be a reason, because it just *doesn't* make sense. I know he doesn't even like her, but that doesn't change what he did.

My lips tremble and I raise my hands to my face as a sob shudders through my body. For the second time tonight, I utterly fail at being the positive, 'sunshiney' version of myself I've worked so hard to unearth from the ashes of my past. And it isn't that I wanted to be a princess or that I wanted to live in a palace and have magic and wealth and not a care in the world. I wanted to be *chosen*. For *me*. Because I have spent my life being tossed aside, and some foolish part of me thought things had finally changed. And I wanted *him*. Not the prince, but the man. The quiet, kind, perceptive, socially awkward Kieren.

But Maddox was right. Quinn was right. Life sucks.

I cry until I am spent. Until there's nothing left inside me. Until an odd sort of calm takes the place of the all-consuming despair that had me in its clutches. I lower my shaking hands and take a deep breath. I don't know why I was sent here or how to get home or if I'll outlast the negative effects the magic is no doubt already having on my body, but I can damn well try.

I lift my skirt and step over the gnarled roots that snake

through the undergrowth. An eerie silence hangs over everything, broken by the slither of my dress over the decaying forest debris and the occasional shriek of ... something. As I move further between the trees, an eerie fog rolls in around my ankles. I trip over something and catch myself against the side of a tree, the bark rough and jagged beneath my palm.

A distant cry catches my attention. Words instead of animalistic screeches. The words become clearer until I swear I can hear someone shouting, "Help me!" The cry comes again and again, and ... is it *Shay*? I'm sure I recognize that voice.

I spin around, calling out "Hello!" while trying to determine which direction the cries are coming from. But they diminish rapidly, fading away completely within moments. I stand there, blinking into the darkness. "Hello?" I dare to call, a shiver skittering up my spine as my voice breaks the silence. I didn't imagine her voice. I *know* I didn't. Which means perhaps I wasn't the only one thrown out of that ballroom and into another world.

I continue on, trying to move faster despite my completely unsuitable shoes, looking around for any hint that I might be heading toward civilization. The trees begin to thin, allowing me a glimpse of a clearing up ahead. I hurry toward it, the fog swirling around my ankles. Closer, closer, and then I'm emerging from the trees and running into open space.

And that's when I jerk to a horrified stop, my breath snatched away in an instant and my heart suddenly frozen in my chest. Because there, in the shadows on the other side of the clearing, is Alice's house.

A violent shiver wracks my body.

This isn't real. This isn't real.

Every voice in my head screams at me to run, but I can't move. All I can do is stare, my body beginning to shake, as the front door opens and a figure walks out of the house. That easy gait, his messy blond hair, the face that can't possibly belong to anyone else. My brain has panicked multiple times over the years, startled by someone with a passing resemblance to him. But this time, I know without a doubt.

Caz.

Run! my brain scream at me, but still my body refuses to move. "You're not real," I whisper as he stops a few feet away from me.

His lips twist into a smile. "Doesn't this feel real to you?"

It does. It feels hellishly, horrifyingly real. But I *know* it isn't. It can't be. "You're not real," I repeat.

"Real enough," he says with a shrug. "And now it's just you and me, little Aves. No Alice. No Quinn."

"Stop."

"I know you want me, you dirty little—"

"Stop! Don't you dare call me that." Though I'm almost faint with fear, I refuse to hear those words one more time. They've haunted my nightmares long enough.

He takes a step closer, tilting his chin down as he peers at me through dark lashes. "But it's what you are, isn't it? You were basically begging for me with your—"

"I was *not*. I was a scared girl and you were a sick brute, taking advantage of the small amount of power you had over other people. Because of *you*, I spent years believing all fae were power-hungry monsters, but that was a lie. Everything about you was a lie." My voice is shaking, both with terror and a strange sort of exhilaration that I'm finally getting to say the things I've always wanted to say to him. "You are *gone*, Caz," I say, injecting as much confidence into my voice as I can muster. "You no longer have any power over me, and I do *not* have to be afraid of you anymore."

"Oh, but I have all the power," he whispers with a snicker. "I will always be here, waiting for you in your nightmares." His hand, sickeningly real and strong, wraps around my wrist. "Waiting to remind you just how small and insignificant and unwanted—"

"Get out!" I scream at him, ripping my arm free. "Get out of my head! Get the fuck out! I will *not* let the memory of you control me! We are *done*, okay? Done! Get OUT!" Suddenly I'm lunging at him and shoving him so hard I feel the force of the impact rocket all the way through my body. There's a split second where he doesn't seem to move at all—

And then a shock of power bursts from my fingertips and radiates away from me, bathing the entire clearing in golden light. It turns Caz to an instant cloud of gold dust as it passes through him, doing the same to the little old house a second later. It ripples over the trees, revealing leaves of burnt orange and deepest red, as if a glamor has melted away.

"What the hell?" I gasp, staring down at my hands, my body shaking almost as much as when Caz first stepped from that house. That was *magic*. But it was part of the illusion, I'm sure. There's no way magic could have come from my own hands.

Something growls in the trees behind me. I spin around, my eyes catching the way the leaves shiver before going still again. I wait, heart galloping in my chest. But everything is silent.

And then that growl, low and menacing, and the sound of a twig snapping. I take a silent step backward. Caz is gone. The nightmare is gone. But something else stalks me now. Something *real*.

A blur of motion explodes from the trees, and I catch a glimpse of enormous eyes and tattered wings before I whip back around and start running. I don't know if it's the same kind of creature as the ones that attacked us at the palace, but it seems just as vicious and deadly. I race through the forest as fast as my ballgown and shoes will allow, some tiny, crazed corner of my brain wanting to yell at Finneas, *You see? If you'd only let me wear jeans!*

Branches crack behind me, and I urge myself faster. I lose one shoe and almost trip in the process, then pause a moment to kick the other one off. Forest debris stabs into the soles of my feet as I take off again, but I pay little attention to the pain. Anything to help me run faster. I dodge around another tree and find an enormous twisted branch blocking my path. With nowhere else to turn, I climb awkwardly over it, ripping part of my dress as I yank it after me.

I shove myself away from the branch as the creature lunges after me, sending air gusting across the back of my neck as its wings swipe a little too close. It would have caught me by now if it weren't slowed down by its size and the fact that it has to force its way between the trees.

Keep going, keep going, keep going, I chant endlessly to myself. Somehow, somewhere, this chase will come to an end. I will make it out of here. I've survived everything life has thrown at me so far, and this is no different.

My foot catches on something, and before I know it, I'm face down in the dirt, all the air knocked from my lungs. I roll over, gasping uselessly, and the creature is looming over me, fangs dripping, talons sweeping toward me, and I'm raising my arms as if my fragile human flesh could possibly do anything to defend me against—

A pulse of brilliant light bursts across the space between us. The creature doesn't vanish into a sprinkle of gold dust, but it does rear away from me with a blood-chilling shriek. I scramble backward on my elbows, my thoughts racing wildly. Was that ... that can't have been me. No way, no way, no—

"Avery!"

Kieren.

A dozen conflicting emotions crash over me at the sound of his voice, but the one that overwhelms me is relief. I'm lifted swiftly to my feet. He tugs me against his chest with one arm, and with the other he pulls something around the two of us in the same way one would dramatically sweep a cloak or blanket around oneself. But it isn't material of any sort. It's ... something like the rippling opalescent sheen of the Shimmer. It envelops us, and there's a split second where I see dripping fangs and enormous eyes hurtling toward us, and then everything is gone.

Chapter Thirty-Two

The ripples of shifting light vanish from around us, leaving us standing in another part of the darkened forest. Or a different forest entirely. All I know is that we haven't left Faeworld. The leaves are splashed with the rich hues of autumn, and glowing, golden specks drift through the air beside tiny white petals. It seems entirely possible that my dress, with its rips and dirt, might have been lifted directly from the forest itself.

"What just happened?" I gasp, stepping out of Kieren's embrace. "What did you just do?"

He seems thrown by my question, as if that wasn't where he was planning to begin. "It's ... a way of traveling within this world. Not usually possible in the human world, though my mother concocted a complex version of it to send you and the others directly into the Nightmare Forest. Avery, are you okay?" His hands rise toward my cheeks. "Your face—"

"The *Nightmare Forest*? Is that where I saw ..." I trail off without finishing.

"I'm sorry. I'm so sorry. I tried to stop her, but—"

"Wait." I take a jerky step back as everything that preceded that moment comes rushing back to me. "You chose Natalya," I say in a voice that sounds soft, stunned. *"Natalya,"* I repeat, louder this time, pain and anger etched into the word. "How could you do that? You didn't have to choose *me*—we both know that was nothing more than a silly daydream—but *her*? Out of all of those girls, you had to choose *her*?"

"I didn't *choose* her. Not in the way you think. Not in the way that matters. I had mere seconds in which to come up with a plan, and—"

"Then explain it to me. Explain this *plan*. Because I fail to see how it makes sense."

"I had to choose someone with—" He breaks off and presses a hand to his neck, seeming to choke on something. "The Winter Prince was about to steal you all away—*you* specifically, thanks to the way my mother was suddenly looking at you—and I knew I had to direct his attention away from you and get as many of you out of there as possible. In the moment, it seemed that the quickest way to do that was to end the game officially."

"Why did he want to steal us away? And ending the game like that was still a ridiculous, drastic decision. It's *your court*. I know the Winter guy brought guards with him, but you have far more. You could have—"

"And I had to draw my *mother's* attention away from you. I was trying to make her believe that I had already found the best option, and that you were *not it*, because I can't let her—" He breaks off again, then lets out a furious groan. "I cannot explain out here!" he roars, startling me. I take another step backward. "I'm sorry, I'm sorry. It is not you my anger is directed at. It's this—this damn—I cannot say it!" he yells, a desperation in his eyes that I don't understand. "Please come with me. We need to go somewhere. Somewhere I can explain."

I shake my head. "Why can't you explain here?"

"I can't. It won't—" He makes that strangled sound again before stopping to take a deep breath. "Please. Please believe me. Please trust me. I *want* to explain everything to you. But I cannot do it out here. It isn't possible. We need to be inside the Autumn Palace."

I hesitate. He's never tried to trick me before. After all the time we've spent together throughout this game, I can't bring myself to believe he's anything but genuine and honest. But everything that's happened tonight has made me warier than usual. "The Autumn Palace? Where your family usually lives when you're not at the Glittering Palace?"

"Where we ..." He swallows. "Where we used to live. Long ago. The original palace."

I'm frowning now. I didn't know there was an *original* palace. But that's hardly the point right now. "Why do we have to go there? Because for some reason you *physically* can't explain things to me anywhere else?"

"Correct."

Well, that's weird, but this is a world of magic, so I suppose anything goes. "What if I say no? What if I don't want to go with you?"

He breathes out heavily. "I will not force you to accompany me. You know that." He looks past me and points through the trees. "That way lies the Shimmer and the Glittering Palace. I have no idea what's happening there now. But whether the Winter Prince is gone or not, it is no longer safe for you there. If you want to return to your world, though, I will take you. I can sneak you past the palace without anyone seeing you. Otherwise, if you want answers—" his eyes meet mine again "—we go that way." He jerks his head in the opposite direction.

I pretend to consider my options for a moment, but I

already know that I want answers. Of course I want answers. I haven't examined my feelings too closely—mostly because I've been trying to protect my heart—but it's scarily possible that I've fallen in love with the man standing in front of me, and if I don't give him a chance to explain what the hell is going on here, I may never forgive myself.

Except ... shit. Quinn.

"I-I have to go back there," I stammer as fear grips hold of me. "I have to find Quinn. I have to make sure she's—"

"She will be fine."

"You don't know that. She was—"

"She was nowhere near the ballroom. After the two of you argued, she left with Iris. Iris would have taken her back to the room where all the contestants' loved ones first assembled this evening. From there, Quinn would have been shown to a room in the East Tower, far from the ballroom."

That's right. I remember the itinerary Iris showed me. Our loved ones are all supposed to spend the night at the palace and then join us for breakfast tomorrow morning before they're taken back home. I'm pretty sure that breakfast won't be happening anymore.

"You are the one who's in danger," Kieren adds quietly. "And if you go back there to look for her, she'll be in danger too once you find her."

I let out a shaky breath. I think what he's saying makes sense. Quinn is safer right now if I keep my distance from her. "Then ... answers," I say quietly. "Please. And thank you for saving me from whatever that ferocious beast was. I know I'm angry with you and I don't understand your actions, but I appreciate that bit."

A ghost of a smile finds its way onto his lips. "You seemed to be doing just fine on your own."

"Uh, sure, except that I was on the ground and it was about to chomp me until you showed up and threw some magic at it."

"Avery," he says quietly, holding my gaze, "that was you."

Everything inside me goes still. So very, very still. "That wasn't me," I say in a voice barely more than a breath. I think of that moment in the clearing when I shoved the nightmare version of Caz and something like power burst from my fingertips. The moment I threw my hands out at that creature and something similar happened. But I assumed a second later, when I heard Kieren's voice, that it had been him. I shake my head and repeat, "That wasn't me."

He sighs and holds his hand out toward me. "I will tell you everything. I promise."

I stare at him, my brain still rejecting the idea that that magic came from me. And yet I saw it with my own eyes. The vitamins, I realize. Perhaps they're the cause. In helping our bodies to acclimate to a world of magic, perhaps they've *produced* some kind of magic inside us.

"Avery," Kieren prompts. "You need to hold onto me if we are to travel there the same way we traveled here. Otherwise we will have to walk, and that would take us a very long time."

Hold onto him. Yes. I can definitely do that. Natalya flickers through my mind, but I brush aside the mental image. *I want you*, Kieren whispered to me not even an hour ago. *I want you.* I step closer and wrap my arms around him. "Do, um, do lots of people travel like this in your world?" I think of the evening we first visited Faeworld and drove along the streets of the Golden City to the opera house. I don't think I saw any strange flashes of light and people disappearing.

Kieren shakes his head, his eyes traveling my face. "Like the glamours, the ones that can change a person's appearance, this magic is difficult to master."

"Oh. Okay."

He hesitates, then gently takes my face in his hands. "I'm sorry. So sorry. For the Nightmare Forest. Whatever you saw there." His thumbs trace patterns down my cheeks. Tear streaks through dirt, I imagine, given all the crying I've done and the falling-face-first-on-the-ground part. Then his arm slides down to encircle my waist, and with his other hand he pulls his magic around us. I'm less alarmed this time by the sudden blaze of flickering light encompassing us, but it's just as beautiful and breathtaking.

When the light dims and night returns to take its place, we're at the edge of a forest. I turn around and—

It's right there. The palace. Perched at the top of a slope. And something is very, very wrong with it. My breath catches at the sight of the shadows that writhe and twist around the entirety of the structure, blocking most of it from view. *Where we used to live*, Kieren said. Now I understand why they don't live here anymore. "What happened to it?" I ask.

"A—" The words seem to stick in his throat again. He sighs. "I will tell you once we've fought our way inside."

"We have to *fight* that mass of shadows?"

"Don't worry. I have done it before. Countless times. I will get you inside safely."

We climb the hill, following overgrown paths between wild bushes. We pass fountains that no longer spurt water and cracked stone statues covered in creeping plants. I imagine these were once manicured lawns, perfect palace gardens. But something has gone terribly wrong here.

"The main entrance is difficult to get through," Kieren tells me as we near the top of the slope and approach the building. "There is a sun lounge on this side with a door that isn't locked. That's the easiest way inside."

"Okay." Honestly, I had no idea which side of the palace we were walking toward. Covered in shadows, it's tough to make out any details.

"Stand back," Kieren says, tugging the silver ring off his right hand. The long crystal-like blade flashes immediately into existence. I can't help remembering the horrifying moment he drove that blade into his own body.

"Are these shadows the same?" I ask. "The same as whatever attacked you in the music room?"

"Essentially, yes." He holds the blade out ahead of him as the shadows dart out and try to reach us. Now that we're close enough, I see they're not merely formless wisps. Some of them take on the shape of thorny vines, the ends of which curl into spirals. "And be ready to run to me when I call you," he adds. "I'll pull you inside when I have a clear path to the door."

He steps forward to meet them, and I feel useless standing here in my bare feet and dirty ballgown. He slashes at the dark shapes, swiping left and right, and bits of shadow fly into the night and disappear with a sound like a distant wail. The vines fight back, lashing out and curling around his arms as if made of something more than black vapor. One of them wraps tightly around his shoulder and yanks him further into the writhing darkness.

Without a thought, I launch forward and try to tug him back. The shadows reach for me, and I tense against the pain I know is coming. But all they do is gently brush against my skin before curling lazily away from me. I freeze, still holding onto Kieren's arm, as the shadows peel away from both of us, seeming to create a pathway directly to the door Kieren was aiming for. With shaky breaths and trembling fingers, I slowly reach out with one hand toward the nearest shadow.

"Don't," Kieren whispers urgently. But all the shadow does is curl around my fingers before drifting away.

"So ... has this happened before?" I ask faintly.

"Never. This has never happened."

I swallow. "Great. That's not weird at all. Any idea *why* these creepy shadows are parting for me?"

He hesitates, his startled gaze still traveling the slowly writhing vines. "Some idea, yes," he answers. "Come inside. I still cannot speak of it out here."

We hurry through the door, and he closes it quickly behind us. I realize, as he turns away from me, that I recognize the strange spiral welts and wounds upon his lower arms. "You were here," I say. "The other night. When we were supposed to meet at the opera house, and then I found you injured in your room. This is where you were."

"Yes. As I said, I come here often." He sighs. "Sometimes it is fairly easy to get through the shadows. Other times ... they fight back with more force. Hence the need for a pool full of healing magic."

"Why? Why do you come here all the time to try and fight them?"

Instead of answering, he jerks his head toward the other side of the room.

"What, you still can't tell me?"

"I can only speak of it in the throne room."

He leads me hastily through the palace, through darkened rooms and along shadowed corridors. Finally, on one side of a vast hall, we stop in front of a pair of enormous doors. Kieren presses his shoulder against them and heaves them open. Beyond the threshold I see a gleaming floor bathed in flickering moonlight, arched windows with shadows writhing beyond their glass panes, and on the far side of the room, a magnificent throne crafted from gilded leaves. But the edges appear tarnished and decayed, and the same shadows that surround the palace writhe across the throne.

"Finally," Kieren breathes as we step beyond the doors, the polished floor cool beneath my bare feet. "Finally, finally, *finally*, I can speak of it. The curse, the game, the lifestones. Everything."

I look at him. "Did you say *curse*?"

"Yes." He takes my hands in his. "There is a curse. A curse upon me, upon this court. And this is the reason I did not choose you. The reason I *could not* choose you. Because the winner of *The Princess Game* is going to die."

Chapter Thirty-Three

"What?" I whisper. Then a whole lot louder: *"What?"*

"There is so much that is a lie," he says, turning away from me and dragging a weary hand across his face. "So much. We did not even intend to reveal ourselves to your world. That was an accident. An accident that became the first lie. One of the biggest."

"Stop. Stop, stop, stop." I hold both hands up. "Can we go back to the part where the winner of *The Princess Game* isn't actually going to marry a prince and move in with the royal family? Instead she's going to *die*?"

He faces me again. "I have to go much further back than that. There is so much to explain." He heaves a heavy breath, then gestures to a ledge beneath one of the tall, arched windows. "Will you sit with me?"

I suppose sitting is a good idea. At least I'll be closer to the ground when I pass out from shock at whatever insanity he's about to tell me. I follow him, and what's left of my dress's leafy, flowery train slides over the floor behind me.

"There is magic in this world that runs through everything. More specifically, the magic of each court is connected to its throne and the ruler that sits upon it. It is more than merely a position of leadership. It is a magical bond between that ruler and the land. A continuous flow of power that sustains everything. But the key that makes it possible is the ..." He pauses, appearing to search for a word. "The lifestone, I suppose you could call it. I think that is the direct translation. You wouldn't have an equivalent word because there is no such thing in your world. The lifestone is embedded in the throne, and it aids this continuous flow of power. It has always been this way, since the first rulers." He turns slightly and looks toward the throne. "Do you see it?"

I look past him and notice the dull stone set into the upper part of the throne. A jewel as large as my fist. Squinting, I see lines running across its faceted surface. "It looks like it's cracked."

"Yes. That is where the problem comes in. Years ago, when I was a boy of barely five, the Queen of the Summer Court cursed the other courts. I don't know the details of their curses—I believe they are different—but here, in the Autumn Court, she broke the lifestone and removed its power, cursing the entire court to eventually wither away into nonexistence.

"She fled with the lifestone's power and scattered it across your world where it was absorbed by an unknown number of humans. Hundreds, thousands, I do not know. Most received barely a drop of this power, but there were some whose bodies retained a significant amount."

"There are some humans who have this magic inside them? This lifestone magic?"

"Yes." He gives me a meaningful look, and I know what he's implying.

"No," I say immediately, shaking my head, though it's impossible to deny what I saw out in the forest earlier. I can't forget the feeling of it either, that rush of something flooding out of my body.

I look down as my hands go strangely warm, and flames suddenly burst across my lap, eating through the leaves of my dress. "Shit, shit, shit!" I gasp, jumping to my feet and slapping at my dress.

"It's okay, wait, hang on." Kieren is on his feet in an instant, a cool blast of power streaming from his fingertips and over the flames, smothering them instantly.

"This is not okay," I whisper, still staring at the smoking leaves.

"I know. It's a lot. I'm sure." He urges me to sit again, and I do so without really thinking. I'm not sure I have much control over my body right now. "There is more," he says carefully, "if you are ready for me to continue?"

"Right," I say faintly, staring up at the gilded details of the ceiling far above us. "We haven't got to the part about the winner of *The Princess Game* having to die."

"Avery ..." He trails off. "If you need a little more time to process—"

"No, it's okay. I'll, uh, just file away this gargantuan discovery about myself to freak out over later."

"Avery—"

"No, please." I look at him. "Just tell me everything. Then I can try to process it all in one go."

"Okay. The Summer Queen gave us the terms of her curse after scattering our power. She said the next heir to the throne would spend his or her life hunting through the billions of people in your world in search of a human who possessed enough power to restore life to our court. *If* the heir was lucky enough to find such a person before the court diminished entirely, then the heir would seat that person upon the throne and kill them. In so doing, the lifestone's power would be released into the throne.

"But," he adds before I can say anything about this clearly psychotic Summer Queen, "because of the sacred magic within a throne, the act of murdering someone upon it would, in itself, bring about a different kind of curse upon the heir who did it. His or her reign would be plagued by one devastation after the next. The Summer Queen knew that, because this is an ancient magic that is woven into all of the thrones. So either way, she ensured our court would not return to normal for a very long time, if ever."

"What a maniac," I whisper. "Why did she do this to you?"

"Not to me," he says quietly, looking down. "Not originally, anyway. I was not the heir. My older sister was. But she was ... killed during an accidental and incredibly violent release of magic." His voice sounds strained as he continues. "The same accident that brought about the existence of the Shimmer. We ... did not see the need to share this information with anyone in your world, which is why you are unaware she even existed. Although ... I have mentioned her to you before. When I told you why I no longer play the piano."

I remember him speaking of a woman who also played and then was 'gone.' Someone he was very close to. It never crossed my mind that he might be referring to a sister. "I'm so sorry," I say. "That must have been unimaginably difficult for you." I try to imagine losing a sibling—losing Quinn—while at the same time becoming next in line to inherit both a throne and a curse.

"Yes," he answers shortly. "And to answer your question about *why*, the Summer Queen did this as an act of vengeance. She fell in love with a human man. She wanted him to rule beside her, but her own court would not stand for it. Along with the assistance of the other courts, they killed the man and removed the Summer Queen from her own throne. So she cursed the Autumn, Winter and Spring Courts in retaliation."

"And her own court?" I whisper.

"Gone. Destroyed. There is no Summer Court now."

My eyes trace Kieren's face as I follow this horrifying story. "You were a child back then, so ... your parents? They were the ones who went along with all of this? They just happily killed a man and then defied a whole load of very important-sounding ancient magic to tear a ruler from her own throne, simply because she loved a human?"

With a pained expression, he says, "Yes. There are few in this world who have ever looked favorably upon humans or those who interact with them. That has changed in recent years. We—the Autumn Court—have changed. The Summer Queen's curse, the fact that we have had to search for a human with power, has led to more interaction with your world. We now have a better understanding of how wrong some of our opinions of humans have been."

"So *The Princess Game,*" I say. "That was all part of searching for a human with power?"

"Yes. It was not our idea, as you know, but we decided to go along with it. Before that, we were doing what we had always done. Carefully observing humans, following rumors, finding those with the most magic and attempting to test them without them realizing it. When I was younger, my father would have people stolen from your world and then discarded once it was shown that they did not have enough power. I wasn't fully aware of what was going on, but my sister was. She hated it. And since she was the one who would have to end the curse, she told him she refused to do it that way."

"I like the sound of her," I say. "I wish I could have met her."

He nods, pressing his lips together, and I realize I've probably put my foot in it by mentioning the sister he clearly cared deeply for. "Well. Anyway. *The Princess Game* was a silly idea, but we thought it through and decided it would be a faster way of finding those who possessed some of our magic. The application form had to be filled in by hand, and some of the questions were complex. It required entrants to form ideas about certain things. This meant that the answers themselves were a kind of creation, and when you create something, you pour a part of yourself into it. If you possess magic, part of it would have spilled onto the pages. That was how the Glittering Palace narrowed down the many, many applications to a short-list of those with magic."

"So *that's* why you said they should have chosen me and not Suzanna," I interrupt before he can continue. "It was mostly my ideas that went onto the page, and I was the one writing them."

"Yes, exactly. An odd coincidence that Carwyn and Evanna chose your coffee shop for their reveal and then ended up choosing you too, but I wonder now if it was your music they were drawn to. There is magic in it I doubt you are even aware of."

"There ... there is?"

"Yes. I knew when I first heard it, but I assumed there was only a hint of magic in you. I knew you had ended up on the show by accident, and that blinded me to the possibility that you might have a significant amount of power. I thought ..." He looks away, his face coloring. "It shames me to admit it, but in the beginning, I thought you were nobody."

Even though I know his opinion has changed, it still stings to hear him say it. I have to remind myself that I didn't think particularly highly of him either when we first met. "So, the contestants," I prompt. "We all had some degree of magic?"

"Well, no. Some had no power at all. We had to choose a few who possessed connections or influence instead. They were there to make the idea of the show seem legitimate. To make it appear that the Autumn Court was looking for a strategic match. Instead, those girls were merely distractions."

"And we all thought it was the other way around," I say quietly. "That *they* were the real contenders."

"Nothing in the game happened by chance," Kieren continues. "It was all a test. The drinks at the Opening Ball? They made anyone with minimal magic sick. The enchanted ribbons? Again, you needed a decent amount of magic to be immune to their sting. Those creatures that attacked you in the middle of the night? They only went after those with the most power. A horrifying test I did not want to go along with, but my parents did not need my approval. I demanded they at least make you all forget. And then tonight, banishing you to the Forest of Nightmares. It was my mother's idea and I was not okay with this test either. The only way out of that forest is to fight back with magic, and it requires a significant amount."

Which I suppose I must have, I realize, *if I managed to fight off Caz.* "But ... then you kept girls around who had little to no power. Annemarie? Cadence?"

"Yes. For the sake of the show. It would not have made sense to dismiss them too early."

I stand and pace away from him, trying to make sense of this convoluted lie we've all been living. "So ... so all this time, since we all arrived at the Glittering Palace, you've known that you weren't choosing someone to be your wife. You were choosing someone for death."

His jaw works. He doesn't answer for a moment. "Yes."

"And you just ... went along with it all."

"Do you think I *wanted* any of this?" He's on his feet now too, his expression pleading. "*I do not want to kill someone.* I almost called off this whole ridiculous game multiple times, the more I got to know all of you, unable to face the thought of having to kill one of you. I have never stopped hoping that I might find another way out of this. It's why I have returned to this palace time and again, fighting against the shadows, hoping to seat myself upon the throne and return some magic to our land that way, but the shadows will never allow me close enough.

"So yes, not a moment has passed throughout this game when I have forgotten that it would all have to end with me taking a life. That was why I did not even attempt to become close to any of the contestants. How could I kill someone if I had grown to care for them? I don't even want to kill someone I *don't* particularly care for, like Natalya. But this was why I made that deal with you at the beginning. This was why I needed someone on the inside to tell me who all the contestants truly were. So that ..." A look of utter misery crosses his face. "So that if it came to it, I could choose the worst of you."

I'm blinking tears away by this point. "This is just ... all so wrong."

"Of course it's wrong. It is a *curse*. I grew up watching this burden weigh my sister down, and I have spent the past five years shouldering it myself. This is what it comes down to: Let my court and all its people wither away to nothing, or take a life, thereby saving them but bringing a string of calamities upon my own reign, which will ultimately hurt the entire court."

I swipe at a tear that's made its way down my cheek. "I'm sorry. I know none of this is your fault. I'm ... I don't know.

Trying to make sense of it all, and it's all just so unimaginably horrible."

He crosses the space between us and takes my face gently between his hands. "But you ... you are the light I discovered in all of this. I didn't intend to care for you, but it happened so easily. There was no pressure. I didn't believe you possessed much magic, so there was no chance I would have to kill you. And though I know this story has no happy ending, not for me, I still hoped. I still let myself get carried away. I still dreamed of finding a way for the two of us to be together."

I sniff. "Like killing Natalya, ending the curse, and when your court returned to normal, maybe I'd be okay with all of this insanity and we could start again?"

He shakes his head, lowering his hands. "No. That is not an option for us. I would not want you to be anywhere near me once I have committed murder upon my own throne." He sighs. "Well. A throne that is soon to be mine."

"I just ..." I shut my eyes in a foolish attempt to block out the rest of the world. "I don't know. I don't know. I'm so tired. This night is just ... too much. There was Maddox, and then I fought with Quinn, and then I mentally relived everything with Caz, and then I almost *literally* relived it in the Nightmare Forest, and then some creature tried to devour me, and apparently there's magic inside my own body, and now there's this heartrending story of how your entire world is literally crumbling apart, and it changes what I thought about *everything*, and my heart is breaking for you because it all seems so hopeless, and ..."

"It is a lot," he finishes quietly.

"Yeah. I kinda just want to curl up in a ball right here on the floor and go to sleep."

"Well, this is perhaps not the safest place to do that."

"I don't know," I say with a shrug. "Those shadows didn't seem to want to hurt me. Oh, you said you might have some idea of why they acted strangely around me. Do you think it's because there's magic inside me and maybe I'm meant to end this curse?" A strange kind of thrill races through my body at the reminder that *I have magic*—followed abruptly by a horrifying mental image of me sitting on the Autumn throne with a knife in my chest. "But wait. Shouldn't that make them want to attack me even more? To get rid of me so I can't get rid of them?"

"Yes, I suppose that would be a better assumption. Perhaps it was simply because you have nothing to do with this court. The curse is not upon you, so the shadows don't perceive you as something they need to end. But the shadows are not what concerns me. My parents are."

"Oh."

"They will be looking for us. After I ended the game somewhat dramatically earlier, there is no point in them hiding behind that farce any longer. They will want to attempt to end the curse either with you or with one of the other girls who demonstrated the most magic, as soon as possible."

"Who are the others?" I ask. "The ones with the most magic?" He chose Natalya, so she must be—

"Natalya, Shay and Riya. There could be—"

An echoing thud interrupts him, coming from somewhere outside the throne room. We both turn immediately toward the open doorway. "What was that?"

"This way," he says, reaching for my hand. "Quickly."

We race across the throne room. My bare feet are silent on the cold floor, but his shoes leave an echoing *scuff, scuff, scuff* behind us. He pulls me faster. We round the throne and aim for a door behind it. Then he's dragging me along darkened passageways and unlit rooms until we make it to an exterior door. He's tugging it open and reaching for his ring again when I say, "Wait, let me try." I hold my hand out toward the shadows without hesitation. As before, they curl away from my touch, parting until a pathway forms in front of us. "So weird," I mutter, gripping Kieren's hand as the two of us hurry forward.

We run another few paces, making sure we're out of the shadows' reach, and then he stops and pulls me against his side. His other arm is tugging magic around us a moment later, and then we're surrounded by bright, flickering light.

Chapter Thirty-Four

"Where are we?" I ask, taking a step away from him and looking around. We're near a lake, its rippling surface reflecting silvery moonlight, and all around us are dozens upon dozens of white rose bushes, their lush fragrance filling the air.

"We have several estates across the land," Kieren says. "Numerous properties. This one is near the very edge of our court, where autumn has less of a hold on the land. It's more a cottage than anything else. Far too small for my family and all the staff my mother seems to require whenever we travel. People come for the roses, but I don't believe anyone has stayed in the cottage in years."

"Cool. A dusty old cottage. I'm in." At this point, he could offer me a patch of damp grass and I'd happily curl up on it and go to sleep.

"Old, yes. Dusty, no." When I look at him, he adds, "Fae enchantments. We like our spaces to remain clean while we are away. Well, some of us do."

I smile to myself. Pools that keep themselves clean, homes that never grow dusty. I think I could happily give up things like

TV and internet in order to live in a world like this. The thought is followed quickly by the sobering reminder that this world is slowly falling apart.

We pick our way between the rose bushes, and after rounding the trunk of an enormous tree with drooping branches, we find the cottage. Which is, of course, at least twice the size of anything I picture when I hear the word 'cottage.' It is simple in design though, the only embellishments being the roses entwined around the entrance, so I can see why Kieren's parents might not think much of it. "It's beautiful," I tell him.

"It is quite lovely in its simplicity. I came here a few times shortly after the Shimmer was created and my sister died. I came alone, needing time away from ... everything. So much had changed. It all felt like too much to deal with at times. This place was an escape."

I reach for his hand and give it a reassuring squeeze. "Don't you think your parents will send people to look for you here? If they know you used this cottage as a hideout of sorts in the past."

He shakes his head. "They were never aware that I stayed here. They had plenty of other things to concern them. Come on." He leads me up a stone path toward the front door. He reaches for the handle and pauses before turning it. A ripple of light streaks away from his fingertips and across the door. It opens easily after that.

Inside, we cross a cozy living space and find an even cozier bedroom. "There's a bathroom through there," he tells me, pointing to a doorway that stands ajar. "And you can open those doors if you'd like. To let some fresh air in." He gestures to the far side of the room where a set of French doors lead to a little patio, also covered in roses. "I imagine you probably want to clean up after everything that happened out in the forest tonight. Not that you aren't beautiful as always, even ..." He trails off.

"Even covered in dirt?" I ask.

"I was trying to think of a nicer way to say it."

"No need," I say with a shrug. "I'm aware I probably look terrible."

"No," he says with a small shake of his head. "Just a little bit wild. Which I'll admit I like very much."

I stare at him, warmth heating my cheeks and something else stirring low in my belly. If it were any other night—if I wasn't weighed down by exhaustion and if my mind wasn't tangled with a hundred conflicting thoughts—I would probably throw myself at him and beg him to kiss me.

"I will be back," he says. "The lights and heating still need to be turned on."

"Okay. Oh, what powers this place?" I ask. Surely there isn't electricity out here. I don't think there's electricity in any part of their world.

He gives me an odd look, as if I should know the answer to this. "Magic," he says simply.

"Of course. Right. Oh, wait. Is it okay for me to stay here? In this world, I mean. Because of the magic toxicity. I've never been here longer than a few hours."

"Avery, there is magic inside your own body. If it was toxic to you, it would have killed you long ago."

I blink at him. "Right. I guess so. Wait, that whole vitamin thing. Was that a lie too?"

"Not entirely. It was necessary for the contestants whose bodies have no magic. For others, like you, it was not."

I nod slowly. "Okay." *There is magic in my body. There is magic in my body.* It's going to take a while for that to fully sink in. "Do you think ... am I supposed to be able to *use* this magic?

The way you use yours? Or does it just erupt out of me by chance, like in the Nightmare Forest, and then earlier in the throne room?"

"To be honest, I have no idea. I can try to teach you some things, if you would like. When you are not so tired."

Something akin to excitement ripples through my veins. "That would be cool."

He leaves the room and I open the French doors. Stepping out, I inhale deeply, savoring the heady scent of roses. In the absence of someone to talk to, my mind begins to replay through everything Kieren told me in the throne room. New questions entwine with those I've already asked him. New fears.

What will happen tomorrow? Will I have to say goodbye to him? Will I spend the rest of my life hiding back in my own world, constantly wondering if the Autumn Court is about to find me and try to use me to end this curse? Should I just give up and let them kill me and know that at least my death will have saved an entire court?

No. I don't want to *die*. But I don't want this world—or, at the very least, this court—to die either. Something inside me feels connected to this place. Presumably it's the piece of life-stone magic that somehow attached itself to me. If I was a regular human with no magic coursing through me, I doubt I would feel this yearning to remain on this side of the Shimmer. This strange conviction that some part of me *belongs* here after I have spent my life not belonging anywhere.

I shut my eyes and press my fist to my lips. Kieren and I haven't even spoken about what should happen next and my brain is already spiraling out of control.

"Avery? Are you okay?"

I lower my hand and open my eyes. He's standing beside me. "Yes. Just ... thinking. About everything." My gaze travels across the tiny glowing creatures climbing out of the roses before launching themselves into the air, iridescent purple-blue wings unfolding behind them. "It's so beautiful here. Almost everything I've seen of your world so far is beautiful. When I first looked around at everything, I wondered how much of it was an illusion. We've been taught to believe that fae magic doesn't last. That nothing is *real*."

"It is that way in your world. There is no magic there. Nothing to hold our creations together. When we cast magic to create something, it does not last. That is why humans have always called them illusions."

"And you didn't correct us."

"No. We did not want them to know how truly powerful magic can be, in the right setting. In the right world. It's not as though humans can last long here anyway. It would not be of much use to them even if they did know what our magic is truly capable of."

"Unless you *want* a human to be able to last long in this world," I say, remembering Riya's tale of the Winter Princess and her human lover. "Then there are ways. Correct?"

He's quiet a moment before answering. "Yes. There are ways. Most of which we in the Autumn Court do not agree with."

"The Autumn Court ..." I turn to face him. "Does everyone know about the curse?" I've been thinking about Finneas and Mischa, so excited to dress me up as the perfect princess. To hopefully catch the prince's eye. To make the court believe I belonged beside the Autumn throne. Either they really are the monsters I once believed and they were excited at the possibility of me ending their curse, or they genuinely had no idea that being chosen would lead to my death.

"You know I cannot speak of it out here," Kieren says with a sigh. "Not directly, at least." He runs a hand through his hair before leaning back against the wall beside the open doors and folding his arms. "Everyone does know of the—" He stops as the words catch in his throat. "The thing of which you speak. They know of it, but they do not know all the details. They know of the ... of what surrounds the palace. They know there is ... certain power lost somewhere in your world. But they do not know how this will end for all of us if we don't solve the problem, even though they have seen the way bits of our world are disintegrating and they have questions. And they don't know *how* we are supposed to solve this ... problem. My father bound the knowledge to the throne room so that none of us who were there that day could spread the details."

I nod, relieved. I so badly didn't want to hate Finneas and Mischa. "And that shadowy creature that attacked you in the music room," I say. "You said it was essentially the same as the shadows around the palace. I assume those shadows are trying to keep you from breaking the curse?"

"Yes, I assume so. They come hunting for me. They try to overwhelm me with despair, reminding me of all the terrible things that have ever happened in my life, presumably so that I will not be able to continue my quest to ... solve the problem."

"And ... okay, one last question. I know it's frustrating having to speak in circles around this thing. The way the edges of things are disintegrating is the whole 'withering away' part of the curse, I assume. But why did you think it so strange that I could see it?"

"Because humans are not supposed to be able to. There have been humans visiting our world since we first revealed ourselves through the Shimmer, and no one else has ever mentioned seeing it or asked about it. I even attempted to point it out to a visiting politician once, but she looked right past it. The fact that you could see our world disintegrating made me realize very abruptly that you had far more magic than I first assumed."

He pushes away from the wall and moves to stand in front of me. His hands gently cup my face. "I did not pay attention to you the way I should have. Or rather, I began to pay attention to you, but not to the possibility of magic within you, since I had already—stupidly—dismissed it as an option. Looking back, I see what I missed. The faerie drink had no effect on you, obviously. The ribbons did not hurt you. I thought you were merely lucky that you had hurried out of their way before they began stinging. And those beasts that chased down the girls with the most magic ... From the way you described it, I thought they were there for Riya and Shay, not for you. Clearly I was wrong. The fact that you grew so ill from its bite is the only part that still confuses me. But perhaps that is also something to do with you having more magic than the others."

"And the Nightmare Forest?" I ask in what I hope is a lighthearted tone. "I'm waiting for you to tell me I got out of there in record time."

"You jest, but I found you far quicker than I expected to. I thought you might be stuck in there for a long time. But—oh, hold on. I forgot—" He steps hastily back inside and disappears through the door to the bathroom. I notice the lamps in the room are lit now, and light emanates from the bathroom as well.

I step back inside just as he leaves the bathroom. "The bath is full," he says. "It should be warm enough."

"Oh. Wow. Thank you."

"Surprising, I know. What would a pampered prince know of filling a bath with water?"

I roll my eyes. "I didn't mean it like that. I just meant that I didn't expect you to do that for me, that's all. But thank you."

"Of course," he says with a nod. "I will, uh, give you some space then."

"Okay. Thanks. Oh, I don't have anything else to wear," I blurt out as the realization hits me.

"Yes, I know. I found some clothes in the room I used to stay in. Things I never took back to the palace. I left a shirt on the bed here for you." He gestures to a white garment spread across one of the pillows.

"Oh. Thank you."

"However … I obviously do not have …" He looks away, rubbing the back of his neck. "Appropriate undergarments," he finishes quickly.

"Oh, right. Yeah, don't worry. I'll, uh—"

"But there is a heating stone in the bathroom. For drying clothes upon. You can wash your … uh, things, in the bath, and they should dry quickly on the stone. It is enchanted for such a purpose."

I press my lips together to try to hold my smile back. It's adorable how flustered he is over this. Before I can say anything else, he leaves the room.

The bathroom here is far simpler than the over-the-top space attached to my suite at the Glittering Palace, but the steaming hot bath is so glorious, I almost fall asleep in it. I spend so long floating in the water that my 'appropriate undergarments'—i.e. panties—are dry by the time I manage to muster the energy to get out.

I try not to feel weird as I pull the oversized white shirt on and do up the buttons. The fabric is soft against my skin, brushing over my breasts as I move. I peer down at myself, trying to figure out if the shirt is see-through. Nope. I think I'm sufficiently covered up. Though I'm so worn out from the evening's events and revelations that I don't think I could summon the energy to care about it if I happened to be revealing some part of myself.

I'm sitting on the edge of the bed, my eyes closed as I squeeze the moisture from my hair with a towel, when I hear Kieren's voice: "You look good in that."

I open my eyes. He's wearing loose pants and something that looks like it might possibly be a T-shirt. I didn't know they made such things in this world. I also didn't know Prince Kieren of the Autumn Court ever wore anything other than a suit. He gives me one of his rare smiles.

"I'll be sure to tell Finneas if I ever see him again," I say, lowering the towel to my lap. "Hey, Finneas, you know all those dresses you spent hours designing and making in the hopes that I'd catch the prince's eye while wearing them? Waste of time. You should have just put me in a plain white men's shirt."

"I wouldn't call them a waste of time," Kieren says. "You were spectacular in all of them. But I think this look might be my favorite."

I laugh and end up slipping off the edge of the bed. He catches my elbow and helps me back up. "I'm sorry. You are very tired. You should sleep now." He steps back. "Good night, Avery."

"Wait." An inexplicable fear shoots through me, jolting me awake. I stand up. "I—please don't leave me."

He hesitates, eyes traveling my face. "Do you mean ..."

"I—I just mean that I don't want to be left alone. What with there being people out there who want to put me on a shadow-covered throne and kill me. The, um ..." I toss a look over my shoulder at the bed. "The bed is big. Space for both of us. We could just ... sleep. I don't mean that I want anything else to happen." Shit, why am I so awkward? "I mean, if you don't mind staying in here. If you don't mind just—"

"Avery," he says. "Of course I will stay with you. And I promise I will not touch you, so you don't have to worry about that."

"Well, I mean, you can *touch* me." Crap, that sounded horribly suggestive too. What is *wrong* with me? I shouldn't be allowed to talk when I'm so tired. "Um, not like that," I say, my face burning now. "I mean, like, a hug or touching my arm or—you know what? Never mind. I'm getting into bed."

I turn hastily away and tug back the covers. I climb into bed and sink back on the soft pillows. I stare at the ceiling as Kieren walks around to the other side and slowly climbs in beside me. I realize the French doors are still open, and I consider how much energy it would require to get out of bed and close them—for safety purposes. In case someone does find us. But then I think about the fact that a flimsy glass door isn't going to stop someone if they want to get inside, and I decide it's definitely too much effort.

At a whisper from Kieren, the lights go out. We lie there, and this is weird, because of *course* I had to go and make it weird. But I'm so bone-deep tired, my limbs so heavy they're sinking into the mattress, that sleep will probably consume me before embarrassment does. So at least there's that.

With a great deal of effort, I roll onto my side and watch him through eyes already half-closed. His beautiful face is bathed in moonlight. He turns his head to look at me. "You're supposed to be tired," he murmurs.

"I am," I mumble. "Beyond tired. I'm not actually sure if I'm still awake or if I've already fallen into dreamland."

He reaches over with one hand to tuck a strand of damp hair behind my ear. "Close your eyes. Sleep. Nothing will trouble you while I am here."

So I do.

Chapter Thirty-Five

I hardly move all night until the first glimmer of pale morning light touches my eyelids. A cool, rose-scented breeze drifts in through the open doors, but I'm snuggled up beneath the covers with my back against a warm chest. I blink a few times, remembering everything that happened yesterday, and then close my eyes again, choosing to ignore the worries of the real world.

I'm lying in bed beside a man I think may love. If all I consider is this moment, then life is very, very good.

I reach behind me, find his arm, and draw it over my waist. He shifts slightly, sighing deep in his throat, and tightens his arm around me. With my eyes still closed, I sink back into perfect dreamless sleep.

A little while later, when the light beyond my closed eyelids has changed from pale silver to glowing gold, I sense Kieren shift against me again. His arm moves, sliding over the curve of my waist and then up my arm. He finds the collar of the shirt—loose and gaping—and pulls it gently aside to reveal my shoulder. He slides his finger across my skin before pressing a kiss there. "Good morning," he whispers.

A smile curves my lips. "Mmm," I murmur, too sleepy to form words or open my eyes. I want to stay cocooned in this moment, wrapped in his embrace. Perhaps, if I keep my eyes closed, the real world won't have a chance to intrude.

"I could wake up next to you every day."

My sleepy smile curves higher. "Same."

"Shall we pretend the rest of the world does not exist? Just for a day?"

A thrill shoots through me at the idea. A thrill I have no right to feel when this beautiful land is slowly falling apart around us. But how much will really change if we ignore the curse for just a day? Very little, I assume. It's been around for twenty years already. Besides, it feels as though today may be all we have. When we get up from this bed and leave this cottage, we'll have to leave this cozy, protected moment behind too, and I have feeling I won't get a chance at another one with him. "How about forever?" I whisper, eyes still closed.

"That sounds even better." His hand brushes down over the sleeve again, over my waist and hip, and finds the lower edge of the shirt. He slides beneath it and traces circles across my lower belly. "So, just to clarify," he says as my breathing begins to quicken. "You are happy to stay right here? In this bed?"

"Mm hmm. Yes. Very happy."

His hand glides up, knuckles brushing along the lower curve of my breast. Back and forth, and then his thumb sweeps across my nipple. Heat pools between my legs. I may have been sleepy before, when he first began touching me, but every nerve ending in my body is awake now.

"So ... I should continue with this?"

My answer is a breathy "Yes."

His lips follow a trail up the side of my neck. "You have no idea," he murmurs in my ear, "of the gargantuan effort it took to keep my hands off you last night. But I promised, and I would never break a promise to you."

Shit. His words alone are enough to send desire sparking through my entire body. His fingers travel back down again, dragging lazy patterns back and forth across my bare skin. Lower and lower until my breath catches as his fingers sweep beneath the edge of my panties for just a moment.

"Is this okay?" he asks.

Words seem to be trapped in the back of my throat. "Yes," I manage to breathe.

"If you don't like something, tell me to stop."

I swallow. "Don't stop," I whisper.

His fingers trace down again, below the elasticated edge, and the muscles of my lower abdomen tighten. He sweeps back up, circling my belly button. "What do you want?" he murmurs against my neck.

What do I want? I have no idea. I want *him*. I want *this*, whatever it is and wherever it may be going. But I'm so inexperienced and I haven't desired anything of this nature in so long that I have no idea how to articulate any of it.

Instead of answering in words, I reach with trembling fingers and slide my panties down, my heart thundering in my ears. I push them down to my ankles and slide them off with one foot while Kieren presses his lips to my neck and traces his fingers over my now-exposed hip. I go still against him, my heart thundering so loudly in my ears I swear he can hear it too.

He kisses across the exposed part of my shoulder as his hand slides over my hip, in between my thighs, and gently urges my legs apart. It's the kind of motion that might cause me to panic, to freeze up, but he isn't *on* me. He isn't *forcing* anything. It is the complete opposite, slow and sensual. He nudges my legs a little more, a little further, while kisses scald my shoulder, until I am spread open beneath the sheets. A tremble runs through my body. I'm still covered, but I've never felt more exposed.

"Tell me to stop and I will," he murmurs again, lips just beneath my ear now, hand sliding along my leg.

I shake my head. This is new and terrifying. New and intoxicating. I don't want it to stop. He traces idle patterns along my inner thigh, up and over my hip, then back and forth across my belly, easing me into this intimacy. He understands that I need this to be slow, and I love him for it.

The pressure builds as his fingers stray closer, an aching need throbbing at my core, and when he finally slides down and touches me *there*, a gasp catches in my throat. "Still okay?" he whispers, his finger rubbing slowly up and down, around and around. Sensation shudders through me, almost too much to bear, and I can't trust myself to speak, so I nod instead. *Don't stop*, I'm gasping inside my head. *Don't stop, don't stop.*

His finger slides down, finding my opening and circling it before returning up to press against my most sensitive part. I'm breathless, desire and nervous anticipation clashing inside me. I'm both relieved and achingly disappointed every time he moves down but doesn't enter me. My fear is of the unknown. No one else has ever touched me in this way. But I want it. I want it I want it I want—

He slides into me, deeper than I imagined, and I suck in a sharp breath, pleasure radiating in waves through my body. I arch up against his hand, my body acting instinctively as he slides out and back in again. He moves slowly, allowing me to adjust to this new sensation, then glides back up to circle my swollen center with slick fingers.

His lips trace my neck and shoulder, and he's murmuring

things I can't make out, words in another language, and I barely hear them as my head spins with pleasure. My thoughts are splintering—*oh* and *yes* and *more* and *don't stop*—as his fingers slide over me and into me, again and again, a delicious pleasure that builds and builds. He begins to move faster, pushing deeper inside as I press upward with desperate, aching need against his palm. I'm hurtling closer, closer, closer to an edge I've never known before, until finally I'm tumbling over it into a dizzying abyss of sensation that leaves me shuddering and trembling in its wake.

I didn't know it could be this good. *I didn't know ... I didn't know, I didn't know ...*

I lie against him as the last few waves of pleasure wash over me, my breath trembling across my lips and my splintered thoughts slowly coming back together. Kieren has lifted my arm now and is leaving kisses along the inside of my wrist. I become aware of him pressed against my back. Hard. Not yet satisfied. I want to do for him what he did for me, but I have only vague ideas based on brief scenes in movies of how to actually achieve this. "Do you ... um ..." I swallow. "Just tell me what to do for you, and I'll do it."

"Do not worry about me," he says with a quiet chuckle. The man who barely smiles is laughing quietly against my neck. "This was about you. Just relax. If we have all day in bed, then what is the rush?"

I turn over to face him, embarrassment washing over me as I meet his eyes and think of where his fingers were mere minutes ago. Of the way my body reacted and the gasps that came from my throat. But his heavy-lidded gaze is filled with desire, and there is nothing there that suggests I have anything to feel embarrassed about.

I lift my hand to his face and slowly run my fingers over his cheekbone and along his jaw. I trace the outline of his lips. His eyes slide closed as he sighs. "I told you before that I haven't done this," I say quietly. "I haven't been close to someone like this. So if I'm clumsy, or I do the wrong thing—"

"And I told you that you are perfect." He opens his eyes, gaze intent on mine. "Just perfect. You cannot do anything wrong."

I lean forward and press a hard kiss against his lips before dragging my mouth across the faint stubble of his jaw and down the side of his neck. My fumbling hand finds the edge of his shirt and slides beneath it, traveling up and over the hard planes of his chest. His muscles tense beneath my touch. Then, telling myself that I have nothing to be afraid of, nothing to be embarrassed about, I slowly slide my hand all the way down, beneath the loose waistband of his pants, and wrap my hand around him. I hear his sharp intake of breath—

And in the next second, I hear a shout and the splintering of glass. Bright light blazes across the room, and I'm sitting up, startled and terrified, and then—

Chapter Thirty-Six

There is a pounding behind my eyes as I wake slowly on a cold, hard surface. I have to blink several times before my eyes can focus. I eventually manage to make out gilded, ornamental finishings in a high ceiling, shadows dancing across it. The throne room inside the Autumn Palace.

With a jolt of fear, I turn my head sideways and find Kieren lying beside me. His eyelids flutter as he strains to open them. "Kieren? Kieren!"

"Thank goodness," an anxious voice breathes out from somewhere behind me. "Please alert the king." I twist clumsily —my hands seem to be bound together—until I see Queen Erralee coming toward me, one hand pressed delicately to her chest. "I was concerned you might not wake up. I'll admit our men used a little too much magic in subduing the two of you. It has taken most of the day to revive you."

I manage to push myself up as memories come hurtling back. Our night in the cottage. Our morning tucked away in bed together. Shame burns hot as I think of the state the queen's men discovered us in. I look down, expecting to see myself in nothing more than an oversized shirt, but I find that I've been dressed in a loose-fitting, silvery blue gown of satin-soft fabric. Simpler than most of the evening dresses Finneas designed for me, but still beautiful.

I look up and meet the queen's gaze. "How kind of you to dress me," I bite out.

She gives me a long look before answering. "I am not a *monster*. I wouldn't hurl you onto that throne half naked. I want you to at least have some dignity in your final moments."

"Great. I hope you're not expecting me to say thank you."

"No. Of course not," she says softly. "But *I* will thank *you*. You have no idea of the many, many lives you will save with your sacrifice."

"I do, actually," I tell her in a shaky voice. "*I do!* And I don't want any of those people to die, but *I* don't want to die either!"

"Miss Avery—"

"Do you care at all about what this will do to him?"

"Avery ..." Kieren is stirring at my side, mumbling my name.

Queen Erralee glances at him before returning her gaze to me. "Do not think for a moment that I don't love and care for him," she says fiercely. "Of course I would rather give him happiness than the suffering of having to sacrifice you, someone he clearly cares deeply for. But this curse has given us no choice."

I know that. I know it and I hate it and *I don't want to die*.

"Avery!" Kieren's voice is louder, stronger, as he pushes himself up. His wrists are bound too. I guess his mother knew he would resist this. He pushes himself onto his feet and plants himself between me and the queen. "I will not do this."

"My son." She steps closer, grips his shoulders and presses her brow to his. "I do not want this pain for you, but you have no choice. *You must—*"

"I will not!" he repeats fiercely. "I will not kill her!"

She whispers to him in a foreign tongue, words that sound as though they're meant to be reassuring, but Kieren interrupts with a fierce, "No! Whatever you have to say, I want her to hear it. She is the one whose life you plan to take. At least do her the courtesy of speaking in a tongue she understands."

The queen lets out a shaky breath. "This is the most noble thing she could ever hope to do with her life. Instead of decaying away into nothing, our court will survive. Our people will survive."

"Anyone but her then!" Kieren roars. "Please! I will be the monster you need me to be and kill someone else, but not her! I cannot do it!"

"My love." The queen's hands move to her son's face. Her gentle fingers stroke his cheeks. "I wish it did not have to be her. I *see* that you care for her. And that is precisely why it must be her and not any of the others. You were in this very room with us the day we were cursed. You heard the Summer Queen. But you were very young. You did not understand all the details."

Kieren shrugs his mother off, taking a step back. I climb to my feet and stand beside him. "What did I not understand?" he demands. "I *know* what she said. We have repeated it to each other each time we managed to make it into this throne room, before you decided to give up on coming back here. 'Find a human who possesses the most power and seat him or her upon the throne that will one day be yours. Kill them, and the lost power of the lifestone will return to the throne.'"

"No." Queen Erralee shakes her head. "'Find a human *to love* who possesses the most power.' That is what she said."

He's shaking his head even before she finishes speaking. "She did not say that."

Tears shine in the queen's eyes. "I am sorry I kept this from you. I am sorry I convinced your father to say nothing of it all these years. But I knew it would only make this harder for you. If you had known you had to love someone only to kill them, you would not have been free with your heart. You would not have allowed yourself to love. As it was, you were so adamant at the start of *The Princess Game* that you would not care for any of the contestants, knowing how it must all end. But I was so hopeful that this silly game would give you the opportunity to love someone." She glances at me before returning her gaze to him. "And it has. Thank goodness. Your father's methods with your sister certainly never worked. We had to try something different with you."

"Methods?"

"He had all manner of men and women snatched away from the human world and brought here. After testing them for power, he forced Kelida to spend a brief period of time with them—no longer than a day or two—and then wondered why the curse did not end when he forced a blade into her hand and made her kill them."

I look up at Kieren and see the horror on his face. "How did I not know that?"

"You were still young. We spared you the details. At the time, it did not seem necessary for you to—"

Her words are interrupted by a deep creak and a long, low groan as the enormous throne room doors slowly open. On the other side of them stands King Eldyn. He sweeps into the room, calling out to his wife in their own tongue. She answers him in kind. "Then let us get on with it," he says, coming to a halt beside her. He looks at me with something that might possibly be pain in his eyes. "I doubt this will mean much to you, but I am sorry."

Kieren steps in front of me. "I refuse—" But the words are barely out of his mouth when two uniformed men grip his arms.

He fights back with a furious roar, managing to break his bonds and send one of them sprawling to the ground, but another quickly joins him so there are now three holding him in place as two pairs of hands grip my arms.

Fear shoots through me, icy and paralyzing. I struggle against them, but they're already dragging me toward the cursed throne where dark shadows writhe around the gilded autumn leaves, and I'm thinking, *Will it hurt? Will it be over quickly?* And then I think of Kieren and decide I have to be brave for him. I won't take my eyes off him, and I'll tell him that it's okay and that I forgive him and that I love him—which I abruptly realize is true. I do love him.

Then everything comes to a halt as I sense a shudder of power rippling through the air. The vice-like grip on my arms is abruptly gone as the two guards are thrown to the side of the room and pinned to the wall by an invisible force. I spin around and see that the same thing has happened to the king and queen, to Kieren, to all the uniformed men and women in the room.

Then my eyes land on her. The woman standing in the open throne room doorway. Daisies trail her sheer yellow gown, and wildflowers are caught in her loose hair, which glows golden as if she wears a crown of sunlight. She steps forward on bare feet and opens her mouth.

"Hands. Off. My. Daughter."

Chapter Thirty-Seven

Daughter. Daughter. She said daughter. The air feels as if it's slowly pressing in on me, and I can't hear properly, can't breathe properly, can't think.

Daughter.

She curls her fingers in my direction, and I go skidding across the floor toward her, my arms flailing inelegantly at my sides. Her magic halts me just before I crash into her. There are murmurs coming from the soldiers pinned to the walls on either side of the room: *"Summer Queen."*

Summer Queen.

The woman who cast the curse.

Daughter.

"Do not call her a *queen*," King Eldyn hisses. "She destroyed her court. There is nothing left of it. She is queen of *nothing*."

The Summer Queen's hard gaze moves to him. The afternoon light, mostly blotted out by the curse shadows that writhe outside the windows, dances strangely across her beautiful face. "And soon you will be *king* of nothing. You will not exist at all. My daughter may possess some of the power of your lifestone, but killing her will not end your curse. She is not human. Your heir will have committed murder upon his future throne for nothing."

Daughter.

I still can't comprehend this.

My eyes dart about until I find Kieren. He's looking between the two of us, the Summer Queen and me, with a kind of horror on his face. And something else. Something that tells me he recognizes this as truth. But it *can't* be.

I look at her again. "I can't ... I can't be ... I'm not *fae.*" I take a breath and swallow, trying to banish the shaky quality from my voice. "Fae have to return to this world every few weeks because they can't survive for long without access to magic. But I've lived my whole life in the human world without ever doing that."

She meets my gaze with blue eyes that match my own. "You are half fae. Your father was human. You can live in either world."

Father.

My father.

The Summer Queen's human lover who was killed.

"But—all the stories about humans and fae not being able to have children together—"

"Are true. In your world. But you were conceived here, where the magic that exists in everything allowed you to be created. You are my daughter."

Daughter.

Finally, my brain dares to think the word that goes with it. The puzzle piece that fits perfectly: *Mother.*

"You're my mother," I whisper.

"Yes. I am your mother."

Something shrivels up and dies inside me. The tiny hope I've clung to since childhood. The hope I used to focus on when despair tried to pull me under. The hope that somehow it was all an accident, that I was never supposed to be abandoned, that my mother was someone good and kind who had never stopped looking for me and would one day find me.

That hope is gone. There is no kindness in this woman's eyes. No love. She may have saved me from death in this throne room, but she didn't do it for *me*.

"Avery, don't listen to her," Kieren calls out to me. His father starts shouting for more soldiers, and Kieren adds, "Whatever she says to you, don't—"

"Silence, everyone," the Summer Queen snaps. Her fist closes around the air, and with that single motion, every voice in the room vanishes.

"You cursed this entire court," I say. "Basically an entire *country*. The land and all of its people will become *nothing*. How could you bring yourself to do something so horrific?"

Her eyes narrow. "Did they not tell you?"

"They did. You loved a human, and they—"

"I loved a *human*. Your father. He was everything, *everything* to me, and when I wanted him to rule beside me, my own court found the very idea to be disgusting. But I was their ruler, and they could not act against me on their own. They went to the other courts for help. And the other courts all agreed." Her eyes, hard with malice, settle on Kieren's parents, struggling against invisible bonds and invisible gags. "They killed my beloved and worked together to break the magic that bound me to my own throne. Probably the *only* time in history that they have worked together for anything. That is how much they hated humans. And so I cursed them all for it, including my own court."

"So many innocent people—"

"Yes, so many innocent people who were happy to allow *me* to suffer," she spits, her furious gaze back on me now. "So I cast a true curse. *Pain*, daughter. Pain is how one does it. One has to suffer in order to cause suffering in others. I took all of my pain and heartache—the pain of losing my beloved and the pain of knowing I had been betrayed by every person I had sworn to lead and protect—and bound it into a curse. I went to each court and cursed its heir.

"When that was done, I went into the wilderness that remained of my court, the wilderness that exists between all the courts, and wandered. I discovered wild magic. Ancient magic. Magic the courts have forgotten." She looks past me and smiles at the king and queen. "Magic that makes me more powerful now than I was when I cast your curse."

"And at some point you abandoned me in another world," I say, drawing her attention back to me.

"Yes. I left you there. I could not have you raised by someone in this world when I did not know how much longer any of it would still be here."

"You didn't have to abandon me at *all*! Or if you felt that you had to, you could have at least found my father's family and left me with them."

"I did not know them. I did not care to know them. I cared for nothing in the wake of my beloved's death. All I knew was that I could not bear the idea of raising a child alone. To have a wailing, unwanted babe to worry about while trying to find my way through my heartbreak? No. My grief was too much for that."

Unwanted. Unwanted. Unwanted.

It is the pulse that has beat through my veins my entire life. The pain I tried to wish away every time I dreamed of a mother who might love me and find me. I take a step back and lift my chin. This pain is nothing new. As I told Kieren, I learned to live with it a long time ago. "If I was unwanted," I say roughly, "why not get rid of me completely? Why go to the trouble of dumping me in another world?"

Confusion clouds her expression. "I did not want you *dead*. You are the last remaining link to the man I loved. You are his blood. *My* blood. I had no use for a *child*, that is all. I have watched you from afar these many years, waiting for you to grow into a woman. Someone I might one day have use for. I saw you become a participant of this ridiculous farce the Autumn Court put together. An odd coincidence, I thought. I did not believe you actually possessed any of the lifestone magic they were so desperately seeking. Though I suppose it makes sense, given that you were within my womb when I scattered it across the human world. Still, it never crossed my mind that so much of it—that any of it—would latch onto *you*."

"You were waiting for me to *grow up*?" I demand, barely contained fury in my voice. "For me to become *useful*? I grew up a long time ago, thanks to the life *you* forced me to live. A life you *watched*, apparently, and had no trouble leaving me trapped in. Did you think nothing of the horrors I was forced to endure?"

She frowns. "Those horrors only served to make you stronger. Better still, all that time you spent with the man you ended up killing nurtured your hatred of fae. The same hatred that has burned in my veins for so long. I saw no need to remove you from your situation."

"You saw no need to—wow. And the Mother of the Year Award goes to the heartless Summer Queen, ladies and gentlemen."

Her eyes narrow further. "Enough of this. We are leav—"

"Not that I *want* anything to do with you now that I know

what you're like, but didn't you think it might be useful to bring me here when I was teenager? To teach me about my world, teach me to use magic?"

She scoffs. "You don't need my help for that. You burned that man, did you not? The fae one who tried to hurt you."

"I—what? No, that wasn't—"

"We do love the sun, those of us from the Summer Court," she says, her lips curving upward. "The heat, the flames, the burn. That kind of magic comes so easily. The kind of magic that consumes completely."

I remember the way Caz's body ignited. I think of the flames that leaped suddenly across my dress as I sat with Kieren in this very room while he attempted to convince me of the magic he was certain flowed within my body. And then ... wasn't there that odd little flame that burned a section of one of my couches the night I was so angry at the way Natalya spoke to Iris?

Was that really all *me*?

"And your music," the Summer Queen continues. "You weave magic without even knowing it. You have captivated the entire human world in recent days. If you *really* knew what you were doing," she adds with a conspiratorial smile, "you could enchant them all. Bend them to your will. It is what we were once known for, the Summer Court."

"Until you destroyed everyone."

"Strange that this upsets you when I did it because of their hatred for humans, and until mere minutes ago, you believed you were human too. Now come, daughter. We are leaving." She makes as if to turn. "You will soon grow to hate the courts as I do."

"Don't call me that. You don't get to abandon me for almost twenty years and then call me *daughter*."

She looks back at me, amusement in her expression. "My

blood runs in your veins. Deny it all you want, but in this world, there is power in blood. We are connected by magic, you and I."

I shut my eyes and tell myself to forget my pain and anger. To forget that I hate her for abandoning me and that I never wish to ask her for anything. I have to beg because I have no other option. "Please. Please, please. If you made this curse, then you can break it."

"Break it? Why would I do that?"

I open my eyes. "*Can* you break it?"

"Of course." She faces me fully once more. "I can break anything I created. But I will not. These people will suffer as I suffered, and they will know that their survival is dependent upon the very creatures they have looked down on forever. *Humans.*"

I hesitate, breathing hard.

There is power in blood. We are connected by magic, you and I.

"Fine." I take a step away from her and push my shoulders back. There is an idea nudging at the back of my mind. A dozen little puzzle pieces trying to fit themselves together. Perhaps they *don't* fit, perhaps I'm wrong, but there is nothing else left for me to try. "Fine," I tell her. "I will break it myself."

She laughs. The sound is as glorious and warm as the sun, utterly belying her true nature. "You? You cannot break it. Only I can break a curse I created. *I* am its master."

"But we share blood."

There is a moment of hesitation before she laughs again, not quite so loudly and confidently as before. "That will not work. As I said, *I* am the curse's master."

"But wasn't I part of you when you created it? Just as I was part of you when you scattered the lifestone magic and some of it clung to me? Perhaps it's my curse just as much as it is yours."

I think of the way the shadows writhing around the palace parted and made a way for me. I think of the way the shadowy curse creature that attacked Kieren in the music room simply passed right through my hand. It didn't do that to his guards. They said they experienced the same awful effects he experienced. But the creature did nothing to me. This curse *recognizes* me. It knows who I am.

There is power in blood. We are connected by magic, you and I.

I spin away from her and run for the throne. She releases a furious cry, her magic lashing out and wrapping around me. In an instant, I'm tugged back around, almost slamming into her. Her hand closes around my throat just as a sphere of magic crackles into existence around us, blurring the rest of the throne room. "You foolish child," she hisses. "I will not let you undo this. You understand *nothing* of this world or the pain I've been through."

"Well, if you wanted me to see things your way, *Mother*," I struggle to say as she squeezes my windpipe, "then perhaps you should have raised me yourself instead of abandoning me."

"And this kind of *insolence—*" she shakes me, her hand squeezing ever tighter "—tells me I was right all along wanting nothing to do with raising a child."

Bright spots of white begin to pop in front of my eyes. I claw desperately at her arm, trying to loosen her grip as I struggle to draw breath.

"Now that it is just the two of us," she continues, "let me tell you precisely how things are going to go from here on out. You will—"

A horrendous screeching sound assaults my ears, followed by a flash of light so bright I have to squeeze my eyes shut for a moment. When it dims, I open my eyes to find Kieren with his crystal-like knife in one hand, breathing hard, clearly having just finished slashing right through the Summer Queen's magic.

Then his hand is around my upper arm, tugging me away from her, and there is motion all around the throne room. My dear mother must have lost control of everyone else when she enclosed the two of us inside a ball of magic. Perhaps she isn't quite as powerful as she likes to believe. A handful of soldiers race toward her, but not before she whips out a long blade from among the folds of her dress and hurls it at Kieren. A moment later, the soldiers tackle her to the floor.

But my eyes are on Kieren as he lets go of me. On the hilt protruding from his side. On his crystal knife clattering to the floor and the blood oozing over his fingers as he presses his hand beneath the wound. He staggers sideways before falling onto his knees and then collapsing.

"No, no, no," I gasp, every other thought fleeing my mind. I drop to my knees beside him and take his hand. "You're fine. You'll be fine. Right? This is ... this is nothing."

"Of course," he grunts in response. "This is nothing."

"A blade poisoned by magic isn't nothing." The amused voice of the Summer Queen carries across the throne room. There is something wild, almost crazed in her tone. "Unless there is strong healing magic *very* close by, you will be dead within minutes. And no, your curse will not end with your death, as you well know. The effects will only come upon your land and its people faster."

I look over my shoulder at her, and she laughs as she attempts to fight back against the soldiers. I turn back to Kieren. "The pool. At the Glittering Palace. Can that heal this kind of wound? Can you get back there quickly?"

"I ... I can," he murmurs, but his eyes are sliding shut. "Just ... let me ..."

"Hey, wake up. Wake up!" I pat his cheek repeatedly. "You're not going to *die*, okay?"

"I ... won't," he whispers, but his eyes remain closed.

I glance about wildly, searching for help, but every soldier in the room is either trying to restrain the Summer Queen or standing protectively around the king. Only Kieren's mother is hurrying toward us, unmasked terror in her eyes. "Help him!" I shout at her.

And in that instant, the Summer Queen finally throws her assailants off with a powerful blast of magic. Kieren's mother is swept across the floor before crashing against the wall. I sense all hope begin to slip away.

My desperate gaze lands on the woman who was never going to be my mother. Her smile is brittle. "We are going to wait here until he is dead," she tells me. "And then, daughter, you will know a little something about pain. Then, I think, we will begin to understand each other."

We are going to wait here until he is dead.

My heart cracks. My lips shudder as I press them together. I don't now if it's too late to save him, but as useless as I am in this moment, there is *something* I can do. I stand on trembling limbs and face the Summer Queen, fury pulsing through my veins. I'm burning the same way I burned with hatred the night Caz killed Alice and tried to hurt me. My skin is so hot, so tight, I think I might combust.

The heat, the flames, the burn. The kind of magic that consumes completely.

"We will never understand each other," I say through gritted teeth. "And I know enough about pain already." Then I whirl away and race toward the throne.

"Stop!" she yells, and her magic wraps around my waist like a whip and tugs me backward. I slip to the floor, my fingers outstretched, just as power bursts away from me. Flames lick across the floor and leap up the front of the throne. The shadows writhe and twist beneath them, filling the air with eerie shrieks and wails as the curse attempts to fight back. But the fire is all-consuming. It engulfs the entire gilded structure until every last shadow has been eaten away. I watch, still gasping for breath, as the fire diminishes and the final flame flickers and vanishes.

The Autumn throne stands there, its tarnished, decayed edges restored to gleaming gold, perfect save for the dull, cracked lifestone.

"You ... you ..." Somewhere behind me, the Summer Queen lets out an unearthly scream. I don't wait to find out what she plans to do next. I scramble forward on hands and knees, slipping on the silly satiny dress. Just a few more feet, a few more feet. I lunge forward and wrap my hand around one of the throne legs.

Nothing happens. There is no power bleeding out of me. "Shit," I gasp. Maybe I have to—

An invisible force sweeps into me and hurls me to the floor. My head whacks the polished surface and pain explodes through my skull. For several moments, all I can do is lie there, gasping in pain, my eyes squeezed shut. I hear shouting all around me, but the sound is dull compared to the pain shrieking in my head. Another few moments ... another few moments ...

I don't pass out. I manage to blink and raise myself enough to look around. The Summer Queen is on the floor again, knocked down by ... Kieren? How? I blink again. Is that really him, or did I hit my head even harder than I thought? Soldiers are attempting to help him restrain the Summer Queen, but magic is flying across the room in all directions. Despite the ache throbbing through my skull, I push myself shakily to my feet and stagger toward the throne. I catch myself against one gilded arm and pull myself onto it. Then I reach up and bring my palm down flat against the cracked lifestone.

Golden light bursts instantly from my hand, so bright I have to squeeze my eyes shut. I sense something pouring out of me. A river, a torrent, a deluge, endless and powerful and flowing. I am empty, utterly drained, exhausted. And as the light dims beyond my closed eyelids and my hand slips away from the lifestone, I slide off the throne and fall into nothingness.

Chapter Thirty-Eight

I wake slowly, clawing my way toward consciousness with difficulty. A dull ache throbs through my head, but I'm lying on something deliciously soft. Where did I fall asleep?

Then, in a rush, everything plays through my head in quick succession: the ball, the Winter Prince, running through the forest, the rose cottage with Kieren, the throne room where his parents came so close to forcing death on me, the Summer Queen, my mother, I'm half fae, I'm *half fae*, and then Kieren was stabbed, and then the shadows were gone, and brilliant light poured straight out of me into the lifestone, and *holy shit I'm half fae*.

I sit up, probably a little too fast, and the room spins around me. The room. What room? I have no idea where I am. I blink a few times, waiting for my head to clear, and then slowly begin to make out the details of a magnificent suite. An enormous bed and luxurious rugs. An opulent sitting area and gilded finishings and late afternoon sunlight streaming through open balcony doors. It's at least twice the size of the suite I had back at the Glittering Palace.

I push back the covers and move to the edge of the bed. I'm still wearing the silvery blue dress I found myself in when I woke on the floor in the throne room. The top of the dress is held together by a knot behind my neck. I reach back and rub the spot where the knot has been pressing into my skin. It's easier to focus on this small irritation than the many mind-blowing things that have happened in the last day or two. Has it been a day or two? I don't know. It's certainly easier than focusing on the terrifying question of whether Kieren is still alive.

He's fine. He has to be fine. I'm almost sure he's the one who attacked the Summer Queen after her magic threw me onto the throne room floor.

But there's a quiet terror at the back of my mind that I can't fully ignore. I take a deep breath and look around again. My eyes land on a folded piece of paper lying on the nightstand, a single word written in elegant script on the outside: *Avery*. My heart lurches into my throat as I grab the note and open it.

You're safe here. I'll be back as soon as possible.

- Prince Faerie Face

A sob shudders up my throat and tears blur my vision as I press the note to my chest. *He's okay, he's okay, he's okay.* I read his words again, laughing at the way he signed himself 'Prince Faerie Face.' I knew he had a sense of humor somewhere beneath that overly formal surface of his.

With a final sniff, I return the note to the nightstand and

climb out of bed. I cross the room, moving around the opulent furniture making up the sitting area before stepping onto the balcony. If I had any doubt before as to my general location, those doubts are gone. I'm somewhere inside the Autumn Palace, high above the ground and overlooking the splendid beauty of the Autumn Court. Every shadow that surrounded the palace is gone, and the warm tones of the setting sun bathe everything in gold.

I lean against the railing as I stare across the land. There is so much that's battering at the edges of my mind, trying to get inside. My mother is a faerie queen. She destroyed an entire court and cursed the others. I'm half fae. I'm half human. I can live in either world. There is no longer a curse. I don't think? I wasn't entirely conscious at the end there, but the shadows are all gone, so that seems promising. So maybe ... maybe ... is there a chance? For Kieren and me? But I'm Summer and he's Autumn, and there's the teeny, tiny fact that his parents tried to kill me, so that seems ... complicated.

Too much, I decide, rubbing my brow and turning to walk back inside. I look around and notice the piano for the first time. A grand piano, large enough that I certainly should not have missed it. Is this Kieren's room? *Was* it his room, when his family used to live here before the curse? I wondered where they've lived in the twenty years since then. The Glittering Palace is far more recent and was never a permanent home. He did mention numerous other estates, though. I suppose the royal family probably had at least one other palatial residence they could move to after the curse was cast.

My eyes land on a platter of food on the low table between the couches. Cheese and bread and exotic fruit. A jug of water and a carafe of wine. My stomach tightens uncomfortably, and it suddenly occurs to me that it's been a while since I ate or drank anything. But ... is this for *me*? I look around, but there's clearly no one else here. *Eat,* I tell myself. *Freak out over everything else later.*

I sit on the edge of one of the couches, pour myself a tall glass of water, and down it all while surveying the food. Some of the fruit is completely foreign and very obviously fae, but what about the rest of it? Which world did it originate in? *But I'm half fae,* my brain reminds me yet again. *It doesn't matter.* So I help myself to some of the bread—deliciously soft and fresh—and cut a few pieces of the slightly more normal looking cheese. I try some of the fruit. Apple slices and grapes that I'm pretty sure are actually apple slices and grapes, and something purple in color that's sweet and juicy and could be a cross between a cherry and a citrus of some kind. I drink a little more water and stare through the doors as the sun sinks below the horizon and the golden glow grows a little dimmer.

"Avery!" I lower the glass and rise to my feet, my heart thrumming at the sound of his voice. "I'm so sorry, I wanted to be here when you woke," Kieren says, crossing the room toward me, "but eventually I had to leave to get cleaned up and deal with some things. I tried to get back as soon as—"

"You're okay!" I step into his embrace and wrap my arms tightly around him.

"Yes, I'm okay," he says, sounding a little confused. "I left you a note, in case—"

"I know, I saw it. I know you're okay *now.*" I step back and look up into his face. "I mean back in the throne room. I thought you were *dying*. When I first woke up, I had no idea what happened to you. I was terrified that you might be ..." I trail off, unable to finish that sentence.

"But I told you I would be fine." He's still looking confused. "You mentioned the healing pool, and I knew I would be okay if I could get to it in time."

"And then you closed your eyes and stopped responding!"

"I'm so sorry." He runs his hands reassuringly up and down my arms. "I did not realize you wouldn't understand, but of course ..." He shakes his head. "This is my fault. I'm sorry. It is a way of conserving one's power. Directing it to where it is needed most. One sinks into an almost meditative state. That's why I wasn't responding to you. But I was aware of it when your fire attacked the shadows on the throne. I saw when the Summer Queen's magic threw you to the floor. I had to keep her from hurting you further."

"So you gave up on trying to heal yourself and attacked her instead."

That confusion is still there in his eyes. "Of course."

"That was ... kind of stupid."

He lets out a small sigh, a faint smile tracing his lips. "Perhaps. But for you, I would do it again."

I shake my head, unable to keep a smile from pulling at my mouth. "Do you remember the day we met? In the coffee shop, when you were so rude? You very firmly told me you would not be *dying* for anything in that place."

"Well," he says, one hand rising to gently brush a strand of hair away from my face, "it does not pain me one bit to admit that I was wrong." He pulls me against his chest again, one arm encircling me while his other hand threads through my hair, gently pressing my head to his shoulder.

I squeeze my eyes shut and breathe him in. "The curse," I whisper, needing to know for sure. "Did it ... is it gone?"

"Yes." He inhales a long, shuddering breath and exhales slowly, as if he's trying to control some overwhelming emotion. "Yes. You were magnificent. I cannot believe ... I still cannot believe ... the Summer Queen ... and *you* ... But it is over. The curse is over."

My next breath is even shakier than his. I blink tears away. "I can't quite believe everything that happened in that throne room either," I mumble against his shoulder. "What happened to her? My ... the Summer Queen."

"She is locked away. She will be dealt with in time."

I nod. "It's all ... a lot."

He pulls back enough to look down at my face. "How are you feeling? You scared me when you slipped off that throne and passed out. I was terrified, to be honest. I thought the act of transferring the lifestone magic back into the throne might have ... might have killed you."

So we were both terrified we had lost the other, it seems. "I'm feeling ... shocked. Sad. Happy. Possibly a little bit numb. Slightly less tired. A bit less hungry."

"You're both sad and happy?" he asks.

"Sad to discover who my mother really is. Or at least, the type of person she is. Sad to know that my father is dead."

"And happy because ..."

"Because I belong here. Because something whispered inside me the first time I went beyond the Shimmer that I belong here. Because it was breaking my heart to think of leaving. I know I'm only half fae, but that means I belong here as much as I belong in the world I grew up in. I can choose."

"You're half fae," he repeats softly, then brings his head down to place a gentle kiss on my nose.

"And I'm ... I'm a princess," I add in a tone of mild disbelief.

"You're a princess."

"Of another court."

"Of another court," he confirms. "Which I believe is why that beast that attacked you—the one that followed you and Riya and Shay into your room—made you so ill but had no lasting effect on anyone else. Those beasts are bound to the

Autumn Court and have been used for centuries against the other courts. They contain magic that is specifically meant to weaken someone who is not Autumn."

"Someone like me," I say softly. "Someone who should be an enemy of Autumn. Am I supposed to be *your* enemy? Are you supposed to hate me or something silly like that?" I try to keep my tone light, but this fear has been growing in me since I woke up. "I don't know much of this world's history, but I know the courts aren't friendly with one another, and I'm guessing a Princess of Summer and a Prince of Autumn generally wouldn't end up together."

"Generally, no." He unwinds his arms from around me and brings his hands up to frame my face. "But this particular Princess of Summer was kind enough to save the entire Autumn Court, and this particular Prince of Autumn happens to be in love with her."

"I happen to be in love with you too," I whisper, my gaze captured by his.

He smiles, a full and beautiful smile, and my stomach flips over. I stand on tiptoe at the same moment as he leans down, and we meet halfway, mouths already open, tongues touching, exploring, fingers fisting in hair and bodies pressed together. My hands slide down to his collar. He has a shirt on now, not the T-shirt-like garment he was wearing when we woke in the rose cottage. Aching to feel his bare skin against mine, my fingers go to the buttons of his shirt and start undoing them.

It takes me longer than I expect, but I finally rid him of the shirt, and then my hands move to the top of his pants. They're quicker to undo, and soon he's stepping out of them and kicking them aside as my fingers trail up and down his back—not yet brave enough to remove his underwear—and my mouth presses hot, needy kisses to his.

He moves his head to brush his lips along my cheekbone. "My turn," he whispers, fingers reaching around for the knot of fabric at the back of my neck. "Let us not pretend," he adds, "that I haven't been dreaming of undressing you entirely since that night in the music room." My wildly beating heart takes an extra leap.

Either he knows exactly how to undo the knot—unlikely—or he uses magic to simply slice through the fabric. I feel it suddenly loosen behind my neck, and then the satin-smooth dress slides effortlessly from my body to pool on the floor around my feet.

He looks at me. My breasts pebble beneath the caress of the cool evening air, and this is as much of me as he has ever seen, and I'm burning beneath his gaze. But before I have a chance to feel embarrassed, he pulls me closer and touches his lips to mine, whispering, "You are so beautiful it makes me ache."

His hands slide down my back and dip below the edge of my underwear, fingers pressing into my ass. He walks me backward. Somewhere. Past a couch, I think. I don't know. My eyes are closed and my lips are still attached to his, and every time my breasts brush against the muscled planes of his chest, it sends a zing of pleasure shooting down to my core.

Then he's gripping my thighs and lifting me, and I open my eyes to find that he's lowering me onto the closed piano lid covering the keyboard section. He pulls me flush against him and my legs tighten automatically around his waist. Then his hands are sliding up and down my sides, and his mouth is on my breast, and my head is tipped back as his tongue swipes across my nipple. Liquid fire burns in my veins and pools between my legs, and I'm trying to find my breath. "I don't think ... this is what ... pianos are meant for," I gasp.

"We could change that," he whisper-growls against my skin.

His tongue circles the peak of my other breast, sending a shiver through my body.

I release a shuddery, breathy laugh. "I don't think I'll ever be able to play it after this."

He brings his lips back up to mine and presses a lingering kiss to them before murmuring, "I suppose we can't have that."

He lifts me again and carries me across the room, stopping beside the unmade bed to lower me to the floor. My lips are still on his, and his hands are sliding down my hips, and my underwear is on the floor, and then so is his. He's on the edge of the bed, pulling me onto his lap so that I'm on my knees, straddling him, and then suddenly everything slows down.

I'm breathing heavily, my gaze on his, as I slowly lower myself until I feel the hard length of him pressed along the slick outside of my center. The immediate spark of pleasure sends heat radiating through every inch of my body. His gaze darkens, eyes never leaving mine for a second. His hands encircle my waist, and he pulls me tighter against him. I start rocking, sliding back and forth, and there is a low groan in the back of his throat. I imagine what it would feel like to have him fill me, but I'm far too nervous to attempt that just yet.

I lean forward and bring my lips to his, my fingers threading through his hair as my tongue explores his mouth. His hands alternate between trailing patterns up and down my back and pulling me harder against him. Then he's lying back on the bed, and I'm leaning over him, and before I can really comprehend what I'm doing, I'm rolling sideways and pulling him with me, pulling him over me, almost pulling him *into* me.

Then I stiffen, my eyes flying open, my body suddenly remembering this position. On my back, my legs open, someone in between them. "Fuck, I'm sorry, I'm so sorry," Kieren is saying, lifting himself off me. "I wasn't thinking—"

"Wait." I grab his shoulders and try to keep him there. "It's ... just ... wait." I stare breathlessly up at him, my gaze tracing his features. The dark hair falling across his brow, his defined cheekbones, his irises that are blue at the center, bleeding into silver, ringed in dark gray. He isn't Caz. I *know* he isn't Caz. Whatever part of my brain acts on instinct needs to know this too. I don't want to freak out every time we end up in this position. *I want this.* I want to rewrite the patterns of my brain. I want to overwrite a traumatic memory with something good and special.

"It's okay," I tell him, then lift my head to kiss him. "I'm okay."

"We don't have to," he murmurs against my mouth.

"But I want to. Like this." I try to pull him back down onto me, but he resists.

"I don't want to cause you distress."

"You won't. If you do, I'll tell you. But you won't."

Finally, he nods and says, "Okay." He presses light kisses across my chin. "But slowly," he adds. "We do this slowly. There is no rush."

Part of me disagrees with him. That part of me that craves immediate release. But another part of me is all too happy to keep this sensuous pleasure building and building, to make it last as long as possible. To know that I am definitely ready and not about to freak out when the moment comes. "Okay," I breathe.

He kisses me again, allowing some of his weight to press down on me, and my fingers dig into his back, trying to pull him closer, trying to feel him where I need him most. But he pulls back, his lips beginning a slow journey down my body. My eyes are closed as I inhale a shuddering breath. *Let go, let go.* It's okay to be vulnerable. It's okay to be on my back, exposed.

I tip my head backward, pressing it into the mattress, and

lose myself in the myriad sensations. Hot kisses across my breasts, hands roving up and down my sides, his mouth traveling lower and lower, and his hands gently urging my legs further apart until—

Oh. My hands fist in the sheets and a gasp catches in my throat at the first swipe of his tongue across my center. Hot pleasure radiates through me. Never did I imagine wanting this, never, never, never, but I feel him there again, and my body goes fluid, my legs falling open further, allowing him closer, and I'm pleading silently with every gasping breath for him not to stop. His tongue continues moving against me, circles and swirls and I don't know, I don't know, I don't know my own name anymore.

I don't expect it when he slides his fingers inside me, and there is an explosion of sensation suddenly rocketing through me. I arch against him, the motion involuntary. He grips my hip with his other hand, holding me in place. With his tongue still pressing, caressing, he curls his fingers inside me before pulling out and sliding back in, and I'm almost whimpering at the exquisite dual sensation. I grip the sheets so hard my hands hurt, pressing up against him again as he drives me toward an end that is right there, right there, *right there*, until finally it crashes over me in a tidal wave of sensation, stars exploding behind my eyes and my body trembling as aftershocks ripple through me.

I am finished, spent, a liquid mess of pleasure tangled in sweaty sheets. Part of me thinks I should have the presence of mind to be embarrassed by this current state, but I'm too lost in the waves of pleasure still washing over me, my breath heightened and my heart pounding against my ribs.

"I think," Kieren says, pressing a kiss to my inner thigh, "that you may be—" another kiss on my other thigh "—properly relaxed now."

I laugh, eyes still closed, and mumble, "Understatement."

"You have no idea how beautiful you are," he murmurs. "I was wrong last night when I said that you wearing one of my shirts was my favorite look. *This* is my favorite look on you: Mussed up hair, cheeks flushed, completely at ease."

"And completely naked?" I ask, a smile curving my lips as I open my eyes and find him easing himself back up alongside me.

"That too," he says, answering me with his own smile.

I roll onto my side and hook my leg over his hip. His hand goes to my waist, pulling me against him, and I'm immediately aware of his need for me. I let him pull me all the way over so that I'm straddling his waist, the hardest part of him pressed against the most sensitive—and now very wet—part of me. I'm surprised at the spark of desire that shoots through me, my body already awake again at his touch.

I lean forward, breasts brushing his chest and lips gliding along his collar bone as I begin to rock my hips, sliding over him again and again. He groans against my shoulder, hips thrusting up against me. The sound is intoxicating. I feel oddly powerful, knowing I have the ability to draw such a sound from him. I want to make him do it again. I want this tense, highly restrained man to lose all control. I want him to shatter apart.

I rock forward a little further, a tremor of anticipation coursing through my body as I sense the tip of him pressed against my opening. I want this. Him. No more space between us. "I want you," I gasp against his mouth, and his hands rise to my face as he presses his lips hard against mine, and his answer is a groan deep in his throat as he thrusts upward and slides the full length of himself into me.

My breath is a shuddering gasp against his lips. This is both pleasure and pain, and at first I think it's too much, the sensation of him filling me, stretching me, but his hands move to my hips, rocking me slowly back and forth until the pressure eases, and then it isn't too much, it's just right, just right, just there, there, *there*.

With my mouth hovering above his, I'm gasping at him not to stop, half-formed words that shudder across my tongue. His fingers press harder into my hips, my ass, and he thrusts into me with increasing speed. There's that deep groan in the back of his throat again, and words uttered in another language, and the fact that he is coming undone will be my undoing.

I tilt my hips, pressing him deeper inside me, eliciting another moan from him. We move as one, his hands guiding my hips, his breath coming in ragged gasps. The pleasure builds within me until it's almost unbearable, and I'm hovering right at the edge, not wanting to let go, not yet, not yet, not yet. Everything fades away and all that is left is breath and lips and hands and rough stubble and the feeling of him moving inside me, thrusting harder, faster—

And then he gasps my name as he presses into me one last time and holds me *there*, and I'm shattering, falling, coming apart, my body shuddering around his as waves of pleasure crash over me.

I collapse beside him, and for several moments, all we do is breathe. Then he slides an arm over my waist and pulls me closer. "Remember I told you," he murmurs against my sweaty brow, "when you were concerned about all of this, that you are perfect and cannot do anything wrong?"

"Mm hmm."

"I was right."

I let out a breathy laugh and snuggle closer to him. His hand traces idle patterns up and down my back, over the scars that mark my skin, and it doesn't bother me one bit. I close my eyes and relish this moment, forgetting the rest of the world.

I'm almost asleep when Kieren quietly climbs from the bed and crosses the twilight-bathed room. Through half-open eyelids, I watch him seat himself at the piano. The first few notes linger in the air, each one carrying its own weight before falling into the next. Then he relaxes into the sound, and the music flows from his fingers, tiny beads of sunshine strung together to form the beginning of a lullaby. I close my eyes and fall asleep to the sound of him playing.

Chapter Thirty-Nine

"This is just ... I don't know how any of this is even real," Quinn says in a shaky voice, blinking away tears. "You're ... one of *them*."

The two of us are tucked away in a corner booth at The Grumpy Bean one quiet, sunny afternoon about a week after my entire world tipped upside down and then realigned itself on a new axis. I confirmed with Iris as soon as I could that Quinn had arrived safely back home the evening after the disastrous end to *The Princess Game*, but I knew I needed to talk to her in person. We had to deal with all the things that spilled out between us that night, and I needed to explain everything that's changed since.

I thought it was going to be difficult to confront all the hurtful things she yelled at me, but she apologized over and over, and I decided to move on from that quickly instead of wondering whether, beneath the surface, she still thinks all those awful things about me. But that part of the conversation was nothing compared to everything I had to explain next.

"I'm *both*," I say to her. "Human and fae. And I'm still me. I know you said that I've changed, and I suppose I have, in some ways. I don't think I could have been through everything from the past few weeks and *not* changed. But in all the ways that are important, I'm still the same person."

"I don't know. You're *half fae*, Avery. And a freaking *princess*."

I look around, half expecting members of the paparazzi to jump out from behind one of the other booths at the word 'princess.' Apparently they swarmed this place for several days after the show ended, harassing Quinn about her Glittering Palace experience and hoping to catch a glimpse of me. But they gave up when nothing exciting happened. "Well," I say, returning my gaze to her, "I don't know if you can really call me a princess if my court—my land and all its people—are gone."

She gives me a look. "You're a real princess, okay. Whether your palace or whatever still exists or not doesn't change that. And you're moving an entire *world* away from me! That's a *big deal*!"

This, more than anything, lets me know that she still loves me even if she'll never accept fae in general. The fact that she doesn't want me to leave. "I'll visit you. I promise. I'm not going to disappear forever."

"You sure? I've heard tons of rumors that your daddy-in-law—who tried to kill you, I'd just like to remind you—has suddenly changed his mind about having anything to do with humans and wants to close the Shimmer and demolish the Glittering Palace."

"He's not my *daddy-in-law*," I remind her, my face twisting. "You know I'm not actually married to—"

"Prince Faerie Face, yes, I know—"

"Kieren," I correct.

"—but you probably will be one day," she continues.

"I mean, *maybe.*" Warmth steals its way up my neck. "And if I do marry him, can you please use the term father-in-law and not daddy-in-law when you refer to the king? It sounds less gross."

"Whatever. You're missing my point. They want to cut ties with this world now that their curse is broken—"

"Quinn!" I hiss, looking around.

"Sorry, *now that their curse is broken,*" she whispers, "which means I may never see you again because you've decided you want to live *there* and not here."

"You know that's not true. Fae have been traveling between their world and this one through small portals for centuries, long before we ever knew of their existence. They didn't stop after we knew about them, even though they were supposed to only travel through the Shimmer, and they're not going to stop now. *I'm* not going to stop now."

I don't add that I would miss my new friend Iris if I wasn't able to travel back to this world ever again, or that I wouldn't be able to visit Lina either, who needs to spend time in both worlds until she can remain permanently at Illiam's side. Quinn probably wouldn't appreciate knowing that I care about other people in this world as much as I care about her.

She heaves a long and dramatic sigh. "Fine."

I sit back against the cushioned seat. "Is the whole world still scandalized by the abrupt and unexpected end to *The Princess Game*?"

"You mean that crazy *non*-ending? Yes. Obviously. It's all highly suspish. I mean, Natalya was apparently chosen as the princess-to-be, but then the show is *cancelled* straight after that? And no one's seen her since? And the fae are saying *nothing*? There's a lot of anger over the whole thing, people saying we were all tricked about the show's true purpose. Which, obviously, we were." Quinn rolls her eyes. "Plus there are rumors that some of the other contestants are missing too. I saw an interview with Shay's mom and twin sister, and they said she's back home and she's fine, but they seemed ... weird. I don't know. Like either they were lying or they'd been glamored. I mean, do you know anything about that?"

I hesitate before answering. "I don't know anything for sure."

Quinn narrows her eyes. "You're keeping something from me."

I sigh. "I'm not going to go around spreading rumors when I don't know what the truth is."

"Fine. *Fine.*"

"Hey." I reach across the table for her hand. "Are we still friends? Even after all of this?"

"I mean, you're more like my sister," she says with a roll of her eyes, not looking at me as she takes my hand. "And you can't get rid of sisters even if you want to."

A smile spreads across my face. "I love you too."

She mumbles something and then adds, "I kissed Holly, by the way."

I blink at her. "What? Holly? The barista who replaced me? The one you supposedly *hate*?"

"Yeah." Quinn draws the word out slowly as her pale skin turn a bright shade of red. "Well, she kissed me and then I kissed her back, and it turns out I don't actually hate her. Or I did, but now I definitely don't. I was going to tell you about this when I visited you at the palace, but ... yeah. I didn't get to that bit before everything else fell apart."

"Oh my gosh!" I squeal. "Quinn, this is like your very own enemies to lovers story."

"Shut up," she mumbles, cheeks still burning.

We continue talking as our coffees grow cold beside us, dissecting the new details of my life ("Your mother sounds *terrifying*," she says) and the new details of Quinn's life ("So I know it's super soon, and we're probably crazy, but Holly and I are talking about moving in together."). Things feel almost normal between us. Almost, but not quite. Maybe they'll never be exactly the same again. And maybe that's okay.

I watch the clock as the afternoon sun begins to wane, until eventually I say, "I'm so sorry, but I have to go now. I'm meeting—"

"Prince Faerie Face?"

"Can you please call him by his name?" I ask, smoothing my hands down over my sundress as I stand.

"Fine, fine. *Kieren.* And could you maybe, uh ... please apologize to him for me? For the way I acted after what happened with Maddox?"

I promise her that I will, and then I head away from The Grumpy Bean, walking to the end of the block and turning into the quiet street Kieren left me in earlier this afternoon. He's already there, a miniature version of the Shimmer glistening in the air behind him. "Did it go all right?" he asks when he sees me. He knows I was almost sick with worry this morning about speaking to Quinn.

"It actually did," I tell him with a relieved smile. "Hey, is that thing visible to anyone who walks past?" I ask, pointing at the portal. I didn't think to ask earlier when we arrived here, anxious as I was to get to The Grumpy Bean and finally talk to Quinn.

"Yes. I could glamour it if I wanted to, but it isn't that busy around here. It didn't seem necessary. And I'm very happy you were able to resolve things with Quinn."

"She apologized to you too, by the way," I add as he takes my hand and moves toward the portal with me. The other side isn't what I expect it to be, though. Instead of the grounds of the Autumn Palace, I see a lake. "What are we doing here?" I ask, stepping onto the grass and breathing in the scent of roses.

"You liked it here, didn't you?" He slips an arm around me and bends to kiss my cheek. "You wanted to stay here forever, if I recall," he murmurs against my skin.

My cheeks flush at the memory of that morning, and heat ignites low in my belly. But I won't be distracted. I know we have other things to talk about. "What did you find out?"

He sighs. "Come and sit with me." He leads me toward a blanket laid out beside the water's edge.

We've been waiting for news of the girls who disappeared the night the Winter Prince showed up. Everything was a bit chaotic after Queen Erralee cast her spell and flung some of us straight out of the ballroom and into the Nightmare Forest. A handful of girls, including Lina, made it to safety, but everyone else was either taken by the Winter Prince or disappeared into the Nightmare Forest and never came out. Aside from some of the contestants, there was one other person who disappeared in the forest that night: Kieren's friend Rhylan.

He raced off with Kieren and some of the guards to search the forest for whoever had been sent there, but the only people who emerged were Kieren, me, and—eventually—the guards.

"We had to send spies to the other courts to determine what happened, and it took time to receive their messages," Kieren says, "but they've confirmed that Shay and Rhylan were taken to the Spring Court, while the Winter Prince took the other girls."

"The Spring Court? Why were they taken there?"

Kieren is quiet for several moments before answering. "I did not tell you this before because it was not my secret to share, but Rhylan is the heir to the Spring throne."

I gape at him. "Seriously?"

"Yes. Whatever their curse, he does not agree with the way his family is dealing with it. He could not tell me the details, just as I could not share the details of my curse with him, though I know they need humans for something. And I could not tell him how or why, but I could tell him that *The Princess Game* was intended to end with me breaking the Autumn Court's curse. He ran away from home, planning to stay with us for the duration of the game, to witness how it played out. His family did not know of his whereabouts. It seems, however, that his father's soldiers found him the same night the Winter Prince showed up. He must have been with Shay when they discovered him in the forest."

Shay or Sadie? I wonder silently. "How—how did you even end up friends?"

"We met by accident years ago, neither of us knowing who the other was. By the time we discovered each other's true identities, it did not matter. We were already friends."

"That's ... wow. Okay." Yet another revelation to add to the many that are piling up. "Okay, so ... Shay might be all right if she's with Rhylan, but the others are definitely not okay at the Winter Court."

"I would not be so quick to assume that Shay is safe. The Spring Court is no kinder to humans than the Winter Court."

"But ... then ... I mean, we have to do something."

Kieren looks out at the lake, his jaw clenching. "It is dangerous to interfere with the other courts. My father has no interest in putting our court at risk now that the curse is broken."

"Are you kidding? *They* came to *your* court and stole a whole bunch of people. Doesn't that count as interference? Don't you get to retaliate or something?"

"He doesn't care enough."

"He doesn't—that's ridiculous! *You* care—"

"I do." He looks at me, his gaze intent. "And I am not saying we will do nothing. I am only saying that we do not have the support of the crown, and that whatever we do will be unofficial. It will be dangerous. But we *will* do something."

"Oh. Okay good. Thank you. And, I mean, I guess it's obvious that getting involved in any way will be dangerous. But what's a little extra danger when there are already people out there who want to take your life? Someone tried to poison you at the beginning of *The Princess Game*, and we still don't know who that was. And I've faced death recently and lived to tell the tale, so I should be able to do that again."

He places a hand gently against my cheek. "Do not joke of such things. I cannot lose you. Whether you decide you belong in this world or the one you grew up in, I cannot lose you."

I fit my hand over his. "I told you I've already decided. I want to be *here*."

"And I told you to take your time. Your life has changed dramatically. You don't need to make hasty decisions right now. The answer to the question of where you truly belong may be more complicated than you think."

I shake my head. It isn't complicated. I already know where I belong. "Tell me," I say, attempting to change the subject, "what we're going to do to help the girls who were taken."

"We are going to wait," he says, lowering his hand and placing it on my knee, "as painful as that sounds. I require more information, and I had to send some of my own people after my father ordered his spies to return after confirming who ended up where. I need to know more about the situation at each court before we can act."

"Waiting," I sigh. "I hate waiting."

"Well. There are things that could occupy us in the meantime, Miss Girl Next Door," he says, tugging lightly on the end of my ponytail.

"Oh really? What 'things' did you have in mind, Your Highness?"

He reaches around to the back of my head and pulls the hair tie out. My hair cascades over my shoulders, and he runs his fingers through it. "Things that require you to be a little less Girl Next Door and a little more wild Summer Princess," he said, bringing his mouth to mine.

I smile against his lips. "I think I can do that."

He presses me gently down onto the blanket, and I kick my shoes off as I go. My fingers thread through his hair as his lips move softly, sensuously against mine. His hand glides down over my waist and hip, finding the edge of my dress before sliding up my bare leg. I can't help the hitch in my breath as his fingers hook in the elastic of my underwear and slowly pull down.

"Outside?" I murmur against his lips. "On a blanket?" But I lift my hips so he can more easily remove them.

"Why not? More comfortable than a piano."

"True."

"It's a beautiful evening," he says, his words whispering along my collarbone now, his fingers already moving to the spot I need him most and nudging my sensitive folds apart. "I thought you would like it out here."

"I do," I breathe, eyes closing as his fingers start sliding over me. I don't tell him that the setting doesn't matter, as long as I'm with him.

My dress is soon gone, and so are his clothes—I've had more

practice in removing them over the last few days—and I'm pulling him into me as the sun sets beyond the lake, and we're moving together, soaring together, splintering apart and landing somewhere among the brilliant beams of golden light.

"You," I murmur against his skin. "That's where I belong. With you."

Bonuses

For free (mostly steamy) fantasy romance short stories and other bonus content related to the world of *The Princess Game*, visit lyravincent.com/bonuses

About the Author

Lover of both fantasy and romance, Lyra Vincent spends most of her time in magical worlds (in her imagination, if not physically) crafting memorable characters, fantastical magic, plot twists, and happy endings—and throwing in a sprinkling of steamy spice.

Her favorite kind of fantasy world is the type where a magical realm exists alongside the modern one we know and live in. Because that means that at any moment, she just might walk into it herself.

Website: lyravincent.com
TikTok: @lyravincentbooks
Instagram: @lyravincentbooks

Made in the USA
Columbia, SC
27 May 2024